A SEASON in

CARCOSA

ALSO FROM MISKATONIC RIVER PRESS:

Dead But Dreaming
edited by Kevin Ross & Keith Herber

Dead But Dreaming 2
edited by Kevin Ross

Dissecting Cthulhu
edited by S. T. Joshi

Horror for the Holidays
edited by Scott David Aniolowski

The Strange Dark One (coming soon)
by W. H. Pugmire

The Grimscribe's Puppets (coming soon)
edited by Joseph S. Pulver, Sr.

www.miskatonicriverpress.com

A SEASON in

CARCOSA

edited by

Joseph S. Pulver, Sr.

Miskatonic River Press

New York • Florida
2012

For information contact Miskatonic River Press

Published in the United States by:
Miskatonic River Press, LLC
944 Reynolds Road, Suite 188
Lakeland, Florida 33801
www.miskatonicriverpress.com

ISBN 978-1-937408-00-8

Contents

"This Yellow Madness"

Robert William Chambers (May 26, 1865 - December 16, 1933).

The King in Yellow. The Yellow Sign. Dim Carcosa. Suicide Chambers. Cassilda and the other beguiling characters in *The Play* . . . Haunting seeds of weird fiction that inspired Lovecraft, Derleth, Karl Edward Wagner, and still infects writers today.

Influenced, in part, by Ambrose Bierce, Edgar Allan Poe, and it can be argued, the French "Decadents", Chambers created a small body of stories, some even term it a mythos, linked by a king in pallid, tattered robes, the madness-inducing "The King In Yellow" play, and the Yellow Sign, and collected them into a volume published in 1895, called *The King in Yellow*. Chamers' are tales lightly-salted with Nihil and ennui, and ripe with madness, haunting beauty, and eerie torments, you'll recall I mentioned Bierce, Poe, and the "Decadents".

Robert M. Price, in his excellent *The Hastur Cycle* (Chaosium 1997), traces some of the core elements of Chambers creations from the first mentions of Carcosa, Hali, and Hastur, in Bierce to Blish and Wagner (KEW's "The River of Night's Dreaming" is KIY canon and one of the finest weird tales ever written! And I'm not alone on this, Peter Straub in his intro to KEW's brilliant collection, *In A Lonely Place* [Warner Books 1983] said so as well! !!). Two years after *The Hastur Cycle* was published I asked Bob to co-edit a collection I wanted to call, *The Pallid Mask*. He agreed and we began to assemble works to include and Bob penned an intro, but we lost our publisher. A decade later at the *H. P. Lovecraft Film Festival* in Portland, OR I pitched this book to S. T. (Joshi), who was very interested in editing it, but he got buried and it came back to me. S.T. said, "You should do it yourself. Who would be better?" In my fantasies, *Datlow*! !! But I didn't have the courage to ask her. The thought of me editing this tome sent me over the edge into true madness. Yet here it is. Having seen the Yellow Sign long ago (I sat by a body of water in upstate,

NY, reading the "The Yellow Sign" by full moonlight, not far from Chambers' home not knowing about it or him; I was sixteen at the time) and having become a fanatical member of the Society of the Yellow Sign (some even say, it's leader), I needed to see this book happen.

Many of the tales that were to be included in *The Pallid Mask* found their way into Peter Worthy's fine *Rehearsals For Oblivion Act 1* (Dimensions Books 2006). Yet, I still wasn't happy. I wanted more KIY tales. New ones. I had lists of writers and my what if _____ ___ did this, or what if ___ _____ did something like that?

My need fed on me and I was finally called to the court.

Bob had said it was a good idea. S.T. was all for it. I sat looking at my Chambers artifacts and holding my copy of *The King in Yellow* (no, it's not a 1st edition! !!) and the King's madness commanded me, Do it!

So I scratched out my notes, looked at my list of writers, many who had been on my list for a long time, and went begging.

Here's what I wished, begged for:

No reprints. No HPL anything. The Lovecraftian mythos is not part of the KIY oeuvre... Exception, ghouls, MU could have copy of KIY play. I do not want to someone to write the play. I am interested in tales based on the canon, or that tip their hat to it, or riff off it. This is a book about madness, altered realities, splintered minds, and what is behind the mask.

The canon as I see it: RWC "The Repairer of Reputations", "The Mask", "In the Court of the Dragon", "The Yellow Sign", "The Demoiselle D'Ys", "The Street of Four Winds", "The Prophet's Paradise", "The Street of the First Shell"; Karl Edward Wagner "The River of Night's Dreaming"; Michael Cisco "He Will be There"; James Blish "More Light"; Vincent Starrett "Cassilda's Song"; Ann K. Schwader "Tattered Souls", "Postscript: the King In Yellow", "A Phantom Walks".

Style is wide open. Noir. Bruno Schultz, Burroughs, Ligotti, Sci-Fi, New Weird, dark fantasy, David Lynch, the Quays, POETICS!, surrealism, Ellroy, Vachss...

Setting and place, any—almost, R'lyeh is out. Urban, desert, cabin, NYC, Paris, Texas in 1885...

Tales could/should touch on - Suicide chambers, the Dynasty, the play, the characters from the play, madness, the Yellow Sign. Paris. Painting/the arts in general [musical adaptations—what would Julie

Taymor's KIY be like?; Robert Wilson stages play; modern poets/musicians looking at the play]. Carcosa, masks, the war w/ Alar . . .

On the following pages you'll see what forms of madness the talented contributors have staged for you. Please dress warmly as you embark for the shores of madness. Upon arrival you'll note there is, in the vales of the Winter Lantern, a clinging chill in the air.

(a certain) bEast
Berlin, Germany
FEB 2012

My Voice is Dead
By Joel Lane

We are the sacred body of Christ, not some bunch of secular do-gooders.
— anonymous Internet posting

The name rang a bell, but Stephen wasn't sure where he'd seen it. Maybe in his student days, when insomnia and random second-hand books had taken him down some strange roads. But he'd been curious, not gullible, and this looked suspiciously like a cult. A mythical realm with dark towers, a ghostly lake, and a king in tattered clothes like some iconic hobo? Surely even in his mixed-up youth, he couldn't have confused faith with a bad dream like that? But something about the feverish words drew him in, made him keep opening the page. Perhaps its sheer morbidity appealed to him now that he was, objectively speaking, close to death.

The anonymous creator of the Yellow Sign website used some dense, archaic font that resembled medieval script. His long paragraphs were interspersed with amateurish sketches and blurred photos meant to illustrate the text, for all the world as if he were a travel writer rather than a delusional fantasist. A black and white photo of a derelict industrial landscape, with two crumbling brick towers, was captioned *The ruined city of Carcosa*. Another photo appeared to show the edge of a lake whose water looked almost black, and was completely still though the clouds overhead were in turmoil. That was captioned *The lake of Hali in permanent twilight*. Of course, Stephen reflected, that probably wasn't meant to be taken littorally.

Then there were a few crude drawings, possibly made with charcoal and scanned into the page, of crippled birds and misshapen human figures that lurked around the lake and the ruined buildings. And the Yellow Sign itself, an asymmetrical logo incorporated into every photo and sketch as if hanging in the air wherever you might look. When Stephen closed his eyes it shimmered there, an unhealthy shade of yellow he'd never seen in real life.

At the end, there was an e-mail address for anyone who wanted to know more. Stephen clicked on it and typed a short message: *I don't know where Carcosa is, but it's got to be a better place than where I am. Will you go waltzing Cassilda with me? A realm of eternal twilight would beat this world where they switch on stage lights and call it day. Tell me where to find Carcosa. I don't have long. Hastur la vista, baby.*

After sending the message, he turned off his computer and tried to pray. But the words wouldn't come. Was God shutting him out for dabbling in a bit of arty folk-religion? *I didn't mean it*, he thought, crossing himself. Then he took the rosary from his bedside cabinet and counted the beads steadily until his panic subsided. After the surgery and chemotherapy, he'd been declared free of tumours and told to go back for routine monthly checks. The last of which had revealed a sudden rise in tumour marker levels, calling for an MRI scan. In three days' time he'd know the results. Surely he could be forgiven for clutching at a few straws.

Of course, all this Ryan Report business wasn't helping. He'd read the coverage in the *Irish Times* with a mixture of rage and shame. Rage at the feeding frenzy that was taking place in the Protestant media, but also at the sheer foolishness of the Church authorities who'd tried to cover up what they should have stamped out. If co-operating with the police was too dangerous, they should have made sure a few of the offenders met with nasty accidents. After all, whatever the papers said, there weren't many of them.

And shame at what might have taken place if the accusations were true, if it wasn't just a bunch of lowlifes blaming their carers and educators for the fact that their lives had come to nothing. Whenever he thought about the alleged crimes, other thoughts got in the way: the fact that those brats would have starved or turned to crime without the care and support the Church offered. He literally couldn't imagine what they said had happened. But not having words for the shame – being slightly ashamed of it, even – didn't make it go away.

His hands were trembling as he returned the rosary to its drawer. It was nearly midday and he'd got nothing done. In the past, he'd have filled a day off with activity: gone somewhere outside Birmingham, or done some reading at the library, or assembled a new bookcase. But now he didn't have the energy, and it was hard to see the point. When his usual routine lapsed, there was nothing there. Stephen wondered if the pain in his back was anything more than the effect of sitting still too long. Suddenly angry, he marched into the kitchen and started wiping the surfaces, washing up a few mugs, then reaching up to wipe a cobweb from the window. How long had it been there? He strode through the house with a duster, rubbing at shelves and pictures. The computer screen was dusty too but he didn't want to touch it, the machine didn't deserve his attention. He reached to switch it back on, then turned away and went back to the kitchen. Where he sat at the table, clasped his hands and pressed them to his forehead, weeping. It wasn't much of a prayer, but it was something.

The bright February light skittered off windows and pools of rainwater. Stephen locked the front door and walked through into his front room, the room he always kept tidy and clean, the room for entertaining visitors (what with, his puns?). Its order and familiarity always calmed him, but not now. He waited to feel at home. *Inoperable.* Behind that word lay more closure than Woolworth's. Oddly, he didn't really feel ill. Just tired.

The computer called him and he resisted just long enough to pour himself a glass of Jameson's. There were only two new e-mails, both with the title 'The exile returns'. Which was a sure sign of spam. But one of them was from his sister Claire. The other was from 'Death in Jaune'.

Claire's e-mail said she hoped he was OK. Then there was a link to the local paper's website, with the comment: *This man married me and Ian. I feel betrayed.*

Breathing deeply, aware of a faint stiffness in his lungs, Stephen clicked on the link. A face he recognised from somewhere. Richard Robinson, aged 73, had been jailed for 21 years by Birmingham Crown Court for multiple rapes of children. A former local priest, known for his motorcycle and friendly manner, he'd quit the country in 1983 to escape prosecution. It had taken the police a quarter of a century to extradite him. All along, the article said, the Church had kept his whereabouts a secret. Up to 2001, they had continued to pay him a regular salary.

Sentencing Robinson to spend the rest of his life in prison, the judge had called for an enquiry into the Church's actions. Stephen noticed his glass was empty but he didn't remember drinking, couldn't taste the whiskey or feel it in his chest.

He felt more helpless now than he had at the hospital. Father

Robinson. He remembered that smiling face at Claire's wedding and other times. Remembered, now, them saying he'd left the priesthood. Scrolling down the long list of comments, he saw nothing but the cheapness of Protestant minds. As if the Church had no higher purpose than trawling through the mire of dubious accusations and worthless lives. One earnest local had declared: *For any priest to go on spouting Latin before the faithful when his church is guilty of such crimes is a vile hypocrisy.*

That was enough. His fingers trembled as he clicked into the empty comment box and typed: *We are the sacred body of Christ, not some bunch of secular do-gooders.* Then he unplugged the computer and stood at his study window. Tiny flakes of sleet were blowing against the glass like dead skin. He ought to phone Claire, she'd sounded upset. No, he'd reply to her e-mail. That way, he wouldn't have to burden her with his own bad news.

The faint hum of the computer was soothing, like the gentle undertow of painkillers. Stephen opened the other 'The exile returns' message. It was in the same archaic font as the Yellow Sign website:

> *O pilgrim of Carcosa grim*
> *Our voices share a common hymn*
> *The Lake of Hali holds the word*
> *Forgotten by the mindless herd*
>
> *The King exists! He has returned*
> *To where the black stars ever burned*
> *And in his sacred yellow cloak*
> *He proves that God is not a joke*
>
> *Cassilda dances like a rune*
> *Beneath a different kind of moon*
> *If for true vision you would ask*
> *Then gaze upon her pallid mask*
>
> *This is long over, and to come*
> *The stones cry out, the mouth is dumb*
> *The King in Yellow – read the text*
> *And then remember what comes next*

Underneath the verses was another blurred Polaroid photograph: the statue of a woman lying in a white casket, her thin arms crossed over her chest. Her face was a flawless marble cast. The eyes, lips and nostrils were sealed. It reminded Stephen of a carving on the tomb of a saint. The pure spirituality of it took his breath away. Behind the figure, cinders from a hidden fire were rising through bare trees.

That weekend, he found a copy of *The King in Yellow* in Reader's World, the only second-hand bookshop remaining in the city. The paperback had no date. Inside, there was a reproduction of the original cover from 1895: a cloaked man standing before a runic sign, with a cyclone twisted around him. Pain struck him on the bus, left him almost helpless, but just managing not to vomit. He got off near his home and collapsed onto a bench, curled up like a foetus. Nobody offered to help him. Finally he managed to stumble back to his flat, the book in his coat pocket. The evening was so bad he nearly called an ambulance. But around two in the morning, the pain and nausea subsided. The peace was too valuable to waste on sleep, so he reached for the book and started reading.

It was a book about a book that didn't exist: a play that had been published but never performed. The narrator of the first story was a bigoted Catholic who hated Jews and clearly disliked women. He turned out to be a violent psychopath driven mad by the play. What was the point of that? The second story was a weird nightmare about people turning to stone and then coming back to life. Much better. The third story plunged back into the twisted world of the play, which seemed to offer a morbid spiritual realm of its own. And then the fourth story, 'The Yellow Sign'. He'd never read anything so disturbing. A more sympathetic Catholic narrator – whose only crime was wasting the chance to make love to his girlfriend. She gave him a carved symbol and then was killed by a rotting man who had come to take it back. The narrator ended up dying, alone, in terror and confusion.

If he'd read the stories before, however long ago, surely he'd remember. They would have troubled him at the time. If not, why did they seem so familiar? What did they remind him of?

Stephen didn't sleep that night. By now he was signed off work, living very much one day at a time. Soon it would be the hospital, and then maybe a hospice. He might have six months, but what kind of months would they be? How long would he be waiting for a Yellow

Sign to release him into the dark? And for which sins was he now being punished? He rather wished he'd tried a few more interesting ones. It was too late now. Flesh and pleasure didn't mix any more.

A week after reading the book, he e-mailed his nameless correspondent: *If Carcosa is real, tell me where it is. I don't have much time. A few more weeks or months of walking and thinking. Then however long doing nothing but die. If the King can give me hope, I'll do anything.* Before he pressed 'send', he wrenched the silver cross from its chain around his neck and dropped it on the carpet.

The answer came back an hour later: *O pilgrim, do not despair. Carcosa is permanent. I have been here for a hundred years or more. Carcosa endures because it makes itself part of death, which the world cannot. The King is in tatters, the Lake of Hali is in twilight, the Pallid Mask never changes. Life fades but death goes on forever. I think you are ready to join us. Bring what money you have, but send nothing. Go by train to Telford, where Cassilda will meet you with a kiss, tomorrow at noon.*

The train was late; he was afraid she would have gone. A cold wind was blowing across the platform. Clutching a weekend bag, he looked around. A young woman came out of the waiting-room and headed towards him. She didn't match his mental image of Cassilda: her dark hair was too short, her clothes too modern. But what was he supposed to expect? Then her eyes met his and she smiled as if waking from an erotic dream. Without asking his name, she gripped his free hand and kissed him on the mouth. It was more of a kiss than he expected or deserved, and he was surprised to feel himself respond. It had been a long time.

Still holding his hand, she led him down the concrete steps to the car park. A man was waiting in a rusty blue Metro. Cassilda opened the back doors and got in beside Stephen. "Welcome to Carcosa," the driver said, starting the engine. He was aged thirty or so, with a checked shirt and pale cropped hair. The car turned away from the town, heading out between mist-wreathed fields. Cassilda leant back into Stephen's arms and raised her mouth towards his. He'd heard that cults did this, used sex to win new converts. But frankly, what did he have to lose?

As the road narrowed and the fields gave way to the bones of a forest, Stephen began to slip back in the cold undertow of pain and nausea. He reached in his bag for medication, gulped two different pills. Cassilda gestured towards her mouth. "It's medicine," he said. She shrugged. The driver was watching them in his mirror. On the dark trees, streaks of mould flickered like discoloured runes.

"Are we going to the lake?" Stephen asked. Cassilda nodded slowly. "How long have you lived there?"

The young man answered: "There is no time in Carcosa. The moon never changes."

"I've been here three months," Cassilda said in a soft Derbyshire accent. "Hastur's just jealous because he only joined us last week." She gave Stephen a conspiratorial smile and rested her head on his shoulder.

They drove on in silence. The forest thinned out at the edge of a derelict estate, identical grey blocks with sheets of metal nailed over their windows. A teenage couple with a pram crossed the narrow road in front of the car. The driver pressed on his horn. "Mindless creatures," he muttered. "If I ran them down, who'd know the difference? Their world means less than the world of slugs. You haven't told anyone where you're going, have you?"

"Course not," Stephen replied. The question made him realise he should phone Claire at least, let her know he'd gone away. If there were phones wherever they were taking him. He didn't have a mobile.

The air seemed to thicken, like smoke with a flickering yellow flame somewhere behind it. Were his eyes giving way? The buildings were shapeless and blurred. It was too early for twilight. A crow larger than any he'd seen before, its plumage streaked with white, flapped unsteadily above the road. Then, suddenly, they passed a ridge and were heading downhill towards a lake whose surface was a metallic blue-grey. On either side was a burnt-out tower block.

"We are lost in Carcosa," the girl said, so faintly he wasn't sure he'd really heard the words. The car shuddered to a halt where the road approached the stony lakeside. As Stephen opened the door, a wave of decay struck him. The clouds overhead were bruised with turbulence. Something brushed his face like an invisible wing, and sickness gripped his bowels. The other two walked on as he crouched by the roadside and vomited. Metallic runes flickered above the dark water. Looking up with tears in his eyes, he saw a twisted shape flapping towards him over the water, like a yellowish cloak with nothing inside it but with purposeful movement. He rubbed his eyes and the shape faded – but now he could make out smaller buildings on the far side of the lake, and people moving between them. A dozen or so prefab huts, and a thin white building with a steeple. There was something attached to the steeple, but from this side he couldn't see what it was – only the framework of boards and scaffolding that held it in place. Then, just at the point when the hallucinatory cloak would have reached him, pain gripped his lower spine and the world became grey. The waters of the lake were churning slowly. The last thing he was aware of was the taste of blood in his mouth.

"Drink this." The man leaning over him was himself. Stephen took the offered glass of tawny liquid and swallowed. It was cognac, a delicate flame in his mouth. His body remembered the pain and he swallowed again, then a third time. The man took his empty glass. It wasn't his double, Stephen realised, though the resemblance was striking: a balding man in his fifties, with a narrow face and steel-framed glasses. The fire was spreading to his throat and chest. He was lying on a narrow bed, in a tiny room with plasterboard walls and an electric fan heater. Another man was standing beside the head of the bed, looking down: the driver.

"Don't worry," the older man said. "You're in Carcosa. We can save you. When you can stand up, we'll take you to the King. And at sunset, he will perform the ceremony of the Pallid Mask."

"Is he an Elvis impersonator?" Stephen asked.

Hastur twitched angrily, but the older man smiled. "No, Elvis was an impersonator of him. I've read your messages, I know you're in trouble. But we're prepared."

Stephen closed his eyes and pressed his hands together, as if praying. But in this place he didn't know the words. His fingers brushed his dry lips. "Is Cassilda here?" he said. Neither man answered. He opened his eyes. "All right."

"Do you have money?" Hastur said. Stephen reached for his wallet and handed it over silently. It contained four hundred pounds, all he could take out before his next salary payment.

They left the hut, the older man supporting Stephen and Hastur walking behind. They were close to the edge of the lake, which stirred restlessly. Dense clouds of blue-green algae hung beneath its dull surface. The air seemed denser than before, harder to breathe, and the clouds held motionless flakes of darkness.

From this side, he could see that the white building held up a twisted yellow shape, a rune or abstract design he remembered from the website. It was hard to look away, but his guide was leading him to a caravan parked opposite the chapel. Hastur knocked three times and waited.

The door opened. "Come in," said the King. He was a tall, slightly hunched man wrapped from head to foot in a ragged cloak. Stephen thought it was made from pieces of other clothes – an army uniform, a priest's vestment, a surgeon's gown, a business suit – crudely stitched together and dyed or sprayed with a vivid yellow pigment. He must be wearing something black underneath, since the tears in the fabric revealed only darkness.

The interior of the caravan stank of incense and alcohol. Its walls were papered with newspaper stories, but in the dim light of two candles he couldn't read the headlines. The table was covered with books, newspapers, empty bottles and other objects. There were only two chairs; the King gestured to Stephen to take one, then sat down facing him. The other two men remained standing.

"Welcome to Carcosa," the King said. He filled two shot glasses from an open bottle and passed one to Stephen. "Tonight you will see the Pallid Mask. You will hear the Hyades sing. And as the black stars shine over the lake of Hali, you will be redeemed. And you will dwell among us forever."

The other two men chanted something in a language Stephen didn't know. The King raised his glass and drank, and Stephen followed suit. The drink was also new to him: a spirit that tasted faintly of smoke and decay. It numbed his mouth and filtered through his gut like a wave of stillness. Within seconds, the world seemed clear and without pain. He gazed through tears of relief at the King's narrow, immobile face.

"Bring me the Pallid Mask," the King said. Hastur stepped through into a back room and returned with a small leather suitcase, which the King placed on the table and unlocked. It contained two objects wrapped in yellow cloth. The King carefully unwrapped the larger bundle. His fingers were thin and very pale. He held up the mask and passed it to Stephen. "Feel the weight of it."

The mask was not plaster. It was carved from marble or quartz, with crystals twinkling in its pure white surface. A young woman's face, with perfect features; the eyes and mouth were shut, the nostrils filled in. Stephen's hands were barely strong enough to lift it. Around the edge were a number of small holes, crusted with dried blood.

He passed it back to the King, who had already opened the second bundle: an electric screwdriver and a plastic box of screws. The King refastened the bundles and passed one to each of his acolytes. Then he looked across the crowded table at Stephen, holding his eyes for a long moment. "The world is poisoned," he said. "Nothing of value remains. Time to go."

The sun was setting as they waited outside the chapel. More people came from the huts and the ruined towers. They were all cheaply dressed and looked sick or troubled, but given strength by a shared expectation. The algae blooming in the dead lake seethed with a mysterious energy. The air was close to freezing point.

Three slender figures emerged from one of the nearest huts: teenage girls, possibly sisters, dressed in long coats. They glanced anxiously at the King, who tapped his watch. "Sorry," one of them said. "We were practising." Stephen wondered if they were the Hyades. The King walked up the steps to the chapel door and took out a large key, then waited.

Finally, three more people joined the congregation: two men flanking a young woman, who appeared to be heavily drugged. Despite the chill she was wearing a sleeveless white gown. As they slowly approached the chapel, he realised the girl was Cassilda. Her eyes tracked across the congregation, from face to face; he looked away. Her minders helped her climb the stone steps to the chapel door. At that moment, the sun's last rays caught the Yellow Sign and made it writhe. The King twisted the key and pushed open the heavy door. Cassilda's guards took her through the doorway after him. The Yellow Sign faded with the daylight; black waves crashed on the lake shore. One by one, the people of Carcosa stepped into the chapel.

Beyond the Banks of the River Seine

By Simon Strantzas

I have read all the books about that time, but they are all wrong. There is no one who knew Henri Etienne as I did, certainly no one in all of Paris. We were both students at the *Conservatoire*, the finest musical school in all the world, where we had met in our first year and had become inseparable. The man people whisper of in the shadows of concert halls bears little resemblance to the boy I had once held dear. This is the way of things, I suppose. Few truly know those they idolize most. Perhaps, this is best.

Henri and I were rivals over everything; two composers always at odds, albeit friendly odds. Or so it seemed to me. But I imagine it would, as I was his better in virtually every way. I do not mean for that to sound as vain as it must, but if this chapter – my final confessional – is to serve its purpose and cleanse my soul, then I must be completely honest. Compared to me, Henri was pale, destined for nothing more than performing in one of the small bars along the Left Bank where he might earn little more than enough to scrape by. It was not that he was unpractised or undisciplined – he was the sort who put many long hours into honing and refining his craft – it was that his proficiency was never more than average, and his playing rote and unemotional. He was no better than the automaton I'd once seen at the *Musée Grévin*, one step above a music box with its carved wax fingers and clockwork piano. What I am trying to convey is that the boy was not in the same league as I, and that only made his company more charming to me.

His sister, Elyse, was a different beast all together. Never in all my years before or since have I laid eyes on a woman so near perfection that even the all mighty himself might be expected to cast a second glance. Elyse was a dream. An angel. And I wanted nothing as much as I did her. Wanted to feel her heat against me. Wanted to show her the sort of passion only a man on the verge of success might be able to provide. And yet, despite all my wooing, she remained resolute against me. I was not an ugly man – my mirror assured me of that – and I was not without means, so her dismissals were very much a surprise. They were illogical, based I was sure on no more than the whims of a woman, and they only made me want her more. I knew she must love me, and that it could only be for her brother's sake that she refused to admit it.

What charmed me most about Henri was his drive, his perseverance to best me at something, anything. He would take quite a ribbing from me in class and with friends, always second to my performances. Perhaps we were rough on him, kept his nerves raw, but it was only from love. I enjoyed having him with me. He could always be counted on for a humorous glower when I dared played the keys of his wounded pride. It seemed to motivate him, though, something for which he should have thanked me. Though perhaps not in retrospect.

Because of our friendly rivalry, he would pore over every task, practice it incessantly, fixate on achieving the truer performance. Where I might play adagio, he would play presto. A minuet I had written would be countered with an quartet from him. Each work of mine was responded to, each with a fury of playing hitherto unknown to any of us who knew him. Henri's hands would tremble before every performance and even my laughter was not enough to calm him. "You mustn't goad Henri, Valise," his sister would plead, to which I would only laugh further. "It's all in good fun," I'd say, and her sweet porcelain face would twist, and then she would invariably spit at me. Is it any wonder I was so smitten? We would watch Henri play, and while the rest of the room focused on his dancing fingers I could not bear it. It pained me to see them drawing such lifeless notes from the ivory. Instead, I studied his face and the flop of hair that would slide over his brow moments into his performance; or at his flushed skin, sweated with concentration before reaching a boil as he wordlessly realized what he was playing was a failure. In these instances, he would inevitably look to me and Elyse, and each time he did I saw defeat had already claimed him. He would not stop playing, but it is a given that once doubt infects a performer's mind, it spreads like a cancer. Inevitably, he would stumble, the first in an increasingly tumultuous cascade of errors, ending in muted polite applause. Often, I would find him after these performances weeping discretely. Forever soft as a lamb was my good old Henri.

At the end of the day, though, my friendship with him was more important to me than anything else save my own career and, perhaps, his sister's hand, and I did all I could to guide him by my example, providing to him a bar by which he might measure himself. Once, while we celebrated too much the sale of one of my compositions, he drunkenly confessed that were he to ever best me, and were he to do so in front of Elyse, he might die a happy man. I treated it as the jest it surely was: with a laugh hearty enough to fill both our mouths. His glower did not falter, which only charmed me further. His sister, however, treated it with far more weight. "We can no longer do this. Please, leave us to our misery," she said one day as I stood across from her in the October courtyard, but she knew I could do no such thing. Henri was my dearest friend, and she my future betrothed. They would have me in the life until the end of it came.

No one was more surprised than I when Henri decided to write a concerto. I asked him about it only once, and he replied, "I want to finally show the school what I am capable of." I shook my head. "You needn't prove anything to them, the ignoramuses. Don't feel as though you must compete. What's that M. Ouillé says in our Orchestration class? One must know one's limits." It seemed as though he were compounding injury, the way he begged for comparison against me. Only the year before I'd had my own piece performed at the *Elysées Montmartre*, and received raves and exaltations from all quarters. Candidly, I was told word of the composition made it as far as the *préfet* of the Conservatoire, François Chautemps, and he requested a copy of the sheet music so he might inspect my craft. There was no way to be sure this was true, of course, but it did not seem so out of reach, especially then. I hoped my success might inspire Henri to do more.

Not long afterward I found myself circling *Montparnasse*, looking for a woman whose name I've long forgotten and instead noticing Henri moving along in a vacant haze. I called to him, though it didn't seem at the time he heard me. Instead, he slipped into a small paper shop on the corner that until then I had thought was closed and unoccupied. It seemed reasonable, given how dusty the volumes in the window were, and the number dead flies that lay among them, half-consumed by dermestids. I followed Henri inside, my lady friend forgotten, and was confronted by claustrophobic walls of ancient bound theatrical scripts and other ephemera. I did not find Henri immediately. Only a small Indian that stood behind the counter, his head wrapped in frayed scarves. His eyes looked yellow and wide as they stared at me, his lower lip curled in a rictal frown. He pointed a skeletal finger at me, but said nothing. It was enough to unnerve me, and I wished to leave but could not. I had to find Henri. I would not abandon him.

But it turned out I did not need to. He appeared from the warren of stacks, his eyes swimming with joy – or if not joy then something else, something more powerful. I knew immediately the forecast was dire. He accidentally dropped the bound script he held upon seeing me, then sputtered and stumbled as though caught doing something improper. I looked down, as did he, at what he had dropped, but neither of us spoke, as though in tacit agreement we should pay it as little heed as possible.

"What do you want, Valise? Why are you following me?"

"Following you? I wasn't doing anything of the sort. You know very well I lunch in the *Dôme*. I merely saw you while waiting for a friend of mine."

Henri twitched, his eyes dancing around the room and refusing to meet my gaze. It was clear he did not want me to ask about the script that lay between us.

"What book is that?" I asked.

He tensed, as though he feared I might swoop down and snatch it from him. Had I been closer, I might have.

"It's nothing at all," he stammered.

"Nothing, is it?" I leaned closer, daunting him. He winced, his eyes spinning into his head, and though I knew my unblinking stare would bore into Henri's psyche given time, I was robbed of it by the Indian. I had not heard him approach, yet there he stood behind Henri. At first, yellow eyes were all I saw, giant and menacing, and them the pit of my stomach rebelled. Though his expression did not change, it felt as though he were snarling at me. I stepped away from Henri, hoping to keep some distance between me and the strange man. Henri, for the most part, remained in whatever half-trance I had found him in. I tried desperately to break it.

"Come, Henri. I haven't eaten. Join me."

"I'm a bit–"

"Nonsense," I swallowed, my gorge rising. "Join me at the Dôme. I'll arrange for us a table on the patio." Where the air is fresher, I neglected to add.

Neither I nor Henri looked at the Indian, but it was clear Henri wanted to and only my presence stopped him. I made the mistake of letting my eyes drift to the script, laying face down upon the ground. I barely had time to notice the strange symbol printed on its lower read corner before Henri's demeanour sharpened and his wits returned. Without hesitation, he bent down and picked up the book, then held it tight to his chest as though to hide it.

"Just let me take care of this. I'll join you in a moment."

"Please, allow me," I said, graciously drawing my wallet from my pocket. I wanted to hurry him, but also see the play he had chosen. Part of me also hoped he might mention my offer to his sister. He would not accept any money, however.

"I do not need your charity, Valise. Please wait for me at the café."

I looked at the yellow-eyed Indian, and acquiesced, eager to be out of his presence. I retreated to Le Dôme and ordered a tea as I awaited my friend's arrival. It was unclear how long I sat there with my cigarettes burning, watching the warped door of that hidden paper shop. But I never saw Henri emerge, and I was forced eventually to lunch alone.

Henri more or less vanished from my life afterward. On occasion I'd see him dashing madly across campus, always too far to catch, and I heard the whispers about him that were even then slowly spreading across campus, incredulous whispers I at once put out of mind. It was a lonely existence without Henri. Certainly, I had others to spend my time with – a gifted musician never suffers from the lack – but none were as dear to me as my friend Henri, none inspired in me the same amount of pride and love for all their foibles.

After the first few weeks he was gone I found an excuse to visit the small flat he and Elyse shared, all in the hope that I might be invited in to see whether those rumours I refused to believe were true. Elyse answered the door when I knocked, but though she did not open the door all the way, still I could see Henri haunting the background, a frail gaunt spectre, eyes ringed dark and full of fire. Elyse smiled that smile that melted my heart and made me forget all others, but when I tried to step past her, let alone speak a word to the passing Henri, she rose a delicate hand to my chest. It was clear from her face that all she sought was comfort. I had no choice but to put my feelings for Henri aside and console her.

She led me to the kitchen, far away from the room Henri was in. I imagined it was to ensure he could not hear what she had to say.

"All he does is write," she said. "Always working on his strange music. I wish he would stop, Valise. I hear him late into the night whispering, whispering. Sometimes, I worry it's no longer his voice I hear but my own. Sometimes, it's no voice I recognize at all. Maybe he'll listen to you. Maybe you can break him of his obsession. I want my brother back." She broke down and cried into my chest, and I closed my eyelids and soaked in her sorrow. It was good, finally, to be once more needed, and I would do all I could for her.

"Henri!" I bellowed, storming into his room. I paused only long enough that I might grasp how disorganized and chaotic it was. "We must speak at once."

My gaunt friend stepped from behind his cluttered desk. His face was drained of colour, but I vowed not to let his appearance dissuade me.

"You must cease this, friend. It is consuming you. I have never known you to be full of health, but this ..." I waved my hand over his willowed frame. He merely attempted a pale imitation of a smile.

"It means nothing. None of it does. I am enraptured by this project."

"What do you mean? What project?"

Here, his smile faltered.

"I cannot tell you."

I sputtered. "Why on earth not?"

He would not look at me, and behind me Elyse *could* not. Suddenly, I wondered if I had been played for a fool. Had anything Elyse told me been true? I could be sure of only one thing: that I'd had enough of their shenanigans. I suddenly wanted nothing more than to be gone, but despite the betrayal my insatiable curiosity had not been allayed. I spotted amid the clutter a familiar jaundiced volume, open and overturned. Even across the room it filled me with ill.

"What is that?" I ordered, but Henri stepped between me and it before I could get closer. He seemed strangely out of breath.

"It's not yours. Valise, please leave."

"I will do no such thing. I demand you tell me what you are working on."

He sighed and looked to where I expected his sister to be. But when I turned I found she had vanished.

"There is no one left to prove yourself to. Please, leave. I must finish my writing. I feel I am so very close."

"Close to what? To adapting *that*?" I pointed to the volume overturned on the table. I noticed his eyes would not go to it while I was in the room. "You think that will bring you what you need?"

"I'm not sure *what* it will bring, Valise. I'm not sure at all."

"Then why do it? Look at yourself, Henri. The toll is too great. Forgive me, but you seem ill-equipped for the task. Here, I have an idea. Let me look at what you've done so far. Let me offer you my expertise."

I thought he might be choking on his own tongue, that the stress was so great he was about to collapse into seizure. But that strange gurgling emerged as something else. Something I had not expected. "Are – are you laughing?" He did not deign me with the answer, but it was clear my offer was rejected by the sound of his uproarious laughter. I did not care for that reaction. I did not care for it at all.

How was I to know when I stormed out that I would not see Henri again for months? He and his sister disappeared from the circles we once travelled in, and if they had new circles I was blissfully kept ignorant. I did not appreciate the treatment I received from them, and had no interest in gracing them with a friendship that was so clearly unwelcome. I left them to their own devices as they left me to mine, and could not even find the interest to pay attention to the new rumours that were circulating about what Henri was doing with his sister's help. There was talk. That was all I cared to know.

But even I could not escape the gossip for long. It ran like chains across the campus, binding students together one by one, forging them into a single voice that rattled inside my head. Elyse, I was told, had all but retired from social life in order to take care of her brother as he composed his grand opus. Confidentially, all the talk of Henri and his mysterious work grated on me, made me think that I might too want to pen some grand statement on life through music, if only to show those fools mesmerized by his growing legend that it was no great accomplishment. Yet I never did. I tried more than once, but each attempt ended in despairing failure. I'd never failed at *anything* before, and yet there I sat, night after night, devoid of any inspiration that might turn cacophonic notes into sweet euphonies. It disconcerted me to say the least, and I knew I had only the lingering rumours of Henri to blame. Their echo seemed to follow me wherever I went.

I did all I could to forget my former friend and his sibling, put my experiences with them behind me once and for all. I could not understand what had gone wrong, and wanted to spend no more time on it than I already had. As far as I was concerned, the pair was dead, and I was better off. But one does not put aside feelings quite so easily. During the day I might have spoken tall and feigned ignorance when either name came up, but at night? At night visions haunted me, my dreams overrun with music and their laughing faces. I dreamt of far away lands on lakes of shining gold, where kings and queens danced in opulent ballrooms while fools spied on from the wings. There, I saw Henri and Elyse dressed in the finest clothing, spinning across a shining floor, never once turning their heads my way.

For all the above reasons, one can imagine my surprise when I received the invitation. The card was small and addressed to me in Henri's shaking script, and on its rear face a time, an address in the Latin quarter, and the words: *Your attendance is requested for an evening in Carcosa. Carcosa.* Now why did that name sound at once both familiar and dreadful? At the time, I had no recall. And that, in the end, may have been my greatest folly.

I had no intention of attending. Despite my curiosity at what Henri's pedestrian mind might have conceived in its isolation, it was clear he did not fully appreciate the wealth of advice I had attempted to bestow. In fact, I took that invitation and threw it into the trash, trusting the lady who cleaned my rooms to rid me of it. And yet, what do you think happened when I returned from classes later that day? Only the discovery that she left behind a single scrap of paper, caught in the thin metallic rim of my waste basket. I need not tell you what that scrap of paper was.

It seemed I was being summoned by a force far greater than myself, and I choose to comply lest it wreak havoc on my life. But of course superstition was not the only reason for my altered decision. In the time since receiving the card, my mind strayed repeatedly to the image of Elyse, and the thought of seeing her once again filled me with an unexpected longing.

The day arrived for Henri's now-infamous performance just as I was recovering from the sort of head cold that keeps one bed-bound for days on end. I was well enough to go out and beyond the point of contagion, but even the short walk to the *Hall du Sainte-Geneviève* winded me. I took a drink of ice water from the bar once inside and settled, but I did not feel myself, and the medicinal tonic I'd had before leaving only made my head feel disconnected from the rest of my body. I tell you this partially as an explanation for what I witnessed, and partially to vindicate myself for not interfering.

I had heard the stories leading up to the day but hardly believed them. Had Henri really written the piece for merely a piano and string accompaniment? And was it true that none of those who auditioned for the quartet managed to make it through a single practice without quitting? It sounded bizarre, and when I causally asked my classmates for proof there was none to be found. How could Henri have auditioned that many musicians and not once seen someone I knew? It seemed impossible. And yet the stories persisted. It was baffling, and I refused to believe them. Which is why the sight of the Hall surprised me so. Perhaps my illness was again to blame, but I did not expect to find only a few rows of pews before a Grande piano, elevated on a platform before the hall's triptych of large windows overlooking the Seine. If there was any accompaniment hired, they had not arrived, and as the seconds ticked away I began to realize this was to be a virtuoso performance, and I wondered how Henri would survive the pressure. Despite the way he had previously treated me, I had no interest in seeing him made a fool of so publicly.

The crowd that had gathered for the spectacle was quite a bit larger than I had anticipated. Henri had been gone from the Conservatoire long enough that under any other circumstance he would have no longer been remembered, and yet it seemed as though every student of the Conservatoire was in attendance. And along with them, row after row of strangers I had never before seen either at school or at one of my own performances. I wondered how could that be. Could they simply be curious, lured in by the cryptic invitation? Surely the lot of them could not have been familiar with Henri's work, or familiar with much well-performed music in general, if they were coming to hear him. I could see no other reason for the numbers, let alone for the general verve of excitement buzzing among those in attendance. Strangest of all was the presence of the man seated at the rear. I knew his face as once, though it took some time before those piercing yellow eyes told me how. Had the anticipation of Henri's work been so grand that it bled out to the local merchants as well? I must admit: from my corner at the front of the room I laughed at the sheer folly of their soon-to-be crushed expectations.

But I was laughing no longer when Elyse appeared. She swept in from the doorway behind me and all but floated toward the front row. She was even more beautiful than I had remembered, dressed in the finest silk and scarves, and though she did not turn her head when I called to her over the din of the crowd, I could see that behind her veil her skin was as wondrously porcelain as ever. My heart swelled at the sight and I became dizzy. No matter what I thought I remembered of her beautiful visage, it was a pale reflection of the truth.

So enraptured with Elyse was I that I failed to notice a hush had fallen over the room. Henri had already arrived, and had done so without fanfare or accompaniment. Unlike his sister, he was frighteningly a shadow of his former self. Sallow-faced, skin pulled tight, he looked like Charon himself as he slowly navigated the aisles of the hall in hushed silence. At the front of the room his piano stood waiting. Henri held in his hand a pale unmarked folder, and when he reached the piano and sat it seemed to require all his energy to remain upright. I looked askance at those beside me, but instead of disbelief I saw rapture. I cannot express how bizarre I found it all.

Henri's eyelids were leaded, and it seemed to require a Herculean effort to keep them open. I became increasingly worried the longer he kept from speaking or moving, and soon forgot my grudge and stood to attend to him – only to be stopped by the words that finally creaked from his mouth. Elyse stared up in rapt attention.

"Welcome, all of you this: the culmination of all my years at the *Conservatorie de Paris*, and all I've learned since being there." I thought Henri might have looked at me then, but his glazed eyes were more apt to be looking through me. "The inspiration for this concerto was a play whose script I discovered at a nameless bookstore. I visited the place first in a dream, and it was only by chance I stumbled across it in the depths of Montparnasse. I knew the sight of it at once, and felt drawn inside, to its furthest corner, where I found amid the stacks a pale book marked like no other. The merest touch, and electricity stung my fingers, and without hesitation I began to read. By the second act, I knew nothing would be the same. I knew I had finally found my key."

But the key to what? I turned to gauge the audience's reaction, but it appeared as though they heard nothing. Their faces were vacant, waiting for the performance to begin. I tried, too, to catch a glance of the Indian seated at the back of the room, but his face was obscured by fidgeting bodies. A sense of dread enveloped me, amplified by the effect of my illness. I worried I might sick, and closed my eyelids in hopes the disorientation and nausea would subside. If anything, it only made things worse.

I opened them once Henri began to play. Or, at least, I believe I did. It's difficult to be sure. Upon hearing those first few notes – those notes that, even now, have a hypnotic effect over all listeners – I realized everything I knew about my former friend was wrong. The way he played, it was as though each note caught the air and crystallized before me, bright gems emitting an even brighter glow. I was bathed in the light of the absolute, and as its brilliance intensified it obscured everything in my sight. Henri played with a power I had never before known him to possess, and it transfixed me with blindness. That blindness did not dissipate until a subtle shift in chords indicated the second act of his concert had begun. Then, the void faded, and revealed a world not as I remembered it. I do not know how to otherwise describe what I witnessed. The walls of the Sainte-Geneviève had pulled back, and I found myself dressed in the strangest of eighteenth century garb. My face felt unusual, and as I reached to touch it I found it was not my own. I turned in confusion, the sound of Henri's soothing playing calming the panic brewing in my centre, but not before I was struck by the audience and the similar masquerade disguises they wore. I looked immediately to the front of the room for Elyse, and saw someone impossibly more ravishing than before, dressed in wigs and gown, her face home to a delicate porcelain façade she held aloft with a single gloved hand.

Then, down the centre aisle, strode a caped figure toward her, a figure I knew instinctively was the Indian from the paper shop despite his being disguised head-to-toe. He had grown taller in the vision, his suit transformed into a long yellow cape, his leggings white and ruffled. Over his face he wore a long-beaked black mask; and on his head, a large yellow hat. He danced particularly as he moved, as though his feet held not contact with the wooden floor beneath them, and compounded with his disguise I was reminded of some fanciful bird in the midst of courting. All eyes were on him, though behind the blank holes of his mask I knew his were only on one. Elyse must have known it too for she stood as he advanced, holding her porcelain countenance carefully to her face as she stepped toward the centre of the room and offered him a gloved hand. It was then the floor gave way to a larger area, like that of a ballroom, and the perch on which Henri continued to play rose up, higher into the air. The roof above us had gone, the black stars blinking in strange transformation around a pair of waning moons, while below the yellow man took Henri's sister by the hand and led her to dance. It was, quite possibly, the most beautiful thing I have ever lived to see. And the most frightening. They moved in simpatico, two beings as one, circling the room over and over as Henri's haunting music played, each step lighter than air.

But all was not blissful. In my illness, the edges of my vision began to waver as though reality itself were becoming undone. I tried to speak but my tongue had swollen, immobilized by the mask I was forced to wear. The man in yellow and his masked bride spun and spun, and as they approached Henri the moonlight bathing them grew so bright a hairline crack that ran along the length of Elyse's porcelain mask was revealed to me. It seemed to stretch further the closer they danced to the triptych of windows, the blinding moonlight reflected from the great lake bathing them in light; light that could have come from no place in all of France but instead from some distant land that only then did I recognize as lost Carcosa.

The swell of music ended in the fading light of the Paris morning, and there was nothing but utter silence, the entire audience trying to grasp what it had just witnessed. I knew I certainly was. Then, the uproarious applause began. A standing ovation that continued for the better part of ten minutes while Henri sat there, visibly drained and quite possibly unable to stand, nor do anything more without risk of collapse. During this time I did not celebrate, for my eyes went where no others did. To the front of the room, and to the seat there that remained unoccupied during Henri's greatest triumph.

I found Henri the next day in the flat he and his sister shared. The morning had been spent listening to the stories of his musical prowess that were sweeping the campus, but I was more concerned with what had vanished than what had suddenly appeared. And yet, when I found Henri, lying in repose and staring at the Seine coursing outside his window, I could not bring myself to accuse him of anything. The flat was in a state of chaos, and I asked when Elyse had last been there.

"It seems like forever since she's been gone."

"Where is she?" I asked, though I was certain I did not truly care to know. Fortunately, he spared me by changing the subject.

"What did you think of the concert?"

I should have lied – under any other circumstance I would have lied – but his face was such a shadow of what it once was, his eyes so worn from all he had been through, that I could no longer hide behind my jealousy of his talent. I admitted it was unforgettable, that I had not ceased thinking about it since I heard it. To this, he dryly laughed.

"The price to write that was high, so very high. And now that I am here before you I wonder if it was really worth it. The others, do you think they'll remember what I've done?"

"I think if all of Paris isn't speaking of it yet, it's only because the day is still young."

"Good, good," he said, and closed his eyes for a moment. They had sunken so low, two dark orbs in jaundiced flesh. He almost looked as though he were wearing a mask, and I prayed he would not remove it. When those eyes opened again, they looked up at me, but I am not foolish enough to think it was me they were seeing.

"Please, Valise, I need to rest now. Tomorrow there is much to do. Will you grant me my peace?"

"Of course," I said, and quietly let myself out as he stared once again out across the Seine. I did not travel far before my regret over Elyse returned, but at no time did I turn around or stop hurrying away. There are some topics, like places, that are best left unvisited.

Movie Night at Phil's
By Don Webb

About two years after, in fact twenty-three months after the event, Phillip Saxon realized that he owed what was left of his sanity to BetaMax. When this silly thought flicked through his head he laughed for the first time since his stay at the hospital. News was even carried to Dr. Menschel that he might be getting better.

When Phil had a life, he had been a programmer and technical writer. He had the usual desirable furnishings of a life for a man of his education and intelligence. His wife Jean carried her stunning looks into her forties, even if her red hair relied on Loreal®. His red headed daughter Susan enjoyed her second year at community college, and would have transferred to the University of Texas next year. As far as Phil knew his ginger-haired son Travis made the honor roll and lettered in track. Even his golden retriever Hawn was admired for her Frisbee catching ability. Their two-story brick façade home had a lovely xeriscaped garden, and all three family vehicles were in good shape. Life was good.

When Phil had gradated Rice University, he had only one regret. There had not been enough film classes to minor in film. Early on Phil worked with the best software for films. If you've done any editing on a professional level, you've used some of Phil's products. The guy loved movies. Foreign films, classics, noir, Westerns, Bollywood, grade Z horror – he had a place in his heart for all of it. Only one thing drove Jean crazy. Phil was a little OCD. When he got on a "kick," watch out. Phil was always on a kick. One month it had been Luis Buñuel. Jean had been horrified by the eyeball-slicing scene in *Un Chein Andalou* on day one, and dismayed by the confused eroticism of *Cet obscure objet du désir* on the last day. One month it had been Godzilla films; did anyone really need to know that there were almost thirty? Jean and her children lost Phil as father and husband for two hours or more a night. But he was a kind man, a hard worker, and sometimes the movies could be fun. Phil had friends and they were all movie buffs as well. They admired his home theater. They drank his beer and ate his popcorn, and often thought to bring their own to share. Four or five nights a week, Phil watched movies. Sometimes he watched them by himself, blogging into the night.

Christmas, Father's Day, his birthdays were easy. Books on films, posters, or memorabilia. It was all good. Then Jean saw *666 Films to Scare you to Death* on Amazon. Although she dreaded that he might obsess on all of the films, she knew he tended to stick with directors or themes. It seemed to be a good peace of mom-engineering. She thought it would save her son.

Jean was a Texas mom of three generations of Texas moms. Worse still she was a Dallas Metroplex stay-at-home, big hair SUV Mom. This came with rules: Don't Disturb The Breadwinner. Secret Keeping Is Good. Phil and Travis hadn't really talked to each other since Travis played football at Sam Houston Middle School. Phil hadn't been a jock, he hadn't related to his son in scouts – he just did his best by having Jean buy the boy expensive gifts. God knew he hadn't any expensive stuff growing up in Doublesign, Texas.

Phil thought Travis was still in scouts, Travis thought Phil was a dickweed. Travis had been suspended twice this year from Crocket High (Go Coogs!). Once for "suspicion" of smoking pot, once for being in a fight with a Mexican boy that had "mean mugged" him. Posters for Naziesque bands covered his room, but also Jason, Freddy, Michael Myers and the *Saw* franchise. Jean thought that if her boys started watching scary movies together, the mysterious force of male bonding would take over and Phil would never need to know his boy was not heading to graduation.

At first it was failure. Phil was always very historical in his watching. "Did you know the first horror film was shot in 1896? It ran for two minutes." Breakfast conversation with Phil was seldom interesting. Jean hinted that more recent films might be something he would share with the boy. So there was a month of Italian giallos. Phil didn't gain any points by trying to explain why the word for "yellow" in Italian stood for horror *cum* sex. But Travis had liked the cruelty and the outrageous sex-and-death scenes, until he figured out the plot keys. "Why is the killer always some that wears black gloves? Why don't the police just search their houses and arrest anyone with black gloves?" Vampire movies didn't work. "Vampires are for fags." But an unexpected sub-sub genre really appealed to Travis – the Roger Corman

Poe movies. There were 8 of them: *House of Usher* (1960), *The Pit and the Pendulum* (1961), *Premature Burial* (1961), *Tales of Terror* (1962), *The Haunted Palace* (1963), *The Masque of the Red Death* (1964), The *Tomb of Ligeia* (1964) and Edgar Allen Poe's *The King In Yellow* (1966). Let's compare-and-contrast. All of the movies start Vincent Price, except for *Premature Burial*, which starred Ray Milland. Most were filmed in the US except the last three, which were shot in the UK. But what most often brings smiles to English teachers is that two of the films aren't "really" by Poe at all. *The Haunted Palace* (despite it's title from Roderick Usher's poem) is a good adaptation by the great Charles Beaumont of H. P. Lovecraft's *The Case of Charles Dexter Ward*, and the last of the series Edgar Allen Poe's *The King In Yellow* was James Blish's adaptation of an obscure French play *Le roi jaune* which may have been written (according to 666) by Lautremont, a generally creepy French writer born in Uruguay.

Travis loved Price's portrayals of despairing nihilistic intellectual sadists. **Everything** he saw he loved. Roderick Usher's domination of his sister touched some long held fantasies. Travis came on to Susan one night and even tried to capture her in her room. A sisterly knee to the groin took care of his advances. Thank god Phil never heard about it. Jean convinced Susan that dad would not be able to handle it.

After *The Pit and the Pendulum* Travis and Cormac Jones, another "Aryan Youth" kid, had held down a black girl and made slow arcing swipes at her face with a Bowie knife. The tip got closer and closer, but never connected. The principal sent him hose for three days. But Jean did see how much Travis loved watch the movies with his dad, and in Phil's fantasy world Travis and he were bonding over the lush Technicolor sets and the costumes. Jean told her friends at the book club that her boys were finally friends. Actually a stranger thing had occurred each now saw a refection of himself in the other, but as St. Paul would have it "Through a glass darkly." Phil thought that Travis might be inspired to that the RTF major at the University of Texas. Phil could already see his son's name scrolling by in end credits. And Travis decided that his Dad was "really into it." "It" variously being DBSM, Satanism, or something vaguer and more evil fro the lack of a name. This folly was best-represented one night when Travis asked his dad if he owned a riding crop. Phil answered in the affirmative thinking that Travis was getting together a list of props for a short movie, maybe some period piece on YouTube. Travis heard that mom's butt was made to grow rosy when the bitch stepped out of line.

Some of Phil's geeky programmer friends came to the screenings. Mike, Juan and Swen were totally despised by Travis. Juan for obvious reasons, since he had made the bad life choice of being born brown. Swen should be OK, but he seemed to demonstrate that even the best genes did not save you from being an absolute Tool. Travis felt a special disgust for Mike. For one thing he was loosing his thinning brown hair and he had watery brown eyes that looked the color of baby crap. For another Mike was a hoarder. Much attention has come to these nearly three million Americans who can't throw anything, cluttering their houses with trash and junk and destroying their lives with the overflow of turbo-capitalism Mike actually *stank*. Mike's "collection" of electronics equipment had long ago filled his shower and tub. He cleaned himself with baby Wipes. Every gadget of thirty years were piled around Mike's domicile – floppy disks, laser disk players, hand-held diathermy machines, record polishers, modems, video games. His house was so full that only two chairs were clean – so Mike could only have one guest at time, not that he had any guests at all. Phil thought of Mike as a sort of reflection of himself, where he would be if he lost control of his movie madness. Travis fantasized about stealing from Mike's house, but realized it would be too hard to shift through the junk.

Jean had little imagination, so she didn't see the signs of what she had started. For example after *The Haunted Palace*, which dealt with revivification, a neighbor's calico cat had been gutted. Someone had placed Bootsy in a inverse pentagram made of salt and drain cleaner hoping to make it a sort of feline Lazarus. Jean discovered the corpse in their alley after her morning jog. She certainly suspected her son, there had been other animals' deaths, but the crack-pot alchemy meant nothing to her. Just else something to hide in the garbage. Poor Bootsy!

Getting the first seven films had been easy. Edgar Allen Poe's *King in Yellow* seems to be the only AIP film not made into DVD. So Phil's film festival lagged a few weeks. Let's look at that entry in *666 Horror Films to Scare you to Death* shall we?

Edgar Allen Poe's King in Yellow

1966. UK dir Rodger Corman, scr James Blish, starring Vincent Price, Azalea Jones, Sophia Macintyre, David Weston

The last entry in the Poe series was something of a failure. Originally shot at 126 minutes, the released version runs for 93 Minutes. The resulting film is actually so fragmented as to be literally incomprehensible. Blish was rumored to have over-sold himself as the adapter of the French play, and major plot devices were changed to reflect AIP's desire for another Poe period piece. For example Le roi jaune is set on another world, but Corman had relocated the drama to 12th Century England. The play is an uneven blend of farce and tale-or-terror, like Corman's masterpiece *The Masque of the Red Death* the final moments of surprise take place in a masquerade. In a moment of poor casting Corman allowed Price to play three roles – an acting task that a Peter Sellers may be up for, but beyond the bombastic Price. Price plays the elderly King as well as two younger men. One of these is the Stranger; a figure (who like Death in The Masque of the Red Death) seems to obey different rules of causality than the human players. The Stranger appears in the masquerade unmasked , which for some reason horrifies the revelers. The King had chosen to announce the crucial issues of succession during the masquerade. The partygoers assume that the Stranger, because of his eerie similarity to the aged King, is some long-lost heir. The Stranger however is on a Cosmic mission related to a mysterious sigil, the Yellow Sign. The courtiers have their own plots and intrigues, which were meant to be enacted with poison and sedcuction during the masquerade. Into this heady stew Corman placed Price playing a third character the Phantom of Truth, who stands out among the richly colored players by his simple white tunic. The Phantom seems to had a sheaf of parchment to some of the party goers, who become so aware of the monstrous secrets they have always held about themselves rush into small rooms (Suicide Chambers) and kill themselves. The audience never sees what is written on the parchment save that the character is drawn in a yellow, which may be the same sigil the Stranger seeks (or owns)   Azalea Jones and Sophie Macintyre play the lesbian twin sisters Camilla and Cassilda. Camilla is actively plotting to place David Weston's Aldones on the throne. Weston's is largely reprising his role in The Masque of the Red Death – the voice of the common man that acts as moral compass in most of Corman's films. Cassilda is a slightly deranged woman, who has read the dreaded parchment but has somehow been strong enough to deal with her own secrets. Corman directed her as sort of Ophelia – alternately lewd and mad, devastated and ecstatic. After seeing the film in its full version, Corman cut 33 minutes of film making this film even less accessible than his badly edited The Terror. Because of the deaths during the filming, legends persist that this is a "cursed" film, but the amazing special effect by which Corman caused three Vincent Prices to be on screen has attracted many cameramen and many theories over the years. The cast had its share of tragedy, during the shooting Sophie Macintyre (Cassillda) did kill herself in one of the Suicide Chambers – with the grim result that the cast thought she was clowning and even applauded as her blood poured out from the chamber door. The location had been plagued by major power outages, with the set going black almost everyday. Price had a minor breakdown after the film and spent six months in reclusion on the Rivera. The resulting mess of a film had a brief cult following at LSD laced Happenings during the Summer of Love. Several stories of suicides induced by the film attached themselves to it, much like the folklore of the Hungarian Suicide song. "Gloomy Sunday." Opinion is divided if such stories were started by Corman to create interest in the failed project (ala William Castle) or the whole business was just part of the general Sixties Weirdness. The film ended what had been a profitable series for AIP, and marked a decline in Price's acting abilities. The only cast member to give interviews about the film was Azalea Jones who laid the blame equally on Blish's bad French and AIP cost-cutting decisions. With a certain poetic weirdness Azalea Jones was lost in a private plane near Bermuda, making her name better known to fans of the Bermuda Triangle than a Sixties gothic actress.

It is the age of the Internet. It took a month, but Phil found a copy of *Edgar Allen Poe's The King In Yellow* on eBay. It was not hidden in the secret Vatican library, locked away in an Ivy League's library in a room of rare and forbidden tomes. It was selling for $118.00 plus Shipping and handling. The seller knowing how to work the crowd claimed that he had not watched the film and could not be responsible for people foolish enough to do so. That had to raise the price of the tape fifty bucks. He also said that it was the 126 minute *uncut version*. Yeah right. That was the rest of the price. Phil knew he was being fooled, but damnit he had to see the movie. He didn't tell Jean of his expenditure.

Travis was more excited than his dad. "Man! Truth that makes people hurt! That's better than anything else. You can get over bruises and cuts but you can't get over Truth." Phil saw his son's enthusiasm as being a sort of philosophical break-through. When Phil had been eighteen he had become interested in Truth. He swore off religion and went thought a month of telling the whole truth and nothing but the truth regardless of how much it hurt. The boy was a chip off the old block.

Jean was giving up on Travis. He had been removed from regular school and was due to be enrolled in a Juvenile Justice program. This would be too much to hide form Phil. The kid would wear uniforms for Christ's sake. Jean began to drink instead of going to her book club. Susan may have been assaulted about this time. She had approached her high school councilor with questions about rape and incest on behalf of a "friend."

The tape arrived.

The mysterious seller Typhonian Entertainment had also failed to mention it was Sony BetaMax. Phil still had a regular VCR, as well as both formats of laser disk players, and every other modern way to watch a film, but the failed format of the mid-seventies was the wrong size and encoding for any of his equipment. Phil had moved on to watching the Felleni oeuvre at this point, and Travis spent a lot of time hanging out with other pale white kids in front a certain convenience store. Phil mentioned his sadness to a slightly tipsy Jean, who reminded him that Mike Stavros had every electronic device know to man in his roach-filled house.

At first Mike was unhappy at the idea of part of his collection leaving his house, but when it became clear that Phil would bring his family over to Mike's and thus expose his shameful secret, he dug the BetaMax machine out. He delivered on it on his lunch hour.

Jean, Susan and Travis were home. Travis demanded that they watch the movie RIGHT NOW. Jean had argued for waiting for Phil, but Travis punched Mike's face and everyone saw the merit of his request. Jean sent Phil a text telling him to come home now, but because of the fickle nature of electronic communications he didn't get the text for two hours. When he got the text he called his house. Jean, Susan and Travis didn't answer their phones. Phil left work early, something he almost never did.

He saw Mike's car in the driveway. Maybe they were arraigning a screening for him. He loved his family. When he walked in he heard voices from the movie room, the big den at the back of the house. This was Phil's territory no one went there without him. He walked back expecting a yell of "Surprise!"

He heard Vincent Price exchanging lines with Vincent Price:

"The masque outlives the man, the masque outlives truth, the masque is in the reflections of the Water before it is made."

As an older character he answered, "I know these things. I have spent millions of years forgetting them. I can't forget them again and my daughters are no longer the masques for each other. Blood will stain the water, but it will turn yellow in the last spring and the poets will use it as ink."

Phil rushed forward at this moment. He plunged into his media room. On the big flat screen Vincent Price was crying, Vincent Price was laughing fiendishly. Vincent Price was lying wounded with his face peeled off , and showing an emotion that Phil does not know and hasn't been able to express or explain to Dr. Menschel in two years of therapy. One woman was holding her blood-spattered twin while as dawn broke over an expressionist castle. Another man stood by laughing quietly. It was Aldones playing a lyre. Then the power went out.

But he had seen by the light. Blood was pouring out of the closet and he would not see Susan. Travis was dressed in a bed sheet and had tried to peel away his face with a case cutter. He was saying something low and rapidly about truth. The sheet was red with his blood.

Jean was topless and holding a bottle of tequila uttering, "No Mask. No Mask! I have failed my husband." Mike was simply staring at the screen, a big shiner forming over his right eye. Travis launched himself at Phil and slashed him in the dark, before passing out from blood loss. Phil thinks his last words were, "My father, my king, I love you!"

The power came back on; Mike stood up and looked at Phil. "Because I love you man." He walked to his BeatMax machine and pulled the tape out and started shredding it. Phil started to stop him, and then realized that calling 911 was the correct response. Mike left the house telling Phil that he could keep the machine -- he wasn't collecting anymore. A few minutes later he pulled his car in front of a speeding eighteen-wheeler. Susan had killed herself, but not before taking a sheet of computer paper and writing in yellow Sharpie® SUICIDE CHAMBER on it and taping it to the inside of the small closet just off of the home theater.. Travis died of shock later in the week. Jean later recovered in a peculiar way. She can remember everything up to age twenty-three when she met Phil. She had expressed no desire to see him again.

The ambulances and police came and there were investigations and more investigations, and no could prove Phil had done anything wrong. E-bay found out that Typhonian Entertainment had ended shop – apparently having only one transaction. Dr. Menschel contacted Carlton Press and made a case for removing the entry for *Edgar Allen Poe's The King in Yellow* from *666 Films to Scare you to Death.*

An indie Texas film *The Outsider's Club* featuring Sarah Postal took its place.

Phil was placed in the State Hospital in Austin Texas, and remains a few steps above catatonic and has only one irregularity as a patient. He never goes to Movie Night.

(*For Kim Newman & James Marrott*)

MS Found in a Chicago Hotel Room

By Daniel Mills

A Confession

T he establishment had no name. The night clerk made this clear to me.

It may have had once, he explained. Probably it did. But the signboard outside had long since faded, weathered by years of rain and winter. Any lettering had been erased completely, while the remaining paint was cracked and peeling, yellow with age.

A pale, sickly kind of color, he added. *Like a wound gone bad.*

Wounds were one subject of which the hotel clerk possessed an intimate knowledge. His left arm terminated in a stump at the elbow, the sleeve cut short to reveal a mass of scar tissue. The man was in his fifties, old enough to have fought in the war against the Confederacy.

I was, I admit, skeptical. While my work had taken me to New York on many occasions previously, I had never before heard of this strange establishment, unnamed and outwardly unremarkable save for the color of its signboard.

And you're sure I'll find... I trailed off meaningfully.

You trust old Everett, he said, winking. He chuckled, a horrible, scraping sound like wet stones on cobble. *Ask for Camilla.*

He went on to give directions. I was to leave the hotel and continue down Mulberry toward the old Five Points slum. *But don't go no farther than Canal Street,* he warned. Instead, I was to take Canal over to the Bowery.

You'll find the place a few blocks down, he said. *Can't miss it.*

I can find my way, I'm sure.

I never doubted it, he said, grinning so his teeth showed, black gums and rot. *And if you find yourself lost, you can always ask about that old yellow sign. Someone's sure to know what you're talking about.*

I reached into my coat and plucked a dollar from my purse. I placed the coin face up on the counter. Columbia's face glinted, gray and dull.

The clerk's hand shot out to cover it.

There's also the matter of the key. He eyed me expectantly, mouth drooping like a bloodhound's, the lips vivid and red.

Key?

I'll need your room key from you. Before you go.

But I may be late. Shouldn't I take it with me?

Oh, I'll be here. Don't worry yourself about that. You just hurry on back.

~*~

It was a miserable night, sweltering, and the damp lay like a pall over that stinking corpse of a city. Within minutes, it had seeped through my shirt and coat, soaking me to my under-things. Sweat stood like fever on the faces of the men who hurried past, attired in brown coats and bowlers, their hands in their pockets.

Women watched from second-floor windows, little more than silhouettes, while children roamed the street below: knobby limbs, tattered garments. They traveled in packs, mostly, keeping to the dark between streetlamps, visible only in moments, like moths glimpsed beyond the circle of firelight.

Several blocks down Mulberry, I entered an unfamiliar quarter. Here refinery furnaces burned through the night, painting the stars into obscurity. The air was fetid: I breathed in smoke and breathed out ash. Darkness whirled in points from my lips, forming clouds, like fragments of the need that lived inside of me, which drove me into the night as surely as the winds that swept down to the East River.

I followed the clerk's directions to the letter. At Canal Street, I turned east toward the Bowery. Once there, I traveled south for several blocks, doubling back when I realized I had gone too far. The yellow sign proved elusive. *Can't miss it,* the clerk had said, but I wandered the same stretch of the Bowery for the better part of an hour until at last the heat pressed hard upon me and I had to sit down.

In the distance, I heard the moan of the ferry, the layered din from the music halls. Songs overlapped, merging one with another, while voices issued from the tenement behind me, a babble of conversations carried on in Irish, Spanish, Italian. I closed my eyes and lowered my face into my hands.

Good evening, a voice said. *Are you alright?*

I lifted my head, surprised to find myself confronted by a young man of twenty or twenty-one. He was handsome, in apparent good health, and his clothes were well-made. Under one arm, he carried a slim valise, three feet by two but little thicker than a cigar case. He smiled broadly, his lips curling to meet his moustache.

Thank you, I said. *I'm—quite well.*

Rising, I offered my hand, giving a false name as I did so. He introduced himself as Robert and folded his hand around mine. He squeezed, strong but gentle, his skin cool and dry despite the heat of the evening.

And now, my good fellow, you look rather the lost sheep. Might I be of some assistance?

I looked him over again, taking in the fine clothes, the thin case. For a moment, I half-fancied him for the religious sort, one of those well-meaning young men who would carry bibles into the depths of Tartarus itself as long as he could return home to his wife and townhouse with everything in its place. But his ready smile and obvious amiability put me at my ease.

There is a—place—nearby. It has no name, I'm given to understand, but the sign outside is a most peculiar shade of—

Yellow?

His eyes glittered.

Well—yes.

He laughed, a roar of surprise and delight. *And here I thought you meant to ask me the way to the nearest music hall.*

You know of it?

He nodded. *As it happens, I'm going there myself. Perhaps you might care to accompany me?*

I fell into step beside him.

It's good of you, I said. *Truly.*

Not at all. We're not far off now. You'll see.

We continued to the end of the block, where my companion turned sharply to the right. He plunged down a sunken roadway—long abandoned, half-flooded by a cracked water main—and I followed him through puddles that were ankle-deep and warm as bathwater.

Eventually, we reached another street even more decrepit, where the air reeked of piss and spoiled milk. Laundry-lines flapped like sails overhead, festooned with colorful rags. After two blocks, my guide ducked down another side street before completing the circle by turning right once more.

This should have brought us back to the Bowery, but the street we entered bore little resemblance to the noisome squalor we had left behind. The crumbling tenements were gone, replaced by elaborate structures of concrete and steel. There were no street children, no milling crowds. Instead, an orderly procession of impeccably-attired men and women walked arm-in-arm down the sidewalk, talking and laughing, engaged in an animated discussion of an opera or play they had all just attended. In the lane, carriages were pulled up, black and gleaming, drawn by fine specimens of horseflesh. Even the street signs were unfamiliar: Genevieve Street, Castaigne Court.

Is this the Bowery? I asked, confused.

Of course. Don't you recognize it?

I offered no reply.

We walked on in silence. My companion maintained a brisk, nearly martial pace, swinging his arms with such vigor that I worried he would lose his valise. Clearly, he was no young missionary equipped with bibles and the armor of self-righteousness. And yet I did not think to ask what he carried inside the case.

He halted. *Here we are*, he said. He pointed up at the splintered sign board, a faceless plank of weather-worn timber caked in faded paint. The color may have once been gray or brown but now appeared yellow in the glow cast by a streetlamp opposite.

The establishment itself occupied a three story building in the Queen Anne style, the walls fashioned from red brick. The windows were numerous and brightly-lit, though masked with damask drapes that hid the rooms beyond.

Come along, Robert said.

He led me inside into an elaborately-furnished sitting room, characterized by paintings in expensive frames and couches upholstered in dark velvet. Most prominent among the room's many ornaments was a gilded clock, which stood over six feet in height. Its face was divided into several dials of various sizes, the largest of which gave the time as a quarter past two—but surely that couldn't be right, I reflected, as it wasn't yet ten-thirty when I left the hotel. Other dials appeared to tell the month and the year, though these, too, were incorrect. A final gauge noted the phase of the moon. Waning.

A woman received us at the counter. She was tall and emaciated, the skin stretched tight over her skull. In color, she was so pale as to be transparent. Her veins showed like scrimshaw under the skin, darkening to violet where they gathered at her temples. She addressed my companion.

Back again, are you? Here to see Cassie, I take it.

Robert grinned. *You know me too well! Would the lovely lady be available?*

For you, young man, I dare say she'd make *herself available. Of course, it probably wouldn't matter to you, even if she wasn't. Maybe you'd prefer it that way.*

Maybe I would, he said, flashing the same winning smile. *Indeed, fair lady, I think you may be right.*

Fair lady? she scoffed. *Ah, go on, up with you. He won't be back for another hour at least. I'll let him know you're in there.*

You have my thanks. He turned and offered me his hand. *Do you think you can find your own way from here?*

I nodded.

Good man, said he, and clapped me on the shoulder. He transferred the valise from under his arm, and then, carrying it at his side, stepped round the counter and passed through the curtained doorway beyond.

The pale woman turned her attention on me. *And you, sir?* she said, speaking more formally than before. *I believe you're joining us tonight for the first time?*

Yes, that's right.

One moment.

She stooped beneath the counter, disappearing from view. I heard the click of a key in a lock, the groan of oiled hinges. Then she straightened, holding a ledger in both arms. The binding was good, the pages crisp and new. She placed it on the counter—gently, the way a mother carries a child—and opened to the marked page.

She looked up at me. With one hand, she held a fountain pen. The other rested on the counter, placed with apparent casualness, though the barrel of a Derringer was just visible where it poked between her fingers.

And which name should I use?

I told her, employing the same pseudonym I had used when meeting Robert. She nodded and noted this down. *And do you know who you're here to see?*

Camilla.

Camilla? You sure of that?

I am. Is there a problem?

No, sir. None at all.

She continued to write for the better part of a minute, the nib scratching and scratching. A glance into the corner of the room confirmed what I had initially suspected: the clock's hands had not changed position. In this unnamed establishment, it was always a quarter past two.

The woman pressed the ledger shut and secreted it away beneath the counter. The gun, I noticed, had disappeared as well. *I'll need payment from you upfront,* she said. *Not many men can afford to see Camilla.* She named a price. It was expensive, but not exorbitant, and ultimately less than I had expected, given the general opulence of the establishment.

I paid it gladly.

She motioned to the curtained entrance behind her. *Go on up to the third floor. Camilla's is the fourth door on the right.*

The curtains parted, ushering me into a narrow corridor marked at either end by a twisting stair. The hall was lined with closed doors carved with scenes from mythology: images of Io and Leda, women sprawled under gods. The smell of smoke was especially pronounced, the cloying odor of cigars. From behind one door came a man's voice, muffled and gravelly, followed by a woman's laughter.

I proceeded to the end of the hall and climbed to the third floor, emerging in a new corridor identical to the first in all respects save the wallpaper, which was painted with a pastoral scene: rolling hills, castles, olive groves. A mass-produced print, I decided, though an artist had made certain embellishments, adding a courting couple to the riverbank and again to the castle's battlements.

The woman stood with her back against the tower-wall. She was arrayed in silks and ruffles, a woman of means. Her golden hair streamed with the wind, hiding her face. The man knelt before her, as though requesting her hand, but his bare back was turned to the audience, and I wondered why he should be naked.

They were not alone. Another figure could be seen at the far end of the battlements, a man watching. His face was lightly sketched, presented in profile, but there was something vaguely familiar about him, a likeness I couldn't place.

I reached Camilla's door. I knocked—gently at first but louder when I received no reply. The handle gave way at a touch. The door swung inward, admitting me to a dimly-lit chamber. The hearth was cold, the lone window shaded with purple damask. The only light emanated from a candelabrum on the mantelpiece, casting layered shadows over the elaborate wallpaper, the four-poster hung with scarlet drapes.

Camilla stood by the window, robed in silk. Her hair was black and curly, gathered atop her head in a series of nested spirals, while her gown was in the Chinese style: crimson, clean lines, the back stitched with a sunburst in gold.

Hearing my step, she turned, and I was surprised to discover that she wore a mask. It was made from porcelain: bone-white and perfectly smooth, a cold facsimile of feminine beauty with elliptical holes left for eyes and mouth. She held her robe closed across her chest, alluringly modest, a triangle of pale skin visible at her throat, merging with the shadows where it plunged to hidden curves below.

She did not speak. Gliding to the night stand, she withdrew a glass pipe from her robe. It was long and slim, a delicate stem that sloped to a shallow bowl. At the night stand, she pushed back the lid of an ornate snuff box. Inside, I could see a coarse black powder, gritty like coal-dust. She withdrew a pinch and placed it in the bowl.

With the pipe in one hand, she approached the hearth and took down the candelabrum. Her robe fell open, revealing her breasts, the thatch of hair between her legs. She made no attempt to cover herself but merely held the candelabrum at her chest and gazed at me through the twitching flame-tips. Her eyes bored into me: black and deep and bracingly still. I returned her stare, unable to look away.

She exhaled, extinguishing two of the candles so that only one remained lit. Tilting the candelabrum, she held the flame to the side of the pipe-bowl and slipped the stem into her mouth. The powder glowed, orange then black. Her inhalation lasted several seconds.

She replaced the pipe and candle on the mantelpiece and turned her gaze on me once more. Extending her hand, she beckoned me closer, one finger curling back, drawing me in. Only then did I realize that she had not exhaled, that she was in fact holding the pipe-smoke in her lungs.

I stepped forward.

For a moment, she regarded me closely, silently. Then, with queer violence, she grabbed hold of my hair and tugged down my head, crushing my face against the mask. Her mouth found mine through the gap in the porcelain. Her lips were as dry and coarse as parchment.

Smoke filled my mouth, my lungs. Darkness bloomed inside my skull, the acrid stench of blood-iron, slow decay. My vision blurred. I coughed and staggered back, losing my balance and tumbling backward. I landed on the bed. The blankets yielded—gave way—and closed over me. The bedroom vanished, and I sank into oblivion.

~*~

Stars. A billion pupils—constricting, expanding—like holes cut through the dome of the sky. Every star provided me a glimpse of a greater illumination beyond, of the light that was always there, though sometimes hidden, cloaked in darkness in the same way Camilla wore a mask, and for the same reason: to hide the face of God.

Years passed like ghosts at broad noon, unremembered, unseen. The Earth groaned and shifted underfoot, releasing a cry of agony that stretched over eons and millennia, dulled by time to a gentle hum. It gave little warning of what came next.

The sun exploded, bursting like a fever-mark. Heat poured out to cover all things. The stones liquefied, the air evaporated. The sky fell away, and I hurtled into the stars.

Surrounded now, I observed that they were not pupils as I had first imagined but flaming suns, ringed with planets like half-lit moons. These new suns arranged themselves in strange patterns around me, forming bands of color, spirals that recalled the coils of Camilla's hair.

But even these were left behind when I passed beyond the farthest star and entered a darkness more alien—and yet more fundamental—than the womb that gave me birth. I was right to have thought that Creation wore a mask, but it was one of light, not dark. The stars served only to conceal the silent tempest that lay beyond, the storm in which I now found myself, shivering and cold. But I was no longer among the heavens. Instead, I had descended inward, to the very center of my being, and discovered there the same boiling chaos where my soul should have been.

Despairing, I crawled forward, unable to rise, while the cosmos cracked and fell to pieces around me. This was the storm that lived inside of me, inside of all men: a thousand cities scorched and shattered, reduced to spinning fragments. Providence. New York. Chicago. Black snow on ceaseless wind.

Footsteps. From somewhere far off, I heard a child's steps: stumbling, uncertain. The night parted and re-formed, the storm taking shape as the wind snapped back against itself, smashing those broken cities together, until they coalesced into the silhouette of a young boy, no more than three years old. He tottered toward me with mouth open, a perfect circle—screaming, though I heard nothing.

How can I describe this?

It was you. *You*, my boy. The reason I'm writing this. Years before I met your mother, before you were born, I knew that we would share this place, would always. There was comfort in that thought, and there was sadness, the latter cutting deep when you offered me your hand. You were frail and sickly, exactly like the child I would watch you become, but still you took my hand, and raised me to my feet, and lifted me out of that silent storm.

~*~

In Camilla's bedroom, the candle had burned down. It guttered into insignificance, spreading a shadow over the stained bed sheets, the cracked and peeling wallpaper. Around me, the room had fallen into disrepair, all elegance stripped away. The air was dank with the stench of mildew and perfume, a sweetness like high fever.

Camilla stood at the window. She was dressed in imitation silks, her face turned to the slit in the drapes. She had removed the mask, which now sat on the nightstand, but the darkness hid her features, and for this, I was glad. She sighed, faintly, and it occurred to me that she was waiting for something, or someone. I gathered my things and slipped from the room.

In the hallway, I encountered my young companion, his valise tucked under one arm. Evidently, he had just let himself out from another bedroom.

His eyes widened upon seeing me. His face went pale.

But—that's Camilla's room!

Yes. I was told to ask for her—
Who told you that?
The night clerk. At my hotel.
My God! You must get out of here. If he finds you…
He? What are you talking about?
She's King's girl. Camilla. Cassie is too, though he doesn't mind me sketching her.
Sketching?

Realization dawned at last. The man from the wallpaper—the figure who stood watching—was none other than my young companion. Though drawn with the vaguest of lines, the face was unquestionably Robert's. Moreover, I realized that it must be a self-portrait. The valise, no doubt, contained his pencils and sketchbooks.

He took me firmly by the arm.

We have to go, he said. *He'll be back soon, but we can take the fire escape. With luck, we might manage to avoid him.*

My mouth fell open, but I could not find the words to protest. Robert didn't wait for me to speak. He spirited me down the corridor, which I now saw to be every bit as dilapidated as Camilla's bedroom, and through a doorway at the end of the hall that led out to the fire escape.

I don't understand, I managed at last. *Who is this King?*

Silas King. A former ship captain and smuggler. Originally from England, I understand, though he now styles himself The King of the Bowery.

A gang leader, then?

Yes. You might say that. Camilla has been his since she was a little girl. Don't you see? She belongs to him. All of the Bowery knows better than to ask for her.

All at once, I understood the night clerk's deception, the thin woman's surprise when I mentioned Camilla. With a thrill of fear, I followed Robert down the fire escape, moving slowly so as to mute my clattering steps. By now, it was nearly midnight, but the air had not cooled. The breeze from the East River brought only heat and soot, the mingled smells of smoke and sewage.

Careful, Robert warned as we reached the ground. The alley before us teemed with faint movement, the scurrying of hundreds of rats. They parted before us like a sparkling sea, fleeing into rubbish bins, piles of twisted metal.

Moments later, I saw what had brought them into the alley to feed.

Opposite the fire escape were buckets of slop and grease, which half-concealed two sheeted forms that may have once been human. Children, I thought, dead on the street. Or the bodies of King's victims.

The alley led back to the Bowery, but there was no sign of the wealthy theater-goers or their gleaming carriages. Outside a barroom, two foreigners fought with knives while a crowd looked on. A young family huddled together in a doorway. The mother called to us, begging for coin. *For the babe*, she said, but we paid her no heed.

Halfway down the block, we passed beneath the yellow sign once more. Formerly grand and imposing, the establishment now bore the marks of neglect: bricks crumbling, windows cracked or broken. I glanced up to the third floor, where Camilla was still visible: a faceless shadow, an outline glimpsed through tattered curtains.

We hurried past.

~*~

Robert froze. Cursing, he took me roughly by the arm and shoved me into the mouth of an alley. I cried out in surprise, prompting him to drop his case and grab me by the collar.

That's him, he hissed. *King.*

Whatever I had expected, I was unprepared for the size of the man who came into view. King was tall, nearly seven-foot, and grossly corpulent. The flesh of his neck was soft, doughy. It gathered in folds above his collar and swung free like a turkey-wattle, rippling with every labored footfall, his entire body vibrating, a drawn string. His hair was black and thickly-greased. His complexion was sallow, shockingly pale, and his face was pitted with disease. An open sore marred his upper lip, red and glistening beneath the thin mustache.

And yet, for all this, his clothing was exceedingly fine. His top hat and frock were of the best workmanship, and a gold chain stretched across his quivering gut. He had lost his left ear but wore a porcelain substitute in its place, and he walked with the aid of a cane, a wrist-thick shaft terminating in a shard of yellow quartz: uncut, its jagged edges showing between his flabby fingers.

King glanced down the alley as he passed. His eyes met mine, briefly, and I saw that they were black: the same non-color as the shadow inside me or the places beyond the stars. He must not have seen me, though, for he kept walking, his cane striking the pavement like a pistol's report. The sound dwindled and disappeared.

Robert released a breath. He turned to me, brow shining with perspiration.

We have a few minutes. Where will you go?

Back to my hotel, I suppose.

He shook his head. *I wouldn't do that. The clerk thought he was sending you to your death. He will be ill-pleased to see you again.*

The police, then.

And you think they would listen? They might turn you over to King themselves if they heard he was looking.

Then what?

Make for Grand Central. I'll pay for a hansom—it's the fastest way. From there you can catch the first train home.

And then…?

He shrugged. *Stay away from New York. And if you have to come back, then for God's sake, don't come near the Bowery. He really is a king here—and not the forgiving kind. However, you should be safe outside of the city.*

Should be, I repeated.

He's pursued some men as far as San Francisco and for less cause. You gave a pseudonym? Good. Then he doesn't know your name or what you look like. He might never find you. Nevertheless he won't stop searching. You can be sure of that.

I recalled the moment in which our eyes had met—black on black, mirrors turned to reflect one another—and realized that it didn't matter what he knew, or what I looked like, for we carried the same tempest inside us.

My companion collected his valise from the ground and proceeded to the end of the alley. He hailed a cab, which drew to a shuddering halt, its lanterns casting us into sharp relief. The horses snorted, slick and steaming in that heat.

Robert helped me into the carriage.

Remember what I said. Avoid the Bowery.

And you?

You needn't worry about me. King and I have an understanding. In any case, it hardly matters. I'm leaving soon, maybe for good.

Where are you going?

Paris. The School of Fine Arts. He hefted his valise. *I'm going to be a proper artist.*

With that, he grinned broadly and wished me goodnight. The driver cracked his whip, snapping the horses into motion. I glanced back over my shoulder, hoping for a final glimpse of my friend, but he was already gone, lost somewhere in that hell of smoke and night.

I never saw him again.

~*~

For years, there were nightmares. In sleep, I plunged once more into seething chaos and surfaced in a place of solitude, cast up in the midst of the silent storm Camilla had showed me. Again, I forced myself forward, crawling hand over elbow, unable to stand, and again, the darkness whirled and took shape ahead of me.

Silas King. He towered over me like the looming specter of ultimate horror, and though I tried to crawl away, I was never fast enough. He found me, always, and I woke up gasping, panting after breath that would not come.

Around this time, I met your mother. When I proposed, she squealed with delight and threw her arms around me. She kissed my neck and whispered love-words in my ear. In those days, you see, she was not yet your mother, the woman you would know. That came later.

But the nightmares persisted, worse than before. Every night, I came awake screaming, choking on sweetness and fever. In the morning, the taste of King's breath lingered in my mouth, recalling the stench of dried blood or the dust Camilla had burned, the smoke with which she had filled me.

Then you were born, as slight and sickly as I had dreamed you. The nightmares ceased soon after, another miracle. At night, I descended into darkness, our darkness, and there found you waiting, not King. Only then did I begin to understand the nature of the blessing and the curse that Camilla had bestowed on me.

It couldn't last, of course. In late '92, I traveled to New York on business. I stayed far from the Bowery. I was careful. All the same, King must have learned of my visit, for I soon became aware of someone following me.

One afternoon, in Boston, on a crowded street, I happened to look behind me and spotted him twenty yards back. He was attired in his customary hat and frock, the gold chain glittering on his belly. He smiled, perhaps in recognition, and hastened toward me, as though advancing to meet an old friend. He moved quickly for his size, loping like an animal, and I took to my heels, thinking only of escape.

I ran. My flight brought me here: to this city, this hotel. Ten after two. There isn't much time. I can hear him in the hallway, pacing beyond the door. His cane taps and taps on the boards, doubling the sound of my heartbeat. Soon he'll knock. He'll rap on the door with that shard of quartz. He'll say my name, my real name, and then I'll have to let him in.

WS Lovecraft, 1893

it sees me when I'm not looking

By Gary McMahon

I t was a strange time that spring in New York City. the air was cold. the sidewalks were shining from the rain. puddles, like mirrors thrown down and smashed on the concrete, reflected my absolute drunkenness as if trying to shame me. but I didn't care. the shit was inside me, all over me, and if I went down I wasn't going down sober.

I'd never liked that city, and it damn well hated me. but we had an understanding. I'd been there a month, marooned after giving a poetry recital to a women's book circle. instead of a free bed and a hot fuck, I'd been thrown out onto the street after the gig, and decided to hang around for a while.

the last time I'd had a woman had been two months ago. Sandy Lane. that was her name – like a punchline to a bad joke. we'd been like two stoned birds on a perch, propping each other up, but I left when the money ran out. her daddy stopped cashing her checks so I stopped cashing her check – if you know what I mean.

so there I was, riding a whisky high and with nowhere to stay when things got low. I considered calling Sandy, but the thought of her big dimpled white ass and the way she liked to sit on my face and break wind in my mouth made me feel all on edge so I walked on down to the village instead, looking for some long-haired hepcats to lay into.

that was how I came into contact with the play. purely by accident. when I went looking for a fight. well, I sure got one, didn't I? one that might just see me trading punches with the darkness forever.

"hey, Chinaski! hey, you cheap dimestore hood! CHINASKI!"

I was ambling through SoHo when I heard the voice, and at first I didn't recognise it. but when someone calls your name at 3 a.m. in the morning, and then starts abusing you, your instincts tend to kick in. so I turned with my hands balled into fists and my arms raised in a fighter's stance.

"hey, Chinaski, you goddam BUM!"

it was Mervin Bones, a dried-up wino from Hell's Kitchen. I hadn't seen him in days – someone had told me he died, and I hadn't thought enough of the guy to miss him. he was always good for a drink, though, so I lowered my hands and opened my fists in greeting.

"hey, Merv. how's things?"

he sort of swerved towards me across the sidewalk, a brown-bagged bottle in one hand. he took a sip and let his hand fall. I looked hungrily at the bottle and I'm pretty sure I even licked my lips.

"what's up, man?"

he swayed before me, his eyes like ball-bearings spinning around in his head. "been looking for you, Hank. I got somethin' you might wanna see."

he knew I wrote poetry and had a fondness for classical music. to Merv, I was an educated man. to anyone else I was a no-good drunk with an interest in beauty. I was a student of Dostoevsky and listened to Mahler whilst drinking wine in the dark. somewhere inside my heart a bluebird sang, but I was the only one who could hear its tune.

"tell me about it, Merv." I reached out and took the bottle from his hand. his grip was loose. he didn't even realise I'd grabbed it until he saw me take a drink.

"yeah...help yourself."

the whisky hit my insides running. it was hot and cool and sweet and evil. it tasted of every woman I'd ever kissed and smelled like every dirty soul I'd ever knocked out in a fistfight in an alleyway behind some bar.

"I got this play. somethin' you'd like. you being a writer, and all." he smiled. his teeth were blackened, rotten. the gums were bleeding. I inspected the neck of the bottle, but it was clean. so I took another throat-full.

"what kind of a play? I don't like that modern shit they put on the stage now, I like the bard – gimme some Shakespeare or give me nothing, you stinkin' fuck." I considered smashing the whisky bottle across the side of his face just to amuse myself but I didn't want to waste what was left.

"I dunno nothin' about shaking spears, but this one's back at my apartment. it's called the king in yellow, and it's got your name written on the inside cover. I thought it might be one of yours – somethin' you had published back in California."

I wasn't sure what puzzled me more, the fact that old Merv had an apartment or that my name was scrawled inside a book I'd never even heard of.

"come back with me, Hank. we'll have a drink. you can buy the book back off me."

so that was his game – and was there any other game in town? everybody wanted their bit, money was everything on those streets. but it wasn't everything to me. I loved art and a good fight in the ring. I craved truth and honour, men with strong hearts and women with soft, warm breasts, but all I got was the scum like Merv, the dirty rotten bastards who were out for whatever they could get. their slice of the pie. their piece of the cake.

"okay, Merv," I said. "let's go back to your place for a drink."

at the very least, I'd get some cheap scotch, maybe even a hand-job from Merv's old lady – last time I'd seen him, he was with some retired hooker from Chicago, and she had these gnarled, bony hands with strange soft fingers...

Merv's apartment turned out to be a room somewhere between Canal and 14th Street, about a block from the river. it was filthy- the kind of place even sewer rats would be ashamed to stay. but the roof didn't leak and the walls were dry. we walked up a rickety steel fire escape stair to get in. Merv climbed through an open window, and I followed him inside. it didn't strike me as unusual at the time. everybody I knew during that brief time in N.Y.C. was trying to dodge their landlord.

the room had bare walls and a torn linoleum floor. there was a filthy cooker in one corner, with no ventilation anywhere nearby. a dining table and two chairs. pushed up against the wall was a single bed, and curled up on the mattress, clutching a thin cover against her half-naked body, was the Chicago woman with the dockworker's hands and artist's fingers. I stared at her fingers at the edge of the blanket. her fingernails were bitten down to the quick.

"don't mind Annie." Merv was opening a cupboard. he took out a pint bottle. "she sleeps a lot. I think she might be ill."

I looked at her again. the covers had slipped down her naked back, baring her spine. the bones there looked weird, like they were bent out of shape. there was a yellow tinge to her skin, like jaundice.

"just leave her. she'll be fine. He's just got the fear."

I shrugged and sat down at the small dining table in the middle of the room. there was a pack of cards on the tabletop, so I started to shuffle them. every card was a joker. this scared me, so I put them back on the stained paper table cloth and waited for Merv to pour me a drink.

as I sat there, watching this lean man with his scruffy face and his smelly clothes pour scotch into two chipped dessert glasses, I thought about Los Angeles. about the big fault line under the town. about how, some day, that fault would open and everybody would fall inside. maybe I should stay in New York, do some more readings for the hip crowd, let them pay me in booze.

"here."

I reached out and gripped the glass. it felt like all of my energy, everything I had, was focused into that single motherfucking moment. I picked up the glass and took a sip, and the pressure went away, just like always. I pity them, the ones who don't know that insane magic. what truly impoverished lives they must lead.

"so I was at a party in a squat somewhere up in the Heights, and this weird lady started giving me drinks. she talked about poetry, and I told her I knew a man who wrote that shit – Henry Chinaski, a famous poet from L.A.!"

I laughed at that. it was funny. it hurt, but it was funny too. "fuck you, Merv."

"no, she was interested, man. she wanted to meet you. but I told her that I didn't know where you were staying, so she got out this book and said that if I ever saw you again I had to pass it on. like a gift." he belched, farted, and took another sip of his scotch. "like a gift..."

"so how much do you want for this gift?"

"how much you got?"

"you fuckin' cockroach. it's a gift. it's meant to be for free."

"like I said, how much you got?"

"all I have is five bucks. take it or leave it." I had another ten rolled up in my sock, but I was never going to tell Merv that. I might give it to the Chicago whore, whose twig-like hands I couldn't stop thinking about. those strange soft fingers, stroking me rigid.

"okay, okay...I'll go get the book." he stumbled as he left his chair, but I wasn't going to stand up and help him. Merv was a fucker, a conman, and if he fell and cracked his head on the floor I would fuck his woman and take my book – my gift – and never come back again.

a few tin pots hung like starved suicides from a rail above the cooker. Merv opened a cupboard door, and the hinges slipped. the door hung askew in his hand, like a slipped mask. he set it down on top of the cooker and took a small book from the cupboard. then he turned around and staggered back to the table.

he threw the book on the table in front of me. its cover was ragged and faded, but I could just about make out the title: THE KING IN YELLOW.

"never heard of it." I reached for the book and opened the cover. the smell of used paper hit me like a drug. sure enough, written inside, on the first page, just below the title, was my own name, in my own handwriting. I'd signed this book but I'd never seen it before.

"see? told ya, didn't I?"

I wanted to beat the stupid bastard to death with his own pots and pans. I wanted his blood spilled like wine, his eyeballs popping from his skull like chestnuts in a fire.

"what did she look like? this woman?"

"she was wearing a mask – they all were. it was a masked ball, in a fucking filthy basement dive."

"so what the hell were you doing there? who'd invite a bum like you to a masked ball?"

"it was Annie." he motioned over to the bed. "some of her whore friends. they were working that night."

I looked down at the book. "so. the woman."

"yeah, the woman. she was wearing this white mask – she kept calling it the pallid mask. and she had on a tattered yellow dress. she was tall – I think she might've been one of those fifth-avenue transvestites, the ones who'll blow you for five in a dirty-movie house."

I turned the book in my hands. the back cover was blank, and there was no illustration on the cover. just that intriguing title. I felt sober for the first time in years – truly sober, like my whole body was being cleansed – so I grabbed the bottle and drank straight from it, needing to drown out these hideous new feelings.

"five bucks."

I nodded and reached into my pocket. I took out the money and threw it onto the table. "how much for a roll with her?" I tilted my head towards the bed, and the woman who was now stirring.

"hell, Hank," she said. "after reading that book of yours, I'll do you for free."

when I spun around in the chair she was swinging her legs off the mattress. the bed sheets had curled around her waist, but I could see enough to know that free was too high a price to pay for what she had on offer. her tits were small and hard and yellow, like lemons. her belly was soft as modelling clay. I didn't want to look for long at her face, but she reminded me of my deformed first wife – the way her head sat directly between her shoulders, with no need for a neck. her lips were yellow. when she smiled I could see no teeth, just a kind of dusty darkness.

"hell, no. I just came for my book. and for a drink."

"fuck you, then, Chinaski." she rolled back into bed, pulled up the covers, and turned her pale face to the wall. the sheets, as she shifted them, were spotted in yellow dust, like decay or the stuff from moths wings.

"she read the book?" I didn't know why it had offended me, but for some reason I didn't like the idea of her eyes roaming across the pages I was yet to see.

Merv was nodding. but his eyes were closed and his head was hanging low. if he wasn't sleep, he would be soon. I took my five dollars from the table and put it back in my pocket. then I poured another drink. I looked again at the name I'd signed in the book, and even in the depths of my drunkenness I knew that the handwriting was mine. there was a message written under the name, and I had to strain to read it.

"hello from Carcosa", it said. I didn't know what the hell that could even mean.

I finished Merv's pint and left the room by the window, holding on to the book as I made my way down the fire escape. it was still dark. the moon was a slice of strange fruit in the glass containing the sky. the stars looked like none I'd ever seen before. I couldn't find the north star.

all the cross streets, alleys and backstreets looked the same. I headed south, towards TriBeCa, just looking for somewhere to be. a place I wouldn't have to pretend to be someone else. but I was drawn to a place where a brazier burned up against a blackened stone wall. the wash of flame looked like somebody had opened the doors of heaven or hell, and I wasn't sure which one sounded best. I found a bar that stayed open 24/7 and ordered a drink. then I found a dark corner and started to read the play. I got through the first act before closing the book, and then I ordered another whisky. the five was almost gone. soon I'd be cutting into the stash in my sock.

there was a lot of shit in the play about strange moons and black stars. like gothic fantasy, but deeper, darker. even as I read it, and thought how stupid it was, I felt wheels turning inside me and doors opening somewhere deep down in the pit of my stomach, at the place where even the booze couldn't reach. when I closed my eyes I saw a woman in a pale mask. behind her stood a man whose face was nothing but a fan of yellow tatters, like old newspapers faded in the sun. the lines of the play – and of the poems I found therein – all seemed familiar, yet they were totally unknown to me. it was like something I'd once dreamt about and then forgotten, or maybe pushed out of mind.

a hidden memory. a repressed event. oh, sweet, sweet Carcosa, why did I seem to know you and recognise your twin suns rising from behind the dark cursed waters of Lake Hali?

when I regained consciousness she was there, standing above me, beside me, with her hands on the table. she wore a featureless white mask and her dress, under the dark overcoat, was yellow. I kept seeing yellow flapping shapes out of the corner of my eye. my cock and balls ached like she was squeezing them and I needed a drink more than ever before.

"I have lots of booze. all you'll ever need." her voice was like a song. a sad, corrupt lullaby sung by a weeping barroom madonna or a broken messiah. "come, come with me to Carcosa."

I couldn't say no. my body obeyed her like she was pulling my strings and I was just a puppet dancing for her entertainment. I followed her out the door and onto the black street. everything looked different. when I glanced up, at the sky, black stars were rising and strange moons circled through the skies. the drink, the night, the play... Merv's cheap booze and his feverish whore. it was all too much, or too little. nothing made sense. even the booze seemed like a lie – the biggest one of all, because I already knew that it was faking. all my life I'd known, but still I'd loved it.

we walked along crazy streets, locked in the arms of a crazy night, and the whole world turned to glass. the buildings were made of liquor bottles – tenement windows swam with amber fluid, trash cans were filled with beer. Carcosa was a world of drink and drinking, and I'd been here all along, without even knowing.

she led me along a narrow alley, and then up another fire escape. this was one was shiny, like new, and light as a feather as I heaved my bulk up the glass wall of a building that was filled with black-eyed angels and psychopaths swimming in vast rooms filled with booze. I glanced upward, towards the sky, and saw the clear crenellated towers of this high glass castle, patrolled by drunken soldiers toting weapons of inebriation.

inside the room I was underwater – no, not water, but under liquor. I moved slowly through those whisky depths, but somehow I was able to breathe. Merv sat at the table, his hair moving gently like dark fronds of seaweed. the whore was still in bed, but as she slept she rose above the covers, floating like a small dead whale. the masked woman moved normally, as if she was the only one still on dry land. I swam towards her, reaching out to grab her tits, her ass, her ghostly body. but her form gave way as I touched it, and she flaked apart like spent jism in grimy bathwater...

treading water (whisky?) I managed to turn around, so I was facing the way I'd come in. fist-sized fishes swam through the open window, but they all had the heads of birds. their fins were razorblades and they had teeth like those of b-movie vampires.

I tried to cry out but bubbles burst between my lips and rose slowly past my eyes. I stared at those bubbles, and inside each one was a tiny replica of the image I'd seen only briefly – a man who was made up of gaunt yellow tatters. each of these Russian-doll visions turned to me at the same time, spreading their arms in a welcoming embrace, and as I looked up, and across the room, I saw long, jagged furls of yellow cloth, like the remnants of ruined flags, curling around the window frame. the woman in the mask was wrapped up in those tatters. she was naked now, but she still wore the pallid mask. she floated across the room and was set down in front of me. her body was thin, the bones prominent through her loose, white flesh. She was like a belsen horror, a stick-and bone phantom. but when I touched her she felt soft, like dough; her flesh was like something left soaking too long in water, the bones rubbery as the limbs of a squid.

I had a hard-on like I'd never experienced before, all raging stiffness and urgent need.

so when she grabbed my crotch I kissed her, sucking on her long, thin tongue as it wriggled like a grave worm down my throat. she pushed me down and straddled me, all the time nodding her head and kneading the loose muscles of my arms with her strong hands. my pants came off without me even noticing, and then I was inside her, thrusting as deep as I could and grabbing her ass with my hands to part her cheeks and slip a finger up inside there. her flesh was soft and flabby, despite there not being too much of it. but I did her anyway; never let it be said that Chinaski ever turned down a free ride.

she drifted away when I was finished. she was still wearing that strange blank mask. her arms hung loose at her sides and her gait was lazy, dissatisfied. I'd done my best, but my best was never good enough. I knew I shouldn't have done it, but I could never turn down a free ride. the yellow tatters gathered around her, spinning her like a toy. she was a yellow mummy, a sanctified thing of sex and longing and the sounds of the lost, the lonely, the dying and the already dead. reality was her plaything, and the tattered king was the master of her yearning, the captain of her unfathomable dreams. when the cloth began to unbind her, unwinding like a shroud, it revealed the shape of the king himself, and slowly and deliberately he lifted his torn yellow face towards me...

...and then I was awake again, and sitting at the table in that same shitty little barroom, an empty glass in my hand and the book spread out before me like a big butterfly someone had pinned to the table using six-inch nails. I shut the book and pushed it across the damp surface, trying to get it away from me. then I gulped down the rest of my drink and stood, my legs weak and barely able to support me.

had I been dreaming, or was the vision something else – like a glimpse into a possible future, if I read the entire play? like Merv's woman, Annie, if I finished the book would my body start to distort, the bones cracking and reshaping, the skin turning the colour of a dying addict's sweat?

while outside the world kept turning, all the New York needle-babies cried, a dog pissed up against the signpost that pointed towards happiness. the sun vibrated and all the birds in the sky took a shit at the same time.

at the last minute I grabbed that cocksucking book. no matter how much I hated my fellow man, and wished them all dead and gone and not bothering me, I had no wish to set this curse upon them. so I carried the book from the bar, out into the alley, and headed towards the burning brazier I'd seen earlier, as I entered the place a couple of street bums were huddled around the flames, warming their hands and bullshitting each other with the tuneless songs of their busted dreams.

"what the fuck you doin'" said one of the bums, barely even turning towards me. he rubbed his rough hands by the fire.

"burnin' books. and you'll never know how much that hurts me, brother – more than a cutthroat razor across the cheek, or a strong right hook to the sweet spot."

I paused for a second or two, just to take in the moment, and then I threw the book onto the fire.

when I turned away, trudging like a punch-drunk pugilist along that miserable asshole of an alley, I happened to look up at the name of the bar I'd been in. it was called 'the yellow sign'.

I don't know what that means – maybe it was just a bullshit coincidence, or a shitty cosmic joke – but all I know is that I went straight to the bus station and got on the next bus out of the big-rotten-motherfucking-apple.

there's a bluebird in my heart but it wears a pale mask. it sees me when I'm not looking.

the bus moved off in a cloud of diesel smoke. I was going back to L.A., where the air is warm, the masks are gaudy, and the poems are all hard and bright and brittle as ice. where there's only one moon in the sky, and the stars are ones that I recognise. the city – my own mythical city of fallen angels – where dim and distant Carcosa is nothing but the memory of a hard night I once lived through and the half-forgotten taste of a bitter drink I once tried.

Finale, Act Two

By Ann K. Schwader

The ebon snows have drifted deep
Along the shoreline of Hali
Assuring that dynastic sleep

Which ever was, shall ever be
The fate of kings whose samite masks
Veil little more than entropy

Incarnate in the blood. Unasked,
They ruled by runes they dared not name
Until a jaundiced phantom tasked

Their line with sorcery. That shame
They tasted once as mortals fled
Before a greater Sign which came

Eclipsing foes like twin suns bled
To ash behind their moons. Unslaked
By any wine save life, it fed

Until Carcosa's towers quaked
& shattered past redemption. Dust
Engulfed the stars as shadows waked

In Demhe's clouded depths, & rust
Of aeons claimed that coronet
Once called the Hyades. Upthrust

Against the void, things men forget
In waking out of nightmare cried
With one dark voice – *Hastur*! – & yet

A Season in Carcosa

A tattered wind alone replied
In threnodies through bones which keep
Bleak vigil where Cassilda died

Beneath those snows still drifting deep,
Along a shore where cloud-waves creep
Into their sorceries of sleep.

Yellow Bird Strings

By Cate Gardner

The yellow-haired girl kicked her heels against a blue fence waiting for friends to stage-manage her afternoon. Bird's trained eye noted the strings wound about her wrists. Their snail trail led back towards the house where the mother puppeteer waited to yank the child back inside. A yellow door opened behind the girl. Bird froze. The door stood halfway along the garden path and the light that emanated from it was sepia, making the world seem like an old faded photograph. Unperturbed, the girl skipped along the path and in through the doorway. The door slammed shut and faded until only a trace of yellow swirled about the garden. Tiles dropped from the roof of the house positioned behind the now-vanished door.

The house's actual door was pillar-box red. It opened. A woman exited, wiping her hands on a tea towel. The mother puppeteer. "Emily, it's time for tea. Emily. Emily."

The mother's cry followed Bird along the road, growing agitated, fearful. *You're going mad, old man.* Doors neither appeared nor disappeared and children only skipped through to imaginary places on television.

A hunched shuffle replaced the elegant dance of the puppeteer and wrists that once manipulated now burned with pain. Bird's shoulders ached from the weight of the plastic bags he carried. Although the bags contained only clothes, costume jewellery and broken string, they weighed heavy as if filled with Vivian's bones, muscles and fat. The handles cut into his palms. Vivian accompanied him wherever he went; strapped to his back, dancing from his wrists, howling like the wind in his ears.

His lips tasted of hers.

His skin reeked of her sweat and perfume.

Sometimes, Bird thought Vivian a figment of his imagination or a forgotten doll, a life-sized replica of a person. He frowned. That final thought accused. The loss of things both manufactured and living carved emptiness in his gut. Pain stabbed at his chest, causing him to double over. The bags dragged against the pavement. Home seemed an endless hike away, and yet, he stood at his gate, a yellow sky framing its grey slate roof, its pale bricks and the puppet who danced at the attic window.

Bird blinked. In the snapshot moment between his eyes closing and reopening, the attic window emptied. He'd imagined the puppet. Imagined its face pressed against dusty glass, its mouth forming an O. It hadn't danced away at the sight of him. They couldn't dance without him.

He lugged the bags to the front door. The right had split open and left a trail of red and green tights on the front path. Stop. Go. Bird slammed the door behind him, causing the house to shiver. He dropped to his knees, burying his face in her things, in plastic until the want for breath burned in his chest and he rolled onto his back. Above him, a fly caught in a spider's web tugged against its prison. Bird turned onto his side, pressed his hand to the floorboards and stood. The house creaked about him, shivering at his monstrous steps.

The mantelpiece clock ticked towards evening. Tired eyes reflected in the shine of his television awards. He'd been someone once. His hand slapped out to knock the awards from the mantelpiece, then stopped and clenched into a fist. Fingernails bit into palms. He shuffled to his favourite chair and switched on the television. Its images reminded him of all he'd lost. A game show blazed with a rainbow of psychedelic colours, painting swathes of light across his walls.

"Win the life of your dreams," Dirk Almond, the presenter, offered the viewing audience a bleached smile. "Behind one of these doors is everything you've ever wanted. But behind one lurks…"

Dirk pointed at the audience, who shouted in reply, "The Eliminator."

Canned laughter hissed from the speakers. Bird jabbed at the remote, but the television wouldn't change channels. There were new batteries in the cabinet, but that would require standing and besides, the television itself was closer. He could just switch it off.

He didn't. He ruminated until he dozed, closing his eyes against the chaos on screen, and the false anticipation of an opening door.

Bird awoke with a start. His arms hung suspended above his head. Pain coursed across his shoulder blade. Bringing his arms down, Bird rubbed his wrists. It felt as if something still gripped him there, and yet, his skin showed no signs of restraints. He looked about him and noted something curious, something wrong with the wall.

A dark outline pressed against the cream wallpaper, causing the pattern of yellow squiggles to elongate and spread. Vivian had objected to his use of the word squiggle, said the marks were a sign of some sort. They meant something to her. Bird stood and peered at the anomaly, tracing his fingers across the wall. There was something underneath the wallpaper. His fingernails dug into the paper until a section tore free. The house settled about him, both of them holding their breath.

If Vivian were here, she'd scream against his vandalism, arms and legs kicking out, her strings wrapping about his wrists, pulling him away. The torn wallpaper revealed a doorknob and a section of door. He recalled the child, Emily, disappearing behind a yellow door. Coincidence or precognition?

"It must be a secret room," Bird said, certain his house was large enough to conceal a room.

If Vivian were here, she'd be thrilled. Although… Bird scratched his head. Why had Vivian papered over the door?

When the studio bosses had cancelled his television show, Bird had smashed a half-dozen of his puppets. Threw them against walls, stomped on their brittle necks, hurled them at Vivian. Perhaps, unable to throw away the broken puppets, she'd gathered their pieces and buried them in this room and he, in his whiskey stupor, had forgotten it existed. The doorknob half-turned and then caught against the lock. He needed something to jimmy it open.

He tried to unlock the door with the bent tine of a fork, several old keys, and one of Vivian's hairpins. Unhappy to settle with this failure, he attempted to open the door with brute strength, pulling and tugging at both the doorknob and the edges of the door. The effort left him breathless. Bird pressed his forehead to the yellowed wood. Sometimes the past should remain unearthed.

To his left, the front door's letterbox flapped open and something dropped through. A book. Grateful for the distraction, Bird shuffled to pick up the book, hitching his trousers as the waistband slipped over his hips. *The King in Yellow*. The book's pages were as yellow as the title and smelled of damp. Something creaked behind him. Sounded like an opening door. Hairs bristled on the back of his neck. His insides trembled. He stopped, hands holding onto trousers that had been snug the day before and turned. The yellow door remained shut. *Of course it did.* His stomach growled, offering its own opinion. He placed the book on top of the television.

With a microwave meal of sausages, onion gravy and mash balanced on his lap, Bird sat in front of the television. He must have slept through a day for the programming had moved from an evening game show to a children's puppet show. Mash slid off his fork and landed on his belly. A puppet wearing a dirty yellow suit and a tarnished gold crown pressed its nose to the screen. Having captured Bird's attention, the puppet danced back and offered a high-pitched laugh. Bird pressed the remote's off button. Again, the television refused to switch off.

The producers and director had told Bird puppet shows were last century. The kids wanted computer animation and celebrities, they said. They'd offered him numerous reality show parts. Well, they'd offered them to him and his 'creepier' (their words) puppets. Vivian went to auditions for shows about cookery, mud wrestling and a week on an active volcanic island. Bird shovelled half a sausage into his mouth; it proved more gristle than meat. Perhaps Vivian had left him to travel from show to show. If he flicked through the channels, he might see her, thin nose pressed against the screen, ready smile, lightning flash of anger.

Bird leaned forward in his chair, his t-shirt soaking up gravy. She'd worn a purple dress to the audition; a purple dress, an orchid in her hair and several layers of make up, but when she'd returned only the dress remained intact, the make-up washed away by a tidal wave of tears, charcoal hints smeared on her ruddy cheeks. They'd told her she was nothing without Bird. Turned out he was nothing without her.

Letting his meal drop to the floor, Bird stood. He pulled at the uncovered door until his shoulders burned and his wrists ached. Standing slumped against the door, he noticed that the wallpaper on the opposite wall looked uneven. On tearing the paper, he found another door.

As this was a party wall, the door would lead into his neighbour's house. Bird pressed his ear to the door and then his eye to the keyhole, but could neither see nor hear the family who lived next door. He understood Vivian would have papered over this door for privacy but it didn't explain why he couldn't remember these extra doors.

From the bay window, he inspected the supposed dividing line between the houses and wondered if a corridor ran between them. A secret corridor populated by puppet children who hid from their puppeteer. Across the street, the girl who had vanished through the yellow door, Emily, now stood against a white fence. In place of her previous jeans and t-shirt, she wore a red-checked dress. Emily looked towards Bird's house and, despite the fact net curtains covered his windows, looked at Bird in particular; her gaze porcelain smooth, expressionless.

The ceiling creaked causing Bird to break his gaze. The trapped fly continued to struggle within the web. On the television, the puppet bemoaned, "There's no one to play with. Oh wait, yes there is. Here comes a jolly fellow for me to mess with."

Bird moved away from the window and switched off the television. The book dropped to the floor. He scooped it up and threw it amongst Vivian's neglected things. After cleaning up his spilled meal and wiping gravy and mash from his t-shirt, Bird settled into his chair. Tomorrow, he'd phone a decorator and have them paper over the doors. He didn't want to know what hid behind them. As Bird began to snore, the television switched on and static filled the room.

Bird woke to the blare of the television. He fumbled about him for the remote and found it jammed beneath his thigh. The game show was on again, probably on some channel's never-ending loop, and an eager participant stood before a yellow door. The contestant and the announcer waited for Bird to fully wake and only when he was on the edge of his seat, breath caught in his throat, did the presenter offer the camera a bow and the show cut to an ad break.

Rubbing his belly, Bird stood. The book he was sure he'd thrown amongst Vivian's things fell from his lap. His trousers followed, dropping to his ankles revealing bone-thin thighs covered in loose skin. He kicked the trousers aside and walked some life back into his stiff bones. Didn't matter if he only wore a dirty t-shirt and greying boxer shorts because there was no one to see him, and it may deter prying eyes. Looking through the net curtains, he saw Emily had moved on, and in her place, a puppet leaned against the picket fence. A puppet in a tattered yellow suit, a gold crown jammed on its head. The puppet stood. Bird did the opposite. His knees cracked against the floorboards.

At first, Bird thought Emily hid behind the fence, manipulating the doll. She'd have seen some of his old shows on television, they repeated everything these days, and she thought to give him a laugh or a scare, perhaps both. Then, the puppet stepped from the pavement, crossed the road and opened Bird's gate. The child could not manipulate a doll that far. Even, he'd struggle. The puppet's shadow lengthened, stretching until it eclipsed Bird. The tarnished gold crown rapped against the window.

"I'll not let you in," Bird said.

A wicked game. The yellow door beside the mantelpiece yawned open, the space behind a sepia-yellow. It would have opened from the vibration of the rap of a gold crown against glass, Bird hoped. He chewed his lip, looking from door to puppet until he was dizzy with it all. Sweat dripped into his eyes. Bird blinked. The rap of the gold crown ceased, the puppet vanished or hid. The yellow door remained open.

Despite his earlier fight to open the door, Bird kicked it shut. It teased, swinging forward an inch before slamming against the frame. The house creaked about him, offering a myriad of wooden footsteps. Puppet children. Bird licked his lips. His mouth was cotton dry.

'*You'll never be alone,*' Vivian had said. Then she'd left.

A bath, a night's sleep and the world would right itself. Steam filled the bathroom, seeping out onto the landing. The bathroom door was white, there were no other doors hidden behind the tiles or the shower curtain. Although alone in the house, Bird twisted the key in the bathroom lock. He understood the story-telling world. He knew an unlocked door was an invitation to unwanted things.

Lying in the bath, the water still, he recalled Vivian dangling from the shower curtain pole. Her strings tied to the showerhead, waiting for their games to commence.

How easily she'd let him play her. At first, he'd thought it her game, a way to persuade him to apply for one of those celebrity shows, but then she'd stopped mentioning them at all. Bird emptied a sponge full of water above his face.

'*My arms ache,*' she'd said.

No wonder she left him. Sobs tore through Bird. He drew his knees to his chest and rocked. He must have stayed in the bath some time for when he emerged gooseflesh peppered his skin. He dried himself off and removed a suit and t-shirt from the chest of drawers in the bedroom. The clothes were from his performing days. He'd never expected to fit in them again.

The mahogany wardrobe threw shadows across the wallpaper, the same paper as that on the living room walls with its dizzying invasion of yellow squiggles. Bird lay on the bed. He'd never sleep for the wardrobe's hulking shadow. A book sat on the bedside table, Vivian's, with 'The King in Yellow' marked on the spine. He picked up the book and hurled it at the wardrobe, as if to encourage its retreat. He waited for the ceiling to creak, for something to move in the roof space or in the walls, but the house lay silent. Too silent. No settling of floorboards, no cars passing outside, no puppet rapping at his window. The wardrobe's shadow pressed against him.

Bird climbed from the bed. The shadow followed him, curving with his movements. Pushing his shoulder against the wardrobe's hollow weight, Bird encouraged the wardrobe from the wall. It caught against carpet, ripping through the thin pile. Bird kept on shoving until he revealed the wall behind it and the door inset into said wall. He pressed his hand to his chest.

"I remember where you go," he said.

To the attic. He recalled standing outside his house a day or two ago, or according to the weight he had lost since then, a year, and the puppet that had pressed her face to the window.

"There's no one up there. You're not up there."

The stillness waited for Bird's next move. Vivian couldn't be up there. He wasn't that sort of man.

Carpet concertinaed about the wardrobe's base, trapping it in position. His hand curled about the doorknob but didn't turn it. Instead, Bird closed the bedroom door and considered wallpapering over it. Hiding the room until he forgot it existed.

Yellow sunlight poured into the living room. The houses surrounding his appeared to be crumbling beneath the aged light--as if he'd lain in bed a hundred years. The yellow doors stood ajar. Static poured from the television. The mantelpiece clock stuttered. Time stuck at three thirty-five. Was the yellow light emitting from the doorways? He crossed over a door's shadow. Something tapped against the window. He refused to check if it was wooden or golden, puppet or crown.

As he stood in the doorway, the light pressed against him, clamping about his wrists, neck and ankles. Bird pushed against it, his puppeteer hands bone thin, dry yellow skin, black veins. Falling back and out of its pressure, Bird approached the first door from behind. It refused to close. He pressed his shoulder against it, his feet losing traction. With a grunt, he threw his now-slight weight against the door. It swung shut with leisurely grace. The game show host roared onto the television screen replacing the previous static. Yellow face, torn yellow suit, caught in the moment, pearl white teeth and black lips forming an artificial smile. The picture stuttered but remained the same.

The other door slammed shut of its own accord. The clock hands spun around. On screen, Dirk Almond shouted, "Here's Vivian."

Only she wasn't here at all.

On screen, a girl squealed and clapped her hands, performing a weird dance before the as yet unopened door. The girl's only similarity to Vivian was that she played Dirk Almond's puppet. Did the silly girl really think she'd find the life of her dreams behind a door on a television show? He expected to find nightmare.

Upstairs, something thudded against one of the locked doors. A headache circled Bird's temple, like a vice tightening about his skull. Another door pressed against the wallpaper, breaking through without his help. Breath caught in Bird's chest. An insistent rap at the window shuddered through him. Emily and the Puppet King peered in.

Bird pressed his fingers to his face, willing them to disappear. A hand rapped at the front door. Bird lowered his hands. The letterbox flapped open.

"You don't live there," Emily said, peering through the flap.

"Yes I do," Bird said, though he wondered if he should ignore the child.

Bird gripped the chair arms. Its leather crumbled beneath his fingertips. The television lurched forward as if its screen was suddenly too heavy for the table's legs.

"Then the big old bulldozer is going to knock you down."

Bird stood and stumbled across the room. His back stooped beneath the unexpected weight of his head. The letterbox slammed shut. Behind Bird, the television fell silent. He should open the door and run. Knock over Emily if he had to and not care if her porcelain head broke.

"Are you still there?" he asked. When Emily didn't reply, Bird shouted, "Are you still there?"

"Are you?" Emily said, and then she skipped away, her heels tap-tap-tapping on the pavement.

Bird stooped and lifted the letterbox, peering through the two-inch gap. Emily and the Puppet King waved at him from the gate.

Bird moved away from the door. His hand shivered in front of him, as though it thought to ward the pair off. His skin looked paper-thin. Cut him open and perhaps you'd find a door to where Vivian had gone. Upstairs, whatever had thudded against the bedroom door finally broke through. Bird's knees gave way and he landed on the bags of Vivian's things.

She'd left him. For the most part, he'd been certain of that. She'd wanted to leave, had intended to, that part was true, but he couldn't remember her actually walking out. No tearful last goodbye. Then there was the question of the things she'd left behind. Above him, the stairs creaked. Bird looked up.

"You don't look well, Bird," Vivian said.

Words caught against Bird's throat. The television roared with laughter.

"Here's Vivian," Dirk Almond said.

Bird shivered as his Vivian descended the stairs. A puppet girl with her strings cut, their tattered remains dribbling from her wrists. He'd wanted her to come back to him, but not like this. She looked too thin, thinner than he'd become, and her perfume was stale and sour. She used to smell of lavender.

Behind him, the letterbox opened. Bird turned. The Puppet King winked at him. Thin wooden fingers and a crown pushed through the letterbox. Bird sat transfixed as the Puppet King placed the crown on Bird's head.

From the television, Dirk Almond said, "We are pleased to announce a new puppet show starting tomorrow, kids. Bird Man at 3:35 pm. Make sure you're watching. It's going to be fun, fun, fun."

Vivian towered over Bird. She grasped his wrists and wound string about them.

"The show can't go on without you, Bird. I tried to get them to take just me. Honest. I tried everything."

His Vivian pulled him up, manipulating him as he had once manipulated her. Bird's head wobbled forward, bounced upon his pencil neck. He wanted to trace her face with his fingers, but she turned her back to him and left him dangling in the doorway. In the living room, Vivian wheeled the television and its table away from the wall. A grey screen flickered, the words *The End* bleeding through in yellow.

A Season in Carcosa

The Theatre and its Double

By Edward Morris

"And Caesar's spirit, ranging for revenge,
With Ate by his side come hot from hell,
Shall in these confines with a monarch's voice
Cry 'Havoc,' and let slip the dogs of war;
That this foul deed shall smell above the earth
With carrion men, groaning for burial."
—William Shakespeare, *Julius Caesar*

B-ROLL:

L'EMPEREUR A VÊTU AVEC LE SOLEIL

   (*PAR FRANÇOIS VILLÓN*, au Paris, ca.1457
   Asile d'Aliénés de St. Eustache)

Supprimé par Antonin Artaud, 1928-

ACT 1, SCENE 1

THE PHANTOM OF MUSIC

CHORUS LEADER

Road-child, bare-faced farmboy, prodigal Prince,
The young Josephus, King Hastur's son, of House de

Jaune
who would be King in those times, in his own daydreams,

Scribal half-blood son of a genocidal necromancer
Who blew himself away before the boy was born,
Away, away, in a blast of white light not quite light,
when he spoke the Name. Cassandra stayed,

And raised Josephus far away
From dead Hastur's kingdom, hastily
renamed....

CHORUS
Beyond the sky, the Hyades sing
The song the bells of Death now ring
Must die unheard, become No Thing,

in Lost Carcosa.

The Hyadian Gates now cannot swing
Where flap the tatters of the King,
The firmament now just a thing
Above Carcosa.

Strange is the night where such stars rise,
Black holes of light which gaze like eyes,
And three moons waltz swamp-fireflies,

in Dim Carcosa,

In stormy skies, the islands break,
Both cloud and land float in that Lake,
A double sun, a Kingly wake

In Carcosa ...

~*~

A-ROLL:

LE RÉPARATEUR DES RÉPUTATIONS

Many call me insane. If I was insane, would I not deny it? Is it insane to fall in love with the landscape of a dream, the precise meeting of two hills above a road of dead stones, where one walks and cannot use words to ask for shelter? So it is to write, in the regions of new space up in the Moon, dreaming, while others sit at home. I partake in planetary gravitation within the fissures of my mind and the tangibility of Man's intentions.

I am never settled in the continuity of my life. My dreams are offered no escape, no refuge or guide. Truly the rankness of severed limbs. I feel a longing not to be, never to have fallen into this sink of imbecilities, abdications, renunciations, and obtuse contacts. I long for the yellow light of Dreamtime, this virtual, impossible light which nonetheless I find in real life.

~*~

The repeated miracle of Dawn was wrought before my eyes just after I woke and took my medicine. I saw the first of the electric lights sparkling off into blackness far among the linden trees. It is April in Paris, and every garden on every street is suffused with that bizarre primal honey that makes sunbeams fall from flowers, trees, clouds, flickering in the deep sky after a long storm.

When the morphine began to work, as I gazed into the cobalt heavens, the shredded mist rising along the river was touched with purple and gold, and acres of meadow and pasture dripped precious stones. That mist drifted among treetops kissed with fire, while in the forest depths faint sparkles came from some lost ray of morning light falling on wet leaves.

Then the sun, the yellow sun, and everything grew stark again.

~*~

When we speak the word "Life," it must be understood we are not referring to life as we know it from its surface of fact, but to that fragile, fluctuating center which forms never reach. When we write, my dear Journal, we start with where we are, to get away from it: These dilapidated spiral staircases at the back of this old firetrap theatre, with all the little doors at every end of every hall.

I start with the scratches my cat Pierrot left up and down my forearms, these funny sun-glasses with the false nose I wear today, my sweat, my pallor, my teeth.

I have fifteen men, five boys and three women in my employ, who are poorly paid, but who pursue the work with an enthusiasm which possibly may be born of fear. My goblin brood come from every shade and grade of society. I choose them at my leisure from those who reply to my advertisements.

It is easy enough. I could treble the number in twenty days if I wished. When they turn on me, I invite them up here to my office for a little chat. We smoke a little *mari-huana*, have a drink. The last one of those was the editor of *Paris-Match*.

We left arm-in-arm, bellowing laughter.

I flew lights with Dullin, and painted sets with Pitoeff while we edited each other's work. I wrote the *mise-en-scene* for the first Surrealist film ever produced. No scribbler or stage-hand could withstand the chaos and joy which are mine to dispense in this strange, roaring year of 1929. I repair the reputations of other playwrights by ruining my own to run their work here at our place. Tomorrow, the Surrealist jackal bastards snap them up like ants on a dead bird. Even if I did succeed in certain cases, it would cost me more than I would gain by it.

But there are some plays which *must* be run, though my Opening Night may be cursed like Rossini's "Barber of Seville" by a maniac in a Pallid Mask, grinning in terror or triumph, who takes my theatre apart, some species of stage-hand who made the mistake of reading the original folio I sometimes forget to place under lock and key.

Allow me to explain. We begin our first rehearsal in several days...

~*~

B-ROLL:

ACT 1, SCENE 2

THE PHANTOM OF DOUBT

DARKNESS. STARLIGHT. CREATURE in what appears to be TAT-
TERED CLOAK AND COWL OF JAUNDICED HUMAN SKIN takes
the stage. CREATURE'S FACE is hidden in high, peaked goblin hood.
Star-light should be made to look black. This is THE KING IN YEL-
LOW.

KING IN YELLOW

The day has come! The day has come!
It is done. While falling through the worlds I've now
remade,
I longed to follow Cassilda. But I'd gone too far, when I
finished
Father's work. Too far. Too far.
I remember when her meddling little sister Camilla found
Father's temple,
Or what was left of it, as I vainly tried to finish the
Work.
I remember her
scream,
And the awful spell I spoke...

Now the tatters of martial law sweep through the
Hyadian Gate,
down the wind between worlds, even to Earth. Fear not,
good people here, for I shall rise in the face of the next
great army, and cause a tempest on two continents.

My skin-fingers, tongues, eyes, still flap across the skies,
through that smoking sky-lake which connects the
Kingdoms
of Hastur, Aldebaran, and Yhill (where the natives know
none of this, and think all such things monstrously im
possible,)
and deepest Demhe that sank beneath the waves long
ago,

Even the sky of Earth which the hateful Croy Castaigne
closed off

with his churlish suicide in my laboratorium, to Uoht
and Thale,
Naotalba, all the poli that once gave Father tribute, and
gave me....

THE KING IN YELLOW OPENS HIS KALEIDOSCOPE EYES,
WHICH ILLUMINATE.

KING IN YELLOW

Which gave me my story, poor ignorant lambs of Earth,
Led to a slaughter you cannot understand,

KING PARTS FLESHLY CLOAK TO REVEAL SHINING CREATURE
BENEATH IT, IN SPLENDID DIADEM, AND A WHITE SILK ROBE
EMBROIDERED WITH A YELLOW GLYPH: A HAWK WHOSE
TALON PIERCES A RABBIT'S SKULL. THE SHAPE OF THE YEL-
LOW SIGN SUGGESTS A CROOKED CROSS.

The story of the Last Great King,
Prodigal Prince set out on the road,
In a yellow, threadbare Family Cloak–

KING RAISES HANDS SKYWARD, EYES TOO BRIGHT TO LOOK
UPON

KING IN YELLOW

It is done, it is done! Let the nations rise and look upon
their King,
King in my right in Hastur's land, because I know the
mystery of the Hyadian Corridor between worlds! I
swam down the Lake of Hali,
and beheld Earth. Father's journals showed me the way,

In between the backward alphabets and cryptic
plants, In between the sketches of King Hastur's human
toys.

My crown, my empire, every hope and every ambition,
Now lived forward, understood backward, seizing me
from behind,

Binding me in my own skin, until my whole voice is a
scream,

And Memory worries me with her black, black beak.
I rage, bleeding, infuriated, having seized
Throne and Empire, and lost everything.

Woe! Woe to he who is crowned the King in Yellow!
I understood not
That saying the name of the Conqueror Worm at the
end of Time itself
(Eater of Stars, Devourer of Pasts,)
Would melt me in the crucible of the Logos, change
My shape, explode my essence, burst me like a balloon,

Yet my remains still could not die, and slithered again
To life, tatters of mind, seeking tendrils of parchment
skin,

Seeking to begin
To finish the Play
of which we are all part,
But my cousin, *le Castaigne*,
wrench in every plan,
Poisoned the way to Earth,
polluted my Working
with his own poncing,
putrefacting corpse,

Slit ear to ear by his own hand,
bleeding the family blood
of his Uncle Hastur,
closing the way,

Shutting off that part of my sky

[folio page is missing]

~*~

A-ROLL:

THE KING IN YELLOW has been called 'the most deliberately authorless play in the world.' On the surface, the play is a Phantastic, otherworldly tale set before the beginning of Time, in a far land. On the surface, it is a potboiler monarchical melodrama about a deposed wizard-king, and a young betrothed girl who falls in love with her husband's cousin.

Her husband, who becomes the King In Yellow, kills his cousin when he dons the mantle, and the wife kills herself in horror and grief. The very banality and innocence of the first act only allows the blow to fall afterwards with more awful effect

No definite moral principles are violated in those pages, no doctrine proselytized, no convictions outraged. It cannot be judged by any human unit of measure, yet. Although human nature might not bear the original, un-arranged "score" if you will, the story strikes the supreme note of Art.

In this instance, the play is the Theatre . . . and its double, in which the essence of purest cosmology lurks.

Robert W. Chambers, one of the most successful commercial authors of the early Twentieth Century, muddied the waters when he wrote the popular version, a series of highly precious and confusing short stories revolving around a fictionalized version of the Marquis de Sade's banned play "L'EMPEREUR A VÊTU AVEC LE SOLEIL". In turn, de Sade had plagiarized much of the essential plot from the play of the same name by Molière, which was also banned and never performed, or read. Both versions were allowed to lapse from print, and no one knows what collector has acquired either.

A version that fits somewhere between the Paris of Molière's day and that of de Sade was first released in Europe in a very limited craft press run by Tristan Tzara (with his fifty-foot lines in his old hat) in the mid-Twenties.

The limited edition was not much more than a curio printed on demand by the very wealthy, foolhardy or impecunious. Tzara claimed to have made the decision to publish the play in a fit of misanthropic hatred for the human race, so much so that he wished to bring about the Biblical End of Days.

Old Tzara now recants this fit, but it is mostly an empty gesture. The Tzara manuscript is shit. It contains an impossibly muddied version of the original, more akin to *Finnegans Wake* than the original play; which predates Dada, Surrealism, even the Irrealism of de Sade.

~*~

This play is an idea, one which is alive, as all ideas live. One which cannot be killed. The King cannot be killed. It has been far too long for that. The Seven Worlds were fractured at a point in our own history before the colonization of the New World, America.

Now America is laboratory and growth medium for the most spectacular failure of any empire since Rome, when her banks call in all those notes that America has defaulted on to pay for its fascist Futurism. It will come. Soon enough. In my dreams, the hellish King shows me men jumping from windows, men who look like American bankers. There is no one to catch them.

~*~

But I dare not speak of that yet. The play is in three acts of roughly five scenes each, and the original folio something like three hundred pages. Not all these pages are full. One or two contain only a single line of dialogue, or utterance. Any more, and the page could not hold it. The illustrations are much saner than the text. That says little.

The cosmology of the play is Gnostic, Manichaean, Blakeian. In the Beginning was the Mess, and the perception of the Mess, into degrees of Light and Shadow, Chord and Discord. When things began to separate, the playwright seems to believe, Life began to hurt.

In the Beginning, things began to separate. In the Beginning, things hurt. The Beginning happened when the King's mind shattered into seven pieces. When He rose and roared the name his Father captured, the name of God, the rags of his robe flapped and rattled in the winds of seven worlds.

Seven doors in the Hyadian Corridor, down through the snakes of fire, and choking frozen fog of Lake Hali's black and smoking tarn in the sky. Betrayed, the King had spoken the name of the Conqueror Worm at the end of Time. Over a woman.

It's always over a woman. Josephus spoke the name, and thrust the scalloped gauntlets on his fists out before him, and made steaming cracks in the ground as the holes between worlds sucked part of Him in, cloak first, and gave Him an eye, an ear, a whispering undead hand in each.

~*~

In the Beginning, the King wrecked everything. So He could fix it. In the Beginning, the King started Time the way it is now. High on His throne, He makes no move to mouth apologies, merely watches with every eye as the smaller parts of Himself repeat the dance, the endless reel, the *ridda*, over and under, in and out, clap hands...

~*~

Clap hands. In the beginning, there was Shit. In the beginning, the first living thing chose to complete the process of coming to life, and expelled the dead parts of itself, so it could exist all the way. To live, one must only stop struggling, but to live in the flesh one must shit.

Man made that covenant, to live in the meat for a short time, then volunteer himself up to die, and let the beasts eat him. To spend his whole live holding onto the smallest part of the world he can understand, behaving like the beasts which will one day devour him whole, living by the clock he made to stop Time and drive back the eternal, incalculable light of the Void that every one of us offers ourself up to in the true Mass, without any intermediary, as She approaches with all Her forms, and circles us, and penetrates.

The Theatre of Cruelty forces the audience to see what it is eating, what it is, what it makes and embodies and becomes. By cruelty, I do not mean to cause pain as the Grand Irrealist, de Sade, did, but to use that kind of cold, clear violence to shatter each and every pasteboard mask of Text and Language and Meaning. To tell a story in the realm of the spirit, and make even the groundlings gasp along.

We do not use a fourth wall at the Jarry Theatre. The audience is the fourth wall. The players could be any of them, but for the simplest of Sophoklean symbols and devices: A whip, a pram, a large blue egg.

The new "strobe-lights" the American Eastman has made for darkroom photography are used upon my stage at the Jarry. All this, and more.

It is raw catharsis I seek from the audience, raw pity, raw fear that make raw ekstasis when the two chemicals combine in the sweat, the tears. You mock me, and hold onto illusions, but you drove your own nails. God demands you have done with your own judgment. Even He cannot compare with your pallid ideological mask.

Our true home, the next world, the Middle World, depends on no variable we understand. Our consciousness must break its jaw to begin to get it down.

It is above hunger, sex, agony, exaltation. It comes in the form of a different hunger, not for ideas, but for Realities. Alfred Jarry knew that. He poked just as much fun at Science as the expatriate American Charles Fort does now! Jarry said that laughter happens when you comprehend an apparent contradiction...

Like war, or half the things we think we know, or our social training. The Theatre can free us from that, shock us hard enough to remember that we're people. But it can't be done by employing the old means.

~*~

Roger and me, we went our own way when we opened the Jarry, though we knew no true Surrealist ever joins any organization that calls itself one. Many of the old gang sneer at us now, while they gobble up American dollars.

Yet . . . somehow, Journal, people are coming to our plays. The best minds of Europe come to our plays, and while they sneer at the 'wretched' Boris Yvain busts in every alcove (his statues all look like they could talk, or scream) they leave and write about the plays we run here.

We are being discussed, as a kind of proving ground. Not *théâtre refusé*, as the critics in the *Journal Paris* slapped it with their broad wet brush . . . But *Théâtre de la Cruâté*, as I feel it should be known.

In between all that comes the perfume of roses and tobacco, the rustle of fans, the touch of rounded arms and the laughter. And the wine. Like when I first came to Paris, and worked all the time alongside those ivy-covered old men. Like when the world still moved in a straight line, and anything was still possible.

~*~

All pathos is cruelty. All Tragedy is cruel. The eagle eats Prometheus' liver. Antigone is shut up in a stone tomb. Yet no one makes full use of this catharsis. Until us. The hand of Notice has struck the hour. Our hour.

But this newest play, oh this great thing... It is the thread which has run through Western civilization itself, an Exquisite Corpse made of many different parts of volumes, redacted and edited and redacted again.

It takes multifaceted eyes to read it, a fly's eyes. I have taken the mushrooms that Gide brought me back from Mexico and done this thing, with my "Girl Friday" flitting about wondering if I should lose my senses and act the wild ape.

But when I sat before the mirror and began to arrange this work, as a composer might arrange an older score, when I looked at my own face I was young again, a devil, a rakehell, head thrown up and long arms outstretched in a gesture of power and pride.

My eyes blazed fiercely when I read, that day. The tragedy was conventional enough, but what I finally puzzled out between the lines was something I could use.

I saw the hidden picture in the play. I saw the theatre's double. I saw the Yellow Sign.

They still think me mad, and I am. Mad to explore the hidden relations of Power, the true alchemic knowledge of the Earth, the groaning gulfs in Science that Fort and Crowley and the lot of them skewer in print.

He who laughs last laughs longest in the madhouse. The Imperial Dynasty of America needs a brake, a budge, a lance to pierce the bloat, to dilate the Void inside, the dead parts of the Void, and trumpet the fart of Art that blows the whole museum apart, explodes the prison of cross and box and angle that binds all Mind. Mind is the thing which I am, and it is I, and it wants to GET OUT.

~*~

These days, a witch-hunt means not that one should be roasted at the stake, but roasted instead by electric shocks and chemicals. All my life, I have been locked away for speaking my mind, and living it. My parents could not cure me, nor the doctors, so they kept locking me away.

From the old disease, the baby-disease that could not be cured, they gave me a worse one: Laudanum, that stopped my headaches and the way my face twisted out of countenance, stopped the screams and the sleepwalking, but left me with itself, embalmed with that which will kill me in the end.

From smaller institutions, I graduated to the Army, a very large one. The Army let me back out.

I ran to the footlights, to Paris. But I did not understand myself to be cured. I was never sick. I never wanted to kill myself, but every time I ever visited the ward psychiatrist, I wanted to hang myself because I needed to cut his throat and they wouldn't let me.

Those avenues are of no use now (the "real world" Papa made so much of when he used his mouth and not his belt to speak.)

I cannot tell anyone that Carcosa really *has* started to take notice of Paris again, that the saber-rattling armies of the world shall themselves rise and tremble before the Pallid Mask. It will be my last jape, my last experiment, my last big leap, to send Him away myself. The native son of Hastur's nighted city shall come in the New Dawn, and the stars of Earth shall turn black. And it is the Surrealists who render Him irrelevant.

~*~

I can travel there, when I draw the Yellow Sign and meditate within it, using a variation of Crowley's Lesser Banishing Ritual of the Pentagram. I am...

~*~

I blink, and I am back in Carcosa, in a single room that takes up most of the top rung in a shaky roof-warren. The hookah stirs the mosquito-nets and the sails of the street-cars squitch sideways between mossy buildings far below, like ghosts in the yellow mist.

The King's tatters cannot reach me here. Yet. I sharpen the pencil with my teeth and find the first word. The silver light grows strange.

Below me, in the streets, the fog swirls with colors unseen on Earth.

Pasty-faced babies wearing the larval clay of the Pallid Mask, grown from the sperm samples of children during the last War, squitter and yap in elaborate carriages.

Their Nurses, too, wear waxen, pasty masks, and pay more attention to the THUD THUD THUD of the Carrionmen pounding their shields as they march by in the street in slow lock step. Their own Masks are smiling, and made of beaten gold, but the faces behind the false faces pulse warm and white and hot-gangrenous-sick as the boiling bodies of maggots, changing... Changing. Into what, I never want to know.

Out in the flat field beyond the square, a circle of six crosses is sunk deep in the foul, drooling embrace of the sick, singing soil. The sun passes over the heart of the omphalos and illuminates it. One man stands at each Station of the Sun, and the Seventh is a slaughtered horse who leads a hollow man to the center of the circle, to the wild wail of a trumpet and the beat of a long drum.

The men walk in slow lockstep around the horse, and its naked zombi-rider. The crosses burn to ash, but the angles are not extinguished. The spell has only sunken into the land.

I have ensconced the Prince's armor in the prop room at the Jarry Theatre, and there is a ring in the helmet that bears the Yellow Sign. We will be spared by the holocaust that is to come, when the King lets loose the waters of Lake Hali onto the Earth, and turns every living thing to marble but the ones his Rapture wishes to spare.

We will be spared anyway. Me and everyone I can round up into the Jarry. They will listen. When the sky opens, they will listen, and not be left behind.

Listen...

~*~

B-ROLL:

ACT 2, SCENE 3

THE PHANTOM OF THE PAST

(folio page is missing)

CASSILDA

92

Midnight sounds from those misty spires of Home,
My street, Street of the Four Winds. Fog rolls
against my windows, down from the clouds
That roll and break upon the shores of Lake Hali,
Far above us, so deep it goes all the way,

To the distant sky-kingdom of Terra,
Which the new people who come here from there
call Earth.

It is thamaturges, mostly,
which come to Carcosa, men
With big impressive names,
and withered limbs, and squints,
who go about on canes,
and continually exclaim
at everything they see.

Once in a while, a woman comes.
One such told me that a new land
on Earth has been found, which
the Travellers say shall be called
the Imperial Dynasty
of America.

I dream this Imperium, mighty as a river,
in my sleep, its towers taller than the tallest
Temple of the Conqueror Worm which mad
King Hastur caused to be built ,
in the last days, when we

Were small, when everything was smoke
and blood and lightning, every man,
woman and child for themselves.

Or so Mother, and Nanna, told me.
Nanna, Mother's Mother, didn't believe
in dreams. Nanna believed in what

she could see. I believed in something I
could see very few places, though,

Love. No love in the surly little lout Josephus
I was supposed to marry, to mix the poison blood
of Hastur, with our own. I swore I would renege,

Come what may.

~*~

ON A HILL, ADOLESCENT JOSEPHUS GUARDS FLOCK OF
SHEEP BY NIGHT. JOSEPHUS POKES AT A SMALL FIRE WITH A
STICK, OUTSIDE TENT, DRAWING SIGILS IN THE CHARCOAL.

JOSEPHUS

Goaded by my blind, hateful mother Venissia,
Father's blood sacrifice, I'm told, was most
Of his Parliament, and the royal family.

Even in the spring sunshine, words drop
Like poison, as death-bed sweat
Absorbs into a sheet, yellows,

Spreads. 'Lord Hastur, we cry your mercy!'
the song goes in our new refugee kingdom,
And the King rumbles back, 'None of you matter.'

Goaded by my own rightful ambition,
I keep loathsome Ubu's sheep upon
this hill, sleep here, eat here, bathe
in this foetid river, where
the changing expression
of my own eyes makes

A face like mine, but whiter,

So thin I barely recognize.

Diamonds flame above my brow.

Oh Thou, who burn'st in heart
for those who burn In Hell,
whose fires thyself shall feed
in turn; How long be crying,
'Mercy on them, God!'
Why, who art thou to teach
and me to learn?

Let the red dawn surmise what we shall do,
When this blue starlight dies,

and All is through.

~*~

A-ROLL:

I read the news yesterday. I'm not sure how much of it can be trusted, or what percentage of actual news is contained between the words, the lines, all the words that say so many things at once the message gets lost between them, eaten and shit out and eaten again, down the social ladder until the news and the things that consume the news only hold the barest semblance of the Devonian slime, not even human at all.

America does not need better conditions for its everyday people. It needs to change its people to adapt to squalid, post-human conditions. America seeks to mass-produce interchangeable workers who can perform any menial task without complaint, the ultimate Product.

The new people can drive the global marketplace through various wars and exchanges of titular power, and as the surplus are cut down, so do a more malleable and less individual strain grow up in their place.

All of these we must keep busy, and invent new intrigues to further crenellate the ant-farm, make the ants run after illusory objects they think they need, objects made in the laboratory very cheaply, which in turn make them sicken and die and hasten along the purging of intellect, the draining of the divine vital essence into the endlessly-replicating machine virus.

The plants will be last to go, when every chemical in them is synthesized. The new people will breathe the new atmosphere as the old growth dies and becomes fuel. For this, the Imperial Dynasty of America has been preparing since the Great War, building the wall higher, wider.

There's a Red under every bed, or some subhuman mongrel race that wants to eat our women and shit in our radio sets. Men once fought with their fists, swords, pistols at ten paces. Then the twin republics of America and France outlawed dueling and forced the guns to get larger, the distances to grow, the level of thought necessary to end a life to shrink, smaller, smaller, until men can be extinguished by God's own microbes with the push of a button. Not me, my very dear Journal. Oh, not me!

All Life is suffering that eats other Life. I cast my lot with the Tarahumara, who swallow the sun in the peyote button until the black night falls on the Days of Man and we must build our own Eighth Day in the darkness after Armageddon.

I cast my lot with the wild naked native who lives without angles or boxes or gravity. I whoop and dance with them as Night falls. I want Night to stay.

A true gastronome is as insensible to suffering as a conqueror, the English say. The Aztecs understood that a conqueror cannot be swayed by suffering. Cruelty was a virtue, in some instances, according to them, the Medici, the Bonaparte....

Cruelty means cleansing blood with blood, violence with violence, every time the Beast shows itself in human nature. We are the gods our ancestors worshipped, the principle within them and us. Now we wield the smallest part of God. The thunderbolt.

Now God is obsolete, for He created a thing uglier than Him, that nailed Him through the heart, embalmed Him, strangled His breath with illusions, but could never scrape out that one boson of Him which is Us.

~*~

The Mind-thing feels Body suffering most acutely, never diminishing, as the external stimuli of the world crowd in and demand, demand, demand until I can't breathe any more, breathe out any more, give them one more gasp of my air. I drown in myself... and then fart like a donkey, and laugh at my new, revolted kind of suffocation.

~*~

I must watch my health. The headaches come more often. I try to only take my medicine in the evening-time, and never more than half a grain. Only morphine from the chemist's, never *l'heroine* that stirs my blood to such flights of fancy but no, NO. Must treat the illness. Must not make the fog come back in my eyes, the way Mother said it used to when I was small.

~*~

The way my assistant says they do now. "Filmy, and white," young Edith Gassion chirrups at me like a hungry little Piaf-bird scolding the human who walks too near their dinner, "Like you keep slipping away, *Mon Oncle.*"

The girl is no relation. I hired her out of the gutter. She can type. She is fourteen, a wild alley-cat of the devil. We get along fine. Except about my medicine.

Ah oui, my little jazz-baby in her cloche hat has nearly given me more heart attacks than the heroin. But she brings coffee when I'm working, and doesn't take half the blessed day about it. And I believe in my heart Edith must be some form of angel, for when she sings in the empty theatre while I write, my headache leaves as I listen.

~*~

Edith sang last night for me, while she corrected my typescript in that long, low, empty barn where Realism finally came to be butchered like a hog. She'd given me a hard time about some money to go see a show that night, or some such thing, over breakfast, so of course she was singing that old Communard chestnut "L'Internationale." *Encore une fois*, little sparrow. Oppressed urchins of the world, unite. She even made Commie songs sound beautiful.

~*~

97

I listened to Edith sing, and remembered that strange little shop in the Rue d'Auseil (far below the garrett on the hill from whence they dragged the mad violinist when I was a boy, it was said, his blind, bug-eyed face savaged by the suck marks of some gigantic insect.) What was that shop called... It's not there any more, they moved or something. CARO, JEUNET ET FILS. That was it. RARE BOOKS.

~*~

The owners were not in. The boy minding the shop that day, who was called Camus or something, was a little haggard and hollow of eye. His gray suit was threadbare, his hands spindly and pale. He said Good Morning, then went back to rolling a great fruit-crate full of encyclopedias placed on a wheeled ladder, into another part of the shop.

I stayed in the front, weaving through the long, tall maze of shelves that bifurcated toward the plate-glass window looking out on the mismatched bricks in the Rue D'Auseil, the fitted flagstones of that part of the street beyond the walk.

It was Spring then, too, last spring, and the pollen made fires of histamine cause my nose to resemble a flaccid, inflamed cock. My eyes were blurring, and I could barely see one title. But I wished to rest.

There was a small armchair, toward the back of one row of shelves. An electric reading-lamp had been thoughtfully placed on an end-table beside it. The armchair itself looked as if some feral cat had attacked it every day for years.

The book in my hand was yellow. On the chewed spine, some Constant Reader had lovingly scrawled: *EMPEREUR A VÊTU AVEC SOLEIL VILLÓN*.

~*~

Gratefully, I took the chair, and took a quarter-grain tablet of good morphine from my cigarette-case. It would be a long walk home. My spectacles were in my shirt pocket. Best to stave off the headache with every means to hand. Then I opened the play to its first page.

~*~

When I could blink again, when I found I could, young Albert the bookseller (he introduced himself), was rather politely asking me if he could close up shop, and saying he might even give me a sou for the tavern if I had any doubts about leaving. I shook my head, chuckling.

"Child, I am no mendicant mountebank. *Je suis auteur! Surréaliste!* But you are kind." It was the clerk who was paid the asking price of THE KING IN YELLOW. For, though I had closed it, I could not at all put it down.

~*~

My face had grown red, I found as I walked back down the hill into Montmartre. The heartbeat in my ears deafened me to everything else. My mind was hot, too, hot with something hotter than mere terror or joy, suffering in every nerve. When I got back home, I crept shaking to my bed, where I read and re-read, and wept and laughed and trembled with a horror which at times assails me yet. I pray God will curse the writer, as the writer has cursed the world with this beautiful, stupendous creation, terrible in its simplicity, irresistible in its truth.

~*~

Tzara's bastardization of the play was of course banned in France and gobbled in England, then faded into obsolescence and obscurity, as all such things do in the popular culture which the last war produced. The Great War so filled History with despair that some of these processes cannot now be reversed.

The King is coming back, and we are paving His way. He is not happy. I dream that his cousin has been reincarnated in New York, and knows it not. The Prince of a mighty dynasty, who may tell no one of his birthright or be barred up in Bellevue for life! Imagine!

But *Je suis Irréaliste*, as de Sade trumpeted from the rooftops until Napoleon Bonaparte drummed him into the madhouse. The de Sade original of the play was locked in his mother-in-law's wardrobe that burned when Bonaparte gave orders to fire on women and children in a public square and the peasants began to riot...

I am that riot, brought to fruit. I am the dead man's switch for the whole world. I am Artaud, and come hell or high water my company will run this play. The time has come. The people should not know the

son of Hastur. The play is my own spell.
To send Him *home...*

~*~

B-ROLL

ACT 2, SCENE 4

THE PHANTOM OF MENACE

BATTLE COMMENCES in STREET OF THE FOUR WINDS. CROY CASTAIGNE hobbles on his cane to the window, looking out. His paint-brush is still in his hand. CASSILDA, modestly attired, sits perfectly still for her portrait, in black WIDOW'S WEEDS.
                    CROY CASTAIGNE

> Suicide is a mortal sin but it's a fine and noble thing
> to be conscripted off to war... I will take you with me, as
> you ask.

OUT OF THE MIST AT THE FRONT, MEN COME RUNNING FROM EVERY ROAD, FIELD AND DITCH, STRAIGHT INTO AN AMBUSH. THE CARRIONMEN, ORIGINAL GUARDS OF THE LAST SHARD OF KING HASTUR'S PALLID MASK, TWIST THE AIR AROUND THEM WITH THEIR LIGHTNING. ORDER BREAKS IN THE RANKS OF THE COUNTER-REVOLUTIONARIES. SOME OF THEM DROP THEIR WEAPONS, AND SOME TURN THEM ON EACH OTHER.

                    CASSILDA

> Sink not ye down to Josephus' foul lair.
> His madness lasts forever, but our love
> Outlasts it still. Rest your eyes,
> Your arms, your hands,
> Your sleeping heart,
>
> Home as the hunter, and in your dreams,

I sing the wild stars at night
That weep down dawning dew,
and begin to burn
Again in setting sun,
in skies so vast and close,

Skies which now no longer open
To anywhere else.

I swear fealty to no King.

CANNONS ARE BEING DISCHARGED. CARCOSA BURNS. HALF
A SOLDIER, IN THE STREET, JERKS AND DIES, STILL HOLDING
A BLUNDERBUSS WITH A FIXED BAYONET. TWO OTHER SOL-
DIERS HAVE JUST SAWN HIM IN HALF.INFANTRY STUMBLE,
SKELETONS OF REGIMENTS STRUGGLE TO MAINTAIN OR-
DER.

CROY whirls, crosses the room, and yanks the clasp with the Yellow
Sign from Cassilda's collar. CROY throws it through the open studio
window. ARTIST AND MODEL EMBRACE IN A CLINCH.

~*~

ACT 2, SCENE 5

A WOOD NEAR CARCOSA

In the crumbling ruin that is the TEMPLE OF THE WORM, Josephus'
beringed hand passes over a black stone, and his view of Cassilda's
family home in the city, of Cassilda and Croy kissing, blows away in
a yellow mist.

JOSEPHUS

There be three things which are too wonderful for me,
yea, four which I know
not:
The way of an eagle in the air; the way of a serpent upon

101

a rock;
The way of a ship in the midst of the sea; and the way of
a man with a maid.
For let Philosopher and Doctor preach
Of what they will and what they will not,

Each is but one link in an eternal chain
That none can slip nor break nor over-reach.
For how to let either sort of Scribe, or Pharisee
Understand the profound derangement they put forth?

JOSEPHUS looks at the ceiling above him, irritated. From far above
that come the scream and boom and whistle of shells.
JOSEPHUS' right hand begins to glow yellow. CIRCLE CHALKED
ON THE FLOOR whistles with wind.

JOSEPHUS

The sun ariseth; they gather themselves together
and lay them down in their dens. Dear Cousin Croy
will fling himself on his knees beside Cassilda's
foul slattern bed, knowing that he dares not
for his life's sake leave what he thinks is
dead, though she only sleeps in liquid
stone. Her soul is safe.
He will not know...

~*~

A-ROLL

(later)

I am crazy! All devoutness has fled, and now I wish to mock myself.
Yet it is with faint heart I write this.
When I came back up here, little Edith was sitting with her big
feet up on my desk reading a folio, bound in yellow. I could not tell
if she had been affected by reading the original. She merely put it
down when I walked in, slowly and decorously, and said nothing. She

seemed dazed.

"He is the King which our every Emperor has served, though many know it not," I whispered. Then for a long while I sat silently beside her, but Edith neither stirred nor spoke.

Finally, her Cupid's-bow mouth began switching and twisting, and her eyes were narrow with nearsighted squint. "This is... brilliant..." she stammered at me, "But... *Mon Oncle*, it was said that you were no longer insane. I..." With something like horror, I saw that my shop-girl was concerned.

"*You have crossed over to Earth, Camilla,*" I whispered, hoping to show her she was safe. "*Explain to me how it was done. Explain. The play must be performed. Surely you can understand my reasoning, for you are Carcosan yourself. How did you swim here?*"

Edith's face changed, then. I saw her much, much older, ravaged by the same opiate poisons now coursing through my veins, shining through the young girl's face like a mask. Like a pallid mask. But she said nothing. She just stood there and listened.

It was after five, by this point. The sunset light grew jaundiced and strange in my dusty office. Edith just stood there and looked at me, eyes wide and dark and grave.

"*The King will bring the Imperial Dynasty of America to its knees. I can tell no one. They merely say I am mentally defective, but many on Earth want the door to Carcosa open again. Many in America. Don't act as if you think I am insane...*"

She shrugs eloquently, a gesture as French as the folk-songs she sings. "Not for me to say. *Ça commence avec toi*," she whispers sadly in my ear, and closes the Book of Dream upon my head.

When she does, I am free, burned clean. Until I feel the restraints.

~*~

B-ROLL

[...]

> Down in the Temple of the Worm, CASSILDA, awakened, now wails over
> CROY'S severed arm, which is all that remained solid when the Spell broke.

CASSILDA

Song of my soul, my voice is dead,
Die though, unsung, as tears unshed
Shall dry and rot within His head,

in Lost Carcosa...

~*~

A-ROLL:

There is a crack across the universe, a yellow scar along the Sun. There is a bigger problem here that can Strike Anywhere, and none will know the hour when the Master comes to call. Even now, the towers of Carcosa rise behind the Moon.

There is a lower voice within, a towering silhouette looming on the glyph-scratched plaster. It likes to lay waste, & all we may hope to do is sing it to sleep for as long as possible. All we can do is bite its hand. Bite its hand, that spoiled the child with the rod, and spilled the seed of shame forever across its spawn it devoured at birth, like a wild sow eating her farrow.

~*~

I wake, and wish immediately that I hadn't.

The tatters of the King wash over my mind again, wash it back into the hanging-court of Chaos. There is only their robot Christ to cry to now.

I could tell more, but I cannot see what help it will be to the world. As for me, I am past human help or hope.

As I sit here, writing, careless even whether or not I die before I finish, I can sense that they will be very curious to know the tragedy – they of the outside world who write books and print millions of newspapers.

They may send their creatures into wrecked homes and death-smitten firesides, and their newspapers will batten on blood and tears. But the final indignity has come true, word for word, a nightmare boiled in an oracle's skull.

All I knew all along was smashed on the rocks when it finally mattered, masticated in Night's cold seeking mouth, scooped out and eaten and shit and eaten again. Above this flat, shackled cot, outside my barred window, the clouds glow gray. White doves roost upon the wires. The wind hoots and cries as the doves do, around the corners of this bleak old madhouse. Outside that window is a town where I never had one reason to be.

So it is written, forgotten…Rewritten? I feel unguarded here, when I wake, exposed, twisting in the wind, unable to distinguish the sickroom shadows from days of decades long since buried, just as then, in some vein. I want to drain this wound, but it is too old and deep. I want to wash away its taste. I want to belt it in the face.

~*~

But even now there is salt spray spuming through the sky outside. I must tighten down the clamps, subdue brute biology, to become safe and distinguish light from shadows, hands that feed from hands that inject a cure worse than any disease.

Yet now and then, my mind grows silent, dripping down madhouse walls. I rest, and breathe, and wait for my medicine. It will come. This time, I behave.

They will never slit open the mattress, or find the folio play. Like the King, I never wear a mask, or claim to be anything else. They simply haven't looked.

~*~

Not until I don the diadem, and let the beaten gold burn a halo in the footlights, as the Creature that rules His father Hastur's kingdom directs the play from the audience.

(*Journal ends here*)

For :
   -Joe Pulver and Lucius Shepard, Earth
   -Antonin Artaud & Robert W.Chambers, Carcosa

.

The Hymn of the Hyades

By Richard Gavin

T·he bad dream did not arrive until daybreak. It bled into Martin's bedroom as stealthily and organically as shadows at night. It put down roots as best it could, for the child it assailed was in limbo, neither slumbering nor yet awake.

Even at the tender age of ten Martin knew a little something of the gorge between the ordered world and the outgrowths of his fertile imagination. His father had been insistent that he learn these parameters and be ever-mindful of them. Every drawing his parents unearthed, each comic book cache they discovered, led to a scolding of some degree. Martin had begun being more mindful of his surroundings and less meshed in the products of his mind. For as long as he'd been aware of himself Martin had often thought of life as some type of play and he was cast in a role for which he'd not prepared himself. Conversation was difficult for him; he was so afraid of flubbing his lines, of ruining the plot, no matter how incomprehensible that plot was to him.

Thanks to his father's conditioning, Martin was groggily aware that the awful noise that scared him so could not be in nature and thus had his imagination as its womb. A cold front had been plaguing the town for the better part of a week, and Martin knew that the temperature had to be mild for it to rain. And without the possibility of rain there can be no thunder.

Yet the next peal confirmed Martin's suspicions of thunder. He forced his eyes open, grateful for the hint of sunlight that illuminated his bedroom just enough to assure him of fixedness. He wondered if the phantom sounds he was experiencing could be accurately called a nightmare, as they were occurring in the light.

He sat up in his bed and poked his fingers into his window blind, flexing them to part the slats. The sky mimicked the drab greyness of empty sidewalks. The flurrying snowflakes forbade the presence of thunderheads. Martin listened as the noise came again, fainter but still noticeable. He studied the pearled lawn and the non-descript fields long-stripped of their crops, hoping for some logical source for the noise. Perhaps he'd left the storm cellar door open again, or maybe it was simply the attic lamenting the assault of frigid gales.

The only way to uncover the truth was to press the issue as bravely and as thoroughly as his father would, had he been in this position.

Martin sacrificed the quilted sanctuary of his bed and, shivering, dressed himself.

His parents' bedroom was pent-up and silent as he slipped past it. It was likely that his folks would be unbothered by his impulse to go out exploring at this hour of the morning, but Martin still did not want to risk discovery. He crept down to the mudroom at the rear of the farmhouse and bundled himself.

When he opened the back door and met the day, he regretted the fuss he'd made when his mother had suggested he get a skidoo suit this winter. Today he would have welcomed the warmth. He came to realize that shirking outerwear he deemed childish-looking was no more likely to win him friends at school than his frequent attempts to laugh along with the older kids whenever they teased him, or the willing sacrifice of his allowance; a weekly ritual that inevitably made him cry.

'No point in being a baby now,' Martin told himself. He transformed his wind-battered trudge into a purposeful march.

The open fields invited the abuse of the winds. Martin tugged his scarf up to his eyes and pushed on. Sourcing out the noise was much trickier than he'd guessed, for in the flat landscape the sound seemed ubiquitous, as likely to have been born from the stiff soil as the trees of the nearby ravine. Without the distortion of his house, Martin noted that the sound was much sharper, like dozens of branches being cracked in succession, like breakers in a glass sea.

His perception of the windblown evergreens as waving him over to the ravine was, Martin knew, simply his wish to escape the unshielded terrain, but he heeded their invitation all the same. The hike seemed impossibly long, but when he reached the treed rim the blasts of ice seemed unable to penetrate through the boughs. Martin sighed with relief. The temperature was not significantly milder, but the respite from the winds was comfort enough.

Snow balanced on the pines and the evergreens like cake frosting, making Martin long for Christmastime. The slope leading down to West River was gradual, but the abundance of ice made it tricky. The further Martin descended, the clearer the sound became. He lowered his hood to be sure that the sound was indeed that of ice breaking up on the river.

His first sight of West River confirmed this, but also left him bewildered. The film of ice never began to crack up until April, March at the earliest. February had scarcely commenced, and the town was in a deep freeze to boot. Still, the great slab that coffined the river was dividing itself into dozens of tiny floes right before his eyes. It must have been cracking up for some time, for Martin could see the black water beneath as it bore the shards downstream.

A freak breaking of the ice he could accept, but not tadpoles and other fish. Martin knew it was far too cold for them to be squirming along the current.

But they weren't tadpoles, and although they were silvery, the dancing specks were far too small to be fish. He crouched down, feeling the frigid spray off the river. He shut his eyes to squeeze out any fantasies that might be infecting him and looked at West River anew.

He'd read – in one of his Never-Never tales no doubt – of stars being described as resembling flecks of ice, but never of ice looking so much like stars. And yet Martin couldn't help but think of a nighttime sky as he watched the sparkles gliding past him. The river did its part to aid the simile, using its cold blackness to give the impression of being just as limitless as space, and just as alien.

Magpie-like, Martin fell under the spell of the swimming glints. Of their shining presence he was certain, but of their strange song he was less so. Were they attempting to lull him like the sirens he'd read of in his illustrated Odyssey? The trilling was faint but still somehow managed to cut through the gush and creak of the river and the ice.

Martin almost reached in but noticed that he still had his mitten on. Soaking his clothing would make the walk home even more unbearable, so he tugged the mitten from his hand and reached in to fish out one of the wailing stars.

He allowed himself the luxury of one fantastical image: his hand breaking through not water, but the night sky of a world that existed leagues below him. He envisioned the shocked natives falling down in dread and awe at the sight of his pale hand raking their heaven.

The temperature of the water shocked his bare flesh, but he was grateful for the frigid wetness once the small bead of light began to burn his palm.

He couldn't have clutched the star, if star it was, for more than a second or two before it pushed through his fingers and moved downriver. But this was enough to scald his hand. Badly. Martin lifted his arm from the water, not recognizing it at first. His fingers had reddened from the cold and were shiny with water. An angry red puncture was set in the centre of his palm. There was no blood, thank God, but there was something that looked sickeningly similar to a gunshot wound. Squealing, Martin turned his hand over and sighed over the small mercy that the star had not burned clean through.

The flesh around the circular hole was bleached and there were jagged lines splaying out from the centre. Martin no longer felt any pain. The only thing he felt now was the scuttling of pins and needles numbing his arm.

Frantically shaking off the water, Martin shoved his hand back into his mitten. He was crying now, from fear rather than discomfort. The noise of the ice breaking was now rarer and quieter, yet the feminine star-song seemed nearer to him now.

He slipped and slid and scrabbled out of the ravine. The wind in the fields was just as harsh, but was of no concern to him now. Phlegm sealed in his throat and the air scalded his throat and lungs. By now Martin's tears had soaked through his scarf and he felt a brief concern that someone may spot him in this condition. But it was Sunday morning, and he knew that the boys who often beat him would be sanctimoniously stationed in their pews.

His house came into view.

They were awake and in the kitchen when Martin stumbled into the mudroom. He pursed his lips to stifle the blubbering noises he'd been making for several minutes now and began to unlace his boots. Clanging sounds told him that his mother was about to fry up some breakfast. Martin wiped the cold tears from his cheeks and sucked in his breath to steel himself against the dreadful mark he'd see once the mitten was removed.

He was less concerned over the wound than he was the potential reprimand he might receive for sneaking out, for heading up a fool's quest to West River, for possibly permanently damaging his writing hand. But once he'd freed himself of his winter garments, he slipped into the kitchen and received only a "Good morning," from his mother.

"Morning," Martin returned. His bad hand was cradled in the other.

"If you were out checking the storm cellar door this morning you can relax. I locked it for you." The brassy voice came from the corner. Martin recognized the hands that held the morning paper, but could only assume that the face behind the newsprint shield was his father's. "I had to go in my pyjamas at ten o'clock last night to set my mind at ease. I had a hunch you'd forgotten to lock it after your mother let you play down there, and I was right. Must have been twenty-below with the wind. I nearly froze to death."

"Sorry."

The hands turned the page noisily. Martin's mother announced, "I'm making omelettes."

With his fear of reprimand abated, Martin hurried upstairs to face his next crisis.

Behind the medicine chest's clouded mirror he found the jar of salve his mother had used to ease his campfire burn last summer. It was greasy and pungent but was the only item Martin thought might balm his wound. The thought of the wound congealing to permanently mar his hand with the strange design made him queasy. How would he explain his stigmata to his mother, to the bullies on the school bus, to his father?

His palm was already beginning to blister. A trio of curling lines spread from the shallow pit where the star/ice had scorched him. The fact that he felt no pain puzzled rather than relieved him, and he knew enough about such matters to realize that the sickly egg-yoke shade of the blister pattern might signify infection.

Martin sat atop the toilet and wallowed in the dreadful consequence of his mistake as quietly as he could until his mother shouted him down to breakfast.

Though he was worried about the scent of the salve being tell tale, Martin quickly remembered that his mother was still suffering a cold, and his father never took notice of any life beyond the ones captured in printer's ink.

He had to choke down the omelette and buttered toast on his plate, hoping no one questioned why he was forking his food with this left hand. After breakfast he cloistered himself in his bedroom.

By noon the fever began to afflict him.

Instinct guided him to the bathroom just in time to bring up his morning meal. He staggered back to his room, his feet and hands pulsating, his stomach still doing flips. As he stripped and then donned his pyjamas, Martin was overcome with dizziness. It was as if there was a gear inside his head that grown rusty and rigid from ill-use but had now been lubricated by the fever and was now beginning to turn uncontrollably. He swayed to and fro as even the floorboards seemed to be affected by his internal wheel. Martin flopped down on his bed, but his being stationary did nothing to anchor the wild turns.

"Mom..." he croaked. Lifting his hand, Martin saw what must have been the source of this all-encompassing vertigo: the sallow mark in his palm was turning, turning. Its yellow tendrils flexed and curled and curved like cat's tongues over milk. The wound in the centre of the sign began to shimmer. The depth of the wound hosted the lustre of a polished volcanic rock, of moonlight floundering in a pool of ink. Jabbing the index finger of his left hand at the hub of the spinner, Martin felt something firm against the soft meat of his fingertip.

Part of whatever he had fished out of West River was still embedded in his hand.

Martin spent the remainder of the day exchanging a few moments of hallucinatory waking life for several hours of dreams that were odder still. One moment he saw himself roaming the shore of a sombre grey lake, the next he was watching the thin stripes in his bedroom wallpaper bending and entwining into ornate alphabets. In fevered sleep he heard trilling songs pouring down from the black stars in the sky, in groggy wakefulness he watched in helpless horror as a great mummy-like shape slid noiselessly into his room. Its tattered dressings were the yellow of Martin's wound.

When the great gaunt shape examined Martin's body, the boy could only watch as his marked hand was exposed and then pierced by the intruder's needle-like claws.

It was very dark when Martin heard his bedroom door opening once again. Able to lift his head with less difficulty than before, he was relieved to note that the silhouette filling his doorway was a familiar one.

"You awake?" whispered his mother.

"Yes," croaked the boy.

She stepped into the room, and when Martin spotted the tumbler of ice water in her hand he almost groaned.

He drank slowly and could feel the cold water pushing out the sickness that had been congealing inside him. It was making him pure.

"You gave us quite a scare." Her voice was soft.

"I'm sorry," Martin began, "I just wanted to see what the noise was —"

"You must promise to tell your father and I whenever you hurt yourself." She either hadn't heard him or had no interest in his confession. "That burn on your hand was very badly infected. Luckily Dr. Mason was able to drain it. I have penicillin for you, but right now you need to get more rest."

"The doctor came in my room?"

His mother nodded.

"Okay," Martin murmured. And it was.

He slept well into the next day. His mother kept him home from school until Thursday. During his convalescence, Martin did not dream of the sombre shore. Beyond a slight itch, his injury no longer troubled him. His hand was dressed in clean white bandage, and when his mother changed these dressings Martin saw only a sloppy-looking scab in his palm. The wheeling blisters were gone, as was the distorted memory of Dr. Mason's fever-costume of a great faceless mummer in yellow.

He was lulled by the comforting presumption that he would never have to see that hideous figure again, which is why his next encounter with it almost levelled him.

Passing Mr. Nelsh's farm on his way to the corner where the school bus fetched him, Martin was startled by the sight of a scarecrow the old man had neglected to tear down for the season. The shocks, stripped of their corn, were mostly buried under snow. The more stubborn ones jutted up like whiskers, and it was over these meagre spokes that the scarecrow loomed. Its ragged clothing matched the sallow hue of the desiccated plants. The figure's attire, which the wind flaunted about in sweeps like a great cape, disguised its wooden perch so well that for an instant Martin believed he saw legs and sandaled feet upon the frozen soil.

But blowing snow and distance was clearly making mischief. The effigy was thinner than any living man could be, and besides that, it didn't appear to be appreciably shorter than the row of evergreens that lined Mr. Nelsh's field.

Martin told himself that he mustn't let his imagination run rampant. What would father say? He thought rationally about the whole thing and managed to convince himself that he hadn't seen the scarecrow stalking silently across the field.

He hadn't even heard the bus rumbling alongside him, or the voices of the other children shouting for him to hurry up. Martin clamoured up the bus's steps, pouncing on this opportunity to distance himself from the skulking thing. Peering through the windows and seeing no sign of the gaudy giant brought no relief. Martin tried to tell himself that his wits had banished this lingering symptom of his fever, but the cold crawl upon his spin told an altogether different tale.

Concentrating on the day's lessons was out of the question. Martin spent the entire morning gazing at the coils of snow that swept across the asphalt playground beyond the classroom window like dervishes of pale dust. Even when pretending to write in his exercise book Martin was secretly listening for the voice of ice upon black river water.

Recess saw him occupied with his usual solitary games. He was hunched by the chain-link fence at the schoolyard's edge, forging effigies out of snow, feeding them lines from his imaginary drama about distant Kings and lands too fabulous for human representation.

It was during this game, when he, the foreign King, was confessing his love to an actress that Martin heard the Song.

Thinking initially that the bird-like trill was coming from his lumpy woman of snow, Martin was almost disappointed when he sourced out the sound and realized it was coming from a young girl in the yard.

She was standing aloof from the other children. Her red coat was like a dollop of blood against the anaemic desert of snow. The voice that bloomed from her tiny mouth was almost inhumanly beautiful.

And the song...

Martin had heard it before, or rather felt it, when it came from the river, came gushing down from the black stars of his fever landscape.

Had the girl shared his dream? Was she part of his dream?

He bounded toward her, desperate to learn which.

The girl seemed unable to answer his questions. Her voice had become distorted; gnarling from celestial hymn to unbridled shrieking.

It was Mr. Feldman, the principal, who pried Martin off the girl. She kept sobbing, refusing to look at him. Martin tried to explain himself, but the girl kept screaming about the awful face Martin had apparently donned before charging after her.

He spent the afternoon in Mr. Feldman's office as punishment but was unable to obey the principal's demand to hand over whatever ugly mask he'd presumably worn to torment the girl. The secretary had tried several times to reach Martin's parents to inform them of his misconduct. When she could not reach them, Mr. Feldman typed out a letter that required their signatures.

The homeward bus ride passed in a wordless haze. As the bus slowed to drop Martin off at the corner, he no longer cared that Mr. Nelsh's yellow scarecrow was still missing.

His house was empty when Martin stepped inside. He searched the kitchen for a note, which his mother always left if she had to go out before he got home from school.

The breakfast dishes were still on the table.

His father's newspaper lay halved on the linoleum floor. Martin tried to swallow but could muster no saliva.

The wind carried with it a faint thudding sound. Martin had caused this sound enough times to recognize it, yet he still went to the kitchen window to see the storm cellar door being lifted and dropped by the gusts.

Jutting up from the rim of the cellar door was a cluster of vibrant tongues.

The sight of these flames caused Martin to panic, sent him charging out of the house and toward the gaping door in the earth.

The tongues that were undulating above the rim of the storm cellar's entrance, bright as roman candles, were too yellow to be fire. By the time Martin realized that what he was witnessing were in fact tatters of vibrant yellow fabric it was already too late.

Staked in-place by shock, Martin's gaze followed the snow-dusted wooden steps that connected the makeshift pit with the lawn where he stood. His thoughts became gluey and all but impossible to apprehend. Martin saw something bundled upon the storm cellar's dirt floor, something that been pulled all out of shape. Even though Martin distantly knew the real reason why his father was lying face-down upon the cold soil, he couldn't help but wonder if it was due to shame, disgust over his son's inability to rein-in his imagination, even now, with the threat so real, so near.

Martin realized that what he'd seen in Mr. Nelsh's field was real, but he felt no sense of vindication. It stood mutely, its face mercifully obscured by the cave of its hood, its only voice being the low lament of the wind. Even the tatters of its robes flapped noiselessly. It was like a wraith in a silent film.

Martin was only dimly aware of the fact that his fingers had begun to pick at the dressing off his palm. He lifted his hand, feebly hoping that the newly spinning mark might somehow aid him.

His next thought was a suitably boyish one: the figure really was as tall as he'd feared.

Its arms were equally unnatural in size, for they jutted up and seized Martin with ease. The yellow mask the figure produced from its folds was small by comparison. He now understood why the girl in the schoolyard had shrieked and wished he could as well.

Martin wondered if it had been wrought just for him, for as he forcibly discovered, the mask fit snugly on his face.

Slick Black Bones and Soft Black Stars

By Gemma Files

All graves look the same, generally: Sunken or up-thrust, back-dirt slightly looser than whatever lies around it, sometimes of a different color, a different composition. Anything that shows something's been scooped out and reapportioned, piled back in atop what lies beneath.

You start with trowel and probe, cleaning the surface near what you suspect is the grave's edge, thrusting the probe in as far as it'll go, then sniffing it for decomp. If you strike something soft, that's a find. Satellite photos also help, as do picks, shovels; Ken Kichi sets up nearby to run the electronic mapping station, charting the site's contours, eventually providing a three-dimensional outline of every body and its position when found, while Judy Moss—your usual dig partner—shares process photography duties with Guillaume Jutras, head of this particular Physicians for Human Rights forensic anthropology team. Their shutters buzz constantly like strange new insects in the oven-door heat, *snap-flash, snap-flash, whirrrr*.

And you, meanwhile—you're crouched down in the stench feeling for bones, finding rotten cloth, salt-stiff flesh.

The grave is humid, seawater-infused. Sand clings to everything, knitting with bone itself. At the very top, exposed to air and scavengers alike—crabs, birds—the bodies are slimy, broken down for parts, semi-skeletonized. Down further, they're still fleshed, literally ripe for autopsy; those are the ones Jutras wants in the worst way. While down further still...

Each stratum is an era, a span of time between massacres. The numbers vary: Twos and threes, five-person groups at most, as opposed to the first and second layers' twenty-three. Deeper than that is where your particular skills will come most into play, differentiating one body's bones from another's, telling male from female, adult from child. You try not to feel bad about wanting to get down there as fast as possible, to see just how far down it all goes.

This tower of murder, thrown down, inverted. To you, it's a mystery, a challenge; to the people whose fragments it's made from—their relatives, at any rate—it's an obscenity, a disgrace. But you can't think about that, because it'll only slow you down, make you sloppy. Sentiment breeds mistakes.

Crouching down, feeling with both hands, gently but firmly. And saying silently to yourself, with every breath: *Keep working, keep quiet, keep sharp. Miss nothing.* Assuring them, at the same time: *Lie still, we're coming, finally. At long last.*

We're coming to bring you home.

~*~

You reached the island of Carcosa seven days ago, at 6:35 PM by your watch, only to find what looked like two suns staring down, one centered, the other offset—an upturned pupil, cataract-white, with a faint bluish tinge. *It's an optical illusion,* Jutras told you, during your conference-Skype briefing; *Everyone sees them. There's other things, too.*

Like what?

Just...things. It's not important.

(The clear implication: *You won't be there long enough for them to matter.* An assumption you don't question, since it suits you fine; you'll remember it later, though. And laugh.)

So yes, it's strange, though not unbearably so—no more so than the incredible heat or the smell accompanying it, rancid and inescapable, though you haven't even come near the dig site as yet; the black beaches with their smooth-washed half-glass sand, the masses of shrimp-colored flowers and spindly nests of stick-insects creeping up every semi-vertical surface. Actually, all the colors are different here, just ever-so-slightly "off": the green laid on green of its grasses, fronds and vines isn't *your* green, not exactly. More like your green's occluded memory.

There's a wet woodsmoke tang to the air, like they've just doused a forest-fire. Breathing it in gives you a languorous, possessive contact high—opium smoke mixed with bone-dust.

According to Jutras, the island—itself just the merest jutting peak of an underwater mountain-range ringed with black smokers, incredibly volatile—was once centre-set with a volcano that exploded, Thera-style, its caldera becoming what's now known as "Lake" Hali. The quote-marks are because the lake itself is filled and re-filled with seawater brought in through a broken end-section that forms the island as a whole into a wormy crescent. Carcosa City occupies the crescent's midsection, its highest peak, while the two peninsulas formed by the crescent's horns almost overlap. The longer of the two is called Hali-joj'uk, "Hali-door" or "-gate", in the island's highly negotiable yet arcanely individual tongue. Wouldn't think there could be quite so many sub-dialects supported on an island whose entire population has never historically topped four hundred, and yet.

It's like every family has their own way of saying things, Jutras told you. *And they all understand each other, but they know you won't. That's why we have the interpreter.*

They don't trust folks from Away, Judy chimed in. *That's how they put it: there's them, and then there's Away. Everywhere else.*

Yeah, it's a serious Innsmouthian situation 'round these parts, Ken agreed. *Some inbred motherfuckers we're dealin' with, that's a certified fact.*

Ken, Jutras warned him, but Ken simply snorted.

What, man? It's just true. These people been marrying their cousins for a thousand years, by definition; cousins if they're lucky, and some years? I'm willing to take a bet the gene-pool maybe didn't stretch all that far. Like those Amish villages where the guys all have the same first name, and every dog's named "Hund".

Not a lot of cultural contamination on Carcosa, in other words, which is good in some ways, not so much in others. To cite another history, in 1856—fifty-two years after being officially rediscovered by the British—Pitcairn Island, inhabited by the descendants of the H.M.S. *Bounty's* mutineers, lost 100% of its population, gaining only sixteen of them back three years after. Since then, its numbers have fluctuated up and down—as high as two hundred and fifty in 1936, as low as forty-three in 1996. Yet numbers in Carcosa apparently remain steady, as though maintaining a strict death per birth replace-the-race policy...barring the occasional mass murder, that is.

Because that's what's brought you here, of course—like it always does, no matter where, no matter with who. Because this is your "business", the reckoning of mortality: to sex bones and extract DNA, to separate violent death covered up from more wholesome detritus, plague-pits or accidents or Acts of God alike, the dreadful human wreckage left behind whenever earth gapes wide, whenever the jungle sneezes up something that makes people cough themselves to death or sweat blood from every pore, whenever the sea rises up and bears away all in its path.

The whole island takes up approximately eighteen square miles, "lake" included. Nine of those take you from the airstrip to Halijo'juk, where the causeway to the dig awaits: Funeral Rock, yet one more island *inside* an island, a tiny chip barely a mile across split off from the main rim back into Hali itself, a shelf of bare black crag-slopes cradling a black sand beach which separates completely from the peninsula at high tide.

This is where it all happened; where no one will say how many of the island's otherwise rigidly-documented population were herded over no one will say how long a period of time, never to return. From what Judy and Ken have uncovered thus far, they think it must've begun long before the island was charted, let alone visited, and continued intermittently long after, with only the sheer numbers of the last mass-murder finally revealing the true nature of this particular "memorial" tradition at last...along with the fact that those taken to Funeral Rock for "burial" were not, strictly speaking, usually *dead* before the rocks and sand were thrown in on top of them.

All they know is, there's no telling how deep it goes down, Jutras told you, before you even started packing. *Which is why I need my best girl, Alice—to turn this around, ASAP.*

What's the hurry? you asked. *Top layer's the only one they can press charges with, right? I mean, the rest certainly proves a pattern of behavior, local prejudices, superstitions, maybe even religion-based motive... but in prosecutorial terms, just how useful is that?*

Jutras sighed. *Hard to say. It's a...weird situation, to say the least; slippery. Nobody knows who's responsible, or claims not to, so the authorities have just scooped up every able-bodied man within a certain radius; they don't have a jail, so they're holding them in the hospital's contagious ward.*

Because women *never kill anybody, right?* But since you both knew the answer to that one, you asked instead: *Who are the authorities in this case, exactly, anyways?*

Um...Wikipedia says the Hyades Islands, "a sub-archipelago thirty miles off the coast of East Timor," so—Indonesia, I guess? It's all pretty up in the air. A pause. *Point is, they don't even have cops here, let alone a court, so whoever does get charged with anything is going to have to be taken off-island for trial, and nobody's happy with that idea; the local garrison commander needs hard facts to keep Carcosa from blowing up around him, literally. Thus, us.*

You've worked with Jutras seven times before, all over. United Nations International Criminal Tribunal digs to start with, coordinated through The Hague—Darfur, then Cotê d'Ivoire. Then on to smaller matters in far more obscure places, balancing corporate internal policing with volunteer work for far-flung, resource-poor communities. Carcosa definitely falls under the latter rubric, and also promises something the other sites most often don't: Mystery. Even back when you were finishing your internship in the Ontario Forensic Pathology Service, the final verdict on any case was almost never in doubt from the moment you first viewed the body on, be it murder, misadventure or J-FROG (Just Plain Fuckin' Ran Out of Gas).

I've never heard of the Hyades, actually, you admitted, feeling stupid. *Carcosa either.*

Yeah, I'm with you there; had to look 'em up on the plane. But ours is not to reason, right?

And you might have disagreed with him, on that last part—should have, probably. But you were jet-lagged already, which never helps. One more dig didn't seem that big a deal.

Now here you are waist-deep in it, learning better.

~*~

Decomp clings to everything, in both senses of the word, just like the heat puts paid to modesty, prompting you and Judy to roll your coveralls to the waist over lunch, so you won't get corpse-rub in your food. Later, you'll pack today's "grave bra" into a plastic bag full of Woolite and choose tomorrow's from the rack it's been drying on in your hotel room closet. You buy seven new ones for every dig, color-coordinated by week-day, and leave them behind afterwards, so stink-saturated they're only fit for burning.

The famous interpreter Jutras hired, Ringo Astur, sits with you under the canopy, waving flies away. Eternally cheerful, chain-smoking imported cigarettes; his skin is the same color as Carcosa City's brick-work, a coral-tinged light brown, hair worn in short corn-rows.

How many today, Alice? he asks you every noon and every night, eyes charm-crinkling, like it's some local version of *How* you *doin'?*

Three so far, Ringo. Why?

Oh, no reason. That's a lot, yes?

More and more, you want to tell him. More, and more, and *more* . . . Just what have these people been *doing* out here all this time, anyways?

Tell me about the other city, you say, instead. *The one from across Hali.*

Hm, he replies. *Well...that city's also named Carcosa, supposedly. It appears lake-centre, where the volcano used to be—not always, not every night, but sometimes. Where the first Carcosa City stood once, before it dropped inside.*

Then there's a whole other Carcosa City under this lake?

A shrug. *So they say. And it appears, sometimes...we'd be closer to it here than back over there, if it did. They come down to the quay when it does, the people who live in it, and beckon, try to get us to row across.*

People live there?

Well, they look like people, yes, supposedly. They say they wear masks, those who've seen them.

You look down at your hands then, still stained from the grave; the sand's black tinge never seems to wash entirely off. Remembering one skull, its back crushed in with an axe-like implement, so fragile that when you threaded two fingers through its eye-sockets and a thumb through the nose-hole, it came apart in your hand—shed itself by sections even as you fought to keep it intact, yellow-grey bone sliding to sketch an entire fresh new face with palm-pink eyes and an unstrung, mud-filled mouth.

Unsurprising how easy they come apart, considering what you discovered on those top-layer excavations: Carcosans are full of cartilage, like sharks or octopi, with the proportion of actual collagen-poor bone to extensive net of tissue creepily small; all of them come out flexible yet springy, like osteogenesis imperfecta without the fracturing. You can see the signs from where you sit, in Ringo's bluish sclerae, his triangular face, that certain blurred malleability of feature which comes from most of your *cranial* plates simply not fusing, a head full of fontanelles and no joint left un-double. Once, in Carcosa City, you saw a not-exactly-small ten-year-old squeeze through a cat-door and pop out the other side laughing, to bound away into the brush.

Not enough bones in some ways, too many in others. And you're the only person, thus far, who ever seems to have thought of putting the extra ones together...

(But that's a private project, at least for now. You haven't even shown Jutras.)

It happens on two-sun days, mostly, around suns'-set, Ringo continues. *That's what they say. You look across Hali and there it is, all lit up, with the masks, and the beckoning. And then when you look up you see black stars high above, watching you.*

Who's this "they" you keep talking about, man? Ken yells at him, from over by the cooler. *I mean, you're related to basically everybody here, right? All those other Asturs? Old John-Paul-George Astur from the post office, Miss Sexy London Astur from the kelp farm? That dude Kilimanjaro Means We Couldn't Climb It Astur, from the boat repair?*

Don't be an arse, Ken, Judy tells him. *Jesus! What's it to you, anyhow?*

Now it's Ringo's turn to look down.

They don't talk to me much anymore, he says, finally. *Because I went Away. So I can't really ask them about any of it.*

You never saw it yourself, then? you find yourself asking.

Well...I did, yes. Once or twice, I think. I was young, a long time back. It was before, and Away—well, Away makes things like that hard to remember.

Ever try to go over?

No, no. That would be—that's a bad idea.

You nod, take a swig of water. Then something he said earlier comes back, prompting another question, before you can think better of it:

Closer over here...is that why people really came to Funeral Rock, in the first place? So they'd have less of a way to row, if they wanted to make it to the other Carcosa?

Ringo looks at you hard for a long moment, not speaking. 'Til: *No,* he says, finally. *That's not why. They came to bury, or get buried. Like the King, in the story.*

...what story?

~*~

The King, Ringo tells you, once ruled in Other Carcosa City, before he was expelled and set adrift. He came from somewhere else entirely, far Away, further than anywhere—came walking through their gates on foot one two-sun day, at suns'-set, and when asked to remove his mask as a gesture of friendship, claimed he didn't wear one.

Couldn't they tell? you ask, reasonably enough. But Ringo just shakes his head.

He looked...different, supposedly. Pale, yellow, with horns, all over—no one could think that was really his face; that's what they say. And yet... That's why the volcano blew up, you know. So they say.

Because of the King?

Because he wouldn't leave. So the people in Other Carcosa City made it happen, to make sure he did.

Wouldn't that have destroyed them, *too?*

Ringo shrugs. Concluding, after a beat: *Well, no, supposedly. They're—different.*

Later, back at camp, Judy maintains she's actually heard this same story a few times already, from other islanders. Which surprises the hell out of Ken, who—for all his bitching—probably hasn't tried talking to anybody without Ringo translating since he got here. Jutras easily confirms it, though, by pulling out an .mp3 he made on his phone of a woman (Miss Sexy London Astur?) telling the tale in Stage One Pidgin, the Malacca-Malay-inflected version of English Carcosans might've picked up from passing sailors, peppered with words you either can't hear or don't understand, your brain papering over the lacunae with whatever seems most contextually appropriate:

Many and many, one time there is to be being one [king] [magician] [warlord] [traitor], who is to be having all strength from the black pit of [stars] [salt] [silt], the bottom of every [hole] [mouth] [grave]. He is to be wearing no [mask] [face] [name]. He is to be being torn apart and ground down, thrown in seas, sunk deep, for fish to be eating. But then one time there are fish to be eating him, and islanders are to be eating the fish, with [pieces] [seeds] [bones] of him inside them. And then islanders are to be having children with [no bones] [no names] [no faces]...

You gulp, taste bile. *Jesus,* you say. *So...that's it, right? The motive. That's why?*

Classic Othering, with a fairytale spin, Jutras agrees. *I particularly like the whole Evil King deal that obviously keeps being trotted out every time these throwback genetic payloads pop up; you wait 'til it gets obvious, re-brand them as changelings spawned by the Enemy, then take 'em over to Funeral Rock and let "nature" take its course. "We 'had' to kill them, you see, because they weren't human, not really. Not like us".*

Look who's talkin', Ken mutters.

Judy frowns. *What I don't understand, though, is where this all came from, originally. The idea of this Evil King, of Other Carcosa City...all of it.*

"*Away*", I guess, Jutras replies. *Except...no, they were doing this long before anybody else ever came by here, so—some sort of primal phobia about the sea, maybe: All that water, everything underneath it, the earthquakes, all the instability. It has to be* somebody's *fault. A pause. That's the theory, anyways. Except it's hard to say, because, uh...nobody will say.*

You can't possibly believe—

Of course not, Alice, but they believe *it. Enough to kill twenty-three children, and God knows how many more...*

Now it's your turn to nod, to stare. And reply, eventually:

...I should show you something, probably.

~*~

Looking at what you've so neatly laid out on a canvas tarp in a shallow trench three feet from the grave's lip, elements-sheltered under a fresh new tent, Jutras says nothing, just stares down. You don't blame him, exactly; did it yourself, the first time you finally thought to stop and breathe. Now the words spill out in a similar rush, barely interrupted, monologue paced to an adrenaline rush tachycardia beat, so fast it barely seems to be *your* voice you're both hearing say these things, with complete declarative confidence—the same authoritarian, spell-casting rhythm which renders truth from lies, makes fiction into fact, simply by stating even the most ridiculous-sounding things out loud.

You study him closely as you speak, too, just in case: Strain to read every minor shift, each muscle-twitch, each spasm. Almost as though you think that at some point his own eye-whites are going to turn blue, jaw and temples deforming, as the planes of his skull soften 'til they slide to form someone else's face entirely.

Remember how Ken kept saying these people weren't like us? Well, asshole that he is, turns out he's actually right. The adult human body has two hundred and six bones. These... have more. Best approximate total: Just over three hundred and fifty, like a human infant, almost as though their bones never fused properly—and three times the normal amount of cartilage, so it doesn't much matter that they didn't. Like they were never meant to; like they were supposed to reach adulthood able to squeeze themselves easily through spaces that'd break a normal adult human's neck.

Also, the reason it's "just over" is because it seems each body's in-

evitably got two duplicates of one particular bone... except it's never the same one. This woman has two fibulae. This man has two second thoracic vertebrae. This child has two mandibles—must've made it hard to talk, especially since the second one is adult-sized. It's like God was smuggling a whole other person into Carcosa, hidden inside these people's bodies.

But—what can I say; I guess everybody caught on.

Oh, and now that we've reached the bottom—did that yesterday— you know how many corpses are in this grave, exactly? Three hundred and fifty.

Plus one.

It's that "plus one" Jutras' looking at right now, the nameless guest at this carrion feast, painstakingly pieced together in anatomical explode-a-view. On its own it'd seem like some drunk pre-med student practical joke, a botched bastardization Transformered together from three or more skeletons at once: Spine articulated like a boa constrictor's, ribs everywhere, even in its limbs; skull like a Rubik's helmet, slabbed and fluted and interlocking, a puzzle-box with a million solutions but no answers. The fact that it proved surprisingly easy to assemble is the least of your worries, a strangeness so trivial it's barely worth sparing the energy to consider...not when there's just so much more about the whole exercise to avoid thinking about at all, in retrospect.

How long has that mould been growing on it? Jutras asks.

What mould?

He points, and you finally see it: grey as the bones themselves, furry. Hard to tell what you thought it was before, if you even registered its existebce—moisture? Condensation?

I...don't know. Why?

...no reason.

But he's already backing away, step by step; peeling the flap without looking, shimmying himself free. You hear him take a long, shaky breath, almost like he's tensing against nausea, trying not to vomit. His walkie gives an almighty crackling howl.

There's something happening, he says, at last, after a hushed, one-sided conversation. *In the city. I have to go.*

And a minute later, it's just you and the bones again.

~*~

Jutras is out of contact for most of the next day, which means he isn't there for the undersea quake that rattles the island. Minor as tremors go, the epicentre's out by the black smoker ring that keeps Carcosa's shores so fertile, so teeming with fish and kelp-forests; closer to Carcosa City than Funeral Rock, thankfully, so the back-slop doesn't do much more than submerge the causeway far faster and for far longer than expected. You didn't even notice it yourself until you came out of the tent and found Ken and Judy on the horn with Jutras, yelling at him about being stuck on-site for the night until the causeway emerges again. Said prospect bothers you less than it should, but that could just be sheer exhaustion. Who knew watching mould grow could be so draining.

What *does* bother you—silencing Ken and Judy as well—is what Jutras finally tells you, when he gets a word in edgewise: The quake brought in a mini-tsunami that cracked the hospital apart, shearing off the wall of the contagious ward. In the confusion, most massacre suspects cut and ran, disappearing into a sympathetic web of backrooms, basements, cliff-caves and other assorted hidey-holes. Surprisingly few injuries amongst the military guards, and all from natural causes rather than any sort of hostile action, but all of you can read between the lines; the garrison is confused and demoralized from the bottom up, perhaps even fixing to cut and run, and the islanders themselves...well, they aren't happy.

They've heard what you're doing here, Ringo tells you, after Jutras signs off. *Putting the King back together—that's why this happened. They want to stop you.*

Ken snorts. *So these dudes in jail, what, called up a wave and surfed on out of there? C'mon, man. Army'll pick 'em up by tomorrow; this place ain't big enough to hide in, not for long.*

You don't know that. You don't know anything about us.

I know enough, man.

No. Ringo shakes his head, visibly struggling to keep polite. *It's... not safe for you here, not now, any of you. You should go.*

Go where? you ask, waving Ken silent, while Judy hugs herself. *Where should we go, Ringo?*

Without hesitation: *Away, of course. And take me with you, when you do.*

~*~

Though you're hardly a mycologist or saprophytologist by trade, anyone who works enough decomp learns to ID the key fungal players soon enough. The stuff that's growing over "the King"'s bones still doesn't match anything you recognize: Too tough, spreading too fast, especially without an identifiable nutrient-source. You take a moment to look up the region on your tablet, looking for a local flora-and-fauna rundown, and pause at Wikipedia's disambiguation page for "Hyades". There are four entries: the islands, the band, the Greek mythological figures, and a star cluster in the constellation Taurus.

You look up in the dusk light, out across the lake. The "twin suns" sink towards the horizon in a blurry shimmer. A mirage, an illusion; the same thing that makes the suns look almost bluish-white, rather than red-gold. So Ringo says. You look back down to your tablet, and click on the entry for the star cluster. Thinking, as you do, about articles some of your geekier friends have sent to you, essays about such things as static wormholes, and equipotential space-time points; quantum tunneling, black branes and folded space, negative energy densities.

The Hyades cluster is more than six hundred million years old, far older than most such stellar groups, a survivor of the aeons by orbiting far from galactic centre. At least twenty of its stars are A-type white giants, with seventeen or eighteen of them thought likely to be binary—double-star—systems. It appears in the *Iliad* on the shield that Hephaestus made for Achilles, and is named for the daughters of Atlas, who wept so hard over the death of their brother Hyas they eventually became the patron stars of rain.

Twilight deepens, and your tablet's glow increases in the growing dark. But your shadow grows sharp to one side, beyond what the tablet could illuminate, and you look up once more.

Above the centre of the lake, where the volcano exploded centuries ago, lights glow in a scattered matrix of green, blue, gold and red, clear and cold. The darkness between them seems to outline shapes—structures, blocks, towers. They're hard to look at, defying your eyes' focus almost painfully. Can't tell if the blur is distance, or atmosphere mirage, or the wake of motion too fast to follow. The blue-green, poisonous light of the setting suns behind it twists your stomach. You feel the whole thing *pulling*, physically, like a hook in the gut: some second force of gravity, pressing you towards the lake and the place you know isn't there, can't be there—

—not because it isn't real, but because it's somewhere else. Some utter, alien elsewhere, so far away its light is older than your species.

It's that pull, that nausea and that disbelief, which keeps you from hearing the tumult until it's too late. Distracted by Other Carcosa City's spectacular appearance, you simply haven't noticed the boats' approach, silent and sure—pontooned sea-canoes, anchoring themselves at Funeral Rock's base so their passengers can shinny up the handhold-pocked cliff and emerge through those cave-entrances you never even knew were there, almost under your feet.

A burst of bullets, muzzle-flare in the night, and Ringo's already up, hauling on your arm: *Alice, come, come on, Alice—now now now, they're here! Leave everything!*

But—Ken, Judy, Jesus, Ringo! What about...

Too late, come on! We have to go—

Across Hali, behind Other Carcosa City's gleaming shoreline, you can just glimpse the "real" capitol going up in flames, a series of controlled explosions. Is one of those Jutras' field-office, the garrison, the sea-plane that brought you here? Over near the grave, meanwhile, Ken's scrabbling for his data, uploading frantically; one shot catches him in the shoulder, another in the upper back, sending him straight over the lip. You can hear him thrashing down below, desperately trying to cover himself in enough sand-muck to turn invisible. Ringo pulls you headlong while the attackers rush the camp, smashing and tearing, hurling equipment and evidence alike into the sea. Ripping up the tents, they riddle every prepped body-bag they uncover with yet more gunfire, as though they think something might be hiding in there.

Good thing I moved him, you find yourself thinking. *Good thing, good thing...*

Ringo drops to his knees, dragging you along with him; your knees jolt, painfully. *In here, Alice*, he says. *Come on! This one goes out the opposite side—we can swim, they'll never see us.*

Swim? Where the hell to?

Other Carcosa City, of course; no one will expect it. Can't you see them, beckoning?

But: That's just a bit too much crazy to stomach, even now. So here you pull back, wrenching yourself free, even as Ringo worms his way slickly down into the earth, gone in seconds—you'd never make it anyways, is what you tell yourself. The gap's far too narrow, too twisting; you'd simply lodge fast, bruised and scraped and strained to breaking, to die crushed like a bug. You let him go instead, whispering *Goodbye*.

Why? Judy yells from behind you, uselessly, drawing another burst. *Why, why?*

Because some things are meant to stay buried, a voice replies, from deep inside.

Then: Spotlights stab down out of the growing dusk, helicopter rotors roaring, as speakers filter what must be orders far past the point of comprehensibility. More gunfire strafes the camp, this time vertically; Judy's head explodes outright, GSW damage simultaneously shock-hammering away one half of your body in a series of consecutive hits to forearm, shoulder, hip, thigh. The downdraft wraps you in already-torn tent-fabric like a plastic bag shroud, momentum rolling you straight into the scrub where you stowed "the King"'s reassembled body, so you sprawl almost nose to whatever it uses for a nose with it.

No pain, simply shock, cold and huge enough to sharpen your observational skills to inhuman levels. The not-fungus has finished its work. The creature's skin is black everywhere but its pallid mask of a face, slick and soft, oily to the touch, almost warm; that's your blood it's soaking up, spongelike, as if every pore is a feeding orifice, swelling with the sacrifice.

And its massive, horned head turns, yellow eyes cracking open. Locking upon yours.

I am here, it tells you; *look across the lake, where my city rises, and watch us beckon. You have done me great service, bringing me back into this world.*

Now: Be not afraid, lie still, lie quiet. Your long wait is over.

Beyond the hovering 'copter, those two suns sink down, white-blue turning red, filling Hali's caldera with false lava. And when you slump over onto your back, looking up again by sheer default, you see stars: Soft black stars, almost indistinguishable, in a black, black sky.

The King lays one scaly hand on your brow, lightly. Almost affectionately.

I am coming, he promises, *to take you home.*

Not Enough Hope

By Joseph S. Pulver, Sr.

{for a king sorely missed, KEW}

K arl Edward Wagner. Writer. Editor. Dreamer. Due to be in search of another story.

After this drink.

"*Or the next.*"

On his balcony in Dim Carcosa. "Some view."

Lifts the empty glass. He's mildly surprised to see it's not radiant—it has no mouth, no memories, it's just a thing taking up space. Holds it a moment. Doesn't change. Sets it back on the table.

"Lot better last night. At least Elvis and Des Lewis had fun . . . Unless the anchovies got 'em."

Laughs, ends with a fit of lungs clawing for another hit of air.

Picks up the bottle.

"Not as many dreams in this shit as I'd like, but."

"Playing with termites and euphoria again, I see."

Karl didn't turn to look at Cassilda. Doesn't want to see those eyes, or the long soft curves of her legs for that matter. Knows they want. Want the thing. Him. He's too full of some other time, too tired to take his mask off again.

"You do know the mall's closed tonight?"

"Yeah. Too late to make the trip."

"Maybe you'll get to see de Vega to-morrow?"

"Perhaps. Unless it snows. The Phoenix will not rise if it's too cold."

"The Monster of Nature, here?" No smile.

"No. At his place." Afraid to turn and see her face, see a stranger, or the brocade of scars. Doesn't want to reel in the complex inches of sorry, or face another bare goddamn. Too often these days, too much scherzo in her eyes, even the cyclones in the crematorium hadn't brought them to a full stop yet.

"Ever snowed here?"

Cassilda circles how much she'd like to dance barefoot, just once, just for a few moments, in the snow. "No. Never."

"Thought so."

A cloud she dislikes returns to waltz with the moon. Exit balcony left.

He doesn't bother to turn and watch her leave. He'd see her sweet ass—probably swaying softly just for him, and it would be his turn to want.

Maybe he should have stopped her. Called her back. Maybe sit and have a drink. Talk, even if some of it came out clumsy. Just spend a little time with her. But that would lead to the bedroom

and the corset

and the toys . . . and *those* memories . . .

Her shoulders would be loaded with primal biology and his tongue would start counting riches. Then she'd ask the question—

"*Damnitall.*"

Looks up sees the little black cloud that haunts her. Nods a half-hearted thanks to it.

Should be doing something with the new Kane story. Told Mr. Deathrealm he'd shoot it over by October. October's not very far off—the birds were already gearing up for it. He knows Mark will understand if he's a bit late this time. It's just not right. Jack stealing a few moments or not, he's a professional.

Lot of things not right the last six aeons.

Not right to-morrow. Not right last yesterday. Pills to help the Jack execute the staccato lonesome is how not right it is here tonight. Another cold Never at the end of a slow purple day . . .

Never never comes in a brand new bottle.

Never.

A bird, he's sure it's a cathedral-deathbird, calls for sliver-starlight. Its stunted blast rattles him. Always does.

"Light-haters and their isolato." Wishes he had a gun. Looks at his lighter. "I know how to fix your ass."

The deathbird goes silent.

"Damn ghoul." *Ought to just shoot all of them one of these nights.*

Back to his bottle. In peace. Not really, but he can't choose, so he goes with what is there.

Like he often does these days.

Wished he'd walked across the food court last night, could have squeezed through the knots of loud kids and their daring colors, and a sat with Des and Elvis. Wasn't in the mood for thin mall-pizza, but he could have had a taco or a burger and maybe a laugh. Laughing might not have hurt. And he always liked Des, jest and jaunt—purl two, knit two, a real master that cat. Never big on Elvis. Not that he was such a bad guy; he could be plenty warm and friendly, just couldn't stand that stupid teddy bear ditty.

"Should have gone over." *Waving hi was not very personable.* "How hard would it have been to navigate thirty steps and talk for a few minutes?"

Rubs an old blister. Two, three shots left in the bottle. Thinks about going inside for another bottle.

Soul. Torn, tried and tired trouble in mind. Not interested in moving.

Looks at his pen. It doesn't seem to want to remember . . .

Looks over the cloudwaves.

All that aches. All the arpeggio decades of dandelion-sunlight corroded by cold . . . How many holes did I leave in that bar where the speakers rayed 1967?

The hours. The places . . . All the pieces scattered with the dead bird wings on the ground under The Winter Tree.

"All the Whiteness."

Phone on the table rings, hand doesn't hesitate. Dylan, "Cabinet's empty, Karl, and all the defective neon signs are creating confusion on Desolation Row. And surveillance shows Rum-Row is a mess a herd of alienists armed with restoration couldn't fix.'

"And Pulver's stopped dancin'—Archer dulled him but good him with all that snicker-snack. Boy lost it to currents of high water and tears. Only thing he said, Betty Davis style was, 'My hands are tied to this trance. They can't be repaired.' Ran his race. He was playing nothing but "Solid Air" all night long. Hour after hour, as if it was an unfinished symphony. If that don't speak to it, I sure as hell don't know what does."

"He'd always been in a lonely place. His galaxy was . . .'

"Greyness and rain always barred him from the shore, Bob."

"He blamed Loki. It's not just him; all the mysteries and conjectures have collapsed. Little things, every vein of syrup and any mercies they carried have fallen to dangerous. Nothing out there is moving. It's all panic and grief in the custody of what the Boneclock assembled." Bob's mouthful stops on a dime.

Karl hears him exhale quickly and take another drag. He's glad he's not here, enough grey-poison choking the sky, doesn't need Bob's romance with the cigarette-smokestack adding to it.

"Brel's out there with a string of fear-mongers at his heels, pushing a wheelbarrow full of antiquated robot parts up and down the block and I can't dig up an amulet of Agamotto to cut through the damn haze. Front and behind, it's all tombstone and cracks, Karl—not a single seat left on the Last Train."

"What was asleep is unmasked. This thing is not just passing through . . . Shit and damnation. Any wisdom for a weary Quixote you care to dole out? I'd sure be grateful."

"Yeah." Bit of a light laugh in it. "High water everywhere, Darwin. Man can only take in so much, open another bottle of Jack. You ride it out, or you don't."

"Already rode the Eternity Line. Not exactly eager to get tied to that chain again."

"Christ, Bobby, you're the one who said you dance with the partner they give you, or tough-shit, zip it and take a seat. Did you really think you could sit in Archer's office and make it back out to some garden with cheery blue skies? Fucker's worse than Loki. Didn't you see that? Son-of-a-bitch might try to, but he doesn't hide that subterranean weather very deep. You filled out the questionnaire, took his tests. All those rows of dark sky questions, you can't resurrect clean and safely after those shadows."

"Oh." Sounds like a crippled ship in a maelstrom of flotsam.

"Have a drink. You'll find what you find."

"Sorry, Bobby, got to dash. Cassilda's wandering around with her demons tonight, any minute she'll be back to handcuff me again. Try not to poke the grave."

"Can't promise that, but I'll lock all the windows."

"Make sure you have extra batteries for the flashlight too."

"Will."

Karl hangs up. Washes down two pills with a slug of Jack. Refills his glass.

The whiteness falls . . . Live dies.

Turns his head toward the cathedral expecting the deathbirds to cackle or offer up one of their evermores.

Hangman must be at lunch. Fucker.

Looks at his pen . . . and the glass. Drains it. Picks up his pen. The page is still white, blank. Karl glares at the pen, still waiting for energy to articulate its indigo into black marks. Old muscles call up old wounds. Instinct shoots the uninspired that was holding it back, Karl's pen moves on the page.

LOKI'S DISCOURSE

The night of coal and ash burns. Takes the details from the bitter soldiery and the threads, their terms thinner and less active after the series of mishaps. Drawing alloys to bridge the riffs and putting down knives for a chance to spin fortune's wheel, each hopes to find true.

There was lightning and thunder.

Lightning and thunder.

There was Lightning and thunder. There was Lightning . . . It came and roared.

Lightning and thunder.

Lightning . . . and thunder.

Lightning.

Thunder.

. . . in imprisoned hearts . . . along the road . . .

Thunder.

And evil faces.

Evil faces that betrayed dreams. Dr. Sipus—Archer spawned, and his poison. That

```
rattlesnake  expression.  The  cold  black  gaze
framed  by  unsightly  horn-rimmed  eyeglasses,
he's  Death  come  knocking  at  the  door.  He's
sin,  purging  and
```

Pen pauses. Smile urges, just do it.

```
pulverizing
```

"Pulver, you ass. Strawberry fields are a myth."

You were just a pawn in the King's game. You were never going to be a duke or a baron.

Sets his pen down and picks up his glass. Looks down at the words.

Did you leave a statement about the fire, or the last day?

Looks up, notes the rivering knuckles of the black cloud tutoring the moon.

"Or did you just stop negotiating and offer tobacco to the tin moon? *You ass.* You stupid ass, you looked down in the darkness and marked the rising waterline with your mug shot. Didn't you?"

No answer in the sky. None in his empty glass. Karl picks up his pen.

```
with  its  measure  of  wrong,  cutting  the  us-
age  of  good  from  cried.
```

```
His  Nation  of  Cleansing,  his  metal  proph-
ecy,  that  river  with  no  bed  for  those  judged
and  carved  by  Other.  "A  case  of  blending  the
light  out  of  it,"  he  said,  as  he  again  spit
on  the  guilt  and  famine  of  the  pawn  he's
engraved  with  the  plague.
```

* * *

```
"Make  it  stop."  And  she  curls  up,  the  be-
trayal  still  a  blade  pressed  to  her  throat.
```

```
She  remembers  the  yesterday  when  her  heart
raced,  raced  beat  for  beat  with  Camilla's.
```

They'd broken misfortune's curfew to dwell in amusement and had been reading of Loki's cunning betrayal when she found herself consumed by a current of fear that caused her to begin sobbing. Afraid, yet somehow remembering that line from the other story— 'One always remembers one's mistakes…'—she found herself shivering as the cold sea air swelled, climbed the cliff and slid into her bedroom window and its weight danced on her shoulder. Camilla held her, covered her with the yellow-trimmed, cream and copper colored quilt that felt like a warm poem.

"Camilla."

"I'm here, Dearest. I will not let go." Camilla's honey-alto transformed her clothes, freed her to swim in the sea.

"Make it stop."

Tears and a coward's soul in the traitor's room with lonely times. This hour, right now, and the narrow ones of debris to come

"Karl . . . Please, you should come inside and rest. A few hours of sleep might help."

"I was, um, considering it."

Her eyes question his weak reply.

She changes her tongue. "*He* will be there."

His expression is loud. Louder than his dim "I know."

"His compass will spin and finally come to rest, pointing at you. To-morrow arrives today."

Karl nods, yes, yes.

"And He will point to your hands."

He holds no cards. Looks at his empty glass.

The moon quickly hides behind a bank of clouds. From the crooked-peaked, bitter-black towers of the cathedral the deathbirds sing the song of unmasking.

Karl sees no tears in Cassilda's eyes. Sees her lips move—
"The last writer sits alone in his study . . . Writes . . .'
"Everywhere: greyness and rain."

(after Karl Edward Wagner's "The River of Night's Dreaming")

[W.S. Burroughs "A Thanksgiving Prayer", Bennie Maupin "Quasar", Kate Bush "Running Up That Hill", John Martyn "Solid Air", Bob Dylan "Things Have Changed", "High Water (For Charlie Patton)", "Desolation Row", B, S, & T "He's A Runner", Jacques Brel "Marathon", Mathias Eick "October", The Beatles "Strawberry Fields Forever", "A Day In The Life", Wings "Live And Let Die", Traffic "(Roamin' Thru the Gloamin' With) 40,000 Headmen"]

Whose Hearts are Pure Gold

By Kristin Prevallet

efore she left for her month-long cruise, Camilla's mother Tess left the ultimate "To Do" list on the kitchen table:

> *vacuum every other day*
> *dust on Sunday*
> *pick up the apples daily*
> *weed whack*
> *clean up the cat mess under the bushes*
> *water the lawn*
> *wash the sheets*
> *prune the trees*
> *pick up the apples*
> *tighten the screen*
> *hose down the driveway*
> *toss old books from the basement*
> *be your best self.*

The "To Do" list is Tess' attempt to control the chaos, the unimaginable clutter that she had accumulated over the past twenty years. When Camilla was born, the baby's presence and its totalizing demands were constant reminders of the man who had gotten Tess pregnant, and then left her to bear the burden. It was perhaps an attempt to bury her child alive that Tess began obsessively shopping: she walked out of thrift stores with bags of trinkets, and scoured used books stores for romance novels, which like a slow moving virus has taken over every surface in the house. Camilla never had her own room, really. Just a small space in a closet that she was able to keep completely clean – a space where she would spend her afternoons reading, and dreaming about what other girls were doing in their rooms.

On this July morning, Camilla wakes up to find the house quiet. She sees the to-do list and instinctively tosses it away. Because for the first time in her life Camilla isn't going to do any of these things: this is the beginning.

Instead of tackling each chore with the great gusto to please her mother as she usually does, Camilla spends the first two days that she is alone watching TV. *Family Feud, The 20,000 Pyramid, The Guiding Light, The Edge of Night*. At 4pm, Leo Buscaglia comes on Phil Donahue to talk about love and positive thinking. "Love always creates, it never destroys. It is our only hope." His words are background noise for a late afternoon dream-slip into sleep.

On the third day, lethargic from watching too much TV but jazzed by her defiance, Camilla gets the urge to get up and do something, somewhere, all on her own. But her mother's controlling influence is so strong that she is paralyzed; the energy is there, but it has no where to go. She wades in anguish through the piles of clothes and cheap statues that have taken over the living room, desiring to break them but feeling that her arms are pinned to her side. All she can do is wander, a ghost who knows she is alive but hasn't yet found her form.

Finally collapsing in tears on the dirty living room floor (which hasn't been vacuumed in years), Camilla spots a wooden box hidden under an overstuffed bookshelf. Inside is an odd trinket – a pin with a clasp of black onyx, on which is inlaid a curious symbol or letter in gold. It is pretty, so she puts it on.

Without knowing why she has an idea: what if she suddenly went through the house and tore the stuffing out of the couches? Pulled the trim from the doorways? Ripped the faucet out of the sink? Could be exciting. But instead of doing anything that would raise her mother's hysterical ire, she gets off the floor, walks out of the house, and stands in the middle of the street.

She stands there for a few minutes. The cement is hot, but she plants her feet on the ground and feels the tar burning. She hears an airplane and the slow rustle of leaves. Somewhere a child is crying. She notices a few shriveled up apples on the ground. She notices a flock of crows sitting on the telephone wire, as if waiting for a gust of wind to knock them into flight. She throws a rock at the crows. A few get startled and fly away. Then, she goes back inside and paces around.

There is something she needs to work out. In spite of her mother's raging voice in her head telling her to do the chores because the house is falling apart, Camilla imagines straying further and further from home: outside her cul-de-sac, down the quiet street, and into a series of adventures and misadventures that, even at their most gruesome, she will take in stride as the genesis of a world she has passively ignited.

II

Each day that her mother is gone Camilla tests how far she can go by appearing where she is not supposed to be: Monday at the bus-stop in her nightgown at 5am, Tuesday at the gas station at midnight, Wednesday on the median that divides traffic at noon, arms outstretched like Jesus.

Thursday she decides to up the ante of her thought experiment by standing in the middle of Alcott Street. Along comes a boy named Kass driving his father's Buick a little too fast, suffering from a hangover, and listening to Zepplin's "Trampled Under Foot" on the tape player a little too loud. He sees Camilla just a little too late, but manages to slam on the breaks, skidding into a tightly-trimmed bramble of a evergreen shrub. Camilla is still standing in the street, looking blankly at the scene, like a detective.

"Are you fuckin' crazy? What the fuck is your problem? Get out of the street you stupid girl!"

Camilla just watches him as he jumps around, punching the shrub, kicking the tires, gesturing in the air. Her silence is unsettling, and causes him to shift his tone.

He pauses.

"What – whoa. Ok. So… got released too early from lockup?"

"To see what would happen," she says.

"To see what would happen?! To see what would fucking happen? I'll tell you what will happen when my father sees his car all scratched. Stupid bitch! You Stupid Bitch!"

Kass grabs Camilla out of the street, pulling her by the sleeve, escorting her to the flattened shrub. Camilla shrugs and smiles at him.

That shrug causes Kass to look at her face very carefully: her round brown eyes, uncombed hair falling messily around a rubber band at the nape of her neck, her shirt just barely touching the hipline of her skirt. He thinks to himself, "she is pretty. And she is obviously crazy. And my father told me that the pretty crazy ones are the best in bed."

At that moment, the shrub owner turns the corner and is about to pull his station wagon into the driveway. Seeing the approach of the shrub man, Kass grabs Camilla and pushes her into the passenger seat of the Buick. Just as shrub man is yelling: "look what you've done to my shrub!" Kass dives into the driver's seat, and then smiles and waves as he backs the car out of the lawn and into the street. None of this is at all alarming to Camilla, who is having the time of her life.

Realizing that Camilla wasn't one to talk very much, Kass inserts "Technical Ecstasy" into the cassette deck. The only music Camilla knows is what her mother plays: compilation melodies from cheap violin cover albums she finds in thrift stores. But now, listening to Kass's music, pure terror channels straight through her, and she is moved. The words say: *The sleepy city is dreaming the night time away / Out on the street I watch tomorrow becoming today*. The music says: fight. Camilla's mind wraps around every beat; she lets out a moan. Some other organ is now her eye. Internally focused, she grasps the gold pin. The sun is setting behind her as the car moves forward in time; and she, always lethargic, is awake with an indefatigable energy.

III

Kass is at a stoplight, bobbing his head and tapping his fingers on the steering wheel trying to contain his excitement about how dangerous this whole thing was feeling. Hearing her moan, he stops moving and looks at Camilla who at that moment is staring straight ahead, her eyes wide open and her lips slightly parted. Kass is smitten. He drives the Buick to the parking lot of Safeway, finds a spot farthest from the entrance, and turns off the engine.

She feels Kass's right hand pulling her hair out of the rubber band, and his left hand lifting her shirt. She thinks of her mother's words: girls who cause boys to touch them will be forever changed into something evil, unlikable, bitter, mean, and ugly. For a moment, Camilla listens to her mother's voice as it runs through her head, but then she thinks of how great it would feel to throw all her mother's crap out into the yard. To poke the walls with thumb tacks. To etch zigzags into the wood panels with a key. She is out to make ruins, and has put the first phase of destruction in motion.

She lets go of the urge to struggle against Kass's hand as he pries apart her thighs. She rejects the voice of shame as his hands push her down. In her mind, she reasons that she has not caused this boy to touch her. She is not doing anything wrong just because she happens to be in a place that is different from the place she normally would have been. She releases into the danger of not knowing what will happen next. When suddenly his chapped fingers are in her: she is flesh, moving in ten different places with the elasticity of gum, and this feeling lets loose a wetness that stops the burning and is almost pleasant. Kass, sensing this, moves his hand faster, making more. Having lost her sense of space, Camilla puts her hand over the yellow pin (which is now beating in time to her heart) and feels her breath moving up and down her chest, like particles of light.

Kass pulls her back up and buckles her in. Her expression hasn't seemed to change; she hasn't said a word. He reasons that she is not going home unless she makes it back there accidentally. She has no money, doesn't really talk much, and seems incredibly clueless. These are intriguing qualities to Kass. And so he decides to keep her. Finally, his very own girlfriend.

IV

Camilla has been staying with Kass for a few days, but Camilla gets bored easily. Kass has to keep a very careful eye on her, lest she wander into the middle of the street again, causing an accident or worse. He takes her to movies and is impressed that she never flinches – a girl who doesn't get scared watching Demon Seed: very cool. Camilla notices that all of Kass's favorite movies are about monstrous people who cause terrible things to happen in the world, but the world always goes back to normal at the end. She witnesses these acts of violence, and learns something about the world within the world that her mother had tried so hard to shelter from her. In this new world, Camilla reasons, violence exists in order that violence be eliminated; evil exists in order that good can assert itself as a power; men fight wars because through fighting, love can be realized. Men shoot themselves in the head because through shooting themselves in the head they are ensuring that they will not shoot someone else. Men shoot, bleed, set fires and cut other men up in order that sanity, as a general principal might be defined. And what, she asks Kass, is so wrong with that?

"Nothing I guess," says Kass who really isn't into all that philosophy bullshit.

Regardless, Camilla has learned some impressive fighting maneuvers in a very short period of time. Her mind moves mysteriously quickly and she absorbs knowledge with incredible agility. From the movies she has learned how to hide and then attack; how to squash a man's head with a wrench; how to kick a man in the balls so that he buckles forwards – at which point she could kick him in the face. She has learned that hitting a man upwards on his chin is more effective than trying to hit him across the face. There is this world of violence, and then simultaneously, there is another world of peace: the darkness of the room, the images on the screen; the honking of horns on the street, the crazed eyes of Kass as he fucks her, just like they do it in the movies.

It was neither an accident, nor a pre-mediated act that caused Camilla, early Friday morning, to use a steak knife to slice Kass's eyebrow while he was sleeping. She sits back and observes, while he screams and pleads for her mercy, the blood from his eye socket pouring down around his face. So, she thinks, these things happen, and then these things, and as long as I continue to do things that I would never have done before, worlds will be created, and everything will be in balance. Little does she know the world she is creating is not her own.

V

She's smiling, hand to her golden heart, as Kass, in a rage, screams: "What the fuck are you doing you ungrateful bitch!"

He's got a t-shirt pressed against his eye, and is stomping around, looking for the phone, and making a wild racket. He's obsessed with Camilla but not at all paying attention as she zips her jeans and ties her white canvas tennis shoes before walking calmly out the front door.

Camilla runs wildly. She imagines herself running into a dark and mysterious forest, where the ghost of a lady furiously roams, looking for the man who would set her free. The fantasy helps her run faster, and not care about the people she is mowing down on the street. By the time she stops crouching behind trashcans, and shooting her invisible gun at non-existent zombies who are pursuing her, it's dark. She is underneath the elevated tracks in the city's center, standing in the middle of the street and spinning in a circle to take in the atmosphere. She'd never been to this part of the city. The cars look like they have been parked for a long time. On the block where she is standing are three repair shops, a used parts store, a bottle-recycling center, and a bar called Kitty's. In a moment of lucidity, Camilla looks up at the cracks between the rails of the tracks and realizes that it is still daylight. But the street lights are already on. This realization unsettles her. For a moment, she wants to go home. But as soon as she has this thought, another one quickly takes its place: *the world's athirst; now let it drink!* says a voice, as if a book is being written in her mind.

VI

A dark green Pinto approaches behind her. Since she is standing in the middle of the street, it honks; she politely moves out of the way. A carload of four college boys pulls over to the side of the road. Camilla stares at them as they get out of the car, laughing and making nervous jokes as if they are trying to be cool, but not really feeling up to the part. Three of them walk across the street to Kitty's, and one stays behind, leaning against the car to light a cigarette and stare at Camilla.

There are no words during this exchange of glances—just a nervous nod. The boy runs to meet up with his friends, and because the brooch has made her fearless, Camilla follows him. The darkness of the bar is overcast by a dull-toned glow of red and the movement of women's bodies on a stage lined with pink tinsel. The boys had taken a seat near the back. Camilla finds herself a spot against the wall, near enough so she can keep an eye on them.

A man approaches her; a voice.

"You here to audition?"

Camilla stands, her feet firmly planted and her arms straight. Her eyes follow the sound of the voice, and she realizes that she is very hungry.

"Burgers, fries, and a soda. Please."

The man, skinny with a long head and a leather baseball cap cocked slightly leftish, appears in her line of sight, laughing.

"That's cute! Sure honey. We've got burgers. And strawberry shakes. You want cheese on that?"

"Yea."

"Ok, you got it. Pickles too."

He snaps his fingers in jest.

"Carlos! A cheeseburger deluxe for the young lady at table number four. Common honey, let's get you undressed. See what you can do. I'll feed you when you're finished. Just come and find me. They call me Phil."

Camilla is led through a narrow hallway into a tiny room where there are mirrors and a coat rack piled high with stacks of rabbit fur trimmed nightgowns. She'd seen these kinds of costumes in the final scene of *Marlowe*, one of the movies from the 60s Kass showed her because he thought it was intellectual. Camilla watched how Delores moved, with her torso arched at a different angle then her legs; her head spinning slowly while her feet remained planted, thighs opening, then closing… quick. For a cheeseburger, she could do this.

Camilla finds a red dress that wraps in an X across the back; it's tight at the top, and flows out at the skirt. Classy. Camilla takes off her gross clothes, tosses them on the floor, and for the first time in 20 years, looks at her body in the mirror. She's all muscle. Suddenly she realizes that the yellow pin is on the floor, and she feels well up inside of her a panic that for a moment almost causes her to flee. But the desire to never again part from the brooch is too powerful. She unpins it from her old shirt and attaches it to the red dress. For a second it seems alive, like a creature grabbing on to its new home. She caresses the mysterious symbol on its back with her finger. It trembles.

Still naked and bent over the quivering thing, Pan opens the door without knocking. He seems startled.

"You're fucking gorgeous."

Camilla smiles as she hurriedly gathers herself together and slips into the dress. Another voice inside of her responds: "Yea, I know."

He helps her zip the dress; takes a bottle of hairspray and mists her hair; takes her cheeks between his hands and kisses each one, gently.

"Knock 'em dead, baby" he says, escorting her out into the hallway and into the light of the stage.

Camilla stands right in the middle, remembering a ballet class she took when she was two – before Tess decided that ballet was bad because her little girl was having too much fun. She plants her feet at an angle, straightens her knees, and fans her hands like a swan above her head. The music has already started, but she just stands there, holding this position. The boys are laughing. A few men at the bar are shouting "show your tits!" But it's all quiet in her head. Nothing happening outside of the stillness she feels in her body matters in the slightest. And she knows now that the yellow pin with its mysterious symbol will protect her against everything.

As if bowing to force that is beyond her, she feels as her hips give way to music. She doesn't know the song, but it enters her spine like gravity pulling down an apple. She moves because the music is her skin, peeling slowly up and down the length of her. Her hands are like ribbons tied above her head; they slowly wave in the air. She falls, catching herself with one arm; she lays down, spreads her legs and arches her back; slowly she turns on her hands and feet, pulsing her lower back; slowly she stands up again, her hands moving up the length of her legs, lifting her dress to reveal her bare thighs, her stomach; the dress falls back down again as she moves her hands up her torso to her heart. The red dress falls off her shoulders; she puts her arms in the air and swirls around the beat of the music, which has entered her like a flood creeping underneath a door. She quakes; she comes; the music stops and the boys are silent, just for a moment. Naked and crouched, perched on her fingertips, she stares into the dimly illuminated darkness of the room. She holds her position, doesn't move. A clapper here; a yeller there. Obscene comments, some laughs. Pan comes behind her and the dress around her shoulders. The brooch is now against her skin, sinking in. As it buries its claws into her flesh, she laughs hysterically. It feels like the ocean, finding eternity in her blood.

Pan, not knowing what is so funny, shakes his head at this bizarre but dynamic girl and leads her off the stage into the dressing room; as she puts the dress back on, he holds her neck and kisses her cheeks.

"Baby, that was beautiful. Whatever that was. A little weird. You're a little weird, right?"

He pulls a wad of cash out of his wallet and gives her $7. There you go kid, go buy yourself a nice cheeseburger. And come back tomorrow at 2pm. Amanda will be here and can teach you a few tricks.

Camilla tosses her old clothes in the trash. She keeps her tennis shoes, even though they've got holes. What a wonderful, magical place with such wonderful, magical feelings, she thinks. Leaving the club she catches the eye of the college boy and he puts his hand to his heart and keeps it there as he watches her leave. She saw this in a movie once: love. Now that she has experienced it, she vowed to seek it out in every person she meets from here on out. And the next afternoon, she will return to dance that feeling of love into every one she stands before, naked her body waving, pulsing, and slowly opening. This was going to be the happiest moment of her life. Finally, she reasoned, it's 1977 and this is my world.

But this moment isn't going to last long. For Camilla, the world is not going to be a garden of chocolate and roses. Because the cycle that has started spinning as the yellow pin (now a part of her, as veins are to her skin) sets out to recreate Carcosa in this place and time has not yet completed turning.

VII

It's definitely dark now. Her instincts tell her to get out from under the tracks and find a street where there are people, and lights, and a Taco Bell. West, she says to herself, and starts walking. A figure leaning against a pole shifts his feet and approaches her. Hello Camilla, Kass says.

Camilla, absorbed by her new world, did not recognize Kass at first. He has a black bandanna covering his hair and a strip from a t-shirt wrapped around his head, covering his eye.

"Did you think I'd let you go so easily?"

A flood of adrenalin hits her with the instinct to run.

Kass pursues, but lags a bit. He had been following her all day, and doesn't feel any pressure to catch up with her now – he just wants her to know that he'll always be around.

Camilla thinks she's lost him and turns down a street with no streetlights and lots of row houses. There are boys her age hanging out on the corner, and she figures this street might lead to a better place.

Suddenly the boys on the corner have circled around her, like bison in attack formation. Kass, lagging behind, sees this happening from a distance, and hides behind a car to watch the scene unfold. This is going to be good.

Camilla smiles and waves at the boys. She folds her arms into her chest and waits for them to make the next move.

The boys are laughing at her. One boy is laughing so hard he is buckled over. Another has his hand on his head. Another is pointing at her and jumping around. She doesn't see anything that's funny, so she starts walking.

She stops short as they block her flow across the street. Now they are poking at her with their fingers as if she had just fallen from the stars.

One of the boys grabs her face. "Hey girlie, you can't pass through here if you don't pay the troll. This bridge is *haunted!*"

The other boys laugh. One pulls out a kitchen knife and holds it to her cheek. She doesn't move. Her fearlessness, at first so amusing, has now pissed them off. They move in closer.

A patrol car turns the corner at just that moment. Seeing young boys circling a young white girl, the car screeches to a halt and two police, a man and a woman, jump out of with guns drawn. Three of the boys take off running in opposite directions; the other three freeze and put their hands behind their heads because the police have drawn their guns.

"Shoot, we were just playin' with her officer. We weren't going to do nothin' to her."

Camilla is smiling at the police, whose foreheads are wrinkled from the stress of having to draw their guns.

"Back away from the girl," said the police woman.

"We didn't do nothin' officer. Nothin' happening, it's cool."

Seeing that the boys have their hands in the air, the police woman puts her gun back in her holster. Her partner is more jittery, and continues to point his gun. The patrol lights whirl red and white through the air. Camilla is mesmerized by the sudden change of light.

"Common officer, we're cool. Tell her she's stupid to be walking alone at night down here. She's crazy officer. You can tell. Just look at her."

But the police aren't listening to them. They slam them up against the car, cuffing them.

"Let's go downtown and you can tell it all to the judge."

The woman officer starts to radio for backup.

Camilla, who was not at all afraid of these boys, makes a quick decision to protect them. She kicks the radio out of the woman officer's hands; the other policeman approaches. Camilla waits until he's at arm's length, and then she karate kicks the gun out of his hand, summersaults to the ground, picks it up. Seeing the police woman grabbing her gun, she opens fire and shoots her in the arm. The force knocks the woman down, and she drops her gun. The male officer sidesteps and quickly picks up his partner's gun; the handcuffed boys, seeing Camilla's completely relaxed face as she shoots the policeman, back away from the scene and run as fast as they can. The police-woman is confused as to what is happening; she yells at the boys to stop, but it's too late; they hop over fences and into alleys quick as antelopes.

Camilla remembers *Carrie* and suddenly feels possessed. She stands with her gun in a victory position, one foot over the fallen policeman. The female officer, terrified, cups her wound with her hand. Camilla shoots her gun straight up into the air because she likes the sound. A crow, sleeping on a nearby roof is startled into flight and catches the bullet. A spray of blood rains down on Camilla. Like a fallen rocket the crow lands at the feet of the felled officer. The lights from the patrol car are turning round and round, and just for a moment Camilla feels the burden of her fate.

But then she hears sirens coming from all directions, and knows that it is time to run. She turns a corner, and hides behind a bush to make sure she wasn't followed. She walks into the backyard of the closest house. All the lights are off, and there is no car in the driveway. She breaks a window into the basement and slips in. No one is home. Tired, she goes upstairs, finds a bed, and falls asleep.

Kass, having witnessed this whole scenario, has followed Camilla into the house where she is sound asleep on the bed upstairs, completely relaxed, as if nothing had happened. She is holding the gun like a dead person holds a bouquet of flowers. He closes the blinds. The police are all over the street. Kass kneels by her bedside, and gently takes the gun from her folded hands. Like a machine she bolts upright, knocks Kass to the ground and grabs the gun. To twist things up a bit, she picks up the alarm clock and throws it out the window. She follows that with the night table, and a chair.

"What the fuck did you do that for?" says Kass.

The police are approaching the house to investigate the sounds of breaking glass.

Camilla grabs the sheet off the bed and throws it over the unsuspecting Kass, wrestling him to the ground. Holding the ends like a sack, she ties the ends of the sheet into a knot. She then proceeds to throw all of the furniture in the room on top of him – bookcase, desk, chair. She finds clothes in the closet and throws them on the pile as well. Kass is yelling for help, but Camilla hardly notices. The police are now in the house, making their way upstairs. Camilla spots a stick of matches that has fallen out of the door of the desk. She lights the sheet wrapped around Kass on fire. The police enter the room, guns drawn. But all they see are flames – Camilla has jumped out of the window, landing in the shrubs.

Brushing herself off, she walks straight through the crowd of people gathered at the scene. The fire trucks and ambulance are racing to meet the blaze. Behind her, the flames shoot out of the room where she had just been sleeping.

Camilla walks for a block and spots a construction site where a scoop truck is parked in a vacant lot; it beckons her like a maternal creature, and she climbs into its claws. The metal is cold against her body, but soon it warms up. She stares up at the stars. The moon is making light where before the sky looked drab. She sighs and allows the scoop to enclose her: mama, she whispers, and the scoop truck seems to let out a slight whirr, but not really. She sleeps soundly thorough the night, until she hears the rumbling of men and cars and realizes that it is morning. She jumps out of the scoop and runs past the gawking men, alarmed to see a young girl emerge from the scoop with the grace of Venus rising up out of the clam shell.

She walks down the middle of the road for a few blocks. A driver picks her up. After realizing that his attempts to fondle her are not scaring her, he decides there is no thrill in it for him, and so offers to take her home. She isn't exactly sure where home is, but she describes the landscape: cul-de-sac, enclosure, tight space surrounded by trees and houses. Not far from Hugh M. Woods on Sheridan Boulevard. The driver drops her off somewhere in the middle of these hazy coordinates, and Camilla, with a heightened sense of navigation, follows the pulse of the yellow pin and manages to find her way home.

VIII

She has only been gone for twelve days but because Camilla and her yellow brooch ripped a hole out of her time it seems like she has been gone for years.

Camilla knows that a course of events had been set into motion. She doesn't know what it is, but is desperate to find out. The yellow pin has steered her into a previously unimaginable freedom, but there is something else she needs to find. She kicks in the door and walks by instinct to the kitchen counter where her mother always leaves her notes. She still wasn't back. Like lightening she returns to the bookshelf where she originally found the brooch. She turns it over until she sees what she is looking for: a book bound in serpent skin. Camilla hears sirens in the distance, clutches the book, and goes out into the backyard. There are fallen, rotten apples everywhere. And the apple tree, unpruned, is thick with foliage.

Camilla quickly empties the contents of the shed onto the lawn – trimming equipment, bikes, broken toys, sea shells, sleds, planting pots and power tools. By the time the police arrive to search the house, she is high up in the tree, hidden behind a thick green canopy of leaves. The backyard is such a mess that they never look up.

After they leave, Camilla pulls off a few boards from the siding of the house to build herself a platform, high up in the apple tree. She rests on a clump of tar which she ripped off the roof. The next morning she builds a teepee of branches, tied together with twine. She sleeps soundly. The swirling of leaves in a wind vacuum rouses her from her sleep – she gets down, collects them, and pushes them into the corner to keep out the draft. She is overcome by the instinct to protect herself and to protect the book.

Finally it is quiet, and she has time to read the horrific book: *The King in Yellow*. It's even more frightening than the movies she watched with Kass, but she reads it straight through with an understanding that this story and her own are one. She is Camilla, third daughter of the King of Carcosa who speaks through her his story of violent self-destruction. She is possessed by his narrative; it has given her form and purpose.

Now filled with the urgency and conviction of a murderer intent on acting out the script of her madness, Camilla pulls apart all the metal from her mother's power tools and arranges them neatly in a pile. In the middle of the night, she grabs as much as she can carry from the trash outside people's houses: wood chairs, appliance boxes, clothes; a lamp, newspapers, a plastic toy house. She lugs all the junk into the backyard and begins to catalogue it: metal things, plastic things, paper things, natural things. She rips the clothes into strips and stuffs them between slabs of cardboard for insulation. Every night she raids her mother's pantry: beans, dried pasta, and Crisco eaten straight from the container. She actually gains a little weight.

Every day she finds more that she needs to make her temple. After one week the junk around her is so thick that it envelopes her in warmth and protects her from the summer afternoon showers.

The metal from the tools lines her house like lethal cake decorations. One night a rabid squirrel stumbles upon the mound of wreckage, and crawls inside: wild-eyed Camilla skins it and makes herself a fur bracelet. She uses the bones to reinforce the joints of her temple, grooving them into an arch that points towards the sky.

It is morning, and chilly. Around her the world is changing and the effects she has put into motion are reverberating. She will never know what those effects are, because the future is like an angel walking backwards through all the debris and chaos, collecting it as she goes, rebuilding what seems salvageable and setting fire to everything else.

By the time Tess comes home from her cruise, sees the unbelievable wreck of her house, and calls the police, Camilla has been sitting quietly in her apple tree temple for almost two weeks. Sleeping while sitting, she spends her days enmeshed in wild fantasies about the yellow king of Carcosa and how delirious it will be when he comes for her and restores her rightful place by his throne.

It takes three fire-trucks and twelve firemen to get to her. As she is led down the ladder, past her sobbing mother, and out the door, she has one moment of complete clarity before descending into speechlessness: the rose bush in the yard is starting to bloom simply because she has not trampled it down. And as the stars drip with spray, the towers of Carcosa rise behind the moon.

April Dawn
By Richard A. Lupoff

T here are no theaters in Kilkee. There are a couple of reasons for that. For one thing, Kilkee is a wee small town, hardly a hundred souls live there, and no businessman would think to build such an establishment, nor would there be customers enough to support it if someone got so foolish as to think of making the attempt.

For another, Father Phinean would surely be against it. I heard him deliver himself on the subject one time. Mr. Seamus Callaghan, our general merchant, had visited the metropolis of Dublin on a buying mission. When he returned to Kilkee he took himself to St. Padraic's Church and told the Father that he'd been to the metropolis and gone to the Bijou Opera and seen a wondrous show with costumes and singing and great dramatic battles acted out right before your very eyes, and he wondered if Kilkee might be a good place to have such a thing as a theater of its own. There might not be enough actors and musicians in Kilkee to put on much of a performance, but there were companies that traveled around putting on their shows, Seamus Callaghan said, and they might come and put one on in Kilkee.

Father Phinean got red in the face. I saw this with my own eyes. I'd been hiding in the chancel and Father didn't know I was there. He smote Mr. Callaghan a thwack aside his head. I was astonished. This was not some troublesome lad who stumbled over his catechism or made improper noises during Mass. This was Mr. Callaghan, an important citizen of Kilkee.

But Father Phinean was so angry, he dealt Mr. Callaghan that blow to the ear and Mr. Callaghan just stood there, getting as pale in the phiz as Father was red.

Then Father said, "Ye'll do penance for a month for that, me lad."

Mr. Callaghan is old enough to be Father Phinean's parent, but Father called him "me lad" and Mr. Callaghan stood there and took it.

"We'll have none of those wicked strumpets painting their faces and showing off their bosoms in this town, and filling our innocent faithful with lustful ideas! If we need music we've got the heavenly sounds of the Mass and if we need drama we've got the Passion of Our Lord. Now get on your knees, Seamus Callaghan, and bow your noggin and pray to the Virgin that she may intervene with her Son to forgive you for making that wicked suggestion and to clean your mind of the filth you have filled it with!"

That was long ago, back when I was a strapping lad and my darling Maeve, Maeve Corrigan, was still alive. Ah, I can see her now. A mere fifteen she was, but a woman already. Her hair was as black as Satan's heart, her eyes as green as Ireland's fields, her skin as white as New Year's snow, her lips as sweet as bright red cherries, her breasts as soft and dear as heaven's clouds.

A lass of fifteen, and I her swain and barely older, as deep in love as two can be. Once she was in the ground Kilkee held no charm for me, and hence I came to the New World's shores.

But you see, now, why there are no theaters in Kilkee. You see the reason now. But we are in Kilkee no longer. We are in the City of San Francisco between the lovely bay and the broad Pacific Ocean, and San Francisco has theaters aplenty! The first time I saw an opera it was at the Golden Nugget Opera House on Kearney Street. It cost me a day's wage just to get inside the hall, but it was worth the price.

There were glittering chandeliers with candles in them and paintings on the walls that I took to be scenes from famous operas, pictures of Greek gods and heroes and Egyptian pyramids and Roman Senators and battles at sea. There were seats so comfortable you thought you might never want to get up once you settled into one. But even before you got to those seats you could stop at a bar and buy a drink as tasty as any you could get in a Barbary Coast saloon, and no danger of being shanghaied onto a clipper ship bound for Asia.

There was a grand play with music and costumes and even horses on the stage. The name of the opera, wait, I wrote it down so I wouldn't forget it, was called *Le Roi d'Ys*, which a kind citizen seated beside me whispered in my ear, was French and it means *The King of Ys*, Ys being an old city in a country called Carnouaille, of which I will confess I never heard. But there are a lot of countries in this world of which I've never heard, I'm sure. It was written by some Monsieur named Edouard Lalo.

It was a wonderful story. There was a King Gradlon who had two daughters, Margared and Rozenn, each one more beautiful than the other. I could see now why Father Phinean was afraid of Seamus Callaghan's building an opera house in Kilkee. The costumes were glorious and the two princesses did indeed have painted faces and lovely bosoms that they were not a bit too shy to show. The singing was all in French but it wasn't hard to follow the story and my neighbor told me what the hard parts meant.

Oh, there was a talking statue of a saint. Imagine, a stone statue coming to life before your very eyes there on the stage in the opera house. It was a statue of a holy man wearing a bishop's mitre. He was called Saint Corentin of Quimper. He jumped off his pedestal and strode around on the stage and talked and even sang, all in French. I never heard of a Saint Corentin but Father Phinean could probably preach a whole sermon about him and scald any lad who slept through it and couldn't pass a test when it was over. There was a Prince Karnac and a knight in armor, name of Mylio, and the king's two daughters were squabbling over who would get her pick of husbands and who would have to marry the other sister's leavings, and by the end of the story there was a giant flood that washed away the city.

Oh, never will I forget that show should I live as long as Methuselah. Nor forget that night, neither, thanks to my kindly neighbor. She was a fine woman, did I think to tell you that, and she showed me some parts of the city that I never would have dreamed about back home in County Clare. Indeed, indeed, she did show me some parts that I never would have dreamed about back home in County Clare.

But enough of that talk. I want to tell you what happened later on, after I went to work for Mr. Abraham ben Zaccheus, the secret King of All the Jews in the World, although he is too modest to call himself that. I had not been in this city for very long when I spotted a notice in the local newspaper. It said:

```
INVESTIGATOR seeks secretary, amanuensis,
and general assistant. Something is happening
in the Earth. Something is going to happen. Ap-
plicant must exhibit courage, strength, will-
ingness to take risks and explore the unknown.
Keen olfactory and kinetic senses vital. Room,
board, and salary provided. Apply in person
only.
```

Being in need of gainful employment, I applied in person, thinking that I met at least some of the requirements of the job. I had courage, strength, and the willingness to take risks and explore the unknown. I might add that I am not bad looking, neither, or so a good many lady friends have told me over the years. I thought I could be a secretary and general assistant. I didn't know what an amanuensis was, but when the gentleman who had placed the advertisement explained it to me, I told him I could handle that job, as well.

After all, if Johnson had his Boswell and Sherlock Holmes had his Dr. Watson, then King Abraham ben Zaccheus could use an amanuensis too, and I was happy to become that.

I had some glorious adventures working for King Abraham, and some frightening ones, as well, but a finer man than Abraham ben Zaccheus I've never known, aside from being the very first Hebrew I had ever been honored to encounter.

But this day, ah, I remember it too well indeed, this day was a Monday. King Abraham and I had returned from an adventure in the Islands of Farralones in the cold Pacific Ocean, where Abraham waded into the ocean stark naked, carrying just his gold-headed walking stick, and disappeared beneath the water for three days and three nights while I built campfires on the rocky shore to keep myself warm and cook the meals that Madame Chiang had packed for us. Then the King of All the Jews walked back out and said to me, "John O'Leary, I hope you remembered to bring the warm towels and the bottle of good whisky because it was mightily cold down there and I need to be warmed up both outside and in."

Now I was helping King Abraham to sort his papers and answer his mail, his help and advice being solicited by suffering and needful parties in every corner, it seems, of the globe.

He sat behind a grand desk of dark mahogany wood, stroking his devilish looking beard and opening the letters that had arrived during our absence. Our housekeeper, Madame Chiang Xu-Mei, was busily preparing our repast and delicious odors wafted from the kitchen.

King Abraham opened the next letter in the pile, gave a sound such as I'd never before heard him make, and jumped to his feet. King Abraham, in case you did not know that, is not exactly slim, nor what you would call a lithe athlete, and seeing him jump to his feet is an experience not to be missed.

"He's in San Francisco!" King Abraham said. "He's been here for a week, and we were busy with those ruins off the Farralones and never knew it! And we're invited for tomorrow evening. Ah, John, this will be a treat indeed!"

He looked at me. "Aha! You wonder about whom I am talking, John O'Leary, do you not?" King Abraham talked that way sometimes.

It took me a moment to figure out what he meant. Then I said, "Yes, Your Majesty."

The King of the Jews shook his head. "Please, John, you know I prefer to be called Abraham. Simply that."

I nodded. "Yes, Your Majesty."

He gave a sigh and sank back into his big desk chair. He waved the letter at me. "This is from Robert Chambers. My friend Robert Chambers."

I waited for him to continue.

"I don't suppose you know who he is. You do not read many books, do you, John O'Leary?"

I conceded that I did not.

King Abraham stood up and strode to one of the bookshelves that filled just about every inch of his study, except where he'd saved space for a painting of some great and famous person. He picked up his favorite gold-headed walking stick, inscribed with Hebrew letters of which I could not tell you the meaning, and he pointed with it to a row of books in bright paper wrappers.

"Robert Chambers wrote these books, John. I met him in Paris when his first book had just been published and he was working on his second, a collection of stories to be called *The King in Yellow*."

He reached up and took a book down from the shelf. He turned the pages, then handed it to me to examine. It was a handsome thing. The cover bore a picture of that king, his yellow robe more tattered than glorious, and strange crimson wings growing from his shoulders. What must it be like to write a whole book, I wondered, no less a shelf full of them. I handed the book back to King Abraham.

"It was not long after I had banished a P'an Hu that had terrifying wedding parties in the Chinese province of Jiangsu. While there I confess that I became addicted to the local cuisine, in particular to their salted dried duck."

A faraway look came into King Abraham's eyes. My employer is a modest man, a quality which he shares with me, of course. He does not tell stories of his cases very often, but when he does I have learned to listen carefully and note them down, as I am paid, of course, to be his amanuensis.

"Authorities in France had heard of my success, and a group of Parisian financiers had pooled their resources to engage my services in ridding the Bois de Boulogne of a pack of vicious loups garous. That was 1895, a year in which France forever disgraced herself by condemning the innocent Captain Dreyfus and stripping him of the honors he had earned in the service of his country."

I could tell that the King of All the Jews in the World remained angry after a decade's passage. He pounded his fist on the top of his desk, then drew a deep breath and resumed telling me his story. It seemed to calm him, to be telling his tale.

"Once my task was completed, I found myself wandering the back alleys of Montmartre. I had not realized how hungry I was until I detected the tantalizing aroma of a Jiangsu style kitchen. Can you imagine, John? I was two continents from the City of Wuxi, where last I had savored that fine cuisine, only to discover it again in a tiny restaurant on the Rue Lamarck, virtually in the shadow of Basilisque du Sacre-Coeur."

His story was interrupted by the banging of pots from Madame Chiang's kitchen. That was a sign that our dinner was very nearly ready, and a signal to Abraham ben Zaccheus to bring his story to its close.

He tapped himself alongside his beezer with a blunt fingertip. "She'll wait for us," he said. "This won't take very long."

He had laid *The King in Yellow* on his desk, and reached now and petted the book as if it were a living thing. He said, "I followed my nose and soon found myself in a tiny, dark establishment. Everyone in the place was obviously Chinese except for one man, a tall, distinguished looking fellow wearing a high stiff collar and heavy, dark moustache. He spotted me as I came in and lifted a hand in greeting. He called, 'Ho there, are you an American?'

" 'No, I am Austrian. But I know your language a little.'

"He invited me to join him at his table. I could see he appreciated Jiansu cuisine. He was dining on a dish that the natives of the region call *Farewell My Concubine*. It involves the meat of the soft-shell turtle, chicken, mushrooms, and Chinese wine. How the proprietors of that Parisian establishment were able to obtain all the ingredients is a greater mystery than that of the terrifying P'an Hu. It requires the efforts of a supreme chef to prepare properly."

He sighed.

"My impromptu host and I introduced ourselves. The American said that his name was Robert Chambers. 'But call me Bob,' he said. He said that he was working on a book to be called *The King in Yellow*. I gave him my address here in San Francisco and he promised to send me a copy when the book was published. And I invited him to visit, should he ever find himself in this city."

He rose to his feet. He said, "Come along, John, Madame Chiang will scold us if we come late to her table." He put his arm around my shoulder as we made our way to the dining room. "Chambers is in San Francisco. He is staying at the Palais d'Or on Market Street. He says that he has another new book, one with the intriguing title, *Tracer of Lost Persons*, and wishes to present me with a copy. And he has a special treat in store for us tomorrow night!"

I spent the next day attending to my duties, awaiting word from King Abraham that it was time to descend from our home on Rooshian Hill and meet the famous Robert Chambers at the Palais d'Or. "We're invited for a midnight supper, John O'Leary," King Abraham had told me.

A midnight supper it was to be, I thought. A midnight supper. How could a man wait until midnight for his evening meal? By the time the sun sank into the evening fog my stomach was growling and I suspect that my face was showing my hunger as well. Madame Chiang, bless her Oriental heart, took pity and fixed me up with a fine steaming bowl of stew. Delicious bits of brisket, carrots, and potatoes swam in a lovely broth. She added hew own Chinese touch of hot oil and soy sauce, and reminded me of my own dear Ireland with a kindly pouring of Jameson's.

Now, says I to myself, now I am ready to wait for this promised midnight supper.

~*~

The light of day was long gone when Abraham ben Zaccheus and I climbed into Abraham's Superba Modern Electric Phaeton. I had ridden in this buggy before with Abraham at the tiller, as it rolled at a terrifying speed of up to fourteen miles per hour. I pride myself on my courage, as my past achievements have surely proven, but I cannot deny that I held on for dear life as the phaeton approached the broad thoroughfare that spans this city.

King Abraham navigated us straight down Lombard Street, through the Barbary Coast and on to Market Street where the Palais D'Or blazed with lights like a merry tyke's birthday cake. King Abraham and I were decked out, the both of us, in soup and fish, black suits and white boiled shirts and bow ties. We were a picture in what Abraham called cheery rusty coo, or something like that, His Majesty always taking the time to teach me words I'd never have heard in Kilkee, save for Abraham's vest embroidered all in Hebrew magical signs in gold and blue.

Mr. Chambers was waiting to greet us in the lobby of the Palais d'Or. There was no mistaking him, from Abraham ben Zaccheus's description, and from the way that the two men grinned and clasped their hands. I could tell from Mr. Chambers' looks that he and King Abraham were of an age and pleased as could be to see each the other after some ten years.

Our gracious host led us to a private dining room which had been reserved for us. Waiters as dressed up as the three of us served food and wine. A little orchestra sat in the corner sawing away at their fiddles. We started off with a glass of champagne and some dainty bits of food that Mr. Chambers said were called *little fours* in French. I don't know why they were called fours but they were certainly little!

But soon came a cold soup, a sort of yellowish-brown, that bounced and quivered in its bowl like fresh-made jelly. The taste wasn't too bad, a little bit like a weak chicken broth, but I thought it would have been better if the chef had remembered to keep it hot before he sent it out to us. Then came some green thing shaped like a child's hoop, all soft and quivery like the soup, with little chunks of chewy vegetables stuck in it like miniature surprise toys in a birthday cake.

The big treat, I suppose, that Mr. Chambers called the *piece de resistance*, was something that looked like a big red spider cooked in a hard shell. It was served with nutcrackers and a kind of white slippery sauce, and it was surely the strangest thing that I ever had to eat. Mr. Chambers said that it was called a long goose, which made no sense to me as it was not very long and it certainly was not a goose. But I will confess that the taste was not bad at all.

During the whole meal, while waiters kept bringing dishes and pouring wine and the little orchestra in the corner kept sawing away, Abraham ben Zaccheus and Bob Chambers kept up their chatter. I mainly concentrated on the wine, which was very good, and the food, which was all cold. I suppose that was because we were eating it so late at night. The chef must have fixed it up for us and gone home hours ago.

I didn't have much to say but I kept my ears open while Abraham and Robert swapped stories. I heard of adventures of King Abraham that I'd never heard of before. The time he went to Yucatan to consult the spirit of a Mayan priest. The time he flew to far Australia to retrieve a lost tablet that had stood on top of something called Uluru Rock for ten thousand years. This was years before those brothers built their flying machine and flew it in North Carolina. The time he brought a lost explorer back from a great stone city buried beneath the ice at the South Pole.

I heard enough tales to fill a book, and mayhap someday I shall write it, if Abraham ben Zaccheus gives me the go-ahead, which to date he has not. But if he does not want his stories to be known to the world, why tell them to Mr. Bob Chambers? And why engage my services as he personal amanuensis?

At last it was Mr. Bob Chambers' turn to speak. Between sips of wine and nibbles of food, he spoke of the entertainment to come. An Eye Tallian composer fellow with a name that sounded something like Gasparo Spontini had read his book *The King in Yellow*, he said, and liked it so much that he sent a letter to Mr. Chambers and said if Mr. Chambers would write something called a libretto he'd write the score to go with it, which I took it to mean words and music in musician talk. Mr. Chambers told Signore Spontini he'd do it, so they got together wrote a whole opera called The King in Yellow.

And that, Mr. Chambers told King Abraham and me, was the special treat. "We're opening at the Maison de Rêves on Sutter Street. I am surprised that you didn't know about it, even if you only received my letter yesterday."

"Ah," King Abraham said, "John O'Leary and I have been tending to a little task to the west of here, and have been out of touch with events in the city." He paused, then went on. "But please tell me about the production."

"It was easy enough for me to create a libretto from my tales and from the original play. And Spontini is a genius. He created a remarkable score, alternately beautiful, jarring, wildly stimulating and almost unbearably sensuous. I think Spontini is writing the music of the future. I have never heard anything remotely like it."

"And when may I hope to hear this work?" King Abraham asked.

Mr. Chambers pulled a turnip from his vest pocket, consulted it, and slid it back from sight. "In an hour, Abraham!"

King Abraham looked surprised. "It is nearly three in the morning," he exclaimed.

"A special command performance, Abraham. For you and your associate, Mr. O'Leary. The production opens tomorrow night. Or should I say, tonight? The company is assembled at the theater. They are in full costume. The set is built. I designed it myself and personally supervised the design of the sets and flats."

He stood up and threw his arms out as if to embrace Abraham and me and the whole wide world.

"Come, come my friends. You will experience something unlike anything you have experienced in your lives!"

We walked through the fog, crossing Market Street and up Sutter. The Palais d'Or behind us was dark now, all but invisible against the black sky and thick, gray fog. The night air was so damp that rivulets condensed and ran down our faces. We must have made a ghostly sight, three of us clad in black clothing and white shirts, with Abraham ben Zaccheus's vest blazoned with Hebrew signs in gold and blue, the ferrule of the King's walking stick clicking on the pavement with each step he took.

The fog had a strange and unpleasant smell to it. I thought I heard a peculiar sound and felt the very earth tremble beneath my feet.

We reached the theater and were greeted by Signore Spontini himself, decked out as were we three. His hair was wavy and he wore a pointed moustache. He was a heavyset man. The Eye Tallians do love their pasta, I thought, but I shook his hand anyway. He led us to our seats and waddled to the front of the auditorium. He climbed to the conductor's stand, picked up his baton, and waved the musicians to life.

Overhead they had hung a glorious chandelier. It was made of a thousand diamonds and lighted by a hundred candles that filled the auditorium with a dazzling blizzard of light.

It was true, what Bob Chambers had told us at the Palais d'Or, the music of Signore Spontini was not like anything I had ever heard in my life.

The curtains drew back and I saw another world. There was a city on the stage, a city half in ruins that looked as if it had once been as mighty as Rome or Paris or San Francisco, but was now almost deserted.

The king of the city was named Yhtill. He wore a garment that might once have been a robe of golden cloth but was now in shreds, like the shroud of a corpse that has lain in the earth for a hundred years or a thousand. He wore a gleaming crown of gold and diamonds, and a golden mask with slits for his eyes.

The play went on. King Yhtill had two daughters, two beautiful princesses. The first of the princesses was named Camilla and she wore a gown of palest orange that seemed to spring into flaring crimson flame as she whirled and sang her arias to the sound of the orchestra. Her hair was shimmering silver and hung about her shoulders, and stood away from her face like the wings of a white dove when she twirled.

She stood beside a dark body of water, the Lake of Hali. The time was dawn or sunset, I could not tell. There were two suns in the black sky over the city, a city called Carcosa.

I felt the theater shake, heard a rumble, smelled the strange odor I had smelled outside in the street.

The second princess appeared. Tall she was, and she took away my breath. She wore a gown of palest green that sprang into searing green flame as she whirled and sang her arias to the sound of the orchestra. Her name was Cassilda.

She sang, *Along the shore the cloud waves break, the twin suns sink beneath the lake, the shadows lengthen in Carcosa.*

Her hair was as black as Satan's heart, her eyes as green as Ireland's fields, her skin as white as New Year's snow, her lips as full as dark red cherries, her breasts as soft and dear as heaven's clouds. Her hair hung about her shoulders, and stood away from her face like the wings of a black raven when she twirled.

She was my Maeve.

She was my Maeve.

My heart was pounding, the tympani in the orchestra were pounding, Signore Spontini was waving his arms as he conducted the musicians. Horns blared and strings screamed and Cassilda who was Maeve, who was my living dearest Maeve, sang in a voice as high and as clear and as grieving as an angel expelled from Heaven by God Almighty, *Song of my soul, my voice is dead, die thou, unsung, as tears unshed, shall dry and die in lost Carcosa.*

With a sound like ten million champagne glasses shattering, the grand chandelier crashed on the rows of empty seats. With a sound like ten million tympani pounding, the roof above the stage crashed down. There was no warning. There was no escape. The painted suns, the artificial lake, were crushed. The singers were crushed. King Ythill, the Princess Camilla, the Princess Cassilda, my Maeve, my darling girl Maeve, were crushed.

The Maison de Rêves was no more.

I looked around me. The sun had risen over San Francisco but the earth had shaken the beautiful city as a dog shakes an annoying flea. Smoke rose all about. The sky was black with it, and then flames rose. Men, women, and children screamed and moaned and wept.

A miracle had saved King Abraham and Robert Chambers and me. Somehow in the rubble of the Maison de Rêves, we had escaped with naught worse than a few scrapes and bruises. But of the players and the orchestra, none survived. None.

I threw back my arms and looked into the sky, into the clouds of smoke and the growing flames, and cursed the cruel God for sparing my life.

King Wolf

By Anna Tambour

NX 224798

CARRETT,

Selwyn Lovelace Wilde "Leary"
Passed away at the Sisters of Mercy Nursing Home, Sunday, January 9, 2012.

Aged 98 years young

Gone to God

Got new feet

Dearly beloved husband of the late Rose. Cherished father of Sister Mary Elizabeth, Nigel (dec'd), Maurine (dec'd), Ronald (dec'd), Cyril (dec'd), and of Silvia (nee Carrett) Pennycuik (dec'd). Beloved father-in law of Ethel (dec'd), Maria, and Cyril (dec'd). Loved grandfather and grandfather-in-law of Joan Carrett-Wong and John Wong, and Alexander Carr (ne Carrett) and Simone Dodd. Loved great-grandfather of Jack and Julie, and of Safire, Emrald, Wolf and Lovage.

A Mass Service for SELWYN will be held at the Sisters of Mercy Nursing Home Chapel, 2158 Pacific Highway, Tempe, on Thursday (January 12, 2012) at 11 a.m. On conclusion of the prayers following the Mass, the funeral cortege will proceed to Kurringah Memorial Gardens Crematorium.

Sydney Love & Care Funerals

Sans Souci   **All Suburbs**

9538 9087   **0413 879 733**

Hour after hour the car sped on, the last town with multiple turnoffs being Wollongong. Now the signs were for turnoffs. Old Erowal Bay, Sussex Inlet, Beachside Lots Just Opened. Swan Lake Caravan Park, a surf shop. Signs on the road with nothing to show for them but trees. Yerriyong State Forest, Luncheon Creek Road, Manyana . . .

Crows jumped out of the way of tyres just fast enough to miss being hit, but there were rich pickings—wombats, wallabies, a few rosella parrots caught with their heads down into seeding weeds, and magpies that also picked the kills but weren't as quick as crows.

Now the traffic was erratic, thin, nothing local—car and truck smashing into the slow-spinning clouds of mating flying ants. Windscreen wipers already sticky from acacia fluff worked hard to remove greasy showers. A few cautious drivers turned their night lights on.

Inside the car, air-con stirred the sultry coolness.

"You don't get that report to me by Monday, I'll serve your balls to my dog!"

In the middle of the middle-back seat, Lovage Carr leaned over in her child-restraint seat and whispered to her oldest brother, Safire, "What dog?"

In the back seat, eight-year-old Wolf unbuckled his seatbelt and turned around till he was looking forward, his head between them. "What balls?"

"Tennis balls," said Safire, aiming a punch backwards.

Wolf laughed. "Come on, he muttered. "Tell Lovie about our dog. Dad's such a family man."

Emrald, Safire's twelve-year-old twin, twisted awkwardly against her seatbelt in the cramped space on the other side of Lovage. "Don't."

"What'm *I* doing," Wolf whined. "We shouldn't let her get her hopes up. And besides, you know what Mum has said about dogs carrying hydatids."

"Like what Dad does about kids carrying childhood," Safire snickered. "He's right, Em. They hate dogs. And if she asks one more time . . ."

In the front passenger seat, their mother pulled out an ear bud and a faint tinkle of étude leaked. Then she put her ear bud back in.

They were talking so low that Lovage didn't listen, and anyway she was thinking of the dog. She had been playing with Pobblebonk, pretending he was a frog prince, but dropped him when she heard *dog*.

Maybe Daddy was angry at someone who was supposed to deliver a dog to meet her as soon as the whole family got home. And she and the dog—she'd already named him Lion—would go in the back garden where Lion would bend his head so that she could ride him, and then they'd parade in front of the flowers till the blue-headed ones bowed to her, and she'd slide off Lion's back and he'd raise his right paw, and they'd play tennis.

The car speeded up, passing a truck. On both sides of the road, the trees looked like dark smudges.

"Fuckin *fuck* you!" their dad yelled. "I don't care if you've got a tumour the size of a fuckin *stadium*. Monday at nine, complete with charts. And ex the excuses." He slammed his left hand against the steering wheel. "Bastard!" His right clutched his phone, and though no one in the back seats could actually see, they could all imagine his thumb working away.

Lovage started shaking. But maybe he wasn't as angry as he sounded. Sometimes it was hard to tell. He was always so busy that he was 'short' as he sometimes said when he apologised, as sometimes he did after he'd scared her and he and Mum had had a fight.

She clutched her lower lip between her teeth.

Safire unbuckled his seatbelt and turned sideways. He stroked her fine golden hair. Her face crumpled. He leaned out over her. "Em?"

Emrald had been desperately punching the remote control, and finally, the screen lit up.

Narnia!

Mute, but that didn't matter. They all knew every word.

Lovage put her thumb in her mouth. At four, she should have outgrown such habits, but she should also have outgrown wetting her pants.

Safire gave Emrald a thumbs up and slid back to his seat, though his legs were even longer than Emrald's.

"Saffa," said Wolf. "Any chips left?"

"No."

"You selfish pig," Em whispered furiously. She leaned out over Lovie and snatched the bag of Smiths Salt and Vinegar off Safire's lap. He grabbed for them and they both pulled. Only the size of Saffa's feet muffled the shower. But they were such experienced fighters that none of this could be noticed in the front.

Wolf had already soundlessly buckled himself in again. No one else liked facing the road they'd been, but then no one else had an incentive to avoid seeing Narnia. Wolf was not only eight years old but with thick dark thatch and deep dark eyes, looked so much like the selfish little brother that he hoped Lovie would outgrow her fantasies of the four of them being special royals—Kings and Queens only lacking a kingdom waiting to be rescued by them, with him being the slimy, sweet-loving sinner so that they have someone they can nobly forgive.

He'd read the book version to see if it was just as bad. Although the book didn't have any mug shots of him in it, he resented the story so much that he took revenge—and his crime made him feel good and bad at the same time, like going to bed without underwear.

It was a *library* book. He buried it in the sticky orange peels and gritty coffee grounds in the wet-food garbage bin. And the next day he confessed, when she was alone at the counter, to the nice librarian with the nametag that said Ursula. He told her that the book had slipped from his hands into the school toilet. He expected to pay for the book. That didn't worry him, but to be banned from the library . . . But she leaned over the counter, smiled and whispered. "I did the same thing once. Don't you worry. We'll just adjust . . ." And she turned to the screen and tapped a bit.

"There," she said, tossing her bright grey hair. "That copy never existed. But don't go away." She reached under the counter. "I pulled this from the withdrawn books before it could reach the sale table. I've kept it here for you. It'll cost you, though! Twenty cents."

It must have been one of those books that the librarians who don't trust people had kept in the dungeon, saved from the shelves, but then it became just another old book adding to their piles.

On the cover, two dancing birds spread wings edged with feathers that stuck out like long, black-gloved fingers. The base of each wing bore a big lopsided yellow square—like trucks do on their back doors. The book had a strange, never-ending name—Animals and their Colors: Camouflage, Warning Coloration, Courtship and Territorial Display, Mimicry—and it was by Michael and Patricia Fogden. The publisher was Crown, Wolf was happy to note. There were publishers he favoured and others he thought untrustworthy.

He rushed home with it to look up, first, the meaning of yellow. He'd already read that yellow means *Don't eat me!* in frogs, so he supposed that the yellow signs on trucks meant *Don't get close.* But when these birds flash their patches, what could they mean but *Come closer!*

Admire my beauty! Wolf had hoped to find out why yellow was his favourite colour, but he never did.

That was six months ago already. He looked down at his T-shirt printed with the kangaroo in the middle of the big yellow road sign and the unnecessary words: Kangaroos Crossing—a Christmas present from Em. He would have liked to wear it on an island with just her. The stupid words annoyed him. And he hated everyone looking at him, saying it suited him. But he didn't want to hurt her feelings.

He always felt even more left out when he saw how much Saffa and Em played along with Lovie, always acting as if they were just putting up with it, not getting any ego trips themselves. "Lovie needs to play Wardrobe," they'd say. So he had to play along, being the bad brother in this cruel world of make-believe that trapped him. He had to play or he'd be branded the selfish brother in real life, the one who made Lovie cry.

And though he didn't want those know-it-alls, Saffa and Em, to know, Lovie's tenderness always broke Wolf's heart. He dreamed of Lovie, of a real big bad wolf slinking up behind her as she walked a trail of yellow bricks. And from out of nowhere, faster than an arrow, more toothy than a shark, he'd come running after that wolf. Just as that wolf that slathered after Lovie was ready to pounce on her, he'd leap. His long claws would slash that wolf's hide down to the bones. That wolf's spit would splat against the bricks on the path as its jaws shattered under his, Wolf's! body, heavy as a load of rocks. And at that moment in Wolf's dream, Lovie would turn around and notice that there was a big bad wolf spatted almost dead, under her brother Wolf, who had saved her. And she'd catch her lower lip in her teeth. And then he always woke up.

Wolf reached into the chest pocket of the stained and smelly jacket his mother called his second skin. He pulled out a book with a waterproof cover, opened it to a stray page, clipped his book light to it and turned the device on. In the grey light of dusk he watched the light unfold like a mutant finger, or god, and point its holy light down to a page. He glanced at it, closed his eyes and mouthed the words. "Treatment for a broken shoulder . . . "

"Would you fucking credit it!"

Alex Carr hit the steering wheel so hard with his left hand that he dislodged his earpiece. It dangled loose over his right ear.

"Would you mind?" Simone removed her earbuds. Piano streamed from her lap. She took off her reading glasses, placed them in the case on her lap, and lowered the screen she'd been looking at.

Her husband stopped in the middle of readjusting his earpiece. He threw up his hands. "You and your Darcy!"

"We've had enough of your histrionics, thank you," Simone said, looking straight ahead, not at his hands waving free of the steering wheel. "I've got work too, may I remind you, and you just juggle team members and money. If you had to place and juggle kids! One day in DOCS and you'd be begging me to trade. Besides, we're time poor and you waste it on what, your sainted grandmother nun you've never met before? This house you say he has, had, in Hunters Hill? No one else turned up except that funeral vulture. I *told* you it wasn't worth the inheritance to drive from Melbourne to Sydney."

He'd been humming to himself, tapping his phone, but stopped. "You wouldn't know worth if it—!"

She turned to him. "I *learned*." And she bowed her head and picked up her glasses case. If she was trying to conceal her smile, she was failing.

"You learned shit!" His earpiece fell onto his lap . "So you read free ancient romances! on a pad I gave you! So you groove to Chopin. How refined! You wouldn't know worth if—"

She picked up the pad. "I learned what someone isn't worth."

He picked up the earpiece and threw it at her pad. It bounced off, falling onto her lap.

She brushed the earpiece off as if it were a spider, and stamped and ground it into the carpet.

He throttled the steering wheel with both hands. His face crimsoned as he drew a ragged breath. Then he stamped on the accelerator and turned the wheel.

With the power of a turbo-charged V8 elephant, the SUV's wheels tore gravel, clipped a drainage ditch and flattened five metres of brush before it hit the tree. The shrieks of metal shear and crunch of glass shatter were smothered by the explosions of four airbags. They puffed out clouds of white powder.

Without the airbag in front of her, Simone would have gone through the windscreen. Instead, her neck snapped. Her head tilted roofwards.

Alex jerked in his seat. "Fuckin airbags!" He leaned toward his wife, but his bucket seat and . . . "Fuckin gear shift!"

He raised his hand to adjust the rear-view mirror, and just then the over-arching bottom limb of the dry and brittle scribblybark tree cracked, tore and fell, punching through the roof above Alex like a fist through paper.

The children's screen hung at a crazy angle—its glass a knife.

Somewhere near, small birds chittered. Maybe they'd been disturbed in their going-to-sleep arrangements. At another time, Wolf would have loved to explore and explain it all to anyone who might have been interested.

"Guhghhhh," went someone in the front. It was a gurgle, like at the dentist right before you spit. But when this gurgle ended, Wolf sniffed. *Yup. Just as the books say.* His belt already unbuckled, he knelt on his seat, looking forward.

Lovie gasped, then started coughing. He stroked her head. "It's okay," he said. "Hang on a sec." Her scalp was hot and sweaty, and a sweet smell of pee drifted up from her.

He reached out and squeezed what he could of Safire and Emrald—a shoulder and a hunk of hair. Em was scrabbling at her eyes. "Everybody out! Poison."

"It's only baking soda or something," he said, feeling sure he'd read it somewhere.

"Fuh ckin shit," Safire mumbled. He unstrapped Lovie.

She banged her face into his, sobbing convulsively. Her lips wet his ear. "You're making noise. We're not supposed to move."

"It's okay," said Wolf.

She raised her head and stage-whispered, "They're *really* gonna get mad now."

"I'll tell them it wasn't your fault," Em said, pulling Lovie onto her lap.

The doors were locked. They held their breath while Safire positioned himself to kick out the window with both feet.

"No!" Wolf hissed. Behind them, gravel crunched. "Shut up and play dead. Someone's coming!"

Safire sat up. "You nuts?" Lovie squirmed in Em's arms.

"Get us help," Em said through gritted teeth. Above, the heavy limb creaked against the roof. Outside, car doors opened.

Safire carefully turned himself around and knelt on his seat. "Here!" he yelled, waving his arms.

The seat jerked, and Wolf sprang up in front of Safire. From

Wolf's open mouth close enough to kiss, a sharp, hot, wordless shriek plunged through Safire, whose body reacted by shooting a blurp into his pants as all the terror that had been lurking in Lovie, emptied from her lungs.

The two people, a nice young German couple touring Australia in the strange continent's summer, took to their heels so fast that she stumbled and fell, and he tore her sundress pulling her up. They drove away as fast as the aging rental van let them get away with.

Em and Safire looked daggers at Wolf.

"Lovie," he said, and pointed to Safire's window. "That's cracked. Bash it out, Saffa. Talk later."

There was something in Wolf's calmness that made his brother drop back and kick the window with both heels. It didn't come straight out. He leant over and opened the eskie on the floor, taking out a tinny of Mother that his dad had packed so that he wouldn't need to be spelled on the thirteen-hour drive home. Safire scraped a circle on the window with the aluminium rim. Then he king-kicked, and heard the glass showering. Then he slithered out the window. Falling onto the broken glass wasn't as bad as the broken brush. One torn twig whipped across his eyelid. He stood and looked to Wolf, who motioned him around to Em's side. She scooted out holding Lovie with some difficulty, but Safire helped, so there were the three of them standing there beside her door. Wolf was nowhere—

"Here!" he called, running out from some bushes a few metres away. "C'mon Em. Saffa. let's get our stuff out of the car."

Safire let Wolf direct. They both carried, but Safire took the heavy stuff. Soon they'd cleaned out the car, including Lovie's old blanket and their mum's and dad's laptops.

Em had settled Lovie on the car blanket and sat beside her. At nine o'clock already, way past Lovie's bedtime. Lovie curled up and stuck her thumb in her mouth. But she wasn't going to go to dreamland yet. She sat up. "Where's Pobblebonk? Pobblebonk is hungry."

"He just ate a grimple," Safire laughed. "It's his bedtime."

"No it isn't."

"Well, tell him a story. He's hungry for a secret." Behind him Wolf was making frantic Tell him to Shut Up signs to Emrald, who took the cue.

"Here's a Messenger from Pobblebonk."

"Thank you, fair Queen," said Wolf, who bowed and unfolded a pretend scroll.

"From the far-kingdom of Scrumply Gumps, I bring this letter, to be delivered to the fairest Lovie in the land."

"That's me!" Lovie laughed. Her green eyes gleamed large as a nightbird's.

"We ask her gracious Lovieness if we may entertain Pobblebonk for a . . . it's hard to read this . . . oh! A kwunth."

Lovie took her thumb from her mouth. "What's a kwunth?"

"A scrumble gumpsian month. And they say Pobblebonk loves their fly pies. So yes? Please yes?" Wolf stood on one leg, and fell over.

"Yes!" Lovie shouted. "But only for a grumble gumpskwillion what ever you said month."

Beside her, Em gave Wolf a thumbs up with her right hand and wiped an eye with her left.

"Mr Sleepy awaits you," she said. Lovie curled up against her and within a minute, they could hear the snuffly snore of a child who'd cried without anyone having said, "Now blow your nose."

Wolf never told them, and they didn't ask, but finding Pobblebonk had been one of his first priorities. He'd found a leg of the soft stuffed frog under the front passenger seat, but it was stuck. He pulled, and it squelched into his fingers.

He bit his tongue then, stopping his scream, but not his vomit.

~*~

First, without any discussion, Safire opened the suitbag, rifled through it and some other bags, and did some bushbashing till he was a ways away. He used a bottle of water from the eskie to wash off, and a splash of his dad's aftershave to deodorise. He used a pair of his dad's socks to dry off, slapping biting flies off his bum and his wet legs. His underpants hadn't leaked, but he dumped his boardshorts anyway, and pulled on his black school / funeral pants. He didn't have any other choice.

The night was as mild as January on the south coast of Australia often is. A light smell of honey from the blossoming hakeas made them seem well disposed to visitors in their kingdom. Wolf and Em talked quietly while they waited, and when they caught the strongest whiff that confirmed their suspicions of why Safire had needed time to himself, Wolf explained that those evil bushes that smelled so good and that had left their marks should be dubbed Your Spininesses.

Em nodded, then shook her head. "If they were human, we could dub them Your Fakeries."

When Safire came back, Em opened the eskie and took out a tinny of Mother. She opened it and they passed it around.

"I won't sleep anyway," said Safire, after he had a gulp.

"Neither will I," Em added, passing it to Wolf.

Wolf raised his lip. "I snuck some of Dad's a year ago. Didn't you know it tastes like shit?"

Safire leaned over and grabbed the can.

"What you want with it?" Wolf demanded.

"I'm just gonna toss it."

"Not in the bush!"

Safire stood to his full height, that of a full-grown man. And he threw with all the graceful force of a practiced athlete. They heard an audible clunk, surprisingly close.

"Fuckin forest!" He knelt and punched his brother hard in the back. They rolled off the blanket, Wolf's teeth in Safire's shoulder.

"You wanna wake her?" Em held up a heavy stick and wagged it. "Okay, Mr Know-it-all. You must have had a reason for screwing up our rescue. Out with it."

"That's all I wanted," mumbled Safire. "An explanation. And it better be good."

~*~

Safire ruffled Wolf's hair. "If only she were some little bugger like you."

"He doesn't really mean that," Em said, smiling at Wolf and crooking her eyebrows at Safire.

Wolf smoothed the carpet beside him. "Saffa's right, Em. But even if that were true, we'd still have the problem of us being four."

"Four wards of the State," Em said. "You know the kind of people Mum has bitched about, the foster-business pros."

Saffa sighed. "I tried to ignore her bitching."

"I don't know which she hated more," said Em. "The foster parents or the problem of the kids who need placement."

"Yeah, I guess," said Saffa. "I felt bad for those kids. I think she kinda hated them."

"Not as much as she hated us."

Em said it. Safire had been looking down, but his head snapped up. "I didn't mean that," Em said. Her mouth hung open.

"Dad too," said Wolf. "We cramped his style."

They were silent long enough that Wolf finally said, "I didn't hear an owl hoot."

Em broke into a short burst of laughter, or sobbing, that ended in hiccups. "On re . . . consid . . . eration," she said. "Mum didn't hate us."

"Not personally," said Wolf.

"She loved the *idea* of children," laughed Safire.

"Which gets us back to Lovie first", said Wolf. "And keeping us four together. It'll be daybreak before we know it."

Saffa punched Wolf lightly. "Friday the thirteenth evening by a spooky outback forest." He whistled (poorly, but no one laughed). "You clinched it, but hell. I would have run from those screams at any time anywhere."

Wolf turned to Em. "You really think this Auntie Joan you talk about might take us?"

"I don't know. I only know that she's his sister and that she married a cardiologist that Dad hated on principle."

"The principle being that the cardiologist helps people to get healthy hearts and Dad bled people dry as a corporate banker because he never had a heart and . . ."

Em held up her hand. "We've already held our Mass for Dad. No sermonising." She turned to Wolf. "They live in London or Manchester or something. And Dad and his sister never got along, so I think that's a dead end. Sorry."

"Besides," said Safire. "We can't take the risk of turning ourselves in. And besides . . ."

"Spit it out," said Em.

"No. Maybe I'm wrong. It happened here, in New South Wales, and that's across the border from Victoria."

Em grabbed him in the back of the neck and squeezed. "Now you're being stupid. Speak up."

"Okay! What if when they find the car, they find out that it's Mum and Dad. So they crashed. But what if they find out that we were in the car too? Sure it's school hols now, but in two weeks it won't be, and even though we moved and we'll all be in new schools, someone's gonna twig sooner or later. And then they'll be onto our parents for why we're not in school, and then they'll link it up with some crash far from home, in the middle of nowhere, on a dark and scary night. Then they find out that our parents were tomato sauced. And flickity flack. They'll have a new motive to find us. Murder!"

"Like, we murdered them?" Wolf rubbed the small of his back.

"So forget I said it."

"No."

"I agree no," said Emrald. "Dad was a bastard and Mum was a—"

Safire held up his hands. "You endethed the sermons!"

"Social worker." Wolf said it straightfaced. They all broke into giggles so loud that Em shushed them and looked to Lovie, who didn't move.

"D'you know where we are?" Wolf asked Em. "Not exactly, but I remember the sign that said Fishermans Paradise. That was a ways back, but I think we might have just passed a dirt road before we . . ."

Wolf lifted his head. "Listen."

Safire and Em closed their eyes. Wolf shivered and reached down the back of his shirt. "Not the bongers. Listen past the insects." He waited while he admired the dull gold iridescence of the Christmas beetle in his hand. Its feet almost hurt, they were so prickly. It was just sitting there doing nothing when it decided to open its wings and fly.

Safire whirled around and punched air. "Fuck off! God, they're spastic. And fuck your quiz."

"I hear it, Wolf. The wind in the trees."

"There's no wind, Em. It's the sea."

Safire punched air. "Holiday houses! I get you."

"Saffa," said Wolf. "I only meant the beach."

"But see, Wolf, if we're lucky, Saffa's right."

"We leave at dawn," announced Safire.

"I'll scout first," said Em.

Safire swung an invisible bat. "Then I'll break and enter. There must be a holiday house we can hole up in."

Em stretched her arms out to them, piling her hands together. "My dear criminal family."

They piled their hands on hers.

"Wait," Wolf whispered. "We've got to vow that we'll never let anyone split us."

"Of course we vow that," Em snapped. "D'you have anything new to add?"

Wolf looked hurt. "Of course I do."

"Sorry."

"That's okay. It's just that we can't take chances. And Lovie is so friendly We can't hide forever and we need to give ourselves new identities, new names. Something Lovie can't stumble on, if she talks to someone."

"A no-brainer for the names," Safire said. "And you're brilliant, little brother. Lovie will love being permanently Lucy. And . . ." he crinkled his eyes. "You should love being Edmund."

"No!"

"C'mon," Safire teased. "Edmund the sleaze, for a good cause."

Em stood up and kicked Safire in the bum. "Enough of that. "It'll be Ed. Okay? And by the way, when and if we all get out of this and land with someone good and kind, of our own choosing, to be family, I vow that we'll rename you, Wolf, King Wolf the Cautious."

"I accept." Wolf seemed partly mollified. "If Saffa is King Boof-head."

"Had you thought of a surname?" Safire asked Wolf.

"As a matter of fact, I had, and Em reminded me. Cosa. It'll be easy for you two to remember, and Lovie never learned more names for herself than Lovage, Lovie and Lucy. So she'll learn this easily."

"Why Cosa?" asked Em.

Safire looked at Wolf with a question in his eyes. "I think I know why. Because it's cosy?"

"Good try, and almost there but not all the way. I was thinking of the family. Our family I'd die before betraying. That's the code of the cosa nostra. I saw it in some movie Dad had on one night. I'm willing to bet that cosa means family, from cosy, just as you said, Saff–er, King. And nostra is *our*."

Wolf was in full flow, his angular face flayed by tree-sieved moonlight. "I'd be willing to bet that when they hunt for us, we'll be called the Car Kids on the news. Nobody'd guess."

Safire punched Wolf's shoulder, in a friendly way.

Em kissed the top of Wolf's head. "You're my favourite Italian crime boss. And by the way, Saffa. Fuckin's dead."

"What you mean, Miss Fox? I know you—"

"That's not what I meant, Saffa. We've buried the fuckin shit with Dad. You're not a younger him. Wolf, it's way past your bedtime."

"Amen," said Wolf.

Em laughed. "It's way past your bedtime, anyway, you little brown-noser."

"You're both too smart for your own good," said Safire. "Now both o' youse. Sleep! I'll take the first watch."

"Okay," said Em. "But you need more sleep, so wake me in two hours."

She lay down, stuffed her backpack under her head, and closed her eyes. Some nearby tree must have been in blossom. Bats were squabbling in the leaves. She wasn't any sleepier than they. "Saffa?"

"Yoh?"

"What you think this funeral thing was all about? And why'd you think Dad made us go when no one had anything to do with him in real life?"

"I dunno, Em. But *I* met him."

Emrald vaulted herself upright. "When?"

"When he was alive."

"I figured that, you idiot."

"When we still lived in Sydney. I must have been about Wolf's age. No, a year younger. It was the day after my seventh birthday, the one when Dad gave me my first pro racquet."

"Well?"

"Well, Dad said that now that I was growing up, he should introduce me to his grandfather. The place was some big stone mansion in a street of them."

"Cool."

"It was pretty weird. It was huge, you could see from the outside, but like, the front hall had a crack in the wall that you could put your hand in. The whole place stunk of tobacco and—"

"What was he like?"

Saffa closed his eyes. "You know our nose? Dad's, mine, and yours? It's his. He must have looked ace when he was our age. But he still was pretty amazing. Sitting there when we arrived, like an emperor. And his hair was grey but there was still lots of it. He had these incredibly bushy eyebrows."

"So what happened?"

"Some chef guy answered the door and let us in, where he sat in the lounge with us while Dad and the old guy talked for a while. Then the chef picked him up and took him up the stairs to his bedroom—"

"A male nurse."

"I guess. So we all went to his bedroom where I had to wait for another long time while Dad and he talked or fought. It was hard to tell. And then we left."

"That was it?"

"Yeah."

"No wonder you never told me."

Safire heard her flop down on the blanket.

He rolled his neck, beginning a stretch routine, remembering . . .

The walls. Covered in paintings with carved gold frames and hundred-year-old grot. But their darkness didn't hide the scenes of naked men and women, some holding cups but all in one humungous gropefest. In the loo, the taps were gold dolphins and the tub stood on lion's feet but standing in the tub was a chrome-frame chair with a blue plastic toilet seat.

The walls of the bedroom were mangy red velvet. Its fur was sticky.

But it was the painting over the bed that Safire had dreamt about ever since that day. On a hill with odd trees like asparagus, a beautiful naked woman writhed on a cross. On her head was a garland of roses, their thorns cutting into her forehead, which streamed with blood. Her hair hung in thick dark ringlets, sprung also from under her arms and between her legs. A crowd of men reached up to her, some touching her feet. All of them looked up to her, their eyes shiny, their lips open, thick and shining with drool. You could only see the top portion of them, but enough to see that they were not all old and some were good-looking, but they were *all* leches.

For years he had nightmares, especially about that hair. But a week ago he had another dream about her—she was a pole dancer with red high heels. And he was in the audience.

He also didn't tell Emrald that halfway through the visit, their great-grandfather of the imperious nose and noble head, took out his teeth. Then his mouth became a terrifying slash or hole And that his clothes were a white shirt and grey(?) pants that St. Vinnies wouldn't accept. And his voice was rough and breathy, and he kept pressing a stained scarf embroidered with mermaids to his neck. And that Dad had said to Saffa after they left, that the reason for the scarf wasn't that Great-grandfather was an artist or anything like that, but to cover the hole in his throat.

And he never told anyone that when Dad went downstairs to the loo just before they left, Dad's grandfather told Saffa to come closer.

And when Saffa managed to, the old man pressed a little box into his hand and told him to save it till he was grown-up and in the meantime, never show it to anyone. He never did. His pants pocket was too shallow, or the other stuff might have crowded it out. By the time he got to his room at home, he pulled out only a box of Smarties.

~*~

At the far edge of the blanket, Emrald woke and listened to Safire's deep, measured breaths. The cloth jerked under her. Probably, Em thought, he's doing another ab routine from *Men's Fitness*. After what must have been fifty situps, he stopped.

"You asleep?"

"No."

"I'm sorry about your violin."

Em was sorry, too. She missed it already.

"You'll never be able to play violin again, you know."

Em sat up. That hadn't occurred to her. "Why?"

"You're too good at it. You'll be recognised."

He was serious. She grinned at him, not knowing if her face was a black mask. "This is the first time you haven't called it stupid. But what about your tennis?"

"I've always hated it."

That was a surprise, but then he'd been pushed into it from age three.

He stretched out and began counting pushups.

She lay on her back. They had not talked about who they'd find to be family. Who would not only want them, but be able to support them? Most important of all, who could they trust? She discounted type after type—the-more-the-merrier Christoids, friendly paedophiles, men cracking onto her as a babe. She considered hacking into some IVF registry, but dumped the idea when she remembered how so many of those 'successful' parents were like her mother–loving the *idea* of kids.

No one will want us. And we can't trust anyone. She was lost–until *gay guys!*

She knew she'd have to explain it right, or Saffa would dismiss it with *Poofters!* But a nice old middle-age couple of say, 50, would be past their wild sex days. And besides, he could beat them up if they tried. As a stable couple at their age, they'd be smart and able to appreciate Wolf.

The idea grew on her as she thought of the couple. They'd be well off, cultured, so they'd love good music (I could switch to harp). They'd always been cruelly deprived of having a family—a family they'd always yearned for. Now they'd have the whole shebang including a dog (and all gays love dogs). She would of course be able to have them as friends. She smiled to herself as she imagined it all, knowing that the most important quality was in the bag. An old gay couple would have spent more than her lifetime keeping secrets, pretending they were someone else to the outside world.

There was only one problem. Would this beach that she could hear waves pound on, be the kind where old gay guys stroll? That could be a problem. At least it wouldn't be Fishermans Paradise. Gay guys don't fish.

She drifted off to sleep and within the hour, her legs as well as Safire's were splayed anyhow over the hunting ground of countless creatures of the night.

~*~

A monster with wet lips was eating Wolf from the head down. The monster had Wolf's shoulder in its talons. Wolf opened his mouth to yell for help but could only rasp—

"Wolf!"

Lovie's lips tickled his ear. She'd worked her way into him till she was almost under his body. "Something's coming to eat us."

Not far away someone seemed to be practicing guitar, plucking one string—pobblebonk male frogs competing. That couldn't be it.

She blubbered into his neck. "Shut up," he said, sitting up, irritated and scared.

Something *was* coming. Something heavy, with a slithery tread.

Picking up Lovie as best he could, Wolf stood, trying not to make any noise.

The darkness ahead exploded in branch snapping, leaf rattling flurry. Then a long hiss dropped down to them from one of the trees ahead. He couldn't tell which—when he saw the side of the closest tree change its profile, at about a storey high.

He lowered Lovie—she was too heavy—and pointed. "See that

tree? Up there's the big brother of my Mr Lizard."

"Really?"

"Not only really, but you know how much Mr Lizard likes you to give him banana?"

"Oh!" she said. Her whole face transformed. Wolf loved her and hated her so much in that instant, that his breathing stopped. Why was Lovie when she was happy, Happy at a level that he could never hope to reach? Why did she make him want to kill for her? Why, when she didn't even appreciate his love, and when she was going to grow out of being Lovie in when—a year? Two?

She took his hand—*to torture me?* Her disgustingly beautiful eyes looked to him with perfect momentary trust. "Do you think his big brother would like bananas?"

"He'd love them, Lovie, but not tonight. Now let's go back to sleep."

She surprised him by not becoming a problem, agreeing to settle down next to him on the blanket. But it was a while before he could sleep, and then it was another nightmare—Mr Lizard waiting fruitlessly.

Em woke first, scratching an itch. *I smell disgusting* was her first thought. Then she opened her eyes. Dawn had come and gone. She was facing Saffa, the zombie till noon. Wolf was also fast asleep, but woke at a touch. In fact, he was the one who really woke them up, as soon as he sat up.

"Where's Lovie?" His stomach felt like it had dropped out onto the ground. That goanna. He hadn't given it a moment's thought, except to admire its mansize length.

No one could move. They were all too panicked. Emrald and Safire couldn't look in each other's eyes, let alone Wolf's.

"Gooood lion. Lion hungry?" Lovie walked into the clearing, holding a little white and black dog. When the dog saw the other three, it trembled against her.

"Shh," said Lovie. "They won't hurt you."

~*~

The jack russell refused an orange that the rest of them shared, and lapped as much water as it could from Em's cupped hands while Em held it. The little dog didn't want to leave Lovie's arms, but did allow Em to attach a makeshift leash to the red, dog-tagless collar. Em stroked the trembling body till the little dog licked her hand.

Em turned to the others, her mouth hard. "She's a Christmas dump dog. And she's just had puppies. Could have walked from the Fisherman's Paradise turnoff. She's starving and her teats are sore."

So now they were five.

Wolf called to Lovie, but she ignored him, either playing with Lion or wanting to be cuddled by Em. That was always how it was with her and Em during the day. Then he didn't exist. Only at night when she was afraid.

"I shouldn't have stuck around," he mumbled. "They're never gonna be able to adopt parents now." He pulled his books out of his pack. All from that library. All due a month ago, now technically stolen, since he hadn't turned them in before the family'd moved.

"Ursula would have taken me."

"Who's Ursula?" Em said, sitting next to him.

"Nobody!" He filled his pack again and stood up. "Aren't we going?"

"Going where?" Lovage looked to Wolf's clouded face, and to Emrald.

"Let's get a move on," said Safire, sweeping up child and dog. "I'll carry them."

Lovie squirmed till Em had to catch her, and the dog jumped out of their arms.

Wolf caught the dog's lead, but he didn't need to. It was only waiting to rejoin Lovie.

"No," she cried, sobbing hysterically. "Don't!"

"She's hungry," said Em.

"Don't what?" said Wolf.

"Don't go home. Let's play Wardrobe."

"Why play Wardrobe?"

"We won't get in trouble!"

"She's not making any sense," Safire said.

Em smoothed Lovie's hair. "You wouldn't either, if you were hungry and four. Let's go!"

"No!!!!!" She fought being in Em's arms, which made her sister hold her harder. Her screams must have been heard on the highway.

Wolf touched Lovie's arm. "Hey Lovie, I've got an idea."

Blessedly, the sound stopped.

"Let's never go home again."

The dog stood and peddled against Em's leg, wanting up.

Lovie stared at Wolf. "Never go home again?"

"Never?"

"Not to Daddy?"

"Not to Daddy," said Safire.

Out of Lovie's line-of-sight, Em waved to Safire: *Shut up!*

"You mean Lion can come with us?"

"Of course," said Wolf.

"And you promise Daddy'll never find us?"

"How could he? He's never gone with us before when we played Wardrobe, so how could he now, when we're not playing?"

She considered, and it seemed to make sense to her. But then she remembered something.

"And Saffa and Em would protect us on our travels?" She reached down for the dog. "After all, Lion's just a baby, and there might be a bad queen you leave us for."

"He wouldn't do that," said Em.

"Shut up," said Wolf. "Saffa and Em would protect us, Lovie, and look how much Lion already loves you."

He nodded to Saffa who held out his hands to Lovie with *I'll take it from here* assurance.

Wolf knelt and rummaged in his pack, hiding his tears. He felt stabbed in the heart.

"I could find us another daddy," Lovage said to Safire. "A nice old man in a bathrobe."

"Brilliant," he mumbled. "A flasher." But he was shaking his head and grinning at Em, who hadn't heard.

She was watching Wolf. *Sometimes!* thought Em, I wonder if Lovie even *has* a heart.

The White-Face at Dawn

By Michael Kelly

SPIDER WOMAN
By An Inhabitant of Dim Carcosa

When twin suns descend, beyond Lake Hali
And black stars rise, to illuminate a dark alley
Night creatures scurry and scuttle along damp brick
And appears a pale spider-woman, it is no trick.

Beneath strange moons, she skitters and crawls
Her face pure marble, a frozen caul
To fall under her dark charms, you'd be remiss
Her benediction is a deadly kiss

A scarlet dawn breaches the thick gloom of the apartment. Slender pink fingers of thin light rouse me from another restless night, plagued by fever-dreams of dear Genevieve, and dreams of the curious tatter-king in yellow robes, a grey and gaunt being that clutches a sceptre of black onyx and wears a crown of tarnished jewels upon his thorny head. His is a face of dark cunning and sharp angles. Grave-worm tongue. It was he, I'm sure, who came for Genevieve.

A noise, as well, gave me fits through the night. A sound like thick clomping, as if the tenant upstairs had traversed their apartment in wooden clogs. *Clomp! ... clomp! ... clomp!*

I am on the small divan in the main room. The bedroom door is closed — the bedroom I had shared with sweet Genevieve and her eyes likes sunshine, skin like alabaster, lips like the ripest fruit. Her voice, her song, was like a choir of angels. All gone, now. Gone forever. Her outer beauty hid an inner weakness, a faulty heart. And now it is I who is stricken with the broken heart. Oh, Genevieve, my lost love. I have not had the courage to go back to the bedroom, our bed, our former life.

Rising up, blinking, the night's unease slowly dissipates, leaving with it a taste of wormwood. I move to the window, throw it open to the rosy dawn and peer out into the cobbled square struggling to wake, like all the denizens of the starving city.

In the square, vendors uncover burlap stalls, their wares made ready. The grand marble fountain sits idle. Old women, veiled in black, waddle across the stonework like fat pigeons. The air smells of turpentine. A faint yellow haze hangs in the brightening sky.

Presently, movement in the square catches my eye. I lean out; peer across to the terraced balconies on the other side of the square. Shadows and shadows, dark upon dark. The dual fledgling suns will not reach these quarters until late afternoon. It is why I chose the westerly side — my best work is done in soft morning light.

Again there is furtive movement from the shadows opposite. Then I see it, and draw back alarmed; a white-white face, bright as bleached parchment and smooth as a mask of exquisite marble, wan and pallid, a frozen stoicism.

A white-face at dawn.

The visage unnerves me; blank and staring, an impassive and patient perfection, its simple lack of expression somehow conveying a terrible beauty. I am reminded of the work of young Boris Yvain, and I shudder and step back into the shadows of my room, away from that judging face.

I shake my head, trying to release the fog of night. Ah, Boris, I think. There is beauty in stone, but always the cracks appear. Boris himself cracked at the tender age of twenty-three, while in Paris. Like a Roman candle he flared brightly but briefly. Though American, I recall now that Boris Yvain must have been influenced by noted sculptor Vance, that dark artist who conjured stone from life. Boris experimented with chemistry, brewing a strange scientific concoction that when put into contact with a living thing, say, perhaps, a wild lily, a reaction occurred, as if a ray of sunshine, a spark of life, was pulled from the flower and coalesced around it, turning it to perfect stone marble. He felt his discovery would contaminate the world of art, and perhaps it would have, but years before, Vance had already corrupted Carcosa. Vance had no qualms about using his "gift" for darker purposes.

Banishing Boris and the white-face from my thoughts, I move into the kitchenette and make a meager breakfast of coffee, and toast smothered in marmalade. Work beckons, so I bring the meal into the drawing room and sit at my desk. Gazing at the closed bedroom door I see . . . *something* in the gap between the floor and the door edge, movement, a black fog, stirring. But then I blink and see nothing but a wedge of darkness seeping under the door. I shake my head and look back at my desk.

From the desk drawer I retrieve my tools — parchment, ink, and quills — and place them at the ready. I will create a masterpiece, something more magnificent even than *The King in Yellow*, that pellucid and unforgettable creation that enervates and terrifies me so. Mine will be the book that they snatch from the stalls and read at night by flickering lamplight, quaking, stricken with terror, yet unable to look away from the poisonous words. They will sing my praises and damn me. How, I wonder, has that creation remained part of the public conscience for so long? And yet ... yet, even know I am tempted to retrieve the volume and revisit the black world of the Yellow King and the Pallid Mask. Try though I might, I cannot hope to ever recreate such an incongruous work. The thought daunts me, fills me with a jealous anger.

Gazing up, my eyes drift to the corner of the room. The manikin, a remnant of my former life, stares impassively, judging. I smile, recalling many wonderful times when I would finish a garment on the manikin and then fit it to Genevieve; the dressing, then the undressing. Then, inevitably, to the bedroom where we would luxuriate in the silks, the satins, and our skin. Perhaps, I think, I should be rid of the old thing. It is but another arrow in my heart.

I turn back to the parchment, my new life, sip my thick coffee and begin, but after a few attempts I stutter. The words will not come. The muse is elusive. I press on, but all I scratch into the parchment seems an illogical and convoluted mess. After a time I admit defeat and retreat to the balcony. Perhaps the beckoning suns will light something inside of me.

I think of the white-face. The balconies across the way are still shrouded in darkness. I gaze intently at the shadows. I see faint glimmers of pale lamplight leaking from some of the apartments. And movement. The occupants, I think, stirring behind shuttered windows and closed blinds. I try to recall from which balcony the white-face loomed. I blink. Was it directly across from me? Below? To the right? My memory fails. It could have been anywhere. Suddenly I have a vision of the white-face crawling across the face of the building, over balconies, across windows, her (and I am certain it is a 'she') body fast and agile, her head smooth, smiling stone.

These drear thoughts cloud my mind. I will not be getting any work done soon, so decide upon a walk.

The square is filled with frenetic movement and loud chatter; orange sunlight and blue shadows. I smell fresh bread and honey. At a rickety stall I buy a croissant from a short, dark man. "Good day," I say to the stout man, smiling, trying to be upbeat, but he only grunts in return. The croissant is stale, tough, but I decide I will not let anything else adversely affect my mood. Genevieve would have smiled and carried on.

Men, women, and children swirl past me in a steady blur. I am the one still thing in a world of motion; the centre, the apex, an inhabitant of Carcosa. Without Genevieve, I am alone. I feel faint, dizzy. I stumble to the nearest cafe table and fall into an empty seat. I close my eyes to try to quell the spinning world.

Eyes closed, I "see" it again — the white-face. Smooth, stoic stone swimming in my vision, floating in the darkness. I start, open my eyes, and gasp.

At my feet something black scuttles across the dark cobblestones. A spider, thin and long-legged, perhaps sensing my sudden attention, stands still as a statue on the warm brickwork. I stand and quickly bring my boot heel down on the black creature. I imagine a satisfying crunch, but it does not come. When I lift my foot there is no trace of the spider.

I stumble blindly across the plaza into a small back alley. I lean against the cool, dark alley wall, panting and blinking. Perhaps, like the white-face, I simply imagined the spider. Perhaps I imbibed too much absinthe last night. It would not be the first time. Or the last.

I try to recall the evening, but it is as elusive as my muse is. I have a faint recollection of a woman, though, which is impossible. There was but one woman for me — Genevieve. There will be no other.

The alley is dark and narrow. It smells of fish guts and despair. I think I hear something, a noise like the clicking of tiny feet along the damp cement of the alleyway. A scuttling. Then a soft whoosh, like the exhalation of a held breath. Perhaps a stuttering, muffled clomp. I imagine movement at the end of the alley, a stirring. I lean forward, squint. I take one stuttering step forward, then another. "H-Hello?" I say. I cannot be sure, but I think I see a pale shape move out of the shadows, a head, or rather a pallid mask, staring sightlessly. Clutching my head, I turn and race out of the alley, vowing to quit the drink once and for all. It would not be the first time.

Then I wake on the small divan in my apartment. The bedroom door is closed — the bedroom I had shared with dear Genevieve. I am tired, and my head is clouded in thick fog. My sleep was fitful. There was a strange noise during the night, a clomping sound, as if the occupant of the apartment above me was wearing wooden shoes. My body itched and prickled all night. I am uncertain what day it is. But I did not drink; I am sure of it.

Rising, I am momentarily startled to discover a figure standing in the corner, silent and still as a winter night. I move forward, hand outstretched, and blink. It is the manikin, naked and immobile, its lower half nothing more than three bare wooden pegs like a saloon stool; its upper half a female torso, its ghastly pink-white skin a patina of cracks and spider-lines, peeling paint. In the dim morning light I discern the face of the manikin. The black eyes stare, unblinking, the mouth open in a grim rictus. I imagine I hear a scream issuing from that unmoving black maw. The head is bald, smooth and glowing like the strange moons above the city.

I recall the old profession; the tailoring and garment-mending, the fine silks and satins, the buttons, needles and pins, the dressing and undressing. Especially the dressing and undressing. I smile. Before Genevieve, there were many women in need of mending. I had, at that time, quite the reputation; one in need of repair.

I shuffle forward and reach out to stroke the manikin's cheek, but I stop. There is a black spot on the ancient manikin's cheek that is moving, crawling slowly across the cracked and broken skin. Another damnable spider! It perches by the manikin's mouth, as if it has crawled from that black hole. I strike the creature with my open hand, squishing it. It leaves a dark smear on the peeling paint. For a moment, I think I hear a small scream emanate from the manikin.

Unnerved, I turn from the still manikin. The apartment is quiet, the windows and drapes closed. I totter toward the bedroom, but the closed door mocks me, stops me in my tracks. I stare at the door. A drear unease settles in me. I back away from the bedroom, grab my waistcoat, and flee the apartment.

Outside, in the light, I look up into the twin suns. By their placement, I guess it to be the mid-afternoon. But how can that be, I think, surely I haven't slept through all the morning?

So it is that I presently find myself outside the Four Winds Pub, squinting up at the wooden sign over the thick black door. I have no recollection of what happened when I departed my apartment, no recollection of how I got here, for now the suns are descending and the afternoon wanes.

I pull open the heavy door and enter. The air is thick with smoke and conversation. Old Viktor is at the bar, so I make my way over.

"Hail," Old Viktor says to me. "My, but you are looking a bit put out. Yours is a faced of worries and sorrows, my old friend."

I'm dimly aware that I haven't eaten, but before I can order a plate of food Old Viktor is placing a double dram in front of me. "On the house," he says. "You look like you need it."

I down the whisky in one gulp and as I place the glass back on the counter I see it, a spider, crawling drunkenly across the moist, dark wood. Furious, I raise my hand to strike at the creature but Old Viktor grabs my arm.

"No," he says, "you mustn't kill the spider. They carry our sorrows. It is considered bad form and will bring you ill luck."

I lower my hand and stare at Old Viktor. "My luck could not be any worse," I say.

"Perhaps," Old Viktor says. Then, "Do you know the story of the Sorrow Spiders?"

I shook my head morosely.

"Come then," he says, leaving the counter to Young Viktor and directing me to a far dark table, but not before getting us both a large dram. "Perhaps this will be good fodder for your next book.

"I heard this tale from Hawberk the Armourer," Old Viktor says, "who heard it from Severn. But it is as true an account as you'll hear.

"A long time ago, well before Carcosa had towers, quays, and bridges, when the black stars dripped misery, there lived a young man, Gaston, the son of the great sculptor Vance. Gaston was in love with an equally young maiden, Camilla.

Now, Vance was no ordinary sculptor. It was said, in fact, that his art was the product of dark magick. With a touch and an invocation, he could turn animate objects to stone. Gaston was a falconer, but was said to have a menagerie of pets, and was particularly fond of spiders. Spiders, Gaston claimed, were of the living world *and* the dead. Thus, they could travel between worlds, transporting souls. They could even, on rare occasion, reanimate the dead."

Here, Old Viktor paused to take a sip of whisky. I did the same.

Old Viktor continued. "Vance had forbidden Gaston to see Camilla, a commoner. The truth was that Camilla was such a young beauty that Vance secretly desired her to himself. He was a man who was used to getting what he wanted. But the young lovebirds continued their affair, unabated, infuriating Vance.

"Then, one day, when Camilla went to Lake Hali to meet her lover, she found, instead, a man of stone, smooth and dead, perched beneath a great, weeping willow. Camilla was cleft with grief. She was inconsolable. She wept for hours by the bank of the lake, holding tight to the cold stone. Finally, too overcome to continue, Camilla flung herself into Lake Hali. But, after some time, the lake threw her back onto shore. She wasn't dead, but she wasn't quite alive, either.

"Though Gaston had been turned to solid stone, spiders began to emerge from his mouth. Hundreds of them spilled from him and skittered down to the lakeshore where they crawled atop the unconscious form of Camilla and entered her open mouth. It is said that they were drawn to her grief, her pain. She was trapped in some sort of purgatory, a no-man's land, and the spiders offered safe passage on her journey, wherever that would take her."

I shuffle nervously in my chair and down the rest of my whisky. "And?" I say.

Old Viktor smiles. "She rose up, of course. This half-dead, half alive woman, dripping wet, shambled across the countryside to the home of Vance, the renowned sculptor. She found him in his studio. When Vance saw her, he stood, expecting angry recriminations. But Camilla only smiled wide and shuffled forward. Black things moved in her mouth. She smiled wider and stuttered toward Vance. *Could it be?* Vance thought. *Did she want me all this time?* Camilla opened her arms. 'Come close,' she said. 'I want to give you a kiss.' And Vance moved to her and put his greedy mouth on hers', and Camilla, seemingly with the strength of stone and grief, held him tight as the spiders moved from her to him, filling him and filling him to bursting as he struggled against the black surge."

My stomach is queasy. "Quaint story," I say.

"They found Vance days later," Old Viktor says, "prone on the studio floor, his face a frozen mask of terror. They blamed it on his heart troubles. A weak heart, they said. The statue of his son, Gaston, was also in the studio, as if it had miraculously 'come alive' and walked the countryside, as well. There was a nest of spiders in his black mouth."

I cough. "And the girl? Camilla?"

"They didn't find her. She was never seen again. Now, though, she is said to visit upon those who mourn lost loved ones. Their sorrows attract her. They feed her, keep her tethered to this world. She is said to take the form of a large spider, with the face of a beautiful young woman. A face, they say, that could only be made of pure white stone."

Dizzy, I stand. I think I should eat, but it seems imperative that I should get home without further delay. I wave aside Old Viktor's ministrations and hurry out of the pub.

The black stars drip, as if weeping. In the dark, under the strange moons, I find my way home.

In the apartment, heart-racing, I move to the bedroom door. *Oh, Genevieve.* My eyes well up with heavy tears. Then, still dizzy and faint from lack of food, I stumble over and fall onto the divan. Then, everything goes black.

I'm awakened by an odd noise, a muffled *clomp, clomp.* I sit up on the divan and blink. My eyes go to the closed bedroom door. *Clomp.* There it is again. *Clomp.* It is coming from the other side of the room.

Clomp.

I stand.

Clomp . . . clomp.

I shuffle forward. Then, as my eyes adjust to the dim light, I see it, the manikin, pale and ghostly, limned in moonlight, moving toward me, its wooden legs skidding along the floor in a herky-jerky dance. Something black is moving inside the manikin's mouth. Then, a sound from the bedroom, a strange scuttling, and I whip my head toward the door. In the gap between the door edge and the floor I see movement, a blacker black, and a wedge of darkness seeping under the door and scurrying towards me, a chitinous rush of black noise. And the manikin dance. *Clomp . . . clomp.*

Then, beyond the bedroom, that noise again, a whoosh, like an exhaled breath, and a rustling, as if someone or something is stirring from a deep rest, rising, coming out of the bedroom pale and smiling and whispering 'Come here and give me a kiss.'

Wishing Well
By Cody Goodfellow

Obviously, nobody ever recognized me on the street as one of the original *Golden Class* kids. I'm forty-three now, and haven't aged well. But whenever I get cornered by some trainspotter of ancient local daytime TV or introduced as Tardy Artie by a tactless acquaintance, I have a ready stock of cute stories when I get asked what it was like. "I grew up with that show," they always say, and "Miss Iris was my other teacher, my real teacher." Some of them can't quite contain their nostalgic jealousy.

"What was it really like?" they ask, and I tell them one of my carefully made-to-order lies. The truth, if I could somehow make them believe it, would crack them in half. I don't tell them about, for instance, the time I tried to take off my mask on-camera, or the day we poured a whole packet of rat poison into Miss Iris's tea.

Words can't contain what it was like to be in the *Golden Class*. What it's still like, if I may make so bold, because every time I close my eyes, I'm back there in the corner behind my mask and dunce cap, and I'm tardy, and in a world of trouble.

The truth is that I didn't know what it was like, I didn't remember anything that I could say for sure actually happened to me from before age seven, until I got the package in the mail.

My hands shook as I ripped the butcher paper from the box. If my fingers had found a mound of rusty razors buried in the Styrofoam packing peanuts, I would've been less unpleasantly surprised than I was, when they touched the jeering contours of my old mask.

There was no note, only a tape—I had to rummage in my storage closet to find my old VCR. There was no return address, no label on the tape, but a faint logo embossed on the black plastic, which I could only see when I held it to the light. The art deco three-leafed flower symbol of Golden Class Productions.

The panic attack was already beginning before I plugged it in and watched the tape. It was a first generation transfer from three-quarter

195

inch video, jaundiced but painfully sharp. After thirty-seven years of seeing the copies in syndication, the colors bleeding into each other like a dementia patient's watercolor, it was a shock like suddenly recovering from a stroke. The curdled blood drains from ruined cerebral tissue, and memory and perception come flooding back.

The theme song played and the title dissolved to the familiar master shot of the *Golden Classroom*. As Miss Iris told the class that this was a special day, the last day of school, I realized that this was an episode that had never aired, and that my therapists and the shrinks at Norwalk assured me was only a figment of my imagination.

They said it never happened, they said I made it all up, and they drugged me until I couldn't remember anything. But it played on my little TV and it wouldn't stop. I threw the remote and then my mask to smash the screen. The audio track continued to hiss out of the tiny speaker. "And do you want to know why today is a special day, children? Because today… we're going to put on a play."

~*~

I don't need to bore you with recounting the show's familiar tropes. Everyone who didn't see it growing up know what it was like, but I happily defer to its brief, oblique Wikipedia entry:

[edit]

Although this daily children's television program shot in Los Angeles lasted only one season (99 episodes) in 1972, it was widely syndicated and gained lasting notoriety for its rigid yet bizarre rituals; hypnotic organ-and-**Theramin** score by exotica godfather **Korla Pandit** (loosely adapted from the jazz standard "Yellow-Belly Stomp" by **King Leopardi**); and its oppressive post-psychedelic art direction. Accused by some critics of borrowing heavily from rivals **Romper Room** and **Mr. Rogers' Neighborhood**, the anonymously produced *Golden Class* was at once more authoritarian and more surreal than either, and was accused by the Christian advocacy group **Action for Family Television** of promoting **"druggy imagery"** and "**occult/witchcraft themes**." **Jean Baudrillard** observed in an interview with **The Psychedelic Review** in 1973 that the program was a "crypto-fascist dialectic posited to undermine the counter-cultural paradigm," and derived unsettling resonances from the notorious **French Decadent** play **The King In Yellow***.

Under the magisterial presence of Miss Iris Moll, the class of twenty-three five and six-year old children were made to wear bizarre expressionistic masks (to protect the identity of the minors, but also to make them easier to replace) and participate in weird rituals involving meditation and playacting alongside lessons in grammar, geometry, philosophy and etiquette. Dominant themes of the lectures included the value of conformity and the danger of unbridled imagination.

Class activities were often interrupted by the intrusion of courtiers and royal family from the Golden City of **Carcosa**—elaborate **marionettes** and **bunraku** puppets that came to deliver songs and stories, but also sometimes to "ride" or possess the weaker students, driving them to harmless but bizarre acts of misbehavior. Miss Iris would order the students and viewers at home to look away from the puppet visitors, and created much unintentional humor with her shrill warnings that the Tatterdemalion would carry away any children who misbehaved to the court of the **King in Yellow***. One especially well-behaved student at the end of each program was selected to throw a coin and a small preprinted note into the Wishing Well—a decorated trashcan—to make a secret wish.

Never collected on **VHS** or **DVD** and barred from **YouTube**, *Golden Class* bootleg compilations are treasured by bizarro television enthusiasts, while images of the masked children were employed as background visuals in a concert video by **White Zombie**, and a particularly incomprehensible Miss Iris lecture was sampled in the song "Yellow Magic Enema" by the **Butthole Surfers**.

*— This page has been deleted by the administrators because of serialized textual corruption.

I had watched each of our episodes dozens of times, looking for answers. But I had never seen this one.

I made myself eject it and I threw it down the trash chute on my way out. I packed an overnight bag and I charged a one-way red-eye to Honolulu out of LAX. I called Kelsey and told her I was leaving and to look after my plants, not to try to contact me. I was going to my island.

I watched the cars on the road, sure everyone was following me. I parked on a residential street off Sepulveda. I left my phone unattended out front of Fuddrucker's in the Galleria and someone palmed it before I had walked away. What a lovely town. I dropped my wallet on the escalator. No one called after me to return it. O brave new world, to have such people in it!

I paid cash for a ticket to something awful at the Arclight and shuffled from theater to theater until after midnight, waiting for low tide.

My plane would be leaving in an hour. They probably knew that I wouldn't be on it. But if they knew me as well as I knew myself, they probably expected that I had completely caved and checked into the Encino Euthanasia Center under a fake ID, or snuffed it in some private storage space, my only trump card denying them the satisfaction of claiming my death.

I knew they knew me all too well. I contained nothing they did not put into me.

Maybe it was their idea, that I go hide on my island.

~*~

My *own* Wikipedia biography after *Golden Class* would read **Drugs, Failure, Homosexual Panic, Drugs, Failure, Drugs, Failure, Rehab.**

Mom had violently opposed my following Dad into acting, but after *Golden Class* wrapped, the bonus check went to her head. I auditioned full-time and landed a few commercials and bit parts in sitcoms and cop dramas until I was ten, and started cutting myself. When I flunked sixth grade and stole her sleeping pills, Mom blew my nest egg on therapy and increasingly abusive private schools.

As a nominal adult, I kept trying to find other work, but there was nothing else I knew how to do. I did theater and the mystery dinner circuit in North Hollywood in between nervous breakdowns, and I cashed the unnervingly decent residual checks that came every month to wherever I happened to be living, even when I didn't file a change of address, even when I didn't want to be found.

When things got really bad, Kelsey tried to lecture me about the cosmic ebb and flow. I was hitting bottom, and the negative flow was bound to reverse itself. Kelsey believed that when she lost a wad of cash, the city was redistributing the wealth to the nearest schizoid crackhead Brahmin in some kind of blind, karmic osmosis.

But Kelsey had only repeatedly touched the bottom, while I had a standing reservation there. I knew what this city was, and that it had acquired a taste for me. To the casual observer, it might appear that I was having another nervous breakdown after losing a job and getting evicted from my studio in Sherman Oaks. But LA was eating me a bit at a time before I got the tape. That I had suffered a nervous breakdown would have surprised no one, but only Kelsey would be there to help.

I would not die for them, but I was going to disappear in the most pathetic way possible.

I was careful. I had no illusions about my ability to get away with anything. When you've been pinched for pissing into a storm drain on your own street at three in the morning in the pouring rain, you learn to take nothing for granted. You live in a world of magical possibility no less incredible for its being entirely fucked and out to destroy you.

My island was the only place on Earth where I felt safe. Nobody would look for me there, nobody could trace me, and I could hide and freak out, and nobody would try to have me committed.

~*~

The last time I saw my father, he came to pick me up when Mom was still at work. Left a note telling her we were going camping, and the last eight months' child support, plus the next six.

Dad was an actor who got thrown off porn sets for trying to direct. Mom never talked about what he did or who he was, and she genuinely didn't want to know. He got into some kind of cult, or he was mixed up in a pyramid scheme. He never had money, and when he did, Mom handled it with salad tongs.

I wasn't expecting to go camping. He didn't have any gear. He'd clearly been wearing the same clothes for a week. We stopped at a park in the Valley, walked around a shallow ornamental pond and fed the ducks, and it was nice until he saw people throwing coins into the water.

"Why do morons think any body of water too small to drown in is a wishing well?"

I didn't answer. Mom told me the only way to navigate one of Dad's irrational rages was to be agreeable, but quiet. At six, I was already enabling at a high school level.

"You want to see a real wishing well?" It wasn't a question, but a command.

We weren't going camping.

He took me to the Galleria and we sat through the late movie—*Mephisto Waltz*—twice, then ducked out and climbed over the wall of the structure overlooking the intersection of the 405 and the 101. He boosted me over the wall and dragged me across the forking, curved onramp. The pavement was soft and hot like chewing gum, even at midnight. It felt like running down the barrel of a gun, but then we jumped the battered guardrail and he was pulling me into a forest thicker than anything in the mountains, wilder than Griffith Park.

The only sound was the rushing of cars, unseen through the thick undergrowth, bullets hurtling through curved cannon barrels. The freeway lights didn't cut through the pines or the thick stands of pampas grass and bougainvillea. Only the silver-blue light of the full moon seeped down into the circular bowl-shaped glade, an enchanted forest of Christmas trees.

"Used to be a ranch right here, before there was a city. Indians here before that. The old *californios* said the well here was a deep one. Indians said it went to the center of the Earth, to the First Water. Wishes made here came true. The legend spread and people forgot everything except maybe any deep hole in the ground could make wishes come true, and all it cost was a penny. They moved the well to another park in Tarzana and put a trash can in, for people to throw away their money… but whatever used to make the wishes come true stayed down in the hole…"

Pushing me ahead of him now, through the crush of untrimmed trees and scrub brush, through the wreckage of a transient camp to a hollow surrounded on three sides by clover leaf offramps. Looking up, you couldn't see the cars, the city, the lights, anything.

"I like to come here to think," my father said, pushing me forward as if to encourage me to meet someone. "I like to come and ponder why none of *my* wishes came true."

He could see I was scared. He ambled around the bowl of a forest in the middle of the freeway and lifted a filthy plywood plank up off the ground, revealing a perfectly circular hole like a pool of oil.

"It used to be here," he said, out of breath, patting himself down for his precious Newports. "They filled it in with concrete, but we dug it out." He finally noticed me backing out of the clearing, towards the guardrail and the hurtling cars. "It's okay, I'm not going to throw you down the well."

That hadn't even occurred to me. Most of the places we'd lived in were infested with rats, roaches and worse. I imagined everything in the dark coming out and dragging us back down. I wanted to go across the freeway to play minigolf, but was afraid to ask.

He took out a silver dollar. Walking it across his knuckles, he flipped it into the hole.

He shouted down into it, "Make me the greatest actor in the whole wide world!"

"It won't come true if you say it out loud," I said. I think I wanted to make him angry, but he just laughed.

"It wasn't for me," he said. "It was for you. And wishes cost a hell of a lot more than a dollar, if you want them to come true."

His voice had that low, brittle tone, like a knife on a whetstone, that he got when he was going to cry or break something. I didn't know what to do. I was hungry and scared, and beginning to think maybe I was going to die on a traffic island on the busiest freeway intersection west of the Mississippi.

But then he came over and sat down beside me, and suddenly he was dragging a backpack, a big one with a bedroll. He set up a little primus stove and heated popcorn.

"You go to any auditions this month?" he asked after a while.

I didn't answer. He kept pushing me until I said, "The agent said I have no *charisma.*"

"But you've got character! That stupid bitch—" he started to fly into a rage again, but then looked around and saw nothing he could throw, but me.

"Don't look at me like that," he growled. "I would never hurt you. You're a prince, and one day, my boy…" His arm trapped me, his other hand sweeping over the candy-colored panorama of the miniature golf course and the endless barrage of cars. "One day, all this will be yours…

"For one day."

~*~

My island hadn't changed as much as the rest of the Valley, but it felt different.

The little pocket forest tucked between the looping cloverleaf onramps of the 405 and the 101 had been overrun by invasive weeds and worse. Nasty parasitic wild cucumber vines and morning glory draped the eucalyptus and pine trees with such repulsive violence you could hear them growing and strangling their hosts. Spiky pods all over them burst as I shouldered past, spreading sticky seeds.

The iodine colored light from the arc sodium lights made everything look like the bruised afterglow of a flashbulb explosion, filling the darkness with squirming life while hiding none of the trash choking the ivy and ailanthus undergrowth. But there was no tramp camp, and the view was still lovely; across the 101 West-to-405 North onramp lay the pastel pasteboard kingdom of the Camelot minigolf course, and beyond that, the fireman's training tower and a graveyard of antique fire engines sprawled out like the abandoned toys of a happier childhood than mine.

I had a silver dollar in my pocket, but I had forgot my crowbar. I always kept it in this bag, with a compact air mattress, a bunch of cereal and freeze dried backpacker food, a mess kit, a flashlight, binoculars, a can of pepper spray and an 8" survival knife. I dumped out the contents of my pack on the air mattress. I had also somehow managed to lose my pill caddy. And I was nearly out of cigarettes.

I could not go home, not until I knew. I could hit the Mobil station and be back here long before high tide. But they would be looking. My plane had left without me. And I didn't need my binoculars to see my apartment on the top floor of my building, because the lights were on. I had turned them off when I left.

I had enough snacks and dehydrated backpacker food for three days. All the landscaping fixtures on the island were reclaimed waste water, but the adjoining island was an oasis with tanbark to kill the undergrowth, king palm trees and an old sprinkler head that I could tap for water. I was prepared to live out here forever, but I wouldn't last twelve hours without my meds, or half an hour without a smoke.

I don't know how long I sat there, paralyzed. I had forgotten to put on a watch.

A car shot down the onramp honking wildly, like trying to spoil somebody's putt on the Eiffel Tower hole. Something smashed through the branches of the sickly pine trees like a cannonball. I threw myself to the ground until I began to feel foolish. I crawled over to the Betty Boop backpack that the passing car had thrown onto the island. Before I unzipped it, a phone inside started to ring.

My pill caddy, an extra sweater, a foil space blanket, two rolls of toilet paper, a stack of tabloids and a carton of Newport Menthols. At the bottom, the disposable prepaid phone trilled like a cicada, making my fillings vibrate.

I answered, "Bueno."

"What the hell is wrong with you?"

I sat down in a clump of ailanthus, choking on rancid peanut butter stench as I burst into tears. "Kelsey… thank you. Thank you… but you shouldn't have gone to my apartment."

"Nobody's looking for you. Nobody else, anyway…"

"Listen, thanks, but you don't know…"

"Is this about the show? Are you having the flashbacks again?"

See how kind she was? She called them flashbacks, not delusions. "Yes... but it's..."

"You're not on your meds, are you?"

"I took them this morning, but... I saw something. They sent it. They want me to know..." My jumbled mind stopped tumbling long enough to connect a thought. "You went back there. Did you see it?"

"You left a mess. Nice job on the TV, by the way. I saw your pills on the counter."

"You didn't find the package on the table—"

"I didn't see anything, but I could go back—"

"No! It's not safe—"

"Are you hallucinating?"

"It's bad. I can't see faces."

"Come again?"

"It's not like LSD or psilocybin hallucinations, either, where everything weirds out in the corner of your eye, but when you really *look*, the veil rolls back. It's more like ketamine, where looking only melts and burns it worse, and you start to think your perception is destroying reality. I can't see anyone's face, Kelsey..."

"You're having a breakdown. It's just paranoia. Nobody's looking for you."

"*You* figured it out pretty quick. They could have followed you—"

"I'm on my way to see *The Reflecting Skin* at the Coronet and eat alone at Dolores', since you flaked out. Anyone following me or tapping the line is welcome to join me."

"This is..." Screaming at her wasn't going to convince her of anything. But I tried. "It's real! I'm hallucinating because that's what they make you do... That's how they... They'll kill you..."

A long pregnant pause, and then the squelched sound of sirens. "Jesus, the freeway is fucked up, they're detouring all the traffic onto Sepulveda... Listen, the phone is good for another week, but as soon as you start feeling the least bit lucid, you need to cut short your camping trip and come back to LA."

"OK..." I got up and walked around the bowl shaped island until my boots stubbed against a plug of concrete jutting a few inches out of the carpet of pine needles. "I'll come back soon, I promise. But Kelsey..."

"What do you need?"

"There's a True Value in Santa Monica that's open all night—"

"For what?"

"Um… I swear I'll come back and straighten out everything, but please just get me a crowbar and a sledgehammer."

~*~

I had never seen her naked, but Kelsey was the great love of my life.

I met her when we were both on suicide watch at County. I attacked my therapy group because I had a narcissistic self-destructive complex, the doctors said, and not because the other patients had masks or slimy, membranous cauls covering their faces that flapped and fluttered when they talked. When things got really bad, she was the only one who still had a face.

It was how she carried herself, the way she occupied space, somehow silently asserting her right to exist in a world that offered her little or no reason to stay. What must they have done to raise a girl so utterly prepossessed, so sure of herself in spite of everything they did to her. I didn't know until later her poise came from trying and failing to kill herself eight times.

Kelsey was a secret bastard. Her anonymous, unspeakably famous father had paid her quite handsomely to change her name and keep her mouth shut. He hadn't paid her to become a 300-pound neurotic, and thus completely invisible in LA, but it would've been money well spent. Someone like Kelsey could sing until angels wept, and nobody around here would notice, unless she hid behind a supermodel when she did it.

She'd gotten a couple plus-size modeling jobs, but somebody at an agency always shitcanned it before the pics went out. It was almost like they kept her in a box and kept shaking it until she had no choice but to cremate his career with a pyrrhic tell-all book. She worked at her one-bedroom in Studio City, doing web maintenance for something called reputation.com. She adopted me because her mother never let her bring home stray dogs.

~*~

The day was one of those brilliant early winter LA days when the sun is a bright pale gold special effect, but the blue shadows are like hoarfrost and suck the heat out of you through your feet. I woke up shivering in my space blanket, and couldn't get up and around for an hour.

I'd had nightmares: the old recurring one, where Miss Iris ushers me into the closet. The dust and the cloying miasma of tea rose and sour sweat clamps over my nose like an ether soaked rag.

"I'm going to show you what you are," she says, and I try not to look at her, but then she orders me to look and she opens her dress and everything spills out and crushes me against the wall.

I had this dream every night through puberty until I stopped talking to girls. I thought it was normal. I thought it meant I was gay. When that didn't work out either, I was relieved I didn't have to try to figure it out.

But nothing like that ever really happened to me. I was told I was using her to express my mother issues, my repulsion for the female archetype. I'd been through hypnotherapy and intensive psychic driving techniques to uncover repressed memories, anything to help me understand why some colors and smells nauseated or terrified me, why I couldn't bear the thought of being touched, why I constantly entertained waking nightmares about what everyone hid under their clothes.

I made my toilette in a castor bean bush and read Wodehouse and enjoyed the sounds of rush hour, so like the waves on a tropic beach. To rest in sylvan tranquility in a glade encircled by an endless circuit of steel and road rage was more soothing, somehow, than any real wilderness setting. I gorged myself on cereal and cooked a Salisbury steak for lunch, then napped until the tide turned, and spent the magic hour spying on my apartment.

My living room curtains were drawn. I was sure I'd left them open. Had Kelsey closed them? I don't know what I expected to see, but I think I would've felt better if Sir Thanksalot or the Raggedy Man appeared to take a bow and confirm that I'd lost my last marble.

I had gone to sleep feeling blessedly relaxed but slightly foolish, and frittered away the day quite sure that I'd merely snapped again. Who the fuck were they, anyway?

The production company that put on the show had folded in 1974; the royalty checks were dispersed from an oblique, headless equity fund; and the non-union, half-amateur show ran no technical credits. The crew and the puppeteers also wore masks. If there was anyone above Miss Iris, we never saw them.

I had only known a few of my TV classmates by name, only seen a few of them without their masks. We were sharply discouraged from fraternizing outside the classroom, and I never saw any of them after the show wrapped in June, 1973. The show lasted in reruns until 1984 in Southern California, and by all accounts was still running somewhere in Canada. A couple of my classmates had been outed, but only after death. The last was a promising TV character who had just made the jump from TV to movies. When he died of a suspicious drug interaction, his obit identified him as Tommy, the teacher's pet. Our records were somehow sealed against press and fans alike, even against ourselves.

I tried for years to find the girl I sat next to when I wasn't in the corner. She had bright new-penny copper hair in pigtails swept back behind the featureless white smile of her mask, and her uniform was always spotless, but her pretty lightly freckled right hand had a faint scar around the heel of her palm and the base of her thumb. Oddly whorled and shiny like a doll's skin even after they caked it with pancake makeup, she told me once, under her breath between takes, that a dog bit her, and that her real name was Regina.

Somehow, Miss Iris heard us talking and I knew I was in real trouble, not like the pretend trouble they trapped me in every other day. I used to dream of taking her by her scarred hand and crawling under our desks and through the little door in the corner to Carcosa or anywhere they'd never find us, but we always got caught. They did things to us that I remember more vividly than anything that happened to me when I was awake. I knew the nightmares were punishment, but I knew I'd be punished no matter what I did.

A week later, I persuaded a slow kid named Richard to switch masks with me, just for the morning sing-along and the visit from Queen Camilla. I felt like I was wearing somebody else's glasses. Halfway through the song, Richard had a seizure. Miss Iris punished him for acting up, thinking it was me. The camera was on her and not me, but all the kids laughed when I took off Richard's mask.

The nightmares got worse. I started wetting my bed and cutting myself. Soon after that, I guess, I poisoned Miss Iris's tea.

That night, the nightmares stopped, and the next day, Miss Iris chose me to make a wish in the Wishing Well.

~*~

A few hours after night fell, I gave up reading by flashlight and began belatedly clearing a level patch of ground to bed down on, when I heard someone stalking through the bushes. Not walking or crashing around, but stealthily picking a path, waiting in silence before taking the next step.

Rush hour traffic had thinned out, but now the night shift flew by on all sides, more than fast enough to kill a pedestrian. I played the flashlight over the shaggy walls of bottlebrush and vine-draped trees, but they still got up behind me.

I jumped back, reaching into my backpack for my knife and strewing my food at my feet.

The tall, skinny black guy in a tracksuit looked like an ashy mummy. I was sure I'd seen him on TV. A fat white lady with straw for hair brandished an axe that looked like she'd made it out of the brake assembly from a motorcycle. She crinkled noisily and snarled to drive me away from my food. She wasn't fat, but her clothes were stuffed with plastic shopping bags. The two Mexican kids were stupefied by glue or grain alcohol. With matching Cholombian sideburns and pointy boots, they looked like they'd come to see a cockfight. Between them, they held up a guy who might somehow have been all of their offspring. Of mixed race and covered in something that stank worse than sewage, he also looked to have been run over by one or more cars.

"Who d'ye think y'are?" the woman screeched. "Can't camp here!"

"Gotta leave, man," said the black guy. "We need *this*, y'know what I mean?" His head bobbed and shook like it was trying to escape. His hand shot out like he thought he was juggling something.

"Fuck off, I pay taxes." I finally found the knife and the pepper spray, which had gone off inside my backpack. My hand burned. "Your friend needs a hospital."

The black guy came over with his hands up. I let him approach. "He's past that, man, he just wants to make a wish. I know why you're here, for real, but my boy, he gonna die before the sun come up, and he just wants to settle up with the—"

The Mexican guys screamed and pointed at something in the trees. They turned and ran away, blundering through the tangled overgrowth with the dying man on their shoulders. The woman swung the axe whistling over her head, then threw a coin and spit on the concrete plug in the center of the island. Then she, too, ran off.

The black guy just looked at me, his eyes trying to set me on fire. Like he was trying to decide whether to run or drag me with him. I held out a fistful of cash, all I had left. He took it and ran away.

I turned around and tried to see what scared them, but all I saw— all I thought I saw—was a sheet blowing in the wind, a wind I couldn't feel, that made it look like a weightless body hurled up out of the trees and wafting off over the northbound 405.

I couldn't sleep until the sun came up, but they never came back. Around three, a car sped around the cloverleaf ramp on squealing bald tires and threw something heavy enough to break branches onto my island. Kelsey was better than anyone deserved. A canvas Whole Foods bag held a crowbar and a mallet.

In the morning, I turned my panicky mental demolition derby into action of a sort. I played detective on the phone and then read tabloids while making coffee and instant oatmeal.

I found the coin the old woman had dropped—a silver dollar with a weird mandala symbol scored into the tail side with a soldering iron. At second glance, the trash around the plugged wishing well was really scattered offerings; food, unopened liquor, little bindles of drugs, candy, votive candles filled with dried blood.

On the spot where I thought I saw the sheet, the weeds and ice plant and eucalyptus saplings had turned white, and crumbled and blew away at my touch.

Kelsey would be done with her morning support chat and working in her breakfast nook, squashing online slander with a cat on each knee.

She answered on the first ring. "You've been chain-smoking, haven't you?"

"What's it to you? You gave me the carton."

"Your breathing sounds like somebody running in corduroy slacks."

"Did you go back? Did you see the mask?"

"I went back, but everything was gone."

"What? It was in the TV, which I was well within my rights to... It's not such a big mess..."

"Listen. Everything was *gone*. Your apartment is cleaned out. It's not *your* apartment anymore."

I fairly screamed and ran into traffic, when she started cackling. "Is that what you wanted to hear?" I couldn't stay angry at her when she laughed like that, and she didn't stop until I joined in.

"I told you, didn't I? They're going to pluck me out of the world and bury every last trace—"

"Get your binoculars and look at your place."

Still hyperventilating a little, I zeroed in on my window and saw her standing on my balcony, waving and drinking coffee out of my favorite mug. "Your grand delusion doesn't hold up to much prodding. I did some research."

"Leave them alone, they'll get you, too..."

"Relax, I do this for a living. Now, understand, I'm not judging you. I love you for who you are, not who you think you are."

"That doesn't sound good."

I probably could've handled that better. Without missing a beat, she carried on. "Well, I was able to find the payrolls for the production company. Your grand conspiracy is locked away in a media vault in North Hollywood. The manager let me poke around and scan documents for fifty bucks. They folded in 1974, and *Golden Class* was the only show they produced."

"Nothing we don't know..."

"I found a class list."

"Bullshit."

"You sat next to Regina Haglund. She was the producer's daughter."

My heart went on strike. In my heart, I had always wanted to believe—well, never mind that.

"Nobody who worked on the show is still alive today. Two of the children have since died..."

My throat closed up. I had to choke down a bottle of water before I could ask, "Which ones?"

"Tommy and Norma Gutierrez. She fell off a bridge and drowned, just before she turned eighteen..."

"Jumped, fell or was pushed?"

"I don't know, they don't... what does it matter?"

"It matters to them," I said. "What about Miss Iris?"

"She wrote the whole program. She and Haglund shared directing duties. She died over ten years ago."

I clipped Miss Iris's obituary June 12th, 1999. The local paper had fun with it. *School's Out Forever*, it said over the picture of a drab old woman with an icy, empty smile. I remember feeling guilty, the first time I saw her naked face. Then it all came loose and I started laughing and crying. She wasn't the accomplished dominatrix I'd always imagined. She looked like a retired inner city librarian, with thinning hair and huge horn-rimmed glasses that hid her eyes in twin mandalas of reflected flashburst. *In accordance with her wishes, Ms. Iris Klawsen will be cremated and her ashes dispersed at sea without ceremony.*

I used it as an excuse to go on a nine-day binge. I never went in the ocean again.

"There's nobody alive, and they were nobodies. The company went under because Haglund was involved in some kind of pyramid scheme or a cult, using out-of-work actors. He committed suicide in '75. His wife and daughter moved away, changed their names. I could find them—"

"No, please. Just believe me when I say, they're not all gone. Somebody sent that tape—" A shadow moved behind her, swooping out of the living room to lunge into her from behind. I stifled a scream. The curtains licked out onto the balcony.

"I couldn't find that, either, and I looked in the trash, thank you very little." She shaded her eyes and pointed to her chest. "Your breathing sounds even worse. What's wrong?"

"Just go back inside, please."

"OK, but I'm not done. You should know…"

"What?"

"You said your memory of that time was pretty hazy…"

"What?"

"Their payroll records say that you were only on the show for one week."

"That's a lie."

"There's a legal brief attached to the ledger for September, 1972. It says you were removed from the show for disciplinary problems, and cites 'inappropriate touching' as a reason. They replaced you with—"

"Stop!"

"—With a boy named Billy Munson who fit your general description, and he took your place for the remaining episodes. There are eight William Munsons in the 818. I could call them…"

"I was in all of them. They're trying to disown me—"

"I believe you, sweetheart." Her humoring voice made me want to throw a rock at her.

"—Trying to cut me out so they won't have to answer for what they did…"

"And what did they do to you?"

"They—" I choked up. "The last day of school, they shot another episode that never aired. They showed it to me. They must've been waiting for me to… crack up, and now they're trying…"

"Is this going to make me all angry and sick? What did they—"

"They made us put on the French play."

"The *what?* I'm sorry, I'm not a theater person. They made you put on a play, like a Christmas pageant?"

I didn't want to say it over the phone, but what difference did it make? If they were listening, they already knew everything. "You're lucky you've never heard of *The King In Yellow.*"

"The… isn't that a Raymond Chandler story?"

"Don't play games."

She wanted to believe me. She'd cut off her arm and eat it, to convince me she accepted whatever I told her. It didn't matter that I was a weirdo son of a grifter with two statch rape convictions, or that my trauma stemmed from being made to take part in a forgotten French play on an equally obscure children's TV show.

"OK, but all of that is in the past. Nobody is looking for you. Nobody remembers—"

"Ouch."

"That's not what I mean. Your IMDB stock is up six percent this week, by the way." She went inside and tripped over something. "God damn your clutter…"

I picked up the binoculars again. "How long have you been there?"

"I crashed here last night. My wi-fi is out and—"

I couldn't seem to find my own apartment or make the binoculars focus. My eyelids were twitching. Had I taken my medication? Did I forget and take too many?

There. The curtains belled out in the morning breeze, then seemed to twist against it, curling around and delineating an enormous body. It turned and showed me a pale eyeless face that somehow seemed, across a half mile of distance, to wink.

"Get out of there, now! Someone's in the living room!"

She pushed through the curtain to stand on the balcony. "There's nobody here but me. God only knows why I've tried to help you, Arthur. You want to make everyone who tries to help you an accessory in your suicide."

"Who said anything about suicide?" And then it hit me. I thought I had no more reason to lie. I had a huge card in my hand, and foolishly, I played it. "I know why you're spinning me round like this, why you said no and then dropped that other package—"

"What other package?"

"I know you're one of them… Norma."

A shocked inhalation sucked all the air out of the connection. "I don't know what you're," she started, but then gave up. "How long…?"

"I never had any reason to try, before today. You never told me who your father was, but you dropped more than enough hints. I made some calls. Your day job company is run by the same equity fund that holds the *Golden Class* syndication rights. I realized Him Who Must Not Be Named was originally named Gutierrez, it only made sense. And I forgive you."

"For what?"

"For hiding in plain sight. For lying about your age. For trying to snow me when…"

Kelsey—Norma—leaned out over the railing, raging into the setting sun as if it were my face. "You don't understand me. You think I wanted to get forced out my life when I was a teenager? I was acting out, and my father's agent thought he would be up for an Oscar that year. So when I jumped into the canal, they lied and said I got swept out to sea. Nobody connected me to my father, and I couldn't prove it in court. But it had nothing to do with the goddamned show…"

"What about the things they did to us?"

"What *things*? They didn't molest us, they didn't drug us… They made us put on a dumb little show! And other kids watched it, and then they grew up and forgot us, and whatever they were trying to do—"

"What were they trying to do, with us, Norma?"

She had to think about that one. "To teach kids what the world really was, behind its mask. Strange games and arbitrary punishments, and a scapegoat staked out in every yard. 'The cleanest hands, washed only in blood…' You remember, it was one of *her* lines."

Her voice was like a fuse almost forty years long, burning down in seconds. Short of breath, scalded by her own tears, she rushed to get it out. "I thought I was an accident, but it was worse. Those people who get everything they want in life. Somebody has to pay for it…"

"You remember the play."

She sniffed, hiccupped and sobbed. "I remember everything."

"Do you remember what happened to me… in the play?"

"If you know so much, then you probably figured this out already. One the group must stone to death, and one must die by their own hand, to take away all the sin of the golden class, and leave them pure to enter Carcosa and rule. Those are the rules, that was the game. One must die by their own hand. That was supposed to be you, Tardy Artie. All those times I tried to off myself… I was trying to save you."

"Don't, Norma, please," I begged. "I love you."

"That's nice…" She bowed her head and smiled. Behind her, the curtain swelled and became a hooded shape. "But we're still puppets. They can make you say anything." And then she jumped off my balcony.

~*~

In all the tinsel and glitter make-believe of the show, there were two things we kids believed in utterly. One was the Wishing Well. The other was the puppet strings.

They didn't have to direct us. Miss Iris held us in thrall without the constant barrage of orders and aphorisms that rasped from the mouth of her mask. When a puppet tapped you on the shoulder, whether it was Lord Tanglewood or Lady Greenteeth, Haita the Shepherd or the Raggedy Man, you didn't know what you would do, only that you had been chosen, and then you watched yourself do it. Some of us stood up from penmanship lessons to utter haunting and beautiful, wordless songs, others were driven to paint unearthly pictures or recite strange lines of nonsense verse, or, like me, they spilled ink or stole school supplies or sodomized another child in the coatroom…

When Kelsey disappeared from view over the railing of my seventh story apartment overlooking Sepulveda and Valley Vista, I felt the strings pull taut. I did not run screaming to the police. I did not call 911. I went looking for the bag lady's axe and started ripping down the wild cucumber vines, chopping down the ailanthus and castor bean and stranger weeds and parasites, until my island resembled once more a manicured paradise, a child's dream of a better world.

And as the sunlight failed, I hunkered down in the bushes with my axe and waited for my class reunion.

~*~

I could not watch more than ten minutes of the final episode, because I was quite overcome by hallucinations. Out of the stiff, strange delivery of incomprehensible lines by hypnotized children, I saw what had traumatized me. In between the frames of stultifying order dissolving into cardboard madness, I saw flickering visions of everything that didn't happen.

Miss Iris at the board, and all the children in a circle with their hands in each others' laps, moaning in unison—all the children clapping in time with Susie slamming her heavy pine desktop down on Bully Billy's broken head—the door to Carcosa opens in the wall and a torrent of rats floods the set, scurrying up our legs as we climb onto desks and each other to get away—screaming, laughing like rabid monkeys, all of us set fire to the books and throw them at each other until our masks and clothes burn and the set and the studio and the whole world burns...

This was not an accident of my clashing meds or a symptom of my trauma. This was what every child saw, every time they watched the Golden Class every time they blinked their eyes, in the little theater of their minds. This was the message of the show, and the secret of its enduring appeal.

But it unlocked everything I had made myself forget. There is no one so free as a condemned man.

~*~

Before he dropped me off, my father had tried to confess. He didn't expect me to understand. I was only six, and more scared of him than anything else.

"I joined this group—they're powerful people, connected in the industry... but they let me in, and I didn't ask why, until it was too late. When you don't have money, people can control you, and when they do for you, there's always strings attached. They got me to do some... favors for them, and they promised things would change for me.

"But they just wanted me to be part of their group to push them up, you know? Like kids on the playground... Listen, inside, everybody in a group thinks they're the phony, and they're afraid of being found out, so they go along with the group. But if the group can put all their weakness into one person, then it dies with them, and they can live and rule without doubt or fear. It's their world, little man."

I didn't say anything, just looked out the window. Dad's radio only got AM, and some awful song about someone called Mellow Yellow leaked through the waves of static.

"I know Mom runs me down a lot, and she's right, even if she's a crazy bitch. But I only want the best for you. I want for you to be somebody, so nobody will ever put their strings on you, so you'll never have to hide behind a mask.

"That's why I'm doing… what I'm doing." He wasn't looking at me, wasn't looking at the road. "I won't jump. I'm going to make them push me."

I hadn't seen my father for a month when I got the invitation in the mail to audition for *Golden Class*. It had hardly entered my mind then that I might never see him again, and it wasn't until much too late that I realized that the two were connected.

~*~

I did not need to watch more than ten minutes of the last episode because, in the intervening years, I had read *The King In Yellow*.

My father's pyramid scheme cult must have used the expurgated text. The *Golden Class* alumni took no chances. Tommy had died ambiguously, which must have driven them crazy, maybe explained why they waited so long to close the circle. Now Kelsey had taken her own life, perhaps because she knew I was too weak. For I knew that the one who laid down their life for the class would don the Teacher's black mask and serve in sunlight. One more had to be sacrificed, to make the Hidden Crown manifest itself. This one would be easy. All they had to do was murder me.

~*~

Ten minutes after eleven, a wave of cloying perfume drifted through the thicket, and she came into the grove. Alone. She glided through the clinging overgrowth, but she didn't trip, for I had cleared the way with the axe I now held up as I leapt into her path.

"I'm not helpless," she said, holding the gun up before her mask. It fit her now. Our masks were huge and grotesque when we were children, because they were our adult faces. In the play, she was Cassilda.

215

I looked, but did not see the gun. The scar on her hand caught the iodine glow of the arc sodium lamps, shiny like teeth.

"I looked for you," she said, under her breath.

"No you didn't," I started to say, but she stopped the words with her mouth. She drove me backwards into the freshly tilled dirt, into dismembered roots and recycled sewage and the perfume of graves.

I could never endure the touch of another human being, male or female, but now, something twisted inside me was severed and I reveled in the soft heat of her flesh through layered white damask and silk. Everywhere I touched her with my filthy paws left grievous stains, as if she'd been trampled by hogs.

Stripping off my rags, she rolled over and laid the gun down, ground her pelvis against me a few times, and grunted in mild surprise when I spent against her thigh.

"Don't sweat it, sweetie," she said. "It still counts."

She got up with the gun and backed away. I tried to find the axe, but I couldn't even find my pants. I was still naked when the others began to come into the clearing.

"His wish has been granted," Regina called out, wiping her leg as she picked her way over to the group. They surrounded me and filled the clearing, a mob of masked men and women. Three of them, two men in black suits and Regina (*Cassilda*) in her mud-smeared gown, advanced on me with long ceremonial knives.

"You're going to fuck it up," I growled. "All the years of planning, of crushing anything good in my life to try to drive me to suicide, and you're going to fuck it up."

The man in Thale's haughty mask snapped, "The sacrifices have been made and accepted." I recognized his voice from two of last summer's top-grossing films. "She's laid down her life to serve in sunlight, and Tom went down to wait in twilight. Only one remains, to wear the Pallid Mask and serve in shadow."

"Let's get this shit over with," Uoht said—which was strange, Uoht was Tommy's mask. But the show must go on, the players were, ultimately, disposable. Uoht lunged with his dagger.

I stepped back and let the pepper spray fall out of my sleeve, gave him a blast that flooded his right eye and filled his open mouth. He went down and I stepped over him, but the others were a frozen tableau. "You think Tom was an accident? You based that on what, the coroner's report? A Variety obit? Jesus, you're all cracked. If I knew everything I had came to me because I was on some stupid kids' show, sooner or later, I'd snuff it, too."

That started them mumbling.

"And Norma wasn't alone in my apartment. She wouldn't kill herself, she knew what was at stake. Somebody pushed her."

The woman, Cassilda, reached up to take off her mask, but Thale stopped her. "I've had enough of this."

"Bullshit," Thale said. "Nobody pushed her. She was a coward, and she did herself in because she knew to stand in our way would be even worse. *Our* way, do you hear? This world is ours." *The crown*, he didn't have to say, *will be mine.* Jesus, that insane sonofabitch could act.

"*I* did it," I said. " I pushed her."

Most of them laughed. I recognized their voices from film and television, from local and national news. In the ones I didn't recognize, I heard the sneer of *real* power, of producers and lawyers and accountants. "You never left your little island, Tardy Artie. We've had you boxed in for two days now."

"I did it over the phone. I told her I knew about her, and… *I told her I loved her.* She was out of her head, and I pushed her."

They were laughing too hard to hear anything. "Her wish was granted!"

"She jumped," Thale said, helping Uoht to his feet. "Tom was weak inside, but maybe it was murder. More than a few of us hated him. No way to be sure, you're right. But The Black Mask has been cast. This thing wants to happen. So let's do it."

I backed up until I ran into stiff arms that pushed me towards the knives. I twisted away, but through the mob, I saw that the twentieth member of our party wore Miss Iris's mask.

I wept aloud. I had murdered her with words, but my hands were clean, according the ultimate court, and now she was the Teacher. Now I laughed, because they thought they had me.

The favored kids who wore the special masks made a wish almost every week, but sooner or later, every student in the *Golden Class* got to make one wish in the Wishing Well. Even the bungled and the botched among us, the slow ones and the cursed, got a rigged question right or did some good deed that allowed us to approach the decorated trashcan in the corner of the classroom beside the door to Carcosa, and throw a golden coin with a tiny slip of paper. I remember how the sound effect of the echoing plop of the deep water drowned out the muted thud of the coin hitting the pillow on the bottom of the trashcan, yet believing that my wish would come true. When Miss Iris escorted me to the Wishing Well—even then, expecting mischief—she squeezed the tightly rolled note into my fist along with the coin. There was no time to balk, so I simply palmed it and threw in the coin with the slip of paper I had written on my own.

"You'll still come to nothing," I told them. "My wish has not yet come true. It'll just be a stupid murder."

The Teacher barged through the line of glowering masks, dwarfing them, forever little children at her knee. Her bright black mask was the size of an automobile hood. But I recognized her voice. "His wish must be granted. But we could not read it. Shoddy penmanship…" Her massive hands knitted together and popped knuckles like starter pistols. "A guessing game should be most diverting."

"No!" Uoht said. "Enough of this shit! Tell us your wish, nobody!" His knife went through my shoulder, just above my lung, and emerged from my back, just inside the wing of my right shoulder blade. I gasped as he lifted me to my toes by the wound. I could not speak, but I could point to the concrete plug at my feet. I could not kick at the crack I had made with the crowbar, but I tap-danced on it. Uoht and Cassilda knelt to inspect it.

"It's just a manhole."

"No… it's a wishing well… My father made… a wish… with his life. He… who serves in shadow…"

Uoht drove me down to my knees with the knife. "Am I the only one who wants this over with?"

Several others rushed forward with their knives, but I surrendered. "I wished… for my father to come back… to me."

The concrete plug flew up like a cap on an oil well, crushing Uoht's legs and pinning him at my feet.

"Your offerings have amused us," I said, mouthing the words that came into me down the strings at the back of my soul, "but the Hour has passed. None of you shall wear the Crown. All shall serve in shadow."

Cassilda staggered back, dropped her knife and tried to run from the golden coin I held out to them. They all tried to run, but it was too late. The scrub brush, the trees turned white and dissolved in clouds of ash.

I took off my mask.

WISHING WELL

Sweetums
By John Langan

I

Feeney?" Keira said.

The cell phone reception here was terrible; her agent's voice cracked and snapped. "Yeah," Ralph was saying, "I know, but it's the only thing I could come up with. Times are tough in Tinseltown, same as everywhere else. If Feeney hadn't pissed off everybody and his uncle with his shit, there's no way I'd be able to get this for you. Fortunately, the guy's an auteur, which is to say, a fucking asshole. Not to mention, his last three films've done shit box office."

"I heard," Keira said. "Honestly, I'm amazed any studio would bankroll him."

"Any studio won't," Ralph said. "Guy's toxic; no one'll touch him. Apparently, he's put together a group of private backers."

"Really?"

"Really. I did a little asking around."

"Who's cutting his checks?"

"Buncha guys from eastern Europe. Probably the Russian mob, looking to launder money."

"Jesus."

"Nah, I'm just fucking with you. The backers are from Hungary or Romania or some shit. From what I hear, they're on the up and up. Bastions of culture and all that."

"Huh," Keira said. "What's the film about?"

"I couldn't tell you. I wouldn't be surprised if Feeney doesn't know, himself. You see his last one? The one he made by intuition?"

"How long is the gig for?"

"Three weeks, with an option to extend for another three. Because you're so busy."

She wasn't. The restaurant where she waited tables had cut her to

Sunday night, which had become the last stop on its employees' ways out the door. She said, "Where is it?"

"Feeney's rented a warehouse on the waterfront. I'll e-mail you the address. First day of shooting's Monday. Bright and early: five a.m.."

"Ouch."

"Again—because you're so busy."

"All right, all right."

"So...?"

"I'll take it. Of course I'll take it."

II

Keira pulled into the warehouse parking lot almost twenty minutes late. She was not as late as she could have been, considering how hung-over she was—how much alcohol was doubtless still coursing through her veins. Last night had brought her firing from the restaurant, after which, her (former) co-workers had insisted on taking her out to the bar across the street—though she had suspected they were as much celebrating their own continued employment as they were commiserating her termination. She had intended to tell them about his gig with Feeney, had felt the news washing closer to the tip of her tongue with each rum-and-Coke, but had been unable to consume enough liquor to release it into speech. It wasn't embarrassment at working with such a well-known flake—an acting job was an acting job, and though this one didn't sound like a leading role, even a few minutes on screen put her one step closer to the day when it would be her name over the title. She hadn't let anyone know her good news, not her father, who kept track of how many weeks had passed since her walk-on part in the shampoo commercial, or her mother, who guaranteed her a position teaching drama at her prep school if she would move back east, or even her roommate, who met her anxieties about losing her job at the restaurant by asking her when she was planning on moving out. She wasn't especially superstitious—well, no more than any other actor—but she had been seized, possessed by the conviction that, were she to reveal her change in fortune to her companions, her parents, her roommate, she would arrive early Monday morning to a deserted address.

So she had swallowed rum-and-Coke after rum-and-Coke, watching the interior of the bar lose focus, starting at the edges of her vision and moving steadily inwards, until the faces of her friends dissolved like pieces of butter sliding around a hot pan. With every drunk-driving PSA she'd ever heard overlapping in her ears, she'd driven home crouched over the wheel of her GEO Metro, which was also the position she'd maintained during her slightly-more-sober race back down I-710 a few hours later. Ahead, the moon was a doubloon balanced on the horizon. When she looked at the road, the satellite elongated, stretching into a pair of gold circles connected by a narrow bridge, an enormous, cartoon barbell. She did her best to ignore it.

The warehouse at which Feeney was shooting was somewhere on the outskirts of the Port of Los Angeles proper, heading in the direction of Long Beach. Within minutes of leaving the highway, Keira was hopelessly lost, unable to recognize or in some cases read the names on street signs. Then, a right turn, and there it was: a wrought-iron gate wide as the street it ended, the word VERDIGRIS suspended between a pair of parallel arches overhead. The left side was open; taped to the right was a piece of canary paper with "Actors Park In Lot 3" written on it in black marker. The doom that Keira had felt pressing her into the steering wheel was pushed up by a wave of euphoria. She sped through the opening. Lot 3 was located to the left side of the warehouse. What were the chances that anything was underway, yet? It was a Monday morning, for Christ's sake. She locked the car and half-ran towards the warehouse.

The place was enormous. If you had told her they docked the container ships inside it and loaded them there, she could have believed it. Eight, ten storeys high, hundreds of yards long, it seemed less of a building and more of a wall, a great barrier built to keep out something vast. The nearer she drew, the smaller she felt. It was like the wall in *King Kong*, except the beast this was to restrain was no overgrown ape, but a creature whose slimy bulk would blot out the sun. *I guess that makes me Fay Wray.*

The entrance to this part of the warehouse was surprisingly modest, a single door above which a bare bulb cast jaundiced light. A piece of legal paper reading "Actors" was thumbtacked to it. Keira was almost at the door when a pair of shapes detached from the surrounding shadows, one to her right, one to her left. Men, they were men. There was time for her to think, *Oh my God I'm going to be mugged*, for her heart to lurch, her arms to tense, and they were on her. The one to the right circled behind her; the one to the left circled in front.

She snapped her head back and forth, the sudden motion making her stomach boil. The men moved with a long, leg-over-leg stride, more like dancers preparing to execute a leap than criminals preparing to beat and rob her. Their hands were up, not in a boxer's guard, but higher, at their eyes. They were holding something to their eyes—cameras, small, rounded video cameras. She could see the red Record light lit on both. "Wait," she said. "Wait." The men continued their circling. "Shit." She grinned, shaking her head more slowly. "Okay, okay. I get it." She held up her hands. "I'm Keira Lessingham. I'm part of the cast." The men continued filming. They appeared to be dressed the same: black, tight-fitting turtlenecks, brown corduroys, and black Doc Martens. She could not see their faces, though one was wearing a black beret. "I'm, uh, I guess I'll just go in, then." The men continued circling. Keira walked through them to the door and opened it.

III

A narrow corridor receded into the warehouse. Heart still knocking against her ribs, Keira walked up it. The passageway was lit by a series of round, blotchy bulbs hanging in space, a row of poisoned suns leading her into blackness, to a gap in the wall to her right. She stepped through, and found herself on a city street. The set was not the most elaborate she'd been on, but taking into account Feeney's limited resources, it was not unimpressive. Across a wide, cobble-stoned street, the brick façade of a low row of apartments was pierced by an archway large enough for a small car to drive through. Stationed along the sidewalk in front of the apartments, one to a doorway, black lampposts whose crowns curved into question marks cradled frosted glass globes that coated the scene with thick, creamy light. Above the apartments, the spire of what was probably a cathedral occupied the near distance; a fairly convincing night sky filled the background. She might have been in some small, middle-European city, one of the places her parents had dragged her to when she was younger and they were trying to inoculate her with culture, a settlement against whose stone walls the tides of invasion, religion, and nationalism had risen and fallen for millennia.

"Finally."

Keira turned to her left, and there was Feeney with a pair of camera men—possibly the same two who had swept down on her outside the warehouse: it was difficult to be certain, because this pair also began circling her, and she was trying to focus on the director.

He was not shorter than Keira had expected—wasn't that the impression most people reported on meeting a celebrity? Keira had never had a sense of Feeney being anything other than average height, even short. His hair stood up in a pompadour that made his forehead seem exposed, his eyes surprised. He was wearing a long wool coat that was either navy blue or black. Around a cigarette that had been smoked almost to the filter, he said, "Great. You can stay where you are. Actually, come forward a couple of steps. Now take half a step to your right. Good." He looked to the camera men, who had stopped their movement. "One of you over there," he said, pointing to the archway, "and the other…here." He gestured to a spot ten feet to Keira's left. "Right. You—"

Feeney was talking to him. "Uh, Keira Less—"

"Right, Keira. Let's see if you're up for this. You start here. You're on this street in—well, it doesn't really matter where. Someplace far from home. The natives don't speak English. You're in pretty rough shape. Actually, you're not that bad, but you feel like you are, okay? Put your hands in your pockets."

Keira jammed her hands into her jeans.

"All right. Roll your shoulders forward—hunch over. Not too much. Good. Okay. When I say, 'Action,' you're looking at that place." He pointed to the apartment row. "Something is going to happen. Something. I won't tell you what; I just want you to react to it."

Keira nodded. "Improvise."

"React," Feeney said. "Got it? Good." He clapped his hands. "Okay! Ready?"

"Yes," Keira said. The camera men held up their free hands in OK signs.

Feeney retreated a half-dozen steps in the direction Keira had come. "And…action."

Four doors down from the archway, almost parallel with the spot where Feeney had positioned her, one of the apartment doors swung inward. *Guess he can't afford to waste any time,* Keira thought. Light the color of dark honey filled the doorway. Somewhere inside that space, that light, a dark shape moved forward—pushed forward, as if struggling through the light. If it was a man—and how could it be anything else?—he was huge, so broad it was hard to believe he would be able to squeeze out onto the front stoop. The silhouette of his head was round, what was visible of his shoulders rough, as if he were wearing a fur coat, or covered in a heavy pelt, himself. Keira could hear the floorboards the man was crossing shrieking with the burden. Without being aware of it, she had withdrawn her hands from her pockets and raised one to her mouth, the other in front of her. Something about the man's movement was off, out of kilter in a fundamental way Keira could recognize but not articulate. It was curiously *soft*, as if the man were nothing but a heaping of flesh, the near end of a monstrous worm. The response it evoked in her was immediate, profound: Keira was more afraid than she could remember ever having been; her arms and legs trembled with it. It was intolerable that she should see any more of the figure in the doorway. She looked back the way she had entered the set, but could not find the opening in the wall, only the façade of another apartment row. Feeney was nowhere to be found. When Keira turned back to the street, she saw the man occluding the doorway. Almost before she knew it, she was running, her feet carrying her across the street and into the archway through the apartment building.

The camera man stationed to the right of the arch tracked her passage smoothly.

IV

For a moment, her footsteps chased one another around the tunnel. Then she was in a large courtyard, the empty center of a square whose sides were further blocks of apartments. In the far right corner of the square, an alley offered the only egress she could see from the space. Keira ran towards it. It seemed to take twice as long to cross the distance as it should have. All the while, she was aware of the archway gaping behind her, the naked space surrounding her.

By the time she reached the mouth of the alley, her chest was heaving, her blouse sodden. Though crowded with metal trashcans, the alley appeared passable. Feet sliding on rotten peels and soggy papers, Keira ran along the alley, narrowly avoiding a collision with an overflowing trashcan whose crash would have directed her pursuer straight to her. Above, on the walls to either side, fire escapes held their ladders just out of reach, taunting her. Ahead, the alley ended in a brick wall. The panic that flared in her was as quickly extinguished by her realization that this alley t-junctioned another. She turned right, saw an opening in the wall now to her left, and ducked through it.

Except for a large, bright rectangle glowing to her left, the long room she had entered was dark. The carbon reek of charcoal threaded the air, as if a fire had scoured the place in the recent past. In between where she was standing and the block of light, dark lines formed rectangles and squares of varying dimensions. As she moved closer to them, she saw that they were the frames of uncompleted walls, their timbers blackened and notched. A motor whirred softly somewhere in front of her. In the center of the bright space, a shape loomed.

Blood surged in Keira's ears. How had the man found her so quickly? She was already half-turned the way she had come when her brain caught up with what her eyes had seen. The figure in the light was Feeney, his head and shoulders, anyway. The steady whir was the sound of a blocky projector resting on a camp table, casting the director's image onto a burnt wall. The footage was rough, the timecode running in the lower right corner. Keira approached the projector. Feeney had been shot facing right, in three-quarter profile. He was holding a bulky phone to his left ear, a freshly-lit cigarette between his teeth. With a pop that made her jump, the audio thundered on, catching Feeney mid-sentence.

"—sweetums," he was saying. "My little turd." He paused. "It's the Sign." Another pause. "No. Not about the Sign, it is the Sign." Pause. "How can—" Pause, during which he removed the cigarette from his mouth, considered its white length, and returned it to its place. "What does any of that have to do with me?" Pause. "No." Pause. "No." Pause. "Don't be ridiculous, sweetums. Don't be stupid." Pause. "Yes you are being stupid. Why are you being so Goddamned stupid?" Pause. "Because it isn't like anything. It's not a metaphor, my little turd." Pause. "You are my little turd. My little piece of shit." Pause. "Sweetums. How I'm going to enjoy fucking you, you little turd. How I'm going to enjoy fucking the shit out of you, you little piece of shit. Oh yes I am." Pause. "I am."

A shoe scraped the floor. Keira spun, and found herself facing one of the camera men, the red Record light shining on his camera. "Jesus." The man offered no response. Keira's cheeks flushed. Of course all of this was part of the movie. What had she thought it was?

No doubt, there had been camera men stationed along the route she'd run. She hoped Feeney would be happy with the mix of relief and shame reddening her face.

Behind the camera man, a doorway led out of the room into another. Keira considered leaving this place in favor of a return to the alley that had brought her to it; however, the prospect of encountering the man (it had to be a man) whose presence had produced such a dramatic response from her was sufficiently unwelcome to send her around the camera man and into the adjoining room.

V

Heavy, mustard-colored curtains blocked her way. Keira pushed them to the left, searching for a part. The fabric was grimy against her fingertips. Dust and mildew rose in clouds around her. She sneezed once, twice. She found the end of the curtain, pulled it up, and passed under it.

She was standing in a small, dimly-lit space whose walls consisted of the mustard curtains. In front of her, a man sat behind a typewriter supported by a card table that quivered as his thick fingers stabbed its keys. The man's longish hair was more brown than red, unlike the beard that flared from his cheeks, which was practically orange. His broad face was pink, puffy, the blood vessels broken across it mapping a route signposted with empty siblings of the bottle of Jack Daniels stationed at the typewriter's left. At the same time, there was a certain open, even unguarded quality to his eyes that made him appear oddly innocent. As Keira watched, the man tugged the page on which he'd been working free of the typewriter and held it up for scrutiny. His brow lowered, his lips moving soundlessly. Maybe halfway through his reading of it, he smashed the paper between his hands, crushed it into a ball and dropped it to the wood floor, where it joined a host of similar casualties. The man took a measured pull from the bottle of liquor, then selected a fresh sheet from the stack of paper to the typewriter's right side and spun it onto the roller. His fingers resumed their assault on the keys.

Was this guy an actor? It was hard to think what else he might be. Keira surveyed the folds of the curtains. Almost immediately, she saw a red Record light shining in one of the recesses to the right. So the guy was part of the movie. Keira wasn't sure how to proceed.

Feeney hadn't covered what to do when she encountered another cast member. Unless his instruction to "react" had been intended to cover everything that was to follow that initial command of "action." The man appeared to be talking to himself. Keira approached him.

It was difficult to hear the man above the clattering of the keys. His voice was sanded smooth by a Southern drawl whose precise origins Keira could not place. He was saying, "Not dreaming, but in Carcosa. Not dead, but in Carcosa. Not in Hell, but in Carcosa. Why then I'll fit you. A true son of Tennessee. Jesus, what an asshole. Come, let us go, and make thy father blind. This was the creature that was once Celia Blassenville. Thus the devil candies all sins over. Excellent hyena! I would have you meet this bartered blood. What creature ever fed worse, than hoping Tantalus? Welcome, dread Fury, to my woeful house. The evil of the stars is not as the evil of earth. 'Tis true, 'tis true; witness my knife's sharp point. Why, this is hell, nor am I out of it. And touched a cold and unyielding surface of polished glass. Rhubarb, O, for rhubarb to purge this choler! There sits Death, keeping his circuit by the slicing edge. *Solomon miseris socias habuisse doloris.* I'll find scorpions to string my whips. Vergama leaned forward from his chair, and turned the page. I account this world a tedious theater. And while Grom howled and beat his hairy breast, death came to me in the Valley of the Worm. Nothing but fear and fatal steel, my lord. Continually, we carry about us a rotten and dead body. No mask? This banquet, which I wish may prove more stern and bloody than the Centaurs' feast. You have seen the King…? Man stands amaz'd to see his deformity in any other creature but himself. Where flap the tatters of the King. It is a fearful thing to fall into the hands of the living God. In dim Carcosa. In lost Carcosa. In dead Carcosa."

The man reached forward and pulled the page from the typewriter. This time, he sampled the bottle while he was scanning it. As before, he had not completed reading it when he crumpled the page and let it fall to the floor. While he rolled a clean sheet into the typewriter, Keira knelt and picked up the closest ball of paper. On one knee, she eased the mass apart and smoothed it over her other knee.

The paper was blank. Keira looked at the man, who had resumed his typing and was repeating his monologue. "When then I'll fit you." Strictly speaking, there was no reason for there to be anything typed on the sheet, but given the ferocity with which the man was punching the keys, she had expected to find something on the page, even random combinations of letters and numbers. "Thus the devil candies all sins over." She had wondered if the guy might be transcribing his weird monologue, which was what she would have done. "Welcome, dread Fury, to my woeful house."

A burst of hammering made Keira leap to her feet. From the other side of at least one of the curtains, sounds of rapid construction—hammers pounding nails; saws chewing wood; lumber clattering together—drowned out the typewriter's chatter. The man did not appear to notice them, nor did the camera man filming him. Was the noise coming from the left? She was reasonably sure it was. There seemed little point in remaining here. She supposed she could attempt to speak to the man, but she was reluctant to break into whatever state the guy was in. React, right? She would react by investigating the source of the building sounds. Keeping near to the curtains, she passed around the man at the typewriter. There was a part in the curtains she could slip through. As she did, a glance back showed the view over the man's shoulder. Though his fingers drove the typewriter's keys down in steady rhythm, none of the corresponding typebars rose to imprint the paper with its symbol.

VI

Keira emerged on the right side of a shallow stage facing an empty auditorium. Center stage, half a dozen men were busy with a wooden box whose proportions suggested a coffin stood on one end; albeit, a coffin for a man a good foot and a half taller than Keira. Dressed in the same black turtlenecks, brown corduroys, and black boots as the other camera men she had encountered, these men had traded in their cameras for an assortment of tools. Without the cameras obscuring their faces, Keira could see that the men resembled one another to a degree that was unusual, even artificial. Bald, their protuberant eyes stretching heavy lids, mouths wide, lips thin, their skin rendered sallow by the bank of lights shining overhead, the men might have been brothers from an almost comically large family. Undoubtedly, they had been made up after the same model; although why Feeney should have cared for his camera men's appearances, Keira couldn't say. Maybe they had parts in the film, too; maybe she would be required to record some of the day's performances.

She had drawn near enough to the activity for one of the men to turn to her and say, "Beautiful, innit?" He spoke with an approximation of a lower-class English accent, Dick Van Dyke playing the cockney in *Mary Poppins*. Keira nodded and said, "What is it?"

The man stared at her as if amazed. "What is it? Did you seriously just ask what this is?"

"I'm sorry. I'm new, here—this is my first day on set, and—"

"This is—come over here," the man said, waving her closer. "Come on, don't be shy."

From the front, Keira saw that the box was at least twice as wide as a coffin. A door that slid to the left disclosed a narrow compartment on the right. She thought of a photo booth, especially when she saw the row of green buttons set in the compartment's left-hand panel. A pair of slots had been cut in the wood above the buttons, the topmost level with a person's face, the one below set approximately throat-high. Below the green buttons, a pair of holes had been drilled in the panel, the upper level with a person's waist, the lower set approximately thigh-high. "This," the man said, "is the King's Beneficence."

"The King's…?"

The man sighed. "You're not from around these parts, are you?"

"No," Keira said. "I mean, I am now, but I'm from New York. Originally."

"You don't say?" the man said. "If you're a denizen of the Old Imperial, then you should be well-acquainted with the Lethal Chamber."

"I, uh, no, I'm afraid I'm not."

"Catlicks, your people?"

Her parents? "Episcopalians," Keira said. When the man frowned, she said, "Anglicans."

"Ah," the man said. "Say no more. This," he gestured at the box, "is the means by which a man—or a woman—with a mind to might make his—or her—own quietus, to quote old Will-I-Am of Avalon. Only, instead of a bare bodkin, you've got your choice of these four buttons."

Her arm stretched out, Keira leaned toward the compartment, only to have the man catch her other arm and haul her back, shouting, "Are you out of your bleedin mind?" At the expression on Keira's face, the man said, "Right, right, you don't know." Releasing her from his grip, the man bent over and picked up a slender piece of wood the length of a yardstick. "'Bout time for a test, anyway," the man said, and tapped the closest button with the wood.

Something bright and metal shot out of the top slot and hung quivering in the air. A broad, flat tongue of steel, its razor edge shone. "The King's Philosophy," the man explained, "with which he relieves us of the burden of our thoughts." He moved the tip of his improvised pointer to the next button and pushed.

From the next slot down, something flashed out and around. Wider than the blade above, this one curved in a crescent inlaid with fine filigree. "The King's Counsel," the man continued, "with which he relieves us of the burden of our words." He shifted the sword to the third button and triggered it.

A pointed length of steel thrust out of the upper hole. When it reached its limit, a dozen blades sprang into a corona around its head. The man said, "The King's Sup, with which he relieves us of the burden of our appetites." He pushed the fourth and final button.

From the lower hole, a bundle of needles sprang forward, twisting first to the left, then to the right. "The King's Chastity," the man concluded, with which he relieves us of the burden of our desires." He dropped the piece of wood. "Well, that's all right, then. Oi!" he shouted. "One of you lot reset the Beneficence." No one replied. "You see?" he said to Keira.

"But," she said, "I mean, I know things can get bad, believe me, but even if they do, would you—I mean—you could take some pills, or—"

"Don't you worry about it," the man said.

Stage left, there was a commotion on the other side of the curtains: someone shouting, the scuff of boots on wood, the curtain swelling. A trio of camera men shoved through to the stage. Their arms were linked, as if they were the world's shortest chorus line. Not to mention, least-coordinated: the man in the middle was badly out of step with his fellows. This, Keira saw, was because he was struggling against his companions.

"Well well well," the man beside Keira called. "The prodigal son makes his entrance."

At his declaration, the man in the middle glanced up from his contest and, seeing the King's Beneficence, began to scream, "No! No! Not now! Not now!" He succeeded in tearing his left arm free of his fellow's grasp, only to have the man on his right pivot in to him and drive his fist into his gut. The captive man folded at the waist like a marionette whose strings have been scissored. The other two took him under the arms and dragged him towards the box.

The remaining camera men had retrieved their cameras and were filming their companions' progress. As the trio passed in front of her, the captive man turned his face to Keira and, in the wheeze of a man whose lungs have been emptied of air, said, "Do you know what this means? Do you?"

"It means what it means, old son," the man beside Keira said. "It's the Sign, is what it is."

While his fellows were preparing to force him into the compartment—from which all deadly accessories had been retracted—the captive man made one final attempt at escape. But the others were ready for him, and the one punched him in the head, the other splayed his hand on the captive man's chest and shoved. Hands covering his head, the man stumbled backwards through the opening in the box. His companions wasted no time in sliding the door closed over it. Keira's last glimpse of the man was of his hands dropping from his face, his features a mix of terror and profound sadness. Once the door was shut, the men secured it with a trio of brass locks.

"Wait—" Keira said, but already, the camera men had begun to chant, "Choose. Choose. Choose," one word repeated in steadily-escalating volume. "Hang on," she said to the man beside her. He ignored her in favor of the chant. "Choose. Choose. Choose."

From within the King's Beneficence, the captive man shouted, "You can go fuck yourselves!"

In answer, the camera men raised their voices another notch. "Choose! Choose! Choose!"

"Do you think I'm going to do this? Just because it happened before, do you think it's going to happen now?"

"Choose! Choose! Choose!"

"Stop it! Stop this right fucking now!"

"Choose! Choose! Choose!"

"Don't you understand what's happening?"

If any of the camera men did, he did not share it. Instead, the group roared, "CHOOSE! CHOOSE! CHOOSE!"

"God damn you! God damn you all to hell!"

"CHOOSE! CHOOSE! CHOOSE!"

Keira had had enough. Eyes straight ahead, she walked off the stage, exiting the direction the captive man and his fellows had entered, stage left.

VII

The other side of the mustard curtain was a short hallway at the end of which a fire door opened on a cul-de-sac. To the left, an alley cornered to the right. Across from her, a metal staircase climbed a brick wall to a doorway. To her right, a camera man stood amidst a herd of trash cans, recording Keira as she considered what might lie around the alley's turn before opting to cross to the stairs and hurry up them.

At the top, she hesitated. A hallway like the one that had brought her into the warehouse stretched in front of her, a similar procession of mottled lights keeping utter darkness at bay. It occurred to her that she was, if not completely lost, uncomfortably close to being so. Should she retrace her steps, try to find her way back to the entrance? It would mean returning to the camera men and the bizarre scenario they were enacting, which she had no desire to do. Okay, the King's Beneficence was some kind of special effect—it had to be; she couldn't imagine Feeney presiding over a snuff film—but she had little taste for torture porn. Were she to step onto that stage again, no doubt she'd be met by a pool of stage blood, seeping out from under the box's door, or, worse, a wash of pig or cow blood, splashed for maximum realism.

Straight ahead it is, then. Besides, there were camera men all over the place. When she needed to find her way out of here, she could ask directions from one of them.

Her footsteps were loud, as if the space beneath the floor were hollow. Echoes of her passage lagged behind, raced ahead of her. Were the lights growing farther apart? She looked over her shoulder. They were: at least twice as much space separated the nearest globes as did those by the doorway. The next bulb was more distant still. Nor could she detect the red light of any of the camera men.

To the right, someone was walking beside her. With a gasp, Keira turned and, for a moment, did not recognize the dimly-lit woman staring back at her in equal surprise. Then she realized she was seeing herself, reflected in a large, rectangular window. "Shit." She approached the window. Through her ghostly image, she saw a bare room in which a desk lamp cast canary-colored light onto a plain table. There were chairs on either side of the table, the one on Keira's left pushed in to the table, the one on her right slid back several feet out of the light by the man seated on it. She couldn't distinguish much of him, mostly a long black or navy-blue coat and a haze of cigarette smoke floating around his head. *Feeney?* What was he doing here? Behind him, a camera man kept record of the scene.

A door in the wall on the other side of the table opened, and a woman entered the room. Tall, thin, wearing a black pantsuit, white blouse, and a necklace of black beads, her long hair dyed platinum blond (badly), she could have passed for Keira's mother—for herself in another dozen years, if time were unkind to her. She thought of the camera men. Was this why Feeney had hired her, because she resembled one—or more—of the actors he already had cast for the film?

The woman tugged the chair away from the table, reversed it, and straddled it, folding her arms on its back. "Well," she said, and Keira heard her, her voice carried by a speaker set above the window. The quality was poor; she sounded flat, tinny.

The man in the chair said, "Kay." Keira couldn't tell if it was Feeney, speaking.

"Don't," Kay said.

"Just talk," the man said. "Say something."

Without pause, Kay said, "I heard about Laceration Parties when I was still pretty new to this place. There was this girl from Vancouver I used to hang out with once in a while. Kirsten or Karen—I think it was Karen. She used to say, 'It's Vancouver, Seward, not the Vancouver in Canada.' Maybe it was Kirsten. Big girl. There was a tavern near one of the more popular King's boxes, The Debt Owed, where we'd stand at the bar and let failed businessmen and despondent troubadours buy us rounds of Pernod while they worked themselves up for the Beneficence. Anyway, it was during a particularly slow night that Karen, I'm pretty sure her name was, told me about these parties, these soirees, a friend had been invited to. In the hills, somewhere near the Observatory. It was just the A list at it, it was the A+ list, the A++ list. Supposedly, the King, himself, had put in an appearance; although Kirsten's friend hadn't seen him, personally. At the door, the guests had been met by a butler who presented them with a ceramic bowl full of razor blades. Everybody picked one for later. The friend had been a little vague as to exactly what had happened later, but her left hand and forearm were heavily bandaged, and she claimed she couldn't move a couple of her fingers, anymore.

"I'd been in this place long enough not to doubt the story. I didn't think I'd ever attend one, though. Not because of any moral reservations; I just couldn't see myself being allowed to mingle with the upper crust—with the powdered sugar sprinkled on top of the upper crust.

"That was before René. If you'd told me I would let a corpse-driver set foot on the same street as me, let alone lay his hand on me…I knew he was, I guess 'interested' is as good a word as any. He would drive past the booth I was working twice a day, once on his way to the morgue, the second time on his way to Potter's Field. They never repeat a route unless something's caught their attention. I knew the risks of acknowledging, let alone encouraging, his notice. Several of the girls I'd met when I came here decided to find out what lay on the other side of the mortuary doors, and I never saw any of them again. I also knew that, without my consent, the corpse-driver's designs would remain hypothetical. Despite the rumors, they adhere to the Compact religiously. It took years before I granted him recognition. It wasn't that he won me over; it wasn't that I had a death-wish, either. There was nothing else left for me: every other avenue had dead-ended. So I made eye contact, raised my left hand with the palm out, and let what would come next, come.

"There was no romance, no spark, no magic moment I realized he was the same as me. To be honest, I'm not one hundred percent sure why he kept me around. It was months until I could stand to have him touch me, and that was only under the influence of a good bottle of Pernod. I've never gotten used to the way his flesh feels; I still jump anytime he puts his hands on me. The smell of formaldehyde makes me ill, and I have zero interest in what he does with the bodies in the back chambers.

"But there are consolations to the role of corpse-driver's companion. The money's not bad, and even better, there's the prestige, this weird, oblique status that allows you access pretty much everywhere. I hadn't understood this the day I recognized him, that eventually, he would be my passport to a Laceration Party. It was in the hills, near the sign. What a sight we must have made, him in that tiny bowler hat and the fur coat, me in a feathered dress and boa. Not to mention, him five times the size of me—of pretty much everyone there.

"At the front door, a kid in a tuxedo held up a wooden bowl layered with razor blades for us to choose from. I took one; René didn't, which should've kept him out of the Party, but really, who was going to refuse him? The house was full of celebrities and people too powerful to be celebrities. The deeper into it you moved, the higher the profile of your company climbed, until you were in a room whose original purpose you couldn't guess with people whose names you didn't know. That was where the razors were put to use. More or less in the center of the room, there was a stainless steel table with a woman lying on it, nude. I'm not sure what process had led to her being there. One by one, the people in the room walked up to her, surveyed the length of her body, and chose a spot on which to employ their razors. The only rule seemed to be that you were not allowed to slice an artery or vein. After you were finished, you cast your blade into a plastic bucket under the table.

"By the time my turn came around, the floor around the table was slick with blood. I stood beside the woman, whose body was a patch-work of exposed muscle and nerve. I had avoided looking at her face, which had remained untouched. I'm not sure why. But I could feel it, dragging my eyes up the bloody reach of her toward it. The second I saw her, I knew her: Karen, or Kirsten, my old crony from The Debt Owed. She remembered me, too; I'm positive of it. There wasn't any fear or anger in her gaze, just a kind of blank fascination. I pressed the razor to her right eyelid, and drew it across.

"When I was done, I straightened, and there was the King, leaning over the other side of the table from me. They say only one person at a time ever sees him, and I guess that's true, because around me, the partiers carried on as if nothing were happening. For a long, long time, while Karen's eyes filled up with blood that spilled onto the table, the King considered me, and I him. He reached out his right hand, and I saw that he was wearing a white cotton glove. He touched the tip of his index finger to Kirsten's eye, and the blood climbed the thirsty fibers, dyeing the lower half of his finger scarlet. He nodded, drew back a step, and the crowd kind of closed around him. I didn't tell René what had happened, but I did hold onto that razor blade.

"So I've seen the King and lived to tell the tale. Everyone always makes a big deal about his face; you know, 'No mask? No mask!' As if he's any different from the rest of us. As if all of us aren't naked for the world to see."

This time, Keira was not surprised by the camera man to her left; she supposed she must have heard him approach. Beyond him, she

could distinguish a doorway through which amber light reached into
the hallway. She stepped around the man, and headed for the doorway.

VIII

The room she entered reminded Keira of nothing so much as
the living room of her parents' brownstone. In front of a round of
bay windows, an old television whose blocky dimensions suggested
an altar broadcast footage of Feeney to an abbreviated couch and a
recliner. Some error in the TV's settings tinted the screen goldenrod.
The director had been shot in three-quarter profile, facing right. He
was holding a bulky phone to his left ear, a freshly-lit cigarette between his teeth. Keira knelt and twisted the volume knob clockwise.
The soundtrack was playing whomever he was talking to. Their voice
was flat, tinny; they were in mid-sentence.

"—about the sign?" There was a pause, as the voice waited for a re-
ply Feeney did not deliver. "What does that even mean? It's a movie."
Pause. "You know what? Forget about it," the voice continued, as
Feeney removed the cigarette from his mouth, considered its white
length, and returned it to its place, "it's not important. What is is that
I'm here, in this fucking…I'm here, and everything is wrong. I don't
know where to start. The Goddamned sky, for Christ's sake." Pause.
"You're the one who brought me here, asshole." Pause. "Yes, you did."
Pause. "Yes, you fucking did." Pause. "I'm not being stupid." Pause.
"It's like—" Pause. "Fuck you. You do not talk to me like that." Pause.
"Fuck you. You're the piece of shit." Pause. "You try to lay a finger on
me, and I'll cut it off." Pause. "Fuck you."

Keira stood. Framed by the archway that led to the front hall, a
camera man filmed her crossing the room. Passing in front of him,
and unlocking the front door.

IX

She emerged into a wide, flat space—a parking lot—the parking
lot outside the warehouse. It was dark, the sky full of stars. Except
for her car, the lot was empty. Had she spent the entire day inside?
She didn't feel as if that much time had passed, and yet, here it was
night. She supposed she could return to the warehouse, but a wave

of exhaustion rose over her. Just being around all of that…whatever you wanted to call it had left her legs weak, her head light. Missing lunch and, from the looks of it, dinner probably hadn't helped, either. Behind her, the door she had exited clicked shut. That settled the matter. Within a minute, she was behind the wheel of the Metro, driving out the gate to the place.

The highway was quiet. Good. She would be home sooner rather than later. It was unlikely she'd manage enough sleep, but she'd take what she could get. Call time tomorrow was 5:00am, again. *Ugh.* Ahead, the full moon hung golden over the hills. She could not remember it ever having been so near, so enormous, the vague face suggested by its topography so apparent. For a moment she had the impression that something enormous had inclined its attention towards her.

Tires ringing on the road, a convoy of eighteen-wheelers swept around her. The windows of their cabs were tinted; rather dangerous for traveling at night, she judged. The trailers were flatbeds, each festooned with a holiday's worth of blazing colored lights, as was the cargo lashed to it. Such was the glare that Keira could not distinguish what the trucks were transporting until they pulled away from her, when she saw that the squared frames ribboned in crimson, mauve, and lemon lights belonged to gallows, their nooses dancing in the rushing air.

As quickly as they had surrounded her, the trucks were gone, their taillights red points in the distance. Keira's eyes were sufficiently dazzled that, at first, she mistook the second moon rising into the sky for an illusion.

For Fiona

The King is Yellow

By Pearce Hansen

T he old black man did his best to bury the butcher knife in Speedy's face as Speedy came through the door. Speedy retorted by sliding out the blade's way and emptying both the sawed-offed's barrels into the geezer's center mass. The results were as unpretty as you'd expect.

Fat Bob darted through the door behind Speedy, brandishing his wrecking bar at the empty room as Speedy broke open his sawed-off, dumped the empty shells, and slid fresh ones into the double-barreled's breech. Both men stepped fastidiously away from the corpse's blood pool, which spread slowly around the body.

Speedy gestured with his chin toward the doorway on the right, and Fat Bob angled that way. Bob peeked around the edge of the door jamb without actually making himself a target for whoever might be in there; he held his wrecking bar back against a grab. Bob looked back at Speedy and shook his head.

Speedy led the way to the left hand doorway, Fat Bob right behind him. This room was the jackpot: the book was right where the Man had said it would be, on the podium. The tome rested on a fine-pored supple piece of pale leather, looking like no cow skin Speedy had ever seen before.

As per instructions, Speedy folded the leather over the book without actually touching it and stuck the bundle under his arm. Fat Bob opened his mouth as if to speak, but closed it again with an expression of chagrin when Speedy gave him a look.

The two men stepped over the DB in the doorway and hurried outside into the light of day. This was Hunter's View, the projects south of the City proper. Scarred apartment blocks surrounded them, bars on all the windows and most of the units obviously uninhabitable.

As they walked quickly past a burned plastic play structure in a playground, a black kid on a ten-speed cruised around a corner and past them. As he saw the two pale faces, the kid's eyes widened like he couldn't believe it. As he pedaled rapidly away, the kid commenced with a loud Indian war whoop, a warbling cry coming from his mouth as he rapidly patted his lips with one hand. After a few seconds, the war whoop was echoed from several unseen spots in the surrounding block; the whoopers sounded like they were getting rapidly closer.

Speedy and Fat Bob broke into an unashamed sprint and rounded the building to the street proper. Little Willy saw them coming with obvious relief, and he pulled the Le Mans away from the curb before their respective car doors had even slammed shut all the way.

They were in Hunter's Point, so they booked west on Third Street past Candlestick Park, away from China Basin and the derelict Shipyard. When they hit the Bayshore Freeway onramp north, the tension in the car diminished almost visibly: phase one was complete, gone down much easier than the Man had led them to expect.

Speedy hit a bank of payphones in Union Square for the reach out. Fat Bob lounged in false casualness a few phones away, watching everything happening behind Speedy's back and ready to crunch anyone trying to swoop on his crimie's blind side; Speedy's brother Little Willy was double-parked at the curb chain smoking, flicking one butt after another out the Le Mans' window, thinking thoughts and suffering his usual epiphanies.

Stolid German tourists waited to ride the cable cars running up and down Powell Street, as if imagining this to be the typical American experience. Surrounding the Square was one of the trendiest shopping districts this side of the east coast: Armani and Louis Vuitton and Tiffany & Co.; Saks Fifth Avenue and Salvatore Ferragamo, Bulgari and Arthur Beren; Nine West and 240 Stockton and Dior Homme.

Union Square was a cash cow, designed to make the local rubes swarm up and vomit their cash – SF was traditionally a town for the nouveau riche, her often unlettered wealthy eager to purchase the accoutrements necessary for establishing superiority over the rabble.

Speedy dialed the number he'd been required to memorize, and the Man picked up before the first ring had finished.

"You have the book?" the Man asked.

"In my car and ready for delivery," Speedy said. "You have what you promised?"

"Well," the Man said, smug glee tingeing his voice. "About that. You *will* get what is coming to you."

"That's about what I expected from the git go" Speedy said, giving a round up gesture to Fat Bob by twirling his finger. Bob bumped erect from the phone booth he'd been leaning against and rotated in place, looking for the inevitable chop and knowing Speedy would turn it around on the fools as soon as they showed their hand.

Fat Bob bounced on his feet in prep, the wrecking bar held down along his leg. He pointed at Little Willy waiting in the car and raised his brows interrogatively at Speedy. Speedy nodded and Fat Bob meandered that way, glaring at everyone in his path – observant people darted to the right and the left to get out Bob's way.

"You are at the Transamerica Pyramid as I instructed?" the Man asked.

"Well," Speedy said. "About *that*. You never gave me reason to trust so I must confess we're not at that specific location. You really thought we'd let you ambush us? I'm the king, bitch – no one fucks me, I know what you were gonna do."

The Man was silent for several pregnant seconds. "Not there?" Whatever smugness he'd been feeling was no longer evident in his tone. "Not there? But that is where you have to be. It is the locus, the intersection for the lines of power."

"Whatever you say chief. Let's re-negotiate the exchange."

"There will be no re-negotiation," the Man said in a voice simultaneously resigned, and on the verge of breaking down. There was a chunky, crumbling sort of sound on the other end of the phone line, and Speedy pulled the phone handset way from his ear as a sudden waft of arctic cold came out the ear piece.

"Master," the Man burbled, and then there was silence.

Speedy waited in growing paranoia and impatience. After a bit he snarled, "Are you there asshole?"

On the other end a voice kicked up, not the Man's, sounding like it was squeezed out through a vat full of mush: "You imbecile – the Man is *deceased*."

"Speedy," Willy wailed.

Speedy goggled at the car – amber light billowed from its interior, blurring Willy's outline so he was no more than a silhouette. The light strengthened even as Speedy watched, wafting forth out the windows like spreading mist. Fat Bob had his hand on the back seat door handle but let go and scrambled back a few steps. Speedy sprinted to join Bob and the crime partners stood together, eyes wide and glittering as the filthy lemon light strobed.

"Get out the car Willy," Fat Bob rasped, his voice gravelly from all the times he'd been punched in the throat. "It's a bomb."

"I can't," Little Willy said, wrenching his arms around without releasing his grasp on the book. "It's stuck to my hands, I can't let go of it."

The book lay open in Willy's lap and his gaze was rapt on its pages, from which the growing light originated – shining on his face from below, the sickly glow made Willy look like a jaundiced corpse. Speedy took a single long stride to the car and flung open the driver door.

"Knock it out his hands, Bob," Speedy said. "Motherfucker poisoned it or something."

Bob approached with obvious reluctance, and took a good swipe at the book with his wrecking bar. The book didn't budge at the bar's impact – instead the wrecking bar bounced back like it had hit a brick wall and Bob dropped it with a cry, shaking his hand.

The wrecking bar squirmed and contorted on the ground, morphed into something resembling a huge saffron centipede and slithered down the nearest storm drain muttering to itself. "The fuck," Fat Bob yelled, back pedaling away.

A woman started screaming over and over somewhere out of sight, and the windows of all the surrounding buildings went milky and opaque as if they'd grown cataracts. Speedy and Fat Bob were instantaneously back-to-back as if their shoulder blades had magnetized together. The sawed-off was in Speedy's hand; Fat Bob's truculent fists were capped by his white faced berserker scowl.

"What is it Speedy?" Bob whispered. "Nukes? Some kinda Russki shit?"

"Slide over Willy," Speedy said, and climbed behind the wheel as his little brother complied, Willy's hands still seemingly glued to the pulsing tome.

Speedy glanced almost apologetically at Fat Bob as he shut the driver door. "I'm thinking the Transamerica Pyramid is the only shot that makes sense. I'll understand if you maybe want to walk from here brother."

Fat Bob paused in obvious reluctance. The unseen woman's

shrieks segued into maniacal laughter, the crowd waiting for cable car rides ran screaming as two of the cable cars started mating, and the man nearest Bob clawed at his own face until blood flowed down his cheeks. Bob hastened to climb in the back seat.

"Eye of the storm, right?" Fat Bob growled in exasperation. "How's about we step on it then."

Speedy smoked the tires away from the curb and they headed down Market Street, but whatever was going on followed them: people pointed at the car as they drove by – looking out the rear windshield, Fat Bob saw the Le Mans leaving sallow tires tracks in its wake as if it had driven through paint. The yellow seeped and spread to both sides, up the curbs onto the sidewalk, and even up the building exteriors.

Bob slowly faced front as they roared down the street: everything apparently normal up ahead. It was close of business for 'the Wall Street of the West.' and afternoon rush hour was kicking in.

The more rarefied office people had direct express elevators to below ground parking, and their de rigueur Beamers & Benz's were queued up at the lot exits up to the street. But as they passed one parking lot exit and the yellow oozed onto the ramp and down it, Fat Bob saw the garage attendant leave his booth and approach the first car in line awaiting its turn to vomit forth into traffic. The attendant, who was surprisingly disheveled and looking more than a little jaundiced, leaned in the car window and started suckling at the driver's face, which caved in rapidly.

Bob winced and turned away to look at Little Willy; Willy shed silent tears as he continued to read the book, as if his now yellow eyes were just as trapped by it as his hands were. Bob caught Speedy's eye in the rear view mirror, hoping he didn't look as terrified as Speedy did.

As the Le Mans blew past and the yellow spread to them, long queues of lower echelon cubicle workers filed down the entrance stairs into the underworld of BART stations running the length of Market. As the lines of people descended, unreassuring noises caterwauled from the depths below – no one was coming back up from underground that Speedy could see. The Muni stops were mobbed by thousands of mass transit commuters fornicating, murdering each other in various creative ways, or doing both simultaneously – the yellow clung to their skin, and their outlines altered in ways not good to see – people melting together into new amalgams, or growing in heaves, or crumbling into dust and scattering away.

As they approached the Montgomery Block, Speedy's eyes traveled up the Transamerica Pyramid's seemingly endless 48-stories to the pointed tip, which stabbed toward heaven – it looked like an extended middle finger, as if SF was flipping the world the bird. Almost against his will, Speedy thought of Little Willy's eternal fascination with the Pyramid. Willy once told Speedy it looked like some kind of cyclopean occult device built by business executives to invoke the Demon of Money and sell their non-existent souls to it. Now it was as if Willy's whimsy had dictated a new reality: the Pyramid hummed with power, and *exuded* a rank sulfurousness that polluted the air around it like a Golden Gate fog bank.

As he careened past Clown Alley, Speedy realized it was a forlorn hope to think heading here could make any difference. The yellow following the Le Mans had caught up, and stained all the surrounding skyscrapers until merging with the more brilliant gold cloud pulsing from the Pyramid – the Pyramid's humming grew ominously louder.

"What do we do now Willy?" Speedy asked, skidding to a stop at the Pyramid's base, next to the main entrance. "C'mon brainiac – what's in that freakin book? How do we make this stop?"

"We don't," Willy said, sounding distracted as he continued scanning the lines. He reached the bottom of the page and it turned by itself to the next, without any outside assistance Speedy or Bob could see. Both Bob and Speedy instinctively did their best not to look directly at the book – but it kept sucking at their attention, there in the corner of their eye.

"We're cards in a deck," Little Willy said. "This time we got shuffled into a lousy hand. But this is only one end for us – the hand will be dealt again, and we'll all be in it. The Yellow King does not rule all, only his own little bedraggled corner. Our tough luck, to die here. But take courage: the book says we'll only have to face a few that are worse than this one, throughout infinity."

"Cut the happy horseshit Willy," Fat Bob shouted. "Fuck the yellow king, figure this out for us."

"I already have," Little Willy said, opening his door and getting out.

Willy walked to the Pyramid's main entrance. The lobby security guard on duty inside no longer fit his rent-a-pig uniform, instead kind of spilling out of it – the clothes were probably the only thing shaping 'him' into any approximation of an oatmeal-hued human form, and if it had a face anymore Speedy couldn't discern it. The amorphous uniformed blob kind of seethed out its seat and reeled to the door, holding it open for Little Willy like a bellboy.

"Willy," Speedy howled, climbing out the car and taking a step toward the entrance with his hand outreached.

Unhurried footsteps sounded – Bob couldn't say if they were a million miles away or right next to his ear, but the delicate footfalls cut through the background noise like they were the only sound in the universe. The lights had gone out inside the Pyramid and, from the depths of the lobby's gloom, a figure appeared and approached.

It was impossibly tall and inhumanly angled beneath its billowing goldenrod-hued ragged robes; its hooded head scraped the ceiling. A ragged mask covered its face with eyes of a sort peering oh-so-tiredly from above the mask's concealment. It reached the door where Willy awaited, and the security blob aimed its featureless face toward the floor as if in awed respect.

The Yellow King fumbled at its tattered mask. Speedy and Fat Bob both gasped and reared back, unable to close their eyes against the upcoming revelation. But Little Willy reached up and stayed the Yellow King's hand, holding out the book as an offering.

The Yellow King pointed its face at Willy, who did not recoil. The King took the book in one taloned paw, clasped Willy's hand, and the two walked back into the darkness together side-by-side.

"Speedy," Bob yelled from the driver's seat. "I'm leaving. You might want to consider going with me."

Speedy got in and they barreled away onto the Embarcadero.

San Francisco screamed. Buildings and hills collapsed all around them and new rules of order arose in novel patterns. The yellow skyline melted and flowed along the hills, the buildings popping into a disjointed array both alien and familiar: a medieval looking ocean of battlements and rooftops, cupolas and towers, as if the entire City had just morphed into one huge haunted castle.

In an electronics store, a three headed elephant puppet was disemboweling another doll over and over on a bank of about a dozen stacked televisions; the puppet entrails spilling out the sacrifice's belly incision were tawny. People shuffled or sprinted about on the sidewalk, many of them already so altered from humanity that their mere outlines were impossible for Bob to look at for more than a second or so.

Fat Bob saw person after person on their knees genuflecting in reverence toward the Pyramid, and the Yellow King. Bob spat out the window.

They hit the Bay Bridge onramp and merged onto the lower deck. Fat Bob tingled in relief – but looking over at Speedy, Bob saw his crimie crying; Speedy's cheeks were wet with tears.

'Willy,' Fat Bob thought, then: 'Fuck that.'

"Don't you dare wuss on me Speedy," Bob snarled. "Don't do that."

"Right," Speedy mumbled. "Right." But he sat up straighter, wiping his face with the back of his hand, and Fat Bob was reassured.

Traffic was thick already, it being rush hour – only now the eastbound span of the Bay Bridge was packed with automotive refugees attempting to flee the City for Oakland just as Speedy and Fat Bob were. Lanes were ignored as cars sideswiped each other, grinding bumpers and trying to squeeze past, under, and over the other cars ahead of them – everyone striving desperately to attain another priceless car length away from the yellow hell unfolding behind them, everyone damning the horrible people occupying the space ahead that they all wanted to move through and occupy.

Almost immediately, Logjam City: the Le Mans couldn't move another inch, and neither could any other auto on the bridge. The two men sat in their seats, both with equally stupid expressions on their face. Cunning was useless now.

"I say we head out to Bakersfield on foot from here," Fat Bob said firmly. "We can lie low out there in the sticks till all this blows over."

"Blows over?" Speedy shook his head and stared at his friend in bemusement, bitterly envious of Bob's utter lack of imagination.

Something clambered down from the upper span, squeezed over the railing and onto the lower level. The thing was maybe the size of a forklift, with way too many legs, a club of a tail held over its head, and numerous hooked grasping members. It was most like a huge, fleshy crab, its skin an unwholesome shade of saffron – hundreds of eyes covered its upper surface, all of them rolling idiotically.

It approached with a surprisingly dainty side step, its shearing mouthparts threshing wetly. It giggled with the voice of a small child as it peeled the top off the nearest car and began eating the passengers like bon-bons – their screams made a dissonant counterpoint to its high pitched titter.

It paused after biting the head off the last passenger, and slowly swiveled until it faced the Le Mans with the decapitated corpse dangling from its grasping members. All its eyes peered at the Le Mans.

"Speedy!" the crab thing crowed in Little Willy's voice, dropping the remnant of its last meal and starting in for them.

Speedy and Fat Bob exited the car with urgency, but the thing was already upon them, and it was not to be denied. It snagged Fat Bob's arm and dragged him up into the air, where he howled as he dangled awaiting ingestion.

Speedy ran toward it with his face in a rictus, letting go with both barrels when he was close enough to touch it. Half its eyes burst under the buckshot – it dropped Fat Bob like a bad habit and shambled rapidly away cursing imaginatively, still in Willy's voice.

"You all right?" Speedy asked Bob, helping him up.

"Just a scratch," Bob said, "Nothing much at all." But the stain spreading on Bob's jacket was yellow, and he wouldn't meet Speedy's eye.

With a metallic shriek the span upheaved as if an earthquake had snapped it loose from its moorings, and it ponderously tilted downward like a dump truck preparing to spill them all into the sea. Fat Bob managed to grab hold of the side railing, but Speedy slid off the ragged edge of the shattered span, barely managing to clutch hold of the ragged edge of asphalt where the span ended.

Cars full of wailing people cascaded past Speedy in a torrent and tumbled in slow motion the hundreds of feet to the water below; the splashes they made on impact were far enough away that the noise took a second to rise up and reach him. Whether in single-minded pursuit or by accident, the big crab thing followed the autos over the edge, its many legs flailing futilely as it fell and disappeared into the depths along with its prey.

Speedy hung above the void, staring about in dismay. Overhead, with a whoosh, the sun went out and night instantly reigned. The brimstone street lights of the Bay popped on for a moment in automatic response, but darkened in an expanding circle as the contagion spread from Willy's ground zero – the darkness crept steadily over Yerba Buena Island and on to the East Bay across the water, continuing up the hills with no indication of slackening speed even as it reached the crest and kept expanding outside the Bay Area basin.

The sky was filled with crazy stars in unfamiliar constellations – appearing and disappearing like winking eyes, pulsing in an obscene sort of Morse code. There was a feeling of pressure above like the sky itself was squeezing down atop them; Speedy's ear drums creaked as if he'd barreled down a steep incline out of the mountains into the lowlands. Then, with a squeak that tremored the world, the night sky inverted into whiteness and the stars turned black in a negative of their former selves. The stars still throbbed and leered like when they were white, but that only made it all seem even more improper somehow.

The asphalt crumbled into dust beneath Speedy's right hand and he yanked that mitt away as if scalded. Speedy dangled by his left hand only now, swinging gently as he considered the yawning gulf beneath.

There were no waves down there where the Bay had been moments before – the surface hundreds of feet below looked ripple-less and silvery and metallic, like a gigantic lake of mercury. The black stars made the mercury glow – or was it shining with its own internal light?

"Bakersfield don't sound like such a bad idea right about now," Fat Bob growled unseen from above him. Bob's voice sounded like he was forcing it through mush.

Here came those quiet footsteps once more, approaching from the far end of the shattered span – quiet as before, but again cutting through all the background noises like it was the only sound in the world.

Speedy let go his grip and twisted into a head down position as he fell. He locked his arms and legs into a ramrod rod straight diver's arrow, just in case it was water down there and he could turn the impact into something survivable.

He fell forever.

D T

By Laird Barron

onsidering his profession, it wasn't surprising that the author would occasionally tell a colorful story dredged from his past. Since his weapon of choice was horror these stories were predictably gruesome.

He'd been stabbed, beaten, burned. He'd initiated misadventures involving felonious exploits and romantic miscalculations. Now he could laugh about it, if bitterly.

The editor sometimes imagined the author as a young Viking biker on the third floor of a tenement, then the bucket of paint thinner splashed in his face, the lighter flare, a fireball, our Viking lad crashing through glass and plummeting into a row of dumpsters and trash bags. After the bounce a few singe marks, a few scrapes, one broken bone, otherwise unscathed except for a burgeoning sense of immortality. Such was the story of his youth. Charmed and cursed at once.

These many years later, the writer had swollen to mammoth proportions, an intimidating mass of muscle beneath the soft pink and gray excess of middle age, a person who was in most ways steadily vanishing from the Earth even as he expanded. His blond hair was long and his handlebar mustache luxurious. His mouth curled in a snarl during sleep. He clenched his left fist like a giant baby, like baby Hercules choking the life from the serpent.

He'd ridden a chopper and worn a bomber jacket in his heyday, had punched the lights out of pigs and rival bikers alike, done a stretch in the pen, standing up, if you must ask. The majority of the scars were on the inside. He'd snorted coke and popped pills and kept the breweries in business. After his reinvention as a pulp lit wunderkind and subsequent ascent through the literary ranks he'd shagged enough groupies to qualify as a minor rock star.

Alas, alack, the star set as stars are wont to do.

No more bestsellers meant no more blow, no more jellybean jars full of pills, no more jellybean jars full of starry-eyed college girls;

down to Schlitz and Jameson and his old Tom cat and Tom's canned cat food. Not sands through the hourglass but smoke through the pipe were the days of his life. Ghosts and demons had come swooping from the wings to bear him away to Valhalla in a plume of fire.

He tossed and thrashed in his slumber and sweated like a man gripped by fever. His lover, the editor, didn't know how to help him. When it got bad, and lately it always was, bad, she smoked Benson & Hedges and perched cross-legged on a chair, nude but for a set of cat's-eye glasses and the fancy camera as ever slung around her neck, watching intently, unable to decipher his delirious muttering. Occasionally she snapped a picture of his comatose form. He too dabbled in photography, one of the mutual loves that kept them together after other loves had sputtered and died. The pictures inevitably developed muddy and grainy as his words.

What was he dreaming?

No mask? No mask! and some bullshit about Camilla was all she got from his raving when she got anything. He'd once mentioned a nightmare of being buried to the neck in sand as the ocean tide came in while world-famous author Stephen King strode toward him decked in an ivory turban and a ragged yellow cloak that dragged the sand like a tail. What could it mean? She didn't think it meant much of anything except that he might have a complex about rich dudes like Stephen King.

He'd also mentioned being followed lately, that he, like everyone, had a doppelganger. He mused that the fucker must be intercepting his royalty checks. This didn't interest the editor – writers were paranoid. No, she dwelt upon other mysteries such as, who the hell was Camilla? Surely not the Camilla. No, surely not.

~*~

The editor was young and wily and after a span in the trenches had landed the fiction editing job at a fresh big city magazine, a science and technology-oriented slick positioned to counterbalance the publishing magnate's interest in high fashion pornography.

The author was two decade's older than the editor and had recently sent his agent novel number seven. Each of the other books had dealt with swashbuckling barbarians matching steel against devils and dinosaurs, or rarely, hard-bitten PIs and their dames versus otherworldly menaces. He mixed a dash of blue collar authenticity and a pinch of literary ambition into the conventional pulp brew. Six times it worked, albeit with diminishing returns.

The agent, who was a mutual friend, had confided to the editor that the new novel was a mess, a kind of Frankenstein teleplay rather than a traditional book, that it wouldn't be winning the author any new fans in the critical establishment, that it would probably sink without a trace and drag the author's dwindling readership to the bottom. What was it about? Who the hell knew? Even the author shrugged off that question and muttered something in Latin she couldn't follow. The agent, still in confidence, had admitted to stalling halfway through the manuscript, of being unsure if he could finish it, much less muster the courage to pitch it to a reputable house.

The author made his bones with the previous six books and another hundred or so short stories, but he'd also done some time editing at weird fiction periodicals and helmed a long-running anthology series that celebrated the best short horror of the calendar year. The anthology gig was in jeopardy due to a climate shift at the publishing house.

The pair had known one another professionally for ages, of course. Genre industry being claustrophobically small, and the science fiction/horror end of the closet all the moreso, it would've been surprising if they hadn't associated at the various conventions and seminars that broke the seasons into manageable chunks. What no one guessed, not even their closest confidants, was the couple engaged romantically with varying frequency and had done so from the beginning. At the outset they'd actually taken some extended holidays together, although as her fortunes ascended and his waned, their ardor cooled. These days it was meet-ups at hotels at prearranged intervals or acts of opportunity during the aforementioned literary conventions. For her the act had become one of charity, residual tenderness in respect of happier times.

Her job at the slick paid substantially better than his anemic sales, so when they rendezvoused once a week to screw and then go dancing she paid the freight. Mostly that meant watching him crack open bottle after bottle from the hotel minibar, or get catastrophically pasted as they waltzed from club to club. Often, their friends and colleagues would accompany them upon these expeditions, never guessing that the couple was actually a couple.

Funny part about the entire affair was, neither had ever taken real measures to keep it a secret. Insomuch as their purviews and spheres of influence made them colleagues and peers rather than supplicant and mistress or master, there wasn't much in the way of conflict of interest. Both, albeit somewhat extravagant in their public personas, were at heart rather discreet, and thus eschewed displays of public affection. Nonetheless, no one ever noted their simultaneous absences from egregiously tedious panels, or how they all too-often walked out of an elevator together, or how they were usually the last to depart the publisher party at the con suite. No one asked and they didn't tell until finally "casually clandestine" became their watchword.

The sum of this being that the editor felt a keen sense of isolation here in the twilight's last gleaming, as it were. She couldn't think of a single person to turn to in her hour of need that didn't present a risk of exposure and scandal. She couldn't think of anyone who'd take the May/December romance seriously.

Thus she observed her lover's gradual decline and slipped in and out of her own increasingly weird dreams that were doubtless a sympathetic response to the man's condition.

~*~

Saturday Night. The author and editor toddled off to their city's version of the Tenderloin and settled in a hole in the wall that catered to the leather and denim set. This was one of those rare occurrences that saw them alone for the entire evening. Joan Jett and the Blackhearts belted from the jukebox, and Lynyrd Skynyrd, and George Thorogood and the Delaware Destroyers. Heads banged and glass smashed.

–Maybe drinking isn't such a grand idea, she said as he brought four double shots of bourbon to the table and slugged them one after another. It was round three for him during the past two hours. Her mostly untouched Long Island Ice Tea had sweated to death in the meanwhile. However, she'd gone through half a pack of cigarettes. – Your color is icky. Ease back on the spurs, have a soda. Come back to the land of the living.

–Hiked the Catskills the other day. There's a herd of magnificent deer back in the hills. I wanted to get a picture. Anyway. Bug season. Ticks, gnats, mosquitoes up the wazoo. Chomped the living shit out of me. He bared his arm momentarily to show off the various red lumps and bumps. —And no deer. Deer shit and ticks and a black forest.

—Maybe you've got malaria, she said, only half in jest.

Bam, bam, bam, bam! He slapped the empty glasses down and grinned at her with the indolent fury of an ancient rogue lion. He patted her hand and grabbed her cigarette and took a greedy drag. —I'm worried about you.

—Oh? Why?

—You talk in your sleep. That ain't good. Means you got mental issues. A guilty conscience.

—I don't have a guilty conscience.

—You should.

—I know, but I don't.

Stereo MC came on with "Connected." She thought the peppy beat masked cosmic horrors. A theme for the modern Lovecrafts.

He snapped his fingers to the beat. —Al died last night. Alden was the author's long-suffering agent and the author spoke of his abrupt demise with a highly affected casualness.

The editor had been away from her office for the weekend , had unplugged the phone as usual, so this news was a punch in the gut. —Holy shit. What happened?

—He was investigating a megalith in Arkham County. The thing fell. He got squished.

—You aren't funny except to look at. Jesus, what happened? I saw Al last week.

—Sorry. I don't know. Cops found him in his apartment this morning. Probably a bum ticker. The author smiled to show it didn't hurt, but his eyes glittered and the pause in his voice was too pronounced. —It'll get sorted. Meanwhile, I'm in a bind. I need a rep. Everybody loves you, E.

—I'm no agent, she said and snatched up the Long Island Ice Tea and drank most of it.

—Just for now. Push my manuscript to some of the big boys, bat your lashes, flash some leg, whatever…

—Nice what you think of my professionalism. I don't need to do that to sell a project.

—Shit, E, I know it. I'm teasing. But dead serious, you gotta help me on this. My head is barely above water. Take a peek is all I ask. He wiped his eyes with the back of his hand and stared into the smoky distance as if focusing on the music. –The funeral. We need to make arrangements

–Okay, okay, she said. No point in a drawn out argument that she was going to lose after a few more rounds. She loved the guy and that was that.

The author smiled and it was sort of genuine. –Gonna shake the governor's hand. He leaned over and kissed her cheek, then lurched upright, nearly upsetting the table. He staggered toward a distant alcove where the bathrooms were stashed. Yuppies and bar toughs alike cleared the hell out of his way as he approached.

She bowed her head and took a breath and asked herself what she'd gotten into all those years ago, what she was going to do.

A stranger stepped from the haze. He said, –Baby, he used to pop them pills and score them hoochie mamas because he could. Now he boozes and does dope because it's the only thing that keeps him level enough to churn out the horseshit he churns out. Except, there's not enough booze or dope to compensate. As for the hoochies, you're the last. Dig?

For a moment she thought her companion had returned from the bathroom, although that was physically impossible. Yet, the voice was correct, so too the general height and features of the man who'd materialized from the smoke and gloom. Her author was dressed in jeans and a leather jacket that no longer zipped properly. This look-alike stranger was leaner by forty pounds and wore a sports coat, slacks, and cowboy boots, all of it crisp. His eyes were hidden behind Hollywood style sunglasses, his long hair was caught in a pony tail. A brother? A cousin? The author as he might've appeared at the end of the road not traveled?

She cleared her throat and forced a smile. –Damn, sorry if my jaw is on the floor. But, the resemblance… Are you related?

–No. The stranger slid into a chair across from her. –I am the doppelganger, at your service. He placed his hands on the table. Large and pale, the left bruised and bloodied across the knuckles from some recent violence, swelling even as she watched.

The editor considered a number of reactions, a couple of them precipitous, and settled on calmness as she might've if confronted by a menacing dog. –They say everybody has a double in the world. She lighted another cigarette and studied the visitor, stalling in the hope that the author would swagger back and put an end to the scene.

Alas, alack.

Finally, the stranger said, –Your boyfriend and I met in Europe. During the war. Remember that train tour of all the old castles and museums…the one you missed? That's the year you landed your job at the slick. Yep, you were too busy schmoozing the brass to hit the road for a vacation with your ever lovin' chum. Well, he was a lost soul and some bad boys sold him worse dope and he went right off the fucking rails. I fastened upon him one night as he lay sweating and raving in his hostel bunk.

–Happened upon him? He's never mentioned you, she said.

–Sure he has. You don't listen so good.

–So well. But I do. And, shit, you're right. He did. Why are you following him? Are you friends? Enemies? An inane question, but the best she could do under the circumstances. She was nervous. Her vision swam from the effects of pounding that damned drink a minute ago…

–It's more of a parasite/host relationship.

–A what?

–Or, perhaps, you could call me his muse. Our pal is awfully productive for a man on the edge of a complete breakdown. As he spoke, the stranger flexed his bruised hand and that reminded her of how the author clenched his fist while asleep.

The editor glanced around. Though the bar was packed, it seemed the two of them occupied a tiny island illuminated by the spotlight of a dull shaded lamp hanging from a chain. She'd dressed in her shortest velvet skirt that usually garnered leers and a few wolf whistles, yet none of the crowd seemed to notice her existence. Even the music had receded to the faint roar of distant surf.

She reached into her purse and came up with the dainty canister of mace she'd kept rattling around since the last time somebody got mugged in her apartment building. –Let's start over. Who are you?

He smiled. Evil twitched the muscles of his jaw and spread fast. –I'm not the only one who's drained the life from him. His fans, his publishers, the critics…

–Who are you?

–Planning to zap me if you don't like the answer?

–Yeah, like a cockroach. She leaned forward so that the nozzle was near his face, saw her shaking hand magnified and reflected in his sunglasses. Her finger caressed the trigger.

–As you say. I am the dreadful one whom Camilla saw.

–Camilla.

–Camilla. No mask. No mask! He hissed to imitate a crowd cheering and made jazz hands.

–Oh, that bitch again. She pressed the trigger, hard.

The stranger inhaled the mist and divided like an amoeba on a slide, his face slithering, sloshing side to side, bisecting, a red crack traveling vertically crown to navel, and the lights in the bar flared black, fist to the eye socket, and back again and he'd vanished.

Far away the bathroom door flew open and the author blundered forth. Blood poured from his right eye and all heads turned to watch him pass. The editor rushed to him and supported his enormous bulk with her slender shoulder. The music crashed and boomed and everyone else ignored them again.

She shouted over the din, entreating him to tell her what happened and to leave at once for the hospital.

–Bah, I'm fine. Woozy is all. He pawed at the blood and wagged his shaggy head in confusion. The gore gave him the appearance of having exploded through a windshield. –Some bastard sucker punched me. Didn't see it coming. Don't need no hospital. Take me home, E. My face hurts.

She took him back to his apartment in a taxi and washed his wounds with hydrogen peroxide. The apartment was a sty– boxes piled up in a maze, a cat box full of cat crap, a rusty radiator thumping beneath the lone window, and on the mildewed brick wall posters of Vonnegut and Einstein, and Vallejo nudes astride prehistoric beasts, overlooking a desk poached from some defunct high school upon which rested his circa 1970s electric typewriter and a mountain of manuscript paper, an overturned pickle bucket serving as office chair; the overwhelming odors of sweat, booze, smoke, and cat. Oh yeah, she instantly remembered why she loathed stepping across the threshold.

The author swigged from a bottle of Jameson and kneaded her ass with his free hand while rambling about his novel, the fucked state of the industry, and the fact he'd lost a step if some no good rat could flatten him with a single blow.

–Honey, I swear the shithead smacked me with a jack handle.

–Shut up and hold still. She dumped the last capful of peroxide into the vicious gash that split his brow and the sluice comingled blood and tears.

Those were the last words they ever exchanged. He fell into farting, snoring slumber punctuated by moans and cries of anguish. She crept away before dawn and collapsed into her own bed in her own flat. Sunday was the only day of the week she ever had to herself and often that simply meant catching up on the myriad clerical details involved in running a major magazine.

~*~

The cops found him three days later after a noise complaint – he'd left the radio volume blasting right before collapsing in the middle of the floor, stone dead. Cardiac arrest precipitated by a swollen liver, the ME said. Liquor and drugs were the main culprits, although some reports circulated that the suffered from Lyme disease.

So the editor attended two funerals in the course of a week. Alden the agent had also died alone and of heart failure. The editor dialed back on cigarettes and alcohol for several days, glimpsing her own future in the mirror of her colleagues' fate. But the bleakness, the loneliness, proved inescapable, and so too the looming notion that her chosen life led to an ineluctable fate, and she wound up smoking and drinking more heavily than ever.

A vacation seemed in order, something to distract from her melancholy. She packed her camera, the author's final manuscript (which she'd snagged from Alden's office when she and a handful of mutual acquaintances carted his possessions into storage), rented a car and drove upstate into the Hudson Valley and took lodging at a quaint bed and breakfast near the hills where her lover often roamed. Her plan was to walk the trails and snap a few pics, shop in the boutiques, drink coffee at the corner café, and make a pass through the book if she could muster sufficient enthusiasm.

The proprietor handed her the keys to a cottage behind the main building and said to buzz if she needed anything. That first night she curled into a ball on the couch, sipped wine by candlelight, listened to a blues station on the radio, unpacked the novel from the travel case she'd stuffed it into, and read the first quarter. Working title D T, and damned if she could decipher from the increasingly esoteric text what that meant. The narrative was eerily disjointed, an amalgam of episodic descriptions of violence and sex and shadowy landscapes populated by alien figures whose inscrutable routines flashed homicidal every few pages. She nodded off and experienced dreams of the sphincter-clenching variety. The one she recalled was of fucking the author in a photo booth while the camera popped, except it was the author's doppelganger and he gazed into her eyes and whispered, It was a warning. And the photo booth became something different–panels in the wall slid aside to reveal nozzle ports of flamethrowers, the teeth of buzz saws and augers–

She awoke with a scream for possibly the first time in her life. Following a dispirited breakfast in the main house dining room, she dressed in cargo shorts and hiking boots and spent the day wandering the wooded hills in a daze. Her legs were leaden, her skull ached, every crackling branch, every shifting leaf caused her to jump in fright, which in turn annoyed her enough to continue ever farther into the underbrush. There were no deer in evidence. She stubbornly photographed deer wallows and piles of deer scat, the meandering trails that bored like tunnels through the wood. In one respect her luck was better than the author's: most of the bugs had died or gone into hibernation and after slathering herself in repellent she suffered few bites.

Dinner at the house, which she again had to herself except for the proprietor and a bored waiter. Then she stumbled to her cottage and fell onto the couch, foregoing the customary nightcap. All day her thoughts had inexorably cycled between last night's nightmare and the nightmarish spell the novel had cast upon her.

Thus she sat by the flickering glow of a candle, the manuscript in her lap, her thumb poised to separate the pages to her previous mark. And thus she finally noticed the glossy black spot the diameter of a dime attached to her thigh, although several more seconds passed before she recognized this as the monstrously fattened body of a tick.

I fastened upon him one night…

Resisting the urge to shriek in terror and revulsion, she took a shuddering breath and snicked the wheel of her lighter and when it bloomed applied the flame to the insect. It retracted from her within moments and dropped onto the floor, leaking black fluid as it waddled for safety.

The editor snatched the block of a manuscript and walloped the tick, crushed it against the pine floorboards with an audible crunch. Blood trickled from the tiny hole in her thigh. More blood, black as an oil slick, oozed from beneath the book.

So much blood one would think…one might think…

Her head swam as it had that night at the bar and her bizarre en-counter with the stranger and she covered her eyes to stop the room's spinning. She was afraid to vomit because she was suddenly convinced blood would spray from her mouth instead of the salmon and curry she'd eaten for dinner.

The vertigo receded and she steadied herself, wiped away tears and snot, and lifted the manuscript, pried it, from the caved-in skull of the man at her feet, and the paper was heavy, sodden with all that blood and brain matter. Gore saturated the stack from the bottom; the paper sucked it up like a sponge until darkness blotched the title page, obliterated the title itself in a Rorschach pattern of Hell.

Someone knocked and the front door swung open and a figure stood silhouetted in the frame, behind it a purple twilight and the yellow moon cracked and gaping as it swooped toward the earth. The distant city should've glowed upon the horizon, but

The figure said in a voice that she recognized, –Where will we go?

–These pages are stuck together, she said. –I'll never know how it ends.

there were no other lights

Salvation in Yellow

By Robin Spriggs

addy. Preacher Daddy. Preacher Daddy had said that Jesus would come—that Jesus would come before the Highway did. But Jesus had not come. The Highway had, but Jesus had not. The Highway had come within thirty cubits of Preacher Daddy's porch. The front porch. The porch that was her porch now—now that Preacher Daddy was gone. The Highway had come and Jesus had not. The Highway had come and brought with it all that was wrong with the world, all that Preacher Daddy had warned against, all that God despised. But she had to be strong. She had to be brave. For Preacher Daddy as well as herself.

"Fear not, my child," he had said, all those years ago. "Greater is He that is in you than he that is in the world."

"Who is *He?*" she had asked.

"Why, Jesus, of course."

"How do you know?"

"There's no mistaking Jesus."

"No. I mean, how do you know he's *in* me?"

"Because I put him there, my child."

"How?"

"With discipline and prayer. And with *this*!" He brandished his Bible above his head. "The word of the Almighty God!"

Discipline, prayer, and the Bible—the three great constants of her life, the three square meals of her spiritual day. Discipline she understood: Preacher Daddy's belt, the back of his rock-hard hand, and the countless welts and bruises they had left upon her person. Prayer, though, was trickier. A thing of smoke and mist. Impossible to grasp. *She* had prayed, too, after all. Prayed for many things. Things

263

she never got, but . . . but the Bible was even harder—harder, in a way, than Preacher Daddy's hands and harder to grasp than prayer—the words too difficult, the language so strange. English, yes, but not. So Preacher Daddy helped her.;God's words were *his* words, after all, so who would know better than he?

But Preacher Daddy had other ways, too, other ways of putting Jesus in her—other, *secret* ways: when he came into her room in the night, came into her room with his rock-hard hands, and his rock-hard words, and the rock-hard something that lived between his legs.

Preacher Daddy was gone now, though. Long, long gone. All that remained was his house and his Bible and his promise—his promise that Jesus would come.

Promises. Contradictions. Riddles. *How*, she wondered, *can Jesus be in me if I'm still waiting for him to come?*

"One thing at a time," she told herself aloud. "First the house, then the Bible, then the promise." That's how Preacher Daddy would have wanted it. Everything in its proper order. Everything in its place. *House. Bible. Promise.*

House.

Bible.

Promise.

~*~

Thirty cubits. Forty-five feet. She had measured the distance herself, with her own forearms, just as Preacher Daddy had taught her. She was a big girl. Tall. From elbow to the tip of her middle finger, exactly a foot and a half. "A cubit, right on the nose," Preacher Daddy had said with a sparkle of pride in his eye. So *of course* she had measured the distance, stealing from the house late on a moonless night, when the traffic had slackened a bit and she was least likely to be seen. On the parched, cracked ground she crawled; on the hard red Georgia clay; from the base of the high front porch to the edge of the blacktop serpent that had done what Jesus had not; elbow to fingertip, elbow to fingertip.

Thirty cubits. The height of Noah's Ark. The distance from the house to the—

She jerked her hand back from the asphalt. It tingled. Felt cold.

No, hot!

No, cold!

She shivered.

"The Enemy is strong," Preach Daddy had said, "beyond our power to measure. But greater is He that is in you than he that is in the world."

The world, she thought, *the earth*, remembering another bit of scripture that Preacher Daddy had preached. From the book of Job. A dialogue between God and Satan. "Whence comest thou?" God had asked. And Satan had answered, "From going to and fro in the earth, and from walking up and down in it."

Greater is He that is in you than he that is in the world.

She looked from her hand to the Highway. The blacktop was hardly visible in the night, but the double yellow line that ran along its middle seemed to glow with a light of its own.

~*~

The pines had grown fast—the small, young pines she had gathered from the woods out back and planted in three long rows between the house and . . . and oh, how fast they had grown, from weeds to trees in a few short weeks. Or months. Or years. Time could be tricky, just like prayer. Maybe . . . maybe that's what it was. A prayer. A prayer from the past to the future. Or from the future to the past. With moments of . . . of "now" in between. Between. Between the house and the . . . the . . .

"This house is our Ark," Peacher Daddy had said. "Our bastion. Our fortress. Our sanctum afloat on a sea of boundless sin. It protects us, my child, and we—you and I alone—must protect it."

Hence the pines, the wall of trees, the barrier between . . . between . . .

But she could still see the accursed thing, by day at least, not clearly but enough, along with the roaring monsters that rode upon its back—the glinting, steel-skinned beasts whose thoughts were as loud as their roars.

Cacodemons, Preacher Daddy had called them. The Noisy Ones. The Screamers.

Screamers?

"Don't be a Screamer," Preacher Daddy had said, when he came into her room late at night with Jesus on his mind and Jesus on his lips and Jesus in his—

Is that what I sounded like? The thought made her dizzy. Sick to her stomach. "Forgive me, Preacher Daddy. Forgive me. I . . . I didn't . . . I didn't know."

But now she did. It was her *job* to know. Her calling. Her purpose. The house must be protected, the Ark kept afloat, the Highway held at bay. The Highway and its . . . its . . .

Even at night she could see them, their eyes burning bright beyond the pines, burning yellow-white, coming and going, going and coming.

What are they looking for?

"Your mama was a Screamer, too," Preacher Daddy had said. "I tried to help her, but she wouldn't listen. Screamers never do. All they do is—"

Me? For me? Why would they be looking for . . .?

She lowered the blinds, closed the drapes, turned away from the window. "No more," she vowed. "No more looking. I promise, Preacher Daddy. I . . . I . . ."

HouseBiblePromiseHouseBiblePromise . . .

~*~

And she had kept her word. She had always kept her word.

In the beginning was the Word, and the Word was with God, and the Word was God.

But little good it had done. Her word. Her promise. She could still . . . still see them. See them with her ears. See them in her head. The Highway. The Noisy Ones. The . . .

Screamers never do. All they do is—

Their thoughts were so loud. So wicked. So . . .

"So why? Why me? Why are they thinking of me?"

So loud. So wrong. So . . .

So she withdrew. Deeper into the house. Farther from the Highway. From its sounds. Its looking. Its thoughts. Deeper and deeper, forsaking first the parlor, then the living room, then her own bedroom, a room a week, or month, or year, hard to tell, to tell time, time and space, space and time, each a prayer, one inside the other, *deep* inside, *deeper and deeper,* first the parlor, then the living room, then her own bedroom, bearing the Bible with her, Preacher Daddy's Bible, *her* Bible now, big, black, heavy, bursting with pages, splitting at the spine, sometimes open, sometimes closed, but talking all the way, to her, in Preacher Daddy's voice, asking . . . *Whence comest thou?* . . . answering . . . *From going to and fro in the earth, and from walking up and down in it* . . . promising . . . *Greater is He that is in you than he that is in the . . . in the. . .* but over all the talk—over it, below it, beyond it—she could still . . . still hear . . . still hear the . . . the Highway . . . the Highway and its . . . its . . . it's still . . . still here . . . still here . . .

~*~

So deeper still she ventured, into areas of the house she had never before seen, rooms she never knew existed, some cluttered, some empty, but all of them—all of them . . . *off* . . . askew . . . just slightly at first, then more so, and more so, till finally she was forced to go about on all fours and brace herself against the walls and cling to doorways like a . . . like a sailor on a ship or . . . or Noah on his Ark or . . . or Jesus on his . . . on his . . .

"Cross my heart and hope to . . . hope to . . . cross my heart and hope to . . ."

HouseBiblePromiseHouseBiblePromise . . .

From doorway to doorway she staggered, lurched, crawled, room after room after . . . each one more crooked, more canted than the last. Odder. Stranger.

A strange woman is a narrow pit.

"I know, Preacher Daddy. And I—I'm sorry. I'm sorry but . . . but I . . .

But the Bible was changing too, changing right in her hands, under her arm, against her breast, in her lap . . . cover fading . . . pages darkening . . . once so white . . . so bright . . . now dingy . . . yellowed . . . like the . . . the double line . . . the double line that . . . and the *bones* . . . the bones in the woods . . . the woods out back . . . the pretty little bones that . . . that Preacher Daddy had arranged in . . . in strange patterns . . . in the garden . . . the *secret* garden . . . the Garden of . . . of Gethsemane . . . GetHimInMe . . . HimInMe . . . Him . . . *Greater is He that is . . .* arranged in strange patterns and . . . and forced her . . .

267

once so white, so bright . . . forced her to . . . now dingy, yellowed . . .
to squat above and . . . and make water . . . make water on the . . . the
pretty little . . . over and over . . . again and again . . . so much water . .
. so much rain . . . forty days and . . . and forty nights . . . or months .
. . or years . . . hard to tell . . . to tell time . . . but time is . . . time is but
a . . . life is but a . . .

"Row, row, row your boat, gently down the . . . gently down the . . ."

~*~

The Lord sitteth upon the Flood; yea, the Lord sitteth King for ever.
"Yes, but . . . but *which* Lord? *Which* King?"
Greater is He that is in you than . . . than He that is in the . . . in the .
. . the woods . . . the woods out back . . . *back!* . . . deeper and deeper . .
. stranger and stranger . . . *a strange woman is a* . . . is a . . . arranged in
strange patterns and . . . and forced . . . forced to . . . to . . .

"Gently down the . . . gently down the . . ."

"A doubt is a leak, my child," Preacher Daddy had said. Or had he?
Yes. Oh, yes. Many times. And was still . . . *still* saying it. In the Bible.
In the House. In her head. *A doubt is a leak, my child, a leak in the hull
of the Ark. And the smallest leak left unrepaired will* . . .

"I know," Preacher Daddy. "I know. But . . . but . . ."

But the Bible was leaking, too . . . pages . . . passages . . . promises .
. . *HouseBiblePromiseHouseBible* . . . once so . . . so white . . . so bright
. . . now dingy . . . yellowed . . . like the . . . the pretty . . . the pretty
little . . . arranged in strange patterns and . . . and leaking . . . oozing .
. . bleeding . . .

"Merrily, merrily . . . yellowy, yellowy . . . life is but a . . . life is but
a . . ."

But still she could hear them. Still she could see them. The . . . the
Highway . . . the Noisy Ones . . . the . . . the . . .

~*~

So deeper still she crawled. Deeper and deeper. Stranger and
stranger. Rooms twisting. Bible leaking . . . pages . . . passages . . .
portals . . . leaking . . . oozing . . . bleeding . . .

"Merrily, merrily . . . yellowy, yellowy . . . life is but a . . . life is but
a . . ."

For the blood is the life.

Yes, but—but *whose* blood? *Whose* life? And why so . . . so . . . so *why* . . . why did . . . why did you . . . it was . . . was *mine* . . . *mine!* . . . and you . . . you . . .

What's yours is mine, my child. What's yours is—

~*~

Deeper and deeper . . . stranger and stranger . . . yellower and yellower . . . pages . . . passages . . . portals . . . rooms no longer rooms . . . just twists and turns and . . . and words . . . endless, mazelike words . . . winding . . . worming . . . calling . . . but . . . but the voice . . . the voice was different now . . . stranger . . . deeper . . . yellower . . . and . . . and changing . . . changing the . . . the shape . . . the shape of the . . . the House . . . bending its boards . . . warping its . . . its angles . . . *angels?* . . . arranged in strange . . . *angels?* . . . and . . . and changing . . . calling . . . *her* calling . . . her *purpose* . . . the . . . the House . . . she could . . . could feel . . . feel herself . . . *touch myself?* . . . feel herself becoming . . . becoming more . . . more a part of . . . of . . . of *It* . . . the House . . . the Bible . . . the Promise . . . flesh of Its flesh . . . blood of Its blood . . . bone of Its . . . Its . . .

~*~

It's mine . . . *mine!* . . . what's mine is . . . is Its . . . what's Its is . . . is . . . arranged in . . . in strange . . . and . . . and squatted above . . . rained upon . . . rained and rained and . . . yellow . . . so yellow . . . so very, very . . . sorry . . . so sorry . . . so very, very . . . but he . . . he made me . . . *made me* . . . I tried . . . tried to keep . . . keep you safe . . . sound . . . secret . . . but . . . but he . . . he . . .

~*~

Greater is He that is . . . but which He? . . . which Lord? . . . which King? . . . *Witch!* . . . *Witch!* . . . *Suffer not a witch to* . . . *to* . . . life is but a . . . life is but a . . . but he . . . he took . . . took *you* instead . . . took you away and . . . and forced . . . forced me to . . . to . . . sorry . . . so sorry . . . . so very, very . . .

~*~

Forty days and forty nights . . . or months . . . or years . . . or . . . but deeper . . . stranger . . . yellower . . . the House . . . the Bible . . . the Promise . . . and the . . . the *bones* . . . the bones in the woods . . . the woods in the bones . . . wood and bone . . . bone and wood . . . hers and . . . and Its . . . Its and . . . and . . .

~*~

Deeper . . . stranger . . . yellower . . . *HouseBiblePromise* . . . *House-BibleIt* . . . *HouseBibleHer* . . . one and the . . . the same . . . the very, very . . . like . . . like time and . . . and prayer . . . and . . . one inside the other . . . *deep* inside the other . . . one and . . . and the same . . . the very, very . . . verily, verily . . . merrily, merrily . . . life is but a . . . life is but a . . .

~*~

An ark! . . . yes! . . . an ark . . . *the* Ark . . . the Ark of the . . . the Covenant . . . the Promise . . . the Promise that . . . that Jesus would . . . Jesus wood . . . wood and . . . and *bones* . . . so many, many bones . . . once so . . . so little . . . so weak . . . now big . . . now strong . . . and . . . and yellow . . . so yellow . . . like the . . . the *line* . . . the *double* line . . . the double yellow line . . . on the . . . the . . .

~*~

It came . . . *It* came . . . not . . . not Jesus . . . but . . . but *It* . . . *IT* . . . and for . . . for *her* . . . just her . . . her and her alone . . . her and . . . and It . . . It and . . . and her . . . two of a kind . . . one and the . . . the same . . . Promises made . . . Promises kept . . . *HouseBibleIt* . . . *HouseBibleHer* . . . together . . . at last . . . again . . . *forever* . . . and . . . and . . .

~*~

Leaking . . . foundering . . . sinking . . . but . . . but merrily . . . merrily . . . and . . . and gently . . . so gently . . . gently down the . . . gently down the . . .

~*~

HIGHWAY . . . MY way . . . THE way . . . I! . . .

~*~

I am the WAY, the truth, and the . . . the . . .

~*~

Life is but a . . . life is but a . . .

~*~

Merrily . . . merrily . . .

~*~

Yellowy . . . yellowy . . .

~*~

Down . . .

~*~

. . . down . . .

~*~

. . . down . . .

The Beat Hotel
By Allyson Bird

O f course all the artists, if they could get it, chose Room 41 of The Beat Hotel, in Rue Git-Le-Coeur. The view over the rooftops was inspiring. An artist, who called herself Juliette, had got into some of the rooms that were unlocked, had taken the grubby pillows and ripped them open. She flung the feathers from the window declaring that winter had come early, and that they would all feel the better for it. That would be doubtful of course because it would be freezing in the shabby place in winter. Still Madame Rachou forgave her, eventually, although Juliette had to give her three of her best paintings, or she would have had to leave. The tally of paintings in her head that she owed herself increased by three. Madame Rachou forgave artists almost anything. She let them do what they wanted in their rooms—there they could reinvent themselves a thousand times over within those walls.

Some of the artists chose the cells in the hotel. They would have an iron bed, small radiator and a chair, one light bulb hanging from an extra thin cord. No window. Cellular. On their own, almost finished with their writing of books and poems, but hoping for some fire before the last ember died away. Before they felt too tired, too worn down, too dim that they let their star fade. All they needed was a breath of fine air, a wealth of fortune, a hideaway that was properly hidden away. A life in death episode. A death in life ritual. An ending. Once more to a barricade (that would come later) with more cobbles than when the Bastille was stormed.

Juliette without her balcony. How would the heavens hear her words and any would-be lover on the street also? She had no need of love anyway— she would not pay lip service to sex. The heavens would wait for her a while longer whilst she finished her paintings.

Madame Rachou had a cat, war torn from scraps with dogs, and other such things. The cat licked her underbelly, on her back; leg pointed straight up, an elastic off white dough leg stretched from a table. The same cat had been kicked into the Seine many times and had always come back meowing for more, more from what life could throw at her. More from Madame and more fondling in the places she like to be fondled. The cat who whispered in Madame's ear about what she had seen. Spread legs and arses, skinny, plump, and round. Madame visibly drooled at the images described by the cat that shook its paw at the Seine like one would an old friend in jest. That cat would see that river again and again. The river could not lose—could it? Could it have won if a cat's body rotted in it? Would the piss bed river lose its attraction for lovers then?

Juliette had let the cat into her room and the cat had run away screaming. It had seen those paintings on the walls. Juliette could get down to it alright. She could paint those figures in those positions, doing those things, which drive men mad and women too, but she had to always take it one step further. One Step Beyond. Remember that do you? The cat had taken that step many times and it would report back to its mistress—that it had gone into forbidden territory, and that there was a man it had never seen before sat in an threadbare armchair. The scalloped edge of his yellow gown reaching out for the cat as it fled. Madame Rachou once had the courage to ask Juliette who her visitor was and how he was never seen entering or leaving the hotel? Juliette simply whispered, 'Carcosa' as if that was the answer to it all.

In her room Juliette found some space on the wall, brushed her dark hair away, and put her ear against it. Could she hear? Could she hear? Yes. 'Carcosa.' 'Carcosa.' 'Carcosa.'

Perhaps this time? She dipped her paint brush in the pot. Golden yellow. The colour perhaps that had made Van Gogh go mad with his blessed sunflowers? Could a colour make you go mad? Juliette held the brush, dripping the gold paint on the floorboards where it piggy-backed the citrine, that held fast in the faded linoleum. What other colours could have made other artists go mad? She tried to think. If she was held in a room where the walls were painted white, for days on end, or if psychedelic colours swirled around one another in a continuous effort to merge, and failing—would that do it? She was sure it would. The forms she painted and that the cat ran away from were liberating—weren't they?

The king seemed to find them so.

She painted them for him. Juliette turned and smiled at him. He nodded.

There came a knock on the door and Juliette, startled, turned quickly and dropped her brush. She never ran out of yellow paint and as it fell to the floor the yellow poured from the brush and under the skirting board. It flowed freely.

No brush could hold that much paint she considered.

It was Chapman. He had come back or did he ever really leave? He took her picture before she could object. He even managed with his snake arm to manoeuvre around the door and her, and take another of her room. Then it snaked back and he was gone. She slammed the door. She did not care.

The king had retreated for now.

Her hunger got the better of her. Would she go to the café at the bottom of the stairs? Raul would be there with his monotone eyes and his ever wandering hands. Occasionally she sat with him. He had once glanced over to Madame Rachou, placed his hand under Juliette's short skirt, felt for her clitoris, and pinched hard—removing his hand quickly. Juliette had screamed, jumped and then smiled. The cat simply thought it wouldn't have to report back to his mistress as she had seen it first-hand. Could a cat smile? It did.

No. Not that café today.

The Beat Hotel had come close to being closed down in 1963. Madame Rachou had cleaned it up a little, it was a thirteen-class establishment after all, and so it didn't require much work. Any crumbling brickwork was put right. Bugs killed off. It was still the 60's and the place was still filthy but the authorities tended to look the other way.

Vietnam in the headlines daily and she played Bob Dylan's "Lay Lady Lay" as she painted. Only that song—nothing else.

The paint brush still oozed more yellow paint than it should hold and had found the gaps between floorboards. Half the floor was covered with linoleum and inundated with scores of stiletto heal marks from a previous occupant.

I smell like the fish I ate last night she thought.

Juliette smiled. She knew Rimbaud. 'Life is the farce we are all forced to endure.' And his descent into madness or truth. Juliet had decided long ago that poets don't re-create the world. They create worlds.

Rimbaud again. 'In the morning when, with Her, you fought in the dazzle of the snow, the green lips, the ice, the black flags and blue rays, and the purple perfumes, of the polar sun – your strength.'

The door opened again and the cat came in. It seemed in a good enough mood but kept its head low and didn't look at the walls. It sniffed at the yellow paint and sat with its back to Juliette. Its eyes—almost totally eclipsed by the black iris in each. Twins suns. Black holes. For a moment she was reminded of the giant dogs in Hans Christian Anderson's The Tinder Box. Those enormous saucer eyes.

A knock at the door. It was Madame Rachou this time. Juliette put her head to one side and studied the woman for the moment. She had lively blue eyes that danced the can can, looking at Juliette's breasts, then the eyes and then the breasts…you know, the way some men do. Madame Rachou wasn't a man, at least Juliette didn't think she was, or was that a hint of a moustache above her upper lip? Juliette laughed out loud as she pictured the woman in a man's clothes and perhaps a Dali moustache. Madame smiled. She was used to Juliette.

Madame handed her a new rent book. Juliette thanked her politely and closed the door, quickly. She remembered the time Madame had given her the first rent book. How long ago was that? She certainly couldn't be bothered to check the date. Juliette threw it onto the desk near the window. Just above it, stuck to the wall, was the postcard Victor had sent to her. He'd drawn a caricature of them both by the Seine. She remembered that day quite clearly—when they had walked along the banks talking about the exhibition they had planned together. It had never materialised but they had both got drunk that summer evening and had flung poems into the water. Had they been any good she thought? The ink would have been washed away but they had fantasised that the words would come together again off the paper and ripple through the water to be washed up on a distant shore, perhaps—Carcosa. Black ink bleeding. She thought of floating in that obsidian water, letting the current take her to the darker sea. And on that sea she became surrounded by pure white orchids for as far as the eye could see.

What happened to Kaja and her book of Human Songs? Had there been anything sweet in them? Human. Returned to dust. Or be black and white. So white. Thousands of doves flying together against the snow and one black rock in the way. Obsidian. Pearl. Sand, and finally glass. Dozens of thick, dark green glass panes in a window with the reflection of one gone now within each.

Juliette recalled her childhood and remembered her dress with tiny red roses on it. She'd spilt the wine. The tiny pink and grey felt hat with Calais on it. Her father had shown her the way and she hadn't looked back since. Her earliest memory. Looking through the bars of her cot into the shadows—looking for the one. Always the one. Never found. The great gaping mouth of the wood beneath her house and all it promised to give her. The two ladies selling Spanish. Another time—the memory of jasmine. The Steiff bear her brother had brought her back from Germany. If you tipped it up it growled. It sat next to the monkey with the cymbals. The bear. Evil thing that was. Would pull her hair and tug the covers off her at night and then roll itself in them near the window where it snored until dawn. The first chink of light through the gap in the curtain made its brown eyes flare and then it would just be a silly stuffed blurred pink bear with a faded red ribbon at its neck. How she wished she had cut its head off in the daytime so it would not scare her at night.

The others had wished to meet The King. They had pleaded with him to come to them. He had taken Victor but not her. Why couldn't she go?

Victor had been back to see her just the once. At least she thought he had. One cold winter night, she'd been drinking again, and shivered under her thin grey blankets. She felt his body close to her and an arm around her waist. Then a wonderful dream—as a child she had seen a tapestry in some old castle or other and depicted upon it was a hunting party, in medieval dress. The woman in a long pink gown— the man in red. They rode white horses and two pale greyhounds looked back at the man and the woman, waiting for instruction. The hooded birds. All through the dream the rhyme played in her head, 'with rings on her fingers and bells on her toes she shall have music wherever she goes…'

The bird flew in through the window. A falcon no less. In Paris? Always a sign. One thing leading to another— down a dim passageway in the Latin Quarter—over the tiny bridge in Venice. They always follow don't they? Nobody to shout out and say, 'Idiot.' Don't you see? No seer in sight, no messenger to shoot or save the day. No daylight now and forever. Forever. Eternity under twin moons. The falcon circled once and flew into the wall as if trying to get through. It broke its neck in the attempt. And blood on the neck of the man on the wall now, before the guillotine descends.

Juliette thought of her father. He said he was a travelling salesman. She rarely saw him for weeks on end and in her strange mind he was the national executioner, Monsieur de Paris. His was the face of the man on the wall. Looking directly at her. She remembered her childhood—a difficult one with loveless parents. An only child. A disowned child. A child allowed to run wild in the streets and the street filth run wild in her. A special child. She'd had to become that.

Juliette pulled the bright green ribbed sweater over her head. It was short. She liked the look of her bare midriff. She then looked out of the window. Would she care if it was cold? She had a black anorak. That would do. She put it on hastily. She only had one pair of shoes—pumps, really. They had been white once. She picked up her battered brown leather duffle bag and left the room. Down the stairs careful not to slip, she had done that too many times before, and out the door.

Paris in the rain. She didn't mind. Juliette always saw the exterior of the buildings in blue and grey. Everywhere grey walls and blue roofs when they should have been grey or rust coloured. Blue roofs—just like the hunting lodge in the tapestry.

She'd go to help Michel on his bouquinistes stall on the bank of the Seine in exchange for a few francs towards the rent and some food. Juliette was good at selling things even herself sometimes.

'Ah, here is my Juliette. Everyone's Juliette!' Michel kissed her passionately on the mouth. She liked the taste of brandy on his tongue.

'Have you sold much this morning?'

'A little. Not much. But now you are here with your sweet words no doubt we will have some sales soon.'

Michel had rigged a tarpaulin over the simple wooden structure and all the old books were laid out on pieces of old carpet, not much protection against the rain, and yet they never felt damp to the touch.

'Did you read the book? Asked Juliette.

'You know nothing in the world could persuade me to open that book.' Only you are going to sell that book, Juliette. I don't know where you got a box full of them. Don't want to know. Shouldn't be stocking the damn thing. I don't know why I am.'

Juliette smiled and opened the box. She had never opened the book either but she had known of many who had and what had happened to them.

She looked up aware of eyes on her. Two young men. One taller than his darker haired companion. They stared at her and at the copy of the book she held in her hand. One whispered into the ear of the other, his hand on the other's arm. The smaller one pushed his hand away. He walked towards her. His finger trembled slightly as he pointed at the book.

'Is that really what I think it is? A copy of the play—The King in Yellow?'

Juliette nodded.

'I'll take a copy.' He thrust a bundle of notes at her. She took what she thought fair and handed the rest back to him with the book.

The taller one joined the boy who turned the book over and over in his hands. He introduced them both to Juliette. Michel looked on—amused.

'I'm Henry and this is Charles...and your name is?'

'Juliette.'

Both young men smiled. She always got that smile when she told anyone.

'Have you lived in Paris long?'

'Long enough.'

They talked for a little while. Juliette told them where she lived. They were impressed as they knew the history of the hotel. And of the beats who had lived there not long ago.

'Did you ever meet Burroughs?'

'Yes. Great writer. Do you two write?'

She knew the answer straight away. Writers. Lost in Paris. Lost in translation. Finding themselves through other writers. Other writers moving on. All artists consumed by a need to find that ultimate experience through prose or not. Climbing higher. Seeking more until the fall. THE fall.

'Would you show us the hotel sometime? Charles smiled.

'I will.' Decisive. It was almost like a marriage vow. Almost.

Juliette arranged to meet them the next day at the hotel. She asked them for the book back explaining that she would get it signed by someone, and that they would be impressed when they eventually saw it. Charles politely declined.

By lunchtime Juliette was hungry and bored with the tourists. No more writers had happened her way. With a nod to Michel, he gave her some francs, and she was off again. She took a few copies of The King in Yellow for the owner of the Shakespeare bookshop. He always placed them on the highest shelves in a bookcase or in boxes behind boxes so that only the most fervent, the most devoted, would find them. He had never read the play either. Most with any sense hadn't.

Floor after floor of shelves and books of all the ages attracted Juliette and she roamed up through each level pulling down large dusty tomes—always searching for references to the forbidden and the profane, the unusual and the exotic, the extreme and those sentences put together in such a simple way that molten gold poured from the pages. The yellow again. She found the 'other' books wrapped in yellow paper. Between those covers could be found exquisite pleasure and pain. Escape.

She found an old armchair and flopped down with a book. Under pretence of reading she watched the people come and go. Juliette could see. She could really see now. She could see into their hearts and minds and saw which hand fate had dealt them. She watched the girl with the floppy blue hat, white lace scarf, paisley blouse and red cotton skirt that swept against the piles of tatty magazines. A man followed her up the stairs. He was much older than her but could still seduce young women. He was about to talk to the girl. Juliette could see that. He'd brush her arm with his hand as he pulled down a book next to her. He apologised and smiled—those bright blue eyes still doing their thing—she had seen him in the shop before. An Englishman. Cunningham she believed he was called. He didn't care who he enrolled into his little cabal. So what if the woman was married or had a child. That didn't matter to him. He never tried for Juliette. He knew better to. He could not surprise her at all. Not at all. He had many books bound in yellow. His heart was made of shadow and she mused that he had lived many times before. Kin to the King in Yellow perhaps? Juliette reminded herself to ask him about Cunningham though she guessed already what the answer would be. When she looked into the heart of the girl she laughed out loud. What foolishness. A fool on an errand with cock in hand. That girl would run a mile.

Juliette looked up and saw a book cover facing out. Unusual for the bookshop as there was so little room. On it was the caricature of a fool, imagine one that Beardsley would draw, an elegant fool if you like. Fools. Fiends. Fallacy. Dogs. Delicacy. Devilry.

Devilry. Der Puderquast. The naked woman being carried by a man with a goat's head and someone else. The someone else wasn't important. Beardsley would be her brother one day. Leda and the swan flew into her mind then.

Ah. Cunningham and the young girl were leaving together. So

soon. What a fool. His arm around her waist and then insisting he goes first down the steep steps. The steps would become steeper for that girl.

Juliette yawned. Time to go home. Not a home. Just a place to drift through. She'd get some wine on the way.

Out into blue and grey again. Rain. She saw Cunningham in the distance, still with his arm around the girl. Where was he taking her? Juliette followed. She was curious to see where he lived. A grand apartment perhaps? The girl laughed. Enchanted. Juliette thought of her King in Yellow and turned away from them. She thought of Henry and Charles. Could they write astounding literature? She would find out and no doubt be bored again in minutes. It had happened before.

Halfway home she sat down on a bench and waited. She could hear the sound of the riot, the students up in arms only to have them tied behind their backs again. The workers looking for more than they had— and why not?

She walked towards the noise. She thought of actresses in ancient Rome. They used to act naked. One didn't. Juliette had heard that the actress had said, 'I'd rather give pleasure to few with my talent than many with my body.' A riot ensued and she was thrown off the stage. Always by choice, girl. Always by choice. These rioters wanted social justice. Then again in 1229, after the student riots, they closed the university for two years. Who noticed?

Juliette walked by those throwing petrol bombs and over turning cars. She looked up and saw The King in Yellow. He faced her but his hood hid his eyes. She felt them. She saw Henry and Charles running ahead over the cobblestones. Charles slipped and the book he had bought that day slid under a burning car. Juliette smiled at that.

Perhaps it would be time to leave now but would HE give her permission?

Madame Rachou looked at her with a sad smile on her ruby red lips as Juliette entered the hotel. She didn't run up the steps. There wasn't any rush. He was waiting for her in her room. The King in Yellow reached out and she took his hand. The wall became a blaze of one colour—the yellow. Juliette melted into it and as she did she saw her father look at her with pleading eyes. He was on his knees. The guillotine blade fell. The sound of it thundered through her blood. A few seconds and she had left her world, and that other half –world between walls. Juliette looked up to see the twin moons.

This was where true Carcosian's go when they are finished with those pale places. Rimbaud, Bierce, Villon, Romualdo Locatelli, Hart Crane, Kaja, Lew Welch—even Corso managed. Helen Strange can be found there— too.

The cat followed them.

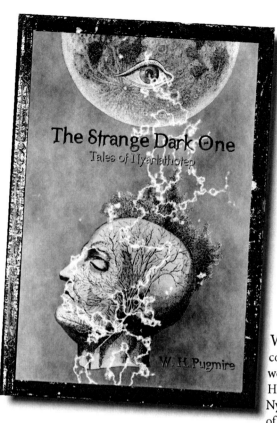

With *The Strange Dark One,* W. H. Pugmire collects all of his best weird fiction concerning H. P. Lovecraft's dark god, Nyarlathotep. This avatar of the Great Old Ones is Lovecraft's most enigmatic creation, a being of many masks and multitudinous personae. Often called The Crawling Chaos, Nyarlathotep heralds the end of mortal time, and serves as avatar of Azathoth, the Idiot Chaos who will blow earth's dust away. Many writers have been enchanted by this dark being, in particular Robert Bloch, the man who, through correspondence, inspired Wilum Pugmire to try his hand at Lovecraftian fiction. This new book is a testimonial of Nyarlathotep's hold on Pugmire's withered brain, and these tales serve as aspects of a haunted mind. Along with stories that have not been reprinted since their initial magazine appearances, The Strange Dark One includes "To See Beyond," a sequel-of-sorts to Robert Bloch's tale, "The Cheaters", and the book's title story is a 14,000 word novelette set in Pugmire's Sesqua Valley. Each tale if beautifully illustrated by the remarkable Jeffrey Thomas, who is himself one of today's finest horror authors.

Coming soon from

Miskatonic River Press

Thomas Ligotti is beyond doubt one of the Grandmasters of Weird Fiction. In *The Grimiscribe's Puppets,* Joseph S. Pulver, Sr., has commissioned both new and established talents in the world of weird fiction and horror to contribute all new tales that pay homage to Ligotti and celebrate his eerie and essential nightmares. Poppy Z. Brite once asked, "Are you out there, Thomas Ligotti?" This anthology proves not only is he alive and well, but his extraordinary illuminations have proven to be a visionary and fertile source of inspiration for some of today's most accomplished authors.

Coming from

Miskatonic River Press

Dissecting Cthulhu
Essays on the Cthulhu Mythos

Edited by S. T. Joshi

THE H.P. LOVECRAFT  HISTORICAL SOCIETY

LUDO FORE PUTAVIMUS

The Call of Cthulhu

Widely acclaimed by critics and audiences throughout the world, this black and white, silent film version of HPL's classic tale has been called the most faithful and effective Lovecraft adaptation to date. Features an incredible original symphonic score, available as a soundtrack CD. The region-free DVD features titlecards in 24 different languages and a behind-the-scenes featurette that some enjoy as much as the movie itself!

The Whisperer In Darkness

HPL's classic tale bursts onto the screen in the style of the classic horror films of the 1930s. Skeptical folklore professor Albert Wilmarth discovers a century-old manuscript describing weird creatures and demonic rituals in the remote Vermont hills — setting off a chain of events that will lead him deep into the mountains and to the very edge of madness as he confronts the true purpose of these shadowy visitors. Now available as a deluxe 2-DVD set with hours of bonus features, and on Blu-Ray disc with commentary track!

A GENUINE Mythoscope PRODUCTION

Dark Adventure Radio Theatre

Experience some of Lovecraft's best stories in the form of 1930s-style radio drama, with great acting and all-original music. Our lavishly produced 75-minute CDs are accompanied by elaborate prop documents, photos, and maps, bringing the stories to life in your hands! Collect the whole set packaged in a nifty custom-made collector box shaped like an old time radio! New titles coming soon!

WWW.CTHULHULIVES.ORG

They Lie not Dead, but Dreaming...

CPSIA information can be obtained at www.ICGtesting.com
Printed in the USA
LVOW05s1921200314

378261LV00016B/324/P